A Note for Readers

The work you hold in your hands took me six years to write and seven months to illustrate.

If you enjoy *A Seat for the Rabble*, and you'd like to make an impact, please consider leaving a review for it on Amazon. Every review counts and will help me promote and finish this multi-volume epic fantasy series.

What should you expect from the series? I've plotted out eight books that will take you through new realms and cultures, mount you astride griffons and dragons, and stun you with the twists and turns visited on characters I hope you'll love and root for. Like this first entry, the series will touch on themes relevant to our lives—themes related to democracy, political upheaval, civil liberty, despotism, and climate change.

I appreciate your time. Thank you for reading!

—Ryan Schuette

What Readers Say About
A SEAT FOR THE RABBLE
and AN END TO KINGS

"An immense yet immersive fantasy about succession and disorder after a monarch's death. . . . Schuette's extensive world is an enticing one. Religion, class systems, and past events play large parts in the conflict. . . . Griffins fly; swords cleave; and the unsuspecting are sometimes slaughtered. . . . Yet the fighting and feuding are matched in such a way to keep the intriguing plot moving swiftly. The competing interests make for a curious, highly detailed, engrossing fantasy."

—*Kirkus Reviews*

"From its electric first pages, Schuette's epic adult fantasy debut grips with a rich, tense, multi-perspective story of a kingdom in unrest. . . . A journalist, [he] writes crisp, compelling scenes that demonstrate an understanding of power, conflicted loyalties, and the ways that history—both ancient and recent, true and made up— powers contemporary conflicts."

—BookLife by *Publishers Weekly* (Grade: A)

"Masterful storytelling and epic worldbuilding make this a must-read for fans of political fantasy. Ryan Schuette weaves a complex world of political intrigue, class conflict, and the pursuit of power in this enthralling epic fantasy. . . . The intricate political landscape, mirroring our own challenging political systems, reflects the power struggles seen in today's world."

—ALEXANDRIA DUCKSWORTH, *Independent Book Review*

"If you like getting marooned in a book, so far removed from real life that there's no need for rescue, then *A Seat for the Rabble* was made for you! . . . [It's] a sumptuous feast for the mind."

—NICKY FLOWERS, *Indies Today* (Stars: ★★★★★)

"How long will an oppressed people endure their chains? How far will those in power go to secure their positions? How can rebels unite under a single cause when they are fighting among themselves? Ryan Schuette lends his absorbing style and real-life political insights to answer these questions with *A Seat for the Rabble.*

"This first installment of *A King Without a Crown* series follows how corrupt machinations of nobles and clergy and a contest for the crown collides with the lives of true-to-life characters. At the same time, the haunting whispers of prophecy echo throughout its pages as readers try to wrap their heads around mysterious cults and socio-political movements. The novel takes the perspectives of vastly different personalities as it follows a bastard prince's wrestling for legitimacy, a boisterous peasant girl's tragic childhood, a romantic lord's passion for reform, a foreign slave's maneuvering of a world that hates him, and a savvy princess' struggle to hold it all together. Schuette seamlessly weaves centuries-old political theory with powerfully human stories, all within a world where a deeper, more ancient force is at work.

"I highly recommend *A Seat for the Rabble* not just to those who love the fantasy genre, but especially to those who seek to answer the underlying question: what happens when the powerless become the powerful?"

—SEAN MALLEN, a reader and fan

"Move over, George R.R. Martin—there's a new voice in epic fantasy. What happens when a corrupted government is finally challenged? A contest to rule, for power, for the crown, begins. In *A Seat for the Rabble* and its stunning conclusion, *An End to Kings*, I found treachery, bravery, sacrifice, honor, and destiny. I was so riveted by this novel that I read it twice, and I highly recommend that you read it at least once.

"Former NPR reporter Ryan Schuette has achieved a remarkable feat in the fantasy genre: an interplay of magic, mystery, and politics in a haunting parable about a ruling class so high on power and privilege that it can't steer itself or society off the road to calamity. This two-volume work grounds the reader in a believable and richly detailed world filled with all-too-human heroes—Machiavellian reformists, zealous revolutionaries, self-interested politicians, religious fanatics, noble outlaws, scheming sorcerers, and a cast of characters caught up in a system too big for them to change.

"A masterful storyteller with a feel for the pulse of our uncertain times, Schuette simply turns this world on us like a mirror so that we can see ourselves and our own fragile systems reflected. A page turner to the last, this epic imparts a warning for modern society wrapped in a fantasy setting with moving story arcs that will leave you smiling, fearful for the characters, and sitting on the edge of your seat. I fully plan to preorder the next installment in Schuette's *A King Without a Crown* series."

—JASON NIEHAUS, a reader and fan

"If you consider yourself a fantasy fan, I recommend you read *A Seat for the Rabble*. Ryan Schuette's tale of social unrest and frail humanity captured my attention like few other works. As grand a fantasy epic as *The Lord of the Rings* or *A Song of Ice and Fire*, it's part morality play and part political treatise, all bundled up with magic, griffons, and prophecy. Schuette's first book in this series is incredibly relevant, engrossingly fun, and hard to put down.

"With this work, Schuette shows us a society unable to pump the brakes, even with the cliff's edge in full view. Drawing on the perspectives of characters like lords, princesses, rebels, hostages, and peasants, he illustrates *why* their country is so divided and why revolution seems inevitable—and for some sympathetic characters, undesirable.

"History clearly inspired this story, and I found parallels to historical events like King Henry VIII and his wives, Oliver Cromwell, and the peasants' revolt of 1381. Even so, you can trace lines between these events and recent turning points in the United States and the world. This lends the story Schuette tells a mildly unsettling feeling that one would hope inspires readers to speak out against injustice, lest we allow our own society to go down the same uncertain path.

"That said, this is a highly entertaining venture into a new world of breathtaking scope. Like George R.R. Martin, Robert Jordan, and Patrick Rothfuss before him, Schuette has written a tale worth navigating that will leave you reaching for *A Seat for the Rabble* and

An End to Kings again and again. I can't wait for what awaits us in the sequel."

—CASSANDRA SHUPTAR, a reader and fan

"*A Seat for the Rabble* is political fantasy *par excellence*. Ryan Schuette delivers a near-perfect balance between mystical fantasy adventure and gripping human drama, all with deep political, social, and economic insights that only a seasoned Washington, D.C., journalist could weave together. It's one of the best fantasy books I've ever read and a triumph for the genre.

"Unlike so many fantasy novels today that riff off of Tolkien, Martin, and Dungeons and Dragons, Schuette has built a world much like our own—one divided by political factions, dark and mystical forces, and various species that render *A Seat for the Rabble* a powerful metaphor for a society coming apart at its seams. In this first book, we get a glimpse of a vast world the author has constructed like a labyrinth, with each turn of the corner deepening the mystery that shrouds the motives of several characters.

"Compellingly, Schuette anchors his world in centuries' worth of political, social, and economic theory, providing at times a radical critique of its ruling classes as well as our own without ever seeming obvious about it. These layers make the book both a fun read and a deep think piece about inequality, justice, social movements, the foundations of Western society, and where humanity is headed.

"What amazed me was how Schuette embodied the abstract in the perspectives of several very human characters grounded in their respective classes. This creates a gripping, character-driven drama as peasants, hostages, revolutionaries, knights, and lords intersect and shape a world filled with griffons, sorcerers, clandestine movements, and still-darker forces. It was mesmerizing and epic, with unforeseen twists and turns that keep you guessing as this house of cards comes tumbling down.

"If you're looking for a book that embodies the best of *A Song of Ice and Fire*, *The Lord of the Rings*, the Dragonlance series, and *Malazan Book of the Fallen*—delivered with piercing social insight about our own dire times—*A Seat for the Rabble* will not disappoint. I can't wait for the next volume in Schuette's *A King Without a Crown* series. Five stars!"

—RYAN ENGEN, a reader and fan

"*A Seat for the Rabble* represents epic fantasy at its finest—addictive, shocking, and rich in world-building complexity. If you want a work with a cutting interpretation of the forces running our own troubled world, this one's written specially for you.

"Ryan Schuette has achieved something special in fantasy with this work and its epic conclusion, *An End to Kings*. He manages to intertwine magic and lore with a parable about the myriad social ills affecting the modern world, blending a cautionary tale about us-versus-them politics with prophecy, subterfuge, and titillating drama. Making a multi-perspective story like this soar—and still carry its weight as an analysis of the corruption in our politics—requires a deftness seldom encountered in an author, and with the written word, this one is a trapeze artist.

"Schuette grounds this richly detailed world in the perspectives of an array of characters, including sorcerers, politicians, outlaws, religious leaders, lords, as well as knights and commoners. He makes these characters come alive by making them so utterly, fallibly human. You empathize with them, feel disdain for their misdeeds and sorrow for their travails, and experience their humanity with the revelry of a Windrider stepping into the minds of catlike griffs and mighty griffons. What befalls them adds heft to the moral of the climax and makes you eager to read the sequel.

"This work is a tour de force. *A Seat for the Rabble* and *An End to Kings* are riveting tomes, and time well spent in a mystical world. Five stars!"

—VICTOR MCDONALD, a reader and fan

A SEAT FOR THE RABBLE

A KING WITHOUT A CROWN: BOOK ONE

RYAN SCHUETTE

BEDIVERE PRESS

ISBN paperback: 979-8-9885986-0-2
ISBN hardcover: 979-8-9885986-1-9
ISBN eBook: 979-8-9885986-2-6
Library of Congress Control Number: 2023911969

Maps by Cartographybird Maps
Cover art by Ted Nasmith
Cover and interior design by Liz Schreiter
Produced by Reading List Editorial
ReadingListEditorial.com

Printed in the United States of America.
www.RyanSchuette.com

For Mom, who took me to speech therapy as
a child, encouraged me to write and draw,
and believed in me.

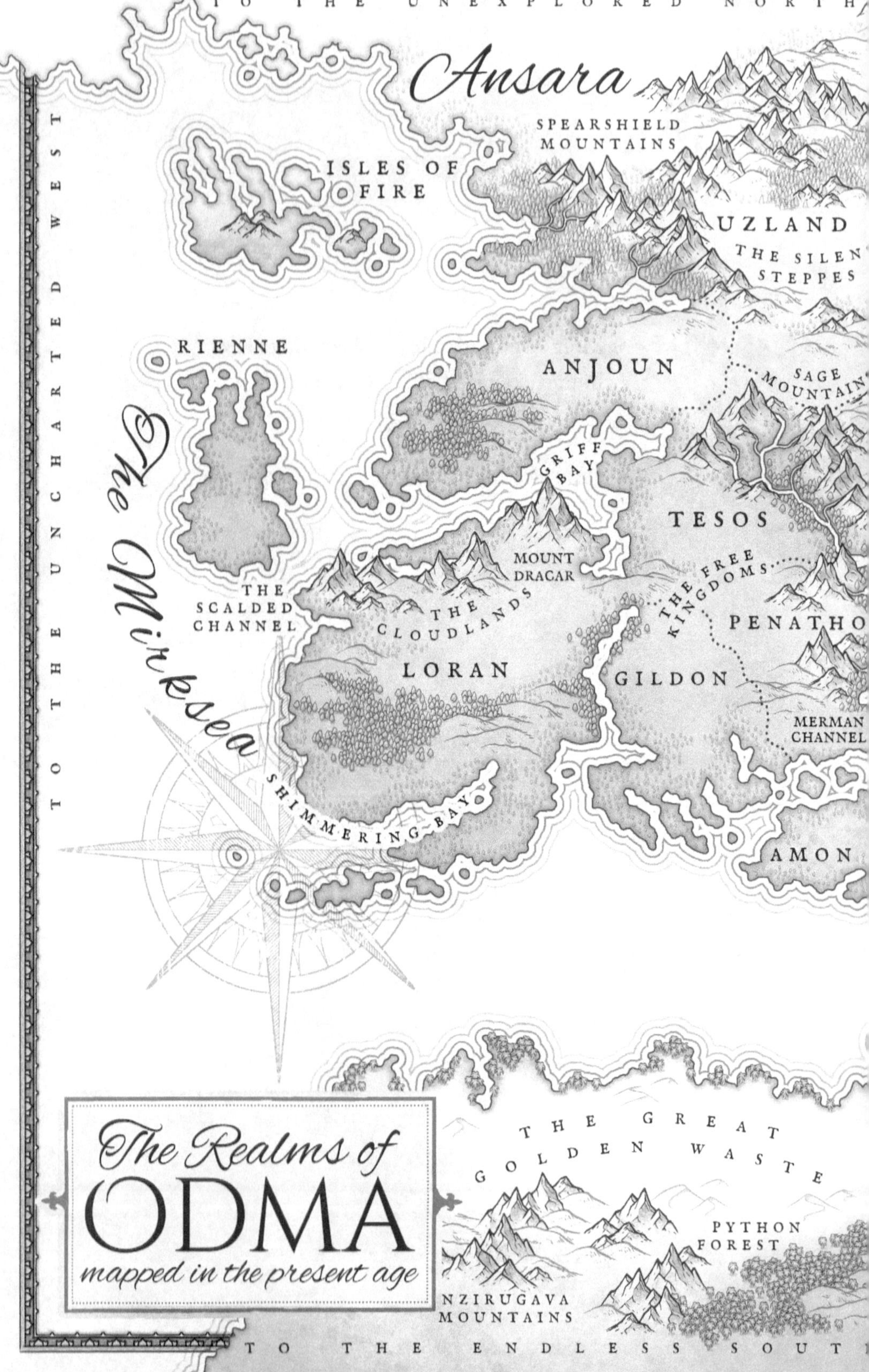

TO THE UNEXPLORED NORTH
Ansara
SPEARSHIELD MOUNTAINS
ISLES OF FIRE
UZLAND
THE SILENT STEPPES
RIENNE
ANJOUN
SAGE MOUNTAINS
GRIFF BAY
TESOS
The Mirksea
MOUNT DRACAR
THE CLOUDLANDS
THE FREE KINGDOMS
PENATHO
THE SCALDED CHANNEL
LORAN
GILDON
MERMAN CHANNEL
SHIMMERING BAY
TO THE UNCHARTED WEST
AMON
The Realms of
ODMA
mapped in the present age
THE GREAT GOLDEN WASTE
PYTHON FOREST
NZIRUGAVA MOUNTAINS
TO THE ENDLESS SOUTH

SLEEPING GIANT MOUNTAINS
MOUNT ROKAR
LAKE OF STARS
EMPEROR'S GULF
The Stormsea
CASVIA
THE ROMARIAN EMPIRE
THE BLACK RIVER
ANJAN'S STRAIT
MAGNES
AMENIS
MEDECIA
DALLA'S BAY
RIDER MOUNTAINS
THE LONELY ISLE
TO THE FAR EAST
The Sea of Dracar
The Brace
The Emerald Sea
NERIMBA
SPHINX RIVER
Casaan
LAKE ELZURA

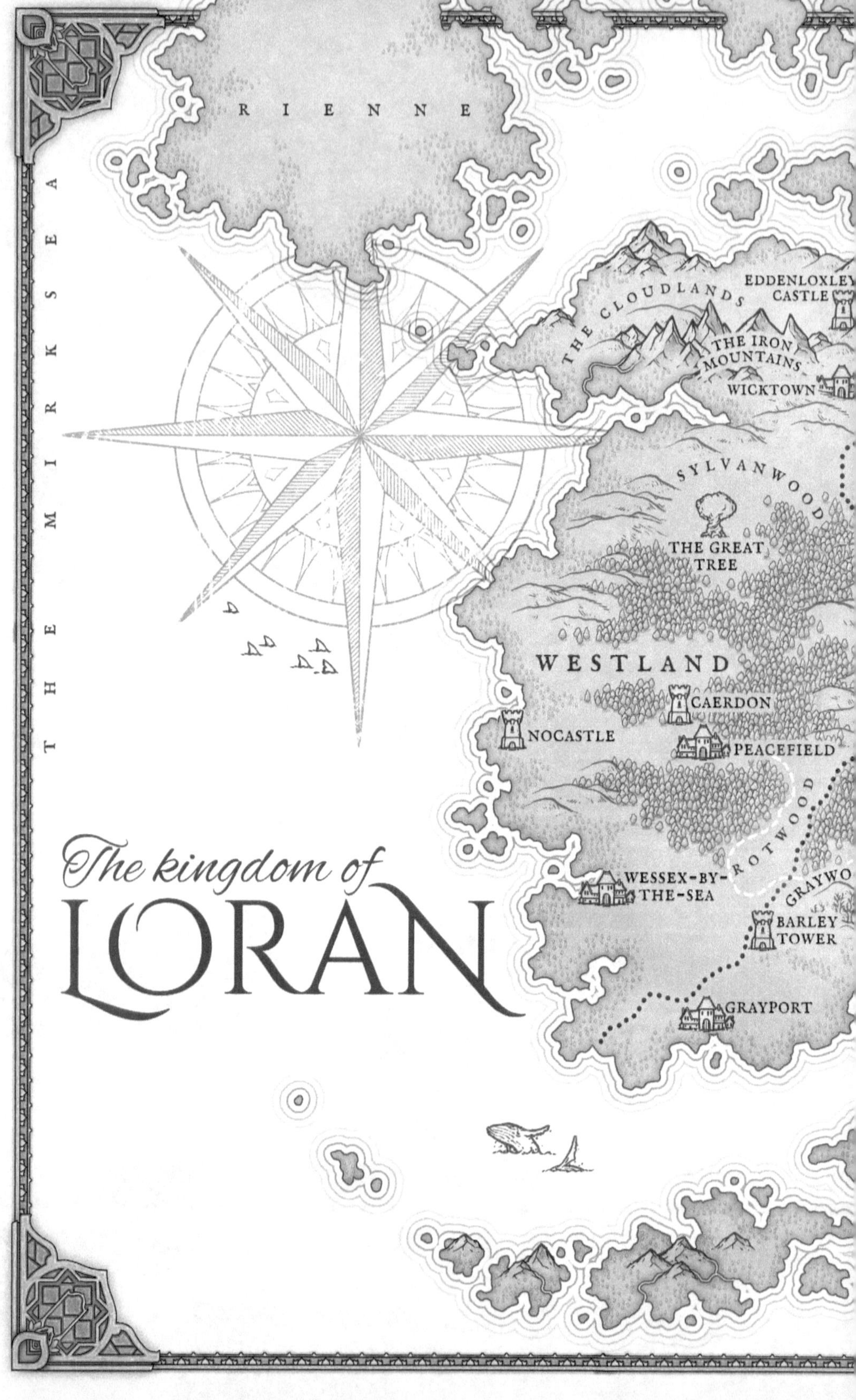

RIENNE
THE MIRK SEA
THE CLOUDLANDS
EDDENLOXLEY CASTLE
THE IRON MOUNTAINS
WICKTOWN
SYLVANWOOD
THE GREAT TREE
WESTLAND
CAERDON
NOCASTLE
PEACEFIELD
ROTWOOD
WESSEX-BY-THE-SEA
GRAYWO
BARLEY TOWER
GRAYPORT
The kingdom of
LORAN

TESOS
THE FREE KINGDOMS
THE RIVER COLOSSUS
THE COLOSSUS
MOUNT DRACAR
NORTHLAND
THE GOLDEN MEADOWS
WESSWOOD
THESSELA
WESTERLICHE
MAJOR SUNDER
SHOALTOWN
EASTLAND
SUNDER WAY
MINOR SUNDER
THE MIDLANDS
HEXWAITE
GILDON
SCYTHE ROAD
BARBARA'S GORGE
SOUTHLAND
THORN'S KEEP
ROSBURY
SOUTHPOINT
SOUTH FARCOMBE
THE WEEPING RIVER
THE SHIMMERING BAY
SAXHOLD
RAMSPORT
Legend
CITIES AND TOWNS
CASTLES AND FORTS
MAJOR ROADWAYS
BORDERS
THE SEA OF DRACAR

A Seat for the Rabble

Go and tell the kings who were:
A tattered cloth shall be mended
With a thread of silver pure,
And the withered vine tended
By hands once and ever sure.

Go and tell the realms of men:
The lame shall rise, the blind see,
And the deaf hear the herald's din
When a king wades through sea
And comes to reign again.

Go and tell those with ears to hear:
He shall shield the few, the fearful last,
Unbowed as shadows circle and sneer,
For o'er man, beast, and blade of grass
The king shall rule far and near.

Go and warn your kings of gilt worth:
Your borders will burn with your keeps
Whilst your paper crowns soil the earth,
For terrors you've sown shall be reaped
Before him, ascendant at birth.
       —"The Ascendant King," a prophecy

Three Trials, three Wings:
Only the Worthy crown kings.
   —A Common rhyme about the Kingstrials

Prologue

ir Damien Sothron was eating breakfast when his squire bolted out of the predawn darkness. The boy tripped on a tree root and tumbled downhill in a cloud of dust.

"It's Spittlelip, he—I saw him take off with Little Lady," Devan stammered as he struggled up. "I think he means to do it himself, sir. To butcher her in the swordwood."

The knight rose from his log by the fire. He retrieved the coil of his leather belt from the barren soil and secured it to his scabbard. "Where did you last see him leading her?" he asked.

The boy pushed moist bangs out of his line of sight. "I'm not sure, I think southeast, sir. Toward that statue we found. Brother Uther told me about it first so I could come and find you." He looked on glumly as the knight probed the sleeves of his chain mail shirt. "He waits for you on the border."

"Did everyone else go with Spittlelip?" Damien slid the mail over his gambeson. He buckled his belt.

Devan shook his head. "Orthos and the rest were with the priest." He ignored his squire's look as he slid on his boots. "Sir Damien, uh, um—what do you mean to do?"

You mean, would a knight sworn to serve a lord kill one of his peasants over a half-mad horse—a creature doomed to die, anyway? Damien thought darkly. *Depending on what Spittlelip has done to her, maybe. And on this day, of all days.*

The knight grimaced. "What I should've done my first day in this accursed wilderness." He slipped on his coif, doused the fire, and trudged uphill, toward the gleam on the horizon that could pass for shoots of morning light.

I'll do it this time, especially if he's hurt that horse, Damien thought with a hand on his pommel. *All it'd take is a push down a swordwood slope, and that'd be that.*

Devan sprinted after Damien, likely trying to discourage him from violence. If so, the squire was nobler in this moment than the knight he served.

Damien stopped and turned about wearily. The tears in his squire's eyes softened his resolve. "Don't worry, Dev," he reassured him. "I swore to protect my lord's subjects. Why would I break those vows?"

But I am breaking them today, he swore inwardly. *I will.*

"It wasn't Spittlelip I was worried over, sir."

The squire thrust a familiar thing into his hand, a small, precious idol he'd forgotten in his fury. Sunlight illuminated the creases in Helsar's gown. Helsar was one of god's twelve faces. His daughter had bought him this Winter Solstice gift with coin her mother had stashed away. You could find better woodwork in Southpoint, but his child had given him this, and Damien Sothron loved her above all else on Odma, above his king, above even his faith.

Helsar guides the brave back to hearth and home. "Thank you, Devan. I'll need Helsar."

"Just think of your daughter, sir. Can't stand to think of what might happen to her if . . . if anything—I mean, if you . . ." Devan trailed off.

If I perish, or must suffer an executioner's blade over my love for that horse.

Damien mussed his squire's hair playfully. "Stay here. You can have my sausages. Oh, and Dev"—he lifted the boy's sleeve, revealing a red sickle of blood—"show care in the swordwood. It's easier than you think to fall in and lose a finger—or worse, if you're a man." He winked in good humor.

The boy smiled only faintly. Damien trudged downhill. Up a ridge, past a brook, and toward the unsettling gleam he went, suppressing a dread that threatened to overwhelm his senses.

He recalled his last conversation with Uthron Morley in the gloom of his court at Thorn's Keep. The Lord Warden, his liege these past twelve years, had summoned the knight for a secret errand he said he could entrust to no one else.

"The Commons are restless, and seeking me to blame for their misery," Morley had said with a vexed look. *Then why not let the Commoners rest?* a small voice inside had pushed him to say. "We need to show the peasants that the Lord Warden of Rosbury knows of their plight and wishes to please the gods."

When the knight had asked his lord *which* gods he sought to please, exactly, the nobleman had replied, as casually as if he were describing his evening plans, "We'll honor the Old Ways. Word has reached me that some peasants think it'd be meet to make a Gift to their old gods." He'd clapped a firm hand on his shoulder. "I need your help to see it through."

The Lord Warden had been vague but all too clear, and it left Damien mute with horror. Some of his fellow villagers—his own *neighbors*—were Sylvanians, he'd realized in that unreal moment. It didn't trouble him that they worshipped trees and stone and dirt.

What troubled was their belief in blood sacrifice.

Things had only worsened from there. He learned that his liege already had a Gift in mind. He'd prayed to the gods in his chapel gardens, he told the knight. He wanted Damien to see to this personally in the swordwood on the Half-Day to Summer Solstice—with witnesses.

Damien had been in disbelief. "But why the horse, my lord?" He'd known Little Lady since the foal could barely stand. His wife thought the courser half-mad, but horses were loyal creatures. *Unlike men,* he thought, then as now. *And why send me on with a cretin like Jacob fucking Spittlelip?*

He'd tried every excuse he could think of to dissuade his liege, to no avail.

Uthron had at least seemed to waver—right up until he crossed looks with that white-haired crone whom the gossips called a witch, and whom the lord called wife. "You will do as I ask, Damien," his liege lord had countered sternly, "or I'll find a knight who *will.*"

And you'll be in a cell beneath Thorn's Keep, Damien knew it hadn't needed saying. What would happen to Rose and Sara then?

Willard Rittman, that's who, the husband and father to a daughter thought grimly as he ascended another barren ridge. Uthron's favorite pug-faced sheriff and taxman followed Rose around market like a shadow, and it was becoming a problem he couldn't seem to resolve without steel. Countless were the times the knight had implored his liege to sack the man, and countless the noble's meaningless promises—and countless, too, all of his excuses for keeping Rittman on.

And that wasn't even the worst of it. Connor Bagman, his neighbor, had told him in the past week that he'd caught the sheriff lingering on Sara.

His daughter was eleven years old. *Why, my liege?* the knight wondered in the present. *Why corrupt your court with apostates and worse? Why even tolerate Rittman and Spittlelip?*

Yet what else could've been done? A knight like Damien had to obey . . . or the wolves would devour his family in his absence. It wasn't lost on him that this service could also shift him back into his liege's favor. So Little Lady had to perish, and by her own rider's hand, surrounded by pagans and worse in a dread wood far from home. *Damn them all.*

With sweat welling in his pits and oiling the backs of his ears, Damien plodded up his last hill. The sun was nearly up by the time he set eyes on a forest frozen in time, the forest that couldn't burn, the forest that peasants said held the remains of a demon deep within.

A haunted forest should've looked the part, all dark and forbidding, but that was what made Graywood so sinister: it seduced the eye. Every trunk, every limb, every leaf reflected sunlight like a riven mirror surface. Stretching southward, the forest canopy rippled like a choppy sea, aswirl with brilliant hues of morning gold and shadowy blue-gray. Even Damien, heartbroken over the task ahead, couldn't dismiss its beauty.

Yet woe to the fool who crossed into that forest thinking it harmless. Graywood was like a poisonous blossom, colorful but deadly to the unwary. A deathwood, men accurately called it: every root, trunk, limb, and leaf could slice through skin as easily as steel through silk, and nothing grew inside the forest except for the number of cadavers.

Hence why they'd wanted to do this thing together in sunlight: to enter that forest in the dark was to stroll into an armory blindfolded. To go alone . . .

A strong wind picked up suddenly, ruffling the strands of his hair but not one of Graywood's leaves. Damien reached into his travelsack and pawed about for Helsar until he found her. *I'll make Uthron's Gift, drink mulled wine to forget, and be on my way to you, my sweet girl, soon as I can,* he thought. *May you forgive me for what I do today, if ever you find out, Sara.*

"Good morning, Sir Damien," came a familiar voice.

Uther Brune, his liege's own cousin, emerged by his side, unsettlingly stealthy for a man his old age. The priest had on his clerical garments, a cream-colored cassock draped with a rich violet cape, a stiff white collar about his wattle neck, and surprisingly little else to protect him in Graywood. On his left hand he wore his lord cousin's favor, an emerald ring wreathed in exquisitely crafted silver leaves. Hair clung to his scalp in cotton-white patches. Seventy-one years of life had stooped his shoulders and ruined his knees, yet his hazel eyes were sharp and discerning.

Damien didn't hide his anger. "*Is it* good, Brother Uther? I was woken to learn the pagans had gone. I left my breakfast cold to set things right with some lip-sucking cretin I should've dealt with years ago—a man you *swore* you'd watch close this morning."

The priest pressed his lips together in contrition. "Yes, I expected you'd be wroth. Forgive an old man his age, sir. I fear sleep steals upon me these days like a thief at night."

"I'm not the one you should ask for forgiveness," Damien said acidly. "Ask *Little Lady* for forgiveness. Not only must she die in this foul wood—no, she has to be *defiled* ere sunrise." His hands tightened into fists.

It wasn't just his wife and daughter he had to watch after. No, the

One True God had seen fit to curse Damien and their village with a goat defiler named Jacob Weeslaw. Most in Rosbury called him Spittlelip on account of the honeycombed scars in his lips that oozed saliva. His shorn tongue hobbled his speech and kept him sucking at his lip for a *shrriping* sound. He'd feel bad for Jacob if the deformity had been there at birth, but he'd brought ruin upon himself.

Damien pointed his finger in the priest's face. "Weeslaw won't get away with this," he swore. "To do that to a horse on *the day* her rider kills her for pagan witchcraft." His hilt lured his hand. "I'll find the hideous bastard and—"

"Kill him? And compound the tragedy?" The old priest had a reproachful look.

"*Tragedy?*" Damien scoffed. "Who'd miss him? His misery is his own fault, priest."

Uther softened. "No. I meant your steed, sir—all this foul business my cousin has sent us on." He touched the knight on his shoulder. "You and I may not be friends in faith, but I'll beg you like one not to do something . . . ill advised."

It didn't need saying. *I'm already on shaky ground with my lord. What worse fate awaits me if I kill one of the peasants we were sent to placate? Even if he is the most reviled one among us.*

Damien stared at the unmoving forest. "I'll do nothing. I have a wife and daughter to think on. We'll do this damn vile thing, and be done, and drink to forget it tonight."

"On that at least, we can agree, parishman. I'll pray to my twelve, and you can pray to your god with twelve faces." Uther patted his shoulder like an old friend. "Come, good sir. Let us find these pagans. Would you lend an old man your arm?"

Damien offered his elbow gently, and down they ambled with what haste they could, the priest and parishioner knight.

He couldn't help but think about what a sight they'd make back in Rosbury. In Loran, a Free Believer would cross the road just to avoid an Elvarenist. Yet their alliance made sense, in the same way sworn enemies might shelter together in a storm. At least the two faiths could still put aside differences when it came to Sylvanian heresies.

The only man in my lord's service worth keeping around, and he wears a collar, Damien mused. *These are strange days.*

After another fifteen minutes of walking, the pair found the rest of their company beneath the shade of a steel-warped tree polished like armor, not a stain of rust upon it.

The older, silver-haired brothers, Orthos and Owen, stood at the front. With them were their other companions, Bill with the eye-patch and toothy-smiled Tom, Sylvanians all, he knew beyond any doubt after weeks together in the wilderness.

"Where's Weeslaw?" Damien barked.

The look he received from Orthos dripped with disdain. He liked Orthos about as much as Jacob Weeslaw. "Aye, we seen 'im," the pagan answered stubbornly. "Rather, we *heard 'im.*" Tom stifled a snicker.

The priest hobbled close. "I failed Sir Damien, but you fail me in turn, Orthos. I told you—Jacob can't be left alone with Little Lady. Lord Uthron would not be pleased to hear a Gift he wanted to make for your folk was mishandled. Where is Jacob? Tell us now."

Orthos looked humbled by the scolding from their lord's cousin. He beckoned to Graywood with a nod. "Like I said, in there," he grumbled. "We lost him. Wasna about to follow."

"We can split up," Owen said helpfully. "Send two parties."

"This swordwood is treacherous even by day," Orthos protested. "If Spittlelip's already in there with the beast, why not let *him* kill the beast? A Gift is a Gift. We can tell the other peasants."

"That would be a lie," Damien said. "If we're killing my horse, we'll do it right. In a circle. Just like our lord told us."

Orthos watched him skeptically.

"I think Owen had the right of it," Uther broke in. "We'll split up. If you find Jacob, you'll trill, bird-like. We'll converge again and make the Gift in a circle, as my lord cousin wanted."

Bill scoffed. "Trill. As if anything lives in Graywood. I'd be careful. The Loyal Company's Pigeons roam these parts."

"We needn't fear those traitors or their footmen." Damien peered into the forest. "They know only idiots would brave this place."

"And here we are," Orthos lamented. "Idiots. All of us."

To Damien's surprise, the brothers offered to accompany the priest so that he could list on their arms. That left him with Bill and Tom, useless, both; the former had just one eye, and the latter cackled like a hyena. Still, he'd rather have five eyes than just two in Graywood. The priest paused with Orthos and Owen before the swordwood, said a prayer, and entered.

Striding past the first few trees, Damien felt his familiar world ebb to trickles of the real. Graywood divided itself into lines of silver lances, too orderly to have ever been living trees. The forest had no discernible smell. Everything green vanished within the first hundred yards, all grass, all weed, all fern, save for dead leaves swept in by wind. Sunlight pulsed off lustrous trees, disorienting him. Damien and his companions constantly watched their extremities, wary of unintentionally straying into tree trunks riven with fierce grooves.

Cursed indeed, Damien thought as his gaze wandered to the dense forest canopy, layers on layers of shiftless silver leaves and branches. Only the long-vanished elves could have wrought this impossible work. *But elves sang music for trees to grow. They would've never profaned the earth with this horror.*

You could choose any number of tales to believe about how Graywood had come into being. Damien heard Bill and Tom finishing each other's sentences about how a dying elk god's blood had blighted the forest with sprouts that turned everything metal. A priest like Uther would cite verse about the demon the First King had buried in the west long ago. Free Believers like Damien held that Graywood was just another one of life's mysteries the god with twelve faces had sent for them to unravel.

But how can anyone examine something this deadly to the touch? Some men succeeded in prying off swordwood and enriched themselves tenfold at the markets. But many more were those who trespassed here, slashed arteries by accident, and bled out, leaving their decomposed remains for wanderers to find.

On and on they wended, listening for a horse's whinny, their trilling companions, Spittlelip's slurping, *anything*. The knight watched, transfixed, as his silver-tipped stubbles and deep-blue eyes slid by in the warped mirrors of trees. Staring too long, he winced from a headache. He pulled off a glove to mop his slick cheeks and massage his temples.

Ahead, corridors of steel blurred together like a desert mirage. *This is a cloudless day,* he realized. *We'll die here if we can't trust our eyes in the heat.*

"We shouldn't have come here," Damien said aloud. "Not even by day. I have a mind to quit this task and risk a cell in my liege's dungeon. As for that goat fucker you call a friend—"

He realized he couldn't hear Bill or Tom. Turning, he found himself completely alone.

Buggering pagans, all of them. He couldn't call for them, lest he alert Spittlelip. Yet he had to do something, because he suddenly realized that he didn't know where he'd entered the forest, or how to even leave. He'd only come here yesterday, when they stumbled upon that frightful statue. In almost every direction, the swordwood looked the same, lines of steel trees plunging with the hills.

The knight found Helsar in his travelsack. *Let me return to my daughter,* he prayed inwardly.

Over the next hour, maybe longer, he wandered through a lifeless labyrinth. Sometimes he called their names, sometimes he didn't. With the sun climbing to noon, the metal forest soon felt as sweltering as a blazing forge. He swabbed sweat off his brow, cursing himself for forgetting his waterskin in his haste.

He was losing patience. "Uther?" he cried out, hearing no reply. "Orthos? *Anyone?*" He was tempted to call for Spittlelip himself. Again and again, he shouted their names.

Suddenly he had an eerie feeling. Someone was watching him. Everywhere he turned, he saw no one and nothing but the gleaming lances of trees.

Shrrip, he heard. "Show yourself, Weeslaw," Damien told the empty forest. "Do it now."

A rustle alerted him. Fifty yards off, a lanky figure trudged through the trees. "Weeslaw," Damien snarled. He closed the distance quickly. "Where's my horse?"

The figure lurched woodenly. He wasn't Jacob Weeslaw. A man he was, naked and limber. Shoulder-length hair curtained his head.

Damien held his breath. The man . . . had no face. Just the shape of one, jawline and cheekbones. No eyes. No ears. No mouth. The pale shallows of eyeless sockets located the knight. Without eyes to see him, the faceless man charged.

In his haste Damien dropped his glove. Wind in his ears, he leapt over a grassless bank, ducked to avoid foliage, and raced past mirror trees. He misplaced his feet and hurled his armored shoulder into a trunk. Trying to slow his speed, he latched onto a tree limb with the bare hand, and cried out at the flood of pain.

He ran and half-ran, for what felt like an hour, breathing haggardly, checking over his shoulder. No matter how many times he looked, he found no sign of a pursuer. *A trick of the eyes. It had to have been. A trick.* Waves of liquid fire coursed through his shredded hand. He wobbled on, passing beneath steel canopy, dribbling blood that pooled in his footprints.

Then he heard it. Little Lady's distant whinny. Birds. His heart filled. *Helsar is with me.* The knight followed their trilling in a daze.

Scaling a hill, he found the statue. Dracar sat cross-legged on his plinth, as if he'd been waiting this entire time. Even with horns, wings, and a snout, the fallen god made for a welcome sight. Left of the tribute to Dracar lay a path he and Devan followed to freedom yesterday; to its right, a sloping hillside.

Damien screwed up his face. Around the statue knelt his companions, hands cupped, heads bowed. Whispering, Bill, Tom, Orthos, and Owen failed to notice him.

"*Uther?*"

The kneeling priest lifted his patchy-haired head. "Ah, you've found us." He gazed at the knight's ruined hand.

Damien approached swiftly, unhinged by anger and fear and the unrelenting throb of his hand. "Aye . . . and you doing blasphemy," he hissed through his teeth. "I know this lot is treacherous. *But you?*" He widened his eyes. "*You* let Weeslaw take my horse. You lied to me, priest. *Why?* Is it my faith—my Free Beliefs—is that why? You'd make sport of me for your own satisfaction?"

"No." The priest's voice had a deepness it'd lacked before. As he rose, the four Sylvanians rose alongside him. Uther had a morose look. "I take no satisfaction."

Something stirred behind him. Damien heard it too late, the *shrrip*. Jacob Spittlelip slammed into the knight with all his weight. As Damien felt his feet leave the ground, he caught one last look of the man with perforated lips and hateful eyes. How he pitied him.

His world whirled. Wind roared in his ears.

Moments later, Damien Sothron was in hell. The fires of hell scorched his body as he writhed. *This isn't hell,* he realized. *This is Graywood.* He bled as a river flows from a hundred cuts. He'd tumbled downhill. He lay paralyzed from the spears of steel branches that lanced through his mail and boiled leather. Steel leaves and needles clung to his shattered arms and legs like forest burs.

He was dying. *Oh, Sara. Forgive me.*

Far above, he thought he saw his squire alongside the traitor priest. Devan wept in shudders. *I was wrong,* Damien thought. *This is hell.*

Uther's voice rang down from above. "As I said, I take no satisfaction in this, Damien Sothron. None of us do." Spittlelip grinned with a *shrrip*. "Give up your life, now, sir. Gift it to the one beside you."

Damien saw the forest shift in the corner of his eye. The faceless one rushed toward him on hands and knees, panting through an emergent mouth. Off to Damien's side lay his wool travelsack, in its dashed contents Sara's Winter Solstice gift. He grasped for Helsar as the creature rose, salivating.

Somewhere, a horse whinnied.

CHAPTER 1

The King's Horn

uran, of the tribe called Nuur, struggled against sleep amid the clinking of coins.

Like every Casaanite at the Silver Walls, he was bound to serve the king, even on his fourteenth birthday. *If I can keep my eyelids open, maybe I'll continue to serve the steward instead of the cooks,* he reproached himself inwardly.

None of the hundred taxmen gathered about the throne room seemed as bored. Grimly, they fixed their eyes on their tormenter, the Chancellor of the Exchequer. Stout, with plump rosy cheeks and a tidy beard, Hanor the Tessian brooded over a checkered table stacked with coins. He pawed inside sacks on stools in his orbit, retrieved golds and silvers, and added to the towers on their white and red checkers.

Hanor reserved white checkers for the noble lords paid up on the king's due, red for those that weren't. Right now, Zur saw, reds outnumbered the whites six to one.

"One-hundred thirty gold lorens from Castle Thessela," Hanor continued drearily, with a side-eye at Zur.

That was his cue. Too late, Zur realized he'd inked the wrong row. He blotted out the sum hastily, leaving unsightly, illegible splotches.

"I think that's in the wrong column, too," a voice rasped near his ear.

Zur half collapsed off his chair, startled. Smiling down at him, Princess Lorana Eddenhold wore a hint of mischief.

Zur clambered up, stifling embarrassment. "Apologies, Highness," he stammered.

His face grew hotter when he saw the princess's servant. Winsome in a fine emerald-green gown, Anyasha had brown eyes that could soften men to butter-melt. With her russet complexion and kinky hair, his kinswoman looked as much a foreigner at court as Zur, yet seemed a better fit.

Zur lingered on the servant's ample amount of cleavage and caught a smirk from the princess. He averted his gaze, embarrassed.

Lorana crossed the chamber swiftly, her gold-and-black brocade gown whispering on the floor, Anyasha shadowing her. Briefly, the princess paused before the Silver Throne, as if fancying herself worthy. She sat in her father's rickety gout chair, the highest a woman could ever dare to climb in Loran.

A herald close by the double oak doors struck floor with staff. "Here sits Her Highness the Princess Lorana Eddenhold," his voice echoed, "daughter of King Hexar and the traitor Alyse, steward of these Walls, doing justice in the king's absence."

Zur bowed his head with the rest of the throne room.

He peeked at Anyasha but settled on Lorana, stirring with pride. With her broad brow and long shoulders, Lorana Eddenhold resembled the king more than even her brothers. She was just as proud.

"I hesitate to even ask, my lord," Lorana sighed. "Tell me, how beggarly are these men today?"

The sheriffs shifted uncomfortably. Most of the kingdom's taxmen had a miserable relationship with the princess.

"We're short by some eight-hundred lorens," Hanor aired, to annoyed shifting and crossed arms from taxmen.

Zur knew Lorana recognized his discomfort by how she looked at him. He stood, feeling as small as a flea in the vast, circular throne room. "It's closer to seven hundred," he said.

The Tessian flitted from Zur to the city of coin towers on his table. "That's incorrect, Your Highness. I know for a fact—"

"I'd trust Zuran with my life, Lord Hanor," Lorana broke in. "And he's had a habit of correcting your counts. Perhaps I'll name *him* to the exchequer, and return you to Tesos, hmm?"

The Tessian weathered the room's laughter. Yet taxmen and guards didn't entirely intend their ridicule for him. No one seriously believed a Casaanite like Zuran could do more than scribble counts on calfskin.

In every one of Ansara's thirteen kingdoms, his hostaged people served highborn men like well-dressed slaves.

Not a day went by that Zur didn't yearn to wear a knight's armor, swear an oath, ride a horse. Elzura's Children could not do such things.

Most considered it laughable to think they ever would.

It might not be so laughable for a Casaanite to rise after today, Zur thought daringly. It was his fourteenth birthday, and the steward had promised he'd leave her service for someone else, likely a chancellor. This mystery lord had lobbied Lorana hard for him, apparently.

There were four chancellors, so only four possibilities. The best by far had to be the king's apothecary. Jon Applewood was half-blind and doddering, but he had an impressive library. If Hanor Graxhold wanted Zur, well, at least he knew the trade; he'd just need to watch how he corrected his counts.

The other two he'd rather not think on. Of those, Drexan Lorrain, Chancellor of the Chancery, felt safer, but not by much. The man dubbed the King's Crow was disliked by lords and priests, rumored to be a sorcerer, even.

But let it not be the king's torturer, Zur thought. *I'd take kitchen work over torture work . . .*

Would that he could serve the king's master-of-arms. Pick up a sword, don the armor. It wasn't far-fetched. The princess herself had teased the possibility of a squirehood all week, pointing out knights around the castle and making suggestive comments.

Make my birthday gift a vellum scroll that allows me to equip a sword, he thought with a wistful look at Lorana. *I've served you well, princess. I deserve your favor.*

"Another poor showing," said the steward, disappointed. "What shall we do? Search their pockets? Call on Lord Charles, have him check them himself?"

The name of the king's torturer only tensed the air. Men muttered angrily, exchanged cross looks. One sheriff, Halford Silverspear, steamed toward the Silver Throne.

The sheriff stopped feet from the princess—inches from an accursed bloodstain none but kings and stewards could near. Armed sentries crossed the chamber to grab him.

Halford, you proud moron, Zur thought.

Halford shook off their hands with a fiery look at Lorana. "We scrape up what we can for our king, and we're *threatened with imprisonment in the Red Tower?*" he blazed. "We collect what we can, but is it ever enough for you, Highness? No. Not while lords like my liege pay theirs fairly and others do not." He suffered a warning shove. "And not to pay for all the wars our king opens up for us like hell's chasms."

"That's your king's daughter, Halford," Hanor warned.

"No, Lord Hanor, I'm steward." Many called Lorana the stone maiden because she could seem cold for a woman. Zur thought it dignified her. "My father—your king—is away for all our sakes, destroying the crown's enemies and protecting us from barbarians."

A telling wrinkle in her forehead caught Zur's eye. How often had she complained bitterly to him and Anyasha about Hexar's costly wars north and east, far from the kingdom?

And yet, appearances. "And so too all three of my brothers," she added. "Insult the king again, Halford, and I'll spare you the Tower. I'll send your head to Traitor's Gate."

Sentries forced the sheriff back behind the table. Lorana reclined in her father's gout chair. "Yet Sir Halford isn't wrong, is he?" she asked openly. "Some lords think themselves above us all, and force what's theirs to pay on those without means."

Zur knew as well as anyone else what she meant. High lords were calling peasant coin their own and faulting their Commoners for what didn't show at court. It was a familiar problem in greedy Loran.

"A drought plagues our Midlands," Lorana went on, "our peasants starve and suffer famine, and yet we gaol them if they don't pay, and separate families if the father hides his children for lack of money." She made a fist, as if she could strike a lord from afar. "All because lords refuse to pay their fair share."

Another sheriff ventured out from the crowd, chin tilted deferentially, feathered cap in hand. His faded red doublet and rumpled stockings told Zur he'd likely been a low shire knight.

"Willard Rittman, would you test the royal presence, too?" Lorana asked loftily.

The man bowed. "Forgive me, Your Highness, but I think I may have another explanation," said Rittman. "If I may."

Lorana nodded her acquiescence.

"Your Highness, I've long enforced King Hexar's will and collected taxes in Rosbury Village," Rittman said. "In that time, I've seen only honesty from noble lords like my own. Truly, it's the *Commoners* who thwart us." Men agreed in murmurs.

"The Commoners." Lorana raised a skeptical eyebrow.

"They've grown restless of late in Rosbury," Rittman said, undeterred. "Talk is on that the Loyal Company wants peasants seated once more in our Worthy Assembly. Roaming vagrants come as prophets to fill their heads with that black treason."

The herald clacked his staff next for Todd Redoak. "What Sir Will says is true," Redoak said. "The lords got nothing to do with this shortfall—it's their *peasants*."

The chamber clamored with approval.

Lorana drummed her fingers on her armchairs. "I do not believe Commoners are to blame for these poor showings, but neither will I dismiss what you say, not without further proof. You lot—you, you, and you"—she made a sweeping gesture at the taxmen—"how much are a sheriff's wages?"

"*Not enough!*" one shouted from the back.

Hanor looked by turns concerned and wary of what would follow. "Most sheriffs who collect taxes receive wages twice above those of the same rank who don't," he offered.

"I imagine this must be so troubling for you," Lorana said. "All of you. To collect the king's due, think you've done right—only to be told it's not enough after all." She shrugged. "We can't very well have our taxmen thinking themselves poor and unliked, can we? Sirs, rise and approach the Silver Throne." She held high the palm of her hand. "Except for Sir Halford, who made trespass and spoke ill of his king. He'll be escorted out."

What could you be doing, princess? Zur thought. Taxmen traded glances nervously. They shuffled around the counting table and gathered before the first stair, careful not to touch the faded bloodstain with their feet.

Lorana stood with her back to the throne. "Kneel," she instructed them, and they did, some slower than others. "Sirs, as steward of these Silver Walls, in the king's absence, I name you justices of the peace in this kingdom. As sheriffs, you are bound to your lords, but as justices you shall be bound to *me*. I charge you with collection of the king's due and enforcement of his will. You shall not serve two roles for the same wages, but for ten times what your lords pay you."

Zur gasped with the taxmen. Hanor looked left and right, incredulous, as if *he'd* been threatened with a Tower cell. "Your Highness, this is, um, most unexpected. The state of—I mean, what I mean is, perhaps we could speak—"

"No need," the stone maiden said in a voice that brooked no dissent. "We'll pay them from the king's due they've brought us today."

Serve as both sheriffs and *justices? And receive wages from the Walls?* Zur wondered. That was sure to anger lords jealous of their power . . . and could *work*, if the justices began to value the crown's monies over what their lieges paid them.

It was clever, and none at all surprising to Zuran when it concerned Lorana Eddenhold.

At the steward's command, sentries took turns laying their swords on the sheriffs' shoulders. "Rise, justices of the peace," she said after their oaths. "Do you swear to serve my father, King Hexar?"

They swore to serve the king, loudly, proudly, as one. "The Head speaks," Lorana declared in the old tradition.

"*The Hands serve*," answered the men with two masters.

All of them, even Free Believers who probably disdained Elvarenist rituals, signed the diamond, hand to hand, thumbs to forefingers. Zur made the sign clumsily; no one noticed.

Lorana ended court. The new justices bowed reverently, thanked the steward, and left one by one, holding their heads somewhat higher. Thick oaken doors groaned shut.

Hanor complained to Lorana about their coffers in low but rising tones. Pretending not to wait on her, on some word about his new assignment, Zur went to tidying up his business, scattering pounce across his pipe roll and blowing to hasten the drying.

The chancellor looked his way and spoke up. "Surely we aren't finished, Your Highness?" he asked. "I'll need a proper accounting of what's been brought—especially since they'll be *wages* now."

Lorana smiled. "I'm afraid you'll need another servant, Hanor. Zuran of Tribe Nuur leaves us today." She crossed the chamber and embraced Zur warmly.

"Forgive me, Ana," Zur said. "I'll be more careful with my marks."

Lorana waved him off. "*Nonsense!* You lasted longer with the Tessian than I normally fare. Besides, my little brother"—she gripped his shoulders and circled him about—"today is your birthday, is it not?"

Anyasha appeared before them with a robe tucked under her arm. Leaning in, she planted a moist kiss on his cheek. His cheeks burned hot as torches. He'd never been kissed.

"That's my gift," Anyasha said with a honeyed smile, "and this is hers."

Anyasha drew the robe out from under her arm. She helped Lorana press out wrinkles. It was a fine robe, shaded with fur black, brown, and gray. Silver threads crosshatched the front. He slipped his arms through the holes; the lining inside felt exquisitely soft.

"Do you like it?" Lorana asked as he modeled the robe. "I had it made from wolfpelt. You'll have to thank Namoni for the embroidery, and—"

Zur threw his arms around her. "*Thank you*, Ana."

Lorana backed away, grinning. The stone maiden was cool to affection. "I've another gift for you. You'll see more swordplay, little brother."

He welled up with excitement. *It's happening,* he thought wildly. *A fine sword in my hand. Gleaming pauldrons across my shoulders.*

"Don't torture him." Anyasha smiled wickedly. "That's for Lord Charles."

The boy's dreams instantly turned dark. *They're sending me to serve the king's torturer,* he thought fearfully. *Dear god.*

Lorana slapped at the girl's shoulder playfully. "What, and quarter him at the Red Tower, far from us? To the South Tower he'll go, and no farther!"

"Lord Drexan . . . I'll serve . . ." He couldn't even complete his protest.

"The very same." The princess embraced him again. His nose tingled from the cloying rosemary in her bosom. "You'll have a good view of the knights from Lord Drexan's window. But I'll miss you in my service, little brother."

Silly fool, he chastised himself. *Casaanites can't be knights.* Indeed, he was worse off than before he turned fourteen. *I'm being made to serve a rumored sorcerer said to turn those who displease him into toads. Damn it all.*

It was late afternoon by the time Zur left the throne room. He headed for the South Tower through a colonnaded walkway that encircled the Silver Walls's sprawling upper bailey, his feet weighing him down like anchors. Silvery light shot along the cliffs of the castle's towering curtain walls, lulling Zur to stop and reflect on the world's greatest manmade structure, if only to stay the inevitable.

But were the Silver Walls made by man? Zur wondered. Elvarenist priests and readers of the Free Beliefs, who agreed on little else, held that Anjan Half-Elf had ordered his builders to erect a fortress that would forever remind the world that it had but one king. A castle to make other castles look like stone rubble piled up by drunkards. A symbol of kingship eternal.

Anjan's castle looked like it'd been brought here from another world. A massive, curved spire rose hundreds of feet above Eduard's Hall, so sparing in straight edges and thicketed by arches it resembled a monstrous cactus plant, to Zur's eye. That strange architecture echoed in the famous defensive walls and huge watchtowers.

Yet it wasn't architecture that'd made the Silver Walls the envy of conquerors for centuries.

It was the stone itself. From twinkling stones in the spire and curtain walls radiated sheets of silvery light that blanketed the castle and spiraled skyward, curling hypnotically over the capital city.

The sound of ringing steel brought Zur out of his trance.

Turning by the Great Hall, he came upon knights clashing in light mail and patchy breeches. Connor Tomas supervised a match between Andrew Windkin and a redheaded squire. The squire made an awkward lunge. Andrew disarmed the boy in a sleight-of-hand move that threw him to the dirt. The observers laughed heartily.

Zur smirked . . . until one of the knights stopped to linger on him. The other men watched him with something between unease and disapproval.

Zur hurried along, suddenly self-conscious. He didn't feel at ease until he rounded statues lined up around the boxwood maze. It was a curse, being a Casaanite in this land—literally. Like any of his kinsmen hostaged at a castle, he spent nearly every waking moment suffering stares and whispers.

New worries replaced the familiar ones when he arrived at his destination.

The South Tower emerged on the other side of the maze, a silver lance jutting through sky, gently pulsing out silverstone light. Peering up, he saw Drexan's high window overlooking the place where the knights liked to cross swords. *It's a solace, princess,* he thought. *I'll be out of their sight, but able to watch their matches.* Walking beneath raised portcullis, he climbed a narrow, torchlit stairway and passed a library and rookery.

At the topmost stairs, Zur halted. Inside a cramped study sat a wiry fellow, hunched over his table, scratching at calfskin with quill. His arm moved with his writing hand, quill feather bobbing diligently. Sunlight glanced off his helm, a thing nearly as alien as the castle of the Silver Walls itself.

Drexan ceased his writing. He looked up from his table. "Are

Elzura's Children deprived even of manners?" came his musical voice. He sheathed his quill in an inkpot. "Was I fool to risk the Grand Inquisitor's wrath in a fight for you, Zuran of the Tribe Nuur?"

Turning, the chancellor rose from his stool. The King's Crow looked the part, stooped over and cloaked in black wool that feathered his ankles. Sunlight silvered his copper beard. Intense green eyes bespoke curiosity, humor, and a courtier's shrewdness. To someone unfamiliar with him, Drexan Lorrain could pass for a kind-faced older man full of stories for young children.

But Zur knew the chancellor's reputation, as surely as he knew that snug helm and the eye that stared back at him from its widow's peak, wreathed in crow-footed script. *The Eye of Guldan,* Zur knew. Only men who'd trained at the Order of Six Sights could display that insignia . . . but who in his right mind would study at a guild for witches and heretics?

Drexan Lorrain would. *And now I'm his servant.*

Zur bowed. "F-forgive me, my lord," he stammered. "By the grace of King Hexar and the Princess Lorana, and the evil of my forebear, I am here to serve you."

A thin smile spread across Drexan's face. "You're wondering why I've asked for your assignment here."

"Yes, my lord."

"Good," the chancellor said resolutely. "I like honesty. It was one of the virtues the First King bade his thirteen knights follow at the Conferral, when his power flowed to them as bolts of lightning, transforming them into his champions." There was a lull. Drexan smiled again. "You want to correct me."

Zur looked up from his feet. "Yes, lord."

"I said I like *honesty,* Zuran. If I am wrong, you should correct me. Now, how did I just lie?"

"Yes, lord. King Anjan passed his power to twelve knights at the Conferral. Not thirteen."

"Indeed." Drexan padded over to his crenelated window. He toyed with a copper-plated pipe raised on a three-legged stand. "And remind me, what was the Conferral?"

Is his question a test, or mockery? Casaanite hostages learned as well as anyone about the Conferral. "It was the day the gods blessed men with magic, if one believes. Cornered by demons on a mountaintop, Anjan Half-Elf and his priest prayed to the twelve gods for deliverance—"

"The god of twelve faces, if you're a Free Believer."

"Yes, my lord." Zur watched Drexan as he twisted a knob. "The god Amath—or his godface, maybe—broke the mountain with lightning. Many stood with Anjan Half-Elf that day, but the lightning bolt passed through only the twelve worthiest men. They became Anjan's Windriders, the worthy ones who rode winged griffons beside the First King as knights ride horses."

"*Worthy.*" Drexan peered through the device's lens. "Tell me, what makes *you* worthy, Zuran? What did Princess Lorana teach you that the King's Crow could use? Apart from that you are exempt from sumptuary laws for your kin, apparently."

He fiddled self-consciously with the edges of his wolfskin robe. "Surely you know? You chose me, lord."

The chancellor flickered with warning. "Insolence wasn't one of the Windriders' virtues. It certainly isn't one here."

Meekly, Zur nodded. He could read, record sums, and dress himself well enough, little else. He told Drexan this. "I kept her confidence and records, and delivered messages for her about the Walls," he added.

"That's all?"

"I also cleaned and refilled inkpots for Lord Hanor."

Drexan harrumphed. "The Tessian is a pea-brained bean counter, but your limited skills will suffice in my service. I will need you to take dictation, relay my messages, and clean my inkpots. I will also need you learned, as the chancery deals in statecraft—the transmission of the king's correspondence to other kings and highborn men. So you shall also need to read, and know the world." Drexan waved him over. "Come, see the world."

The Casaanite went to the window, studying the strange instrument. "What is this, lord?"

"A skyglass—something a king wouldn't share with his Casaanites. Glassmasters made this in Gildebirg. Through it, you can get a closer look at the stars."

Balancing the pipe in one hand, Drexan tilted it so that a still-smaller cylinder shunted out with a tinny *clink*. He pressed one eye to the glass lens near the pipe's butt.

"There it is," Drexan said. "*Breathtaking.* Here, look."

Peering through the lens, Zur beheld a blurry, late sky. The skyglass wobbled as Drexan twisted its knob. Zur blinked to make sure what he saw was real. Dusk bled with brilliant indigos and burnt oranges, wisps of cloud rolling across it. On the edge of night, stars glistened like fine jewels.

It was like seeing the world through a magnifying glass.

"This is amazing," he said softly.

"And yet still nothing compared to what King Anjan and his Windriders saw through the eyes of beasts they controlled."

Zur focused on feathers ruffling on the wings of birds passing through his line of sight. "How is this possible, lord?"

"The Awakening's scholars discovered that we needed clever glass and the right amount of dark to view the heavens," Drexan said. "Let it never be said that their time on earth was unhelpful. Now, what am I showing you?"

"Stars."

"A constellation, more specifically. Which one?"

"The Merman's Trident?"

Gently, Drexan pried him away from the skyglass. "This is the Lame King. Do you know him?"

Zur knew their names easily enough, the heroes and devils and beasts chosen by the twelve gods—or One True God—to dwell in the skies forever. "The Lame King is King Eduard, last of the true line of Anjan Half-Elf," he said.

The chancellor looked through the lens, rotating the knob. "Why is he lame?"

So this is why he questions me—to remind me of my place. Every

Casaanite hostage suffered the link between himself and Eduard, the last known heir of Anjan Half-Elf. "He was hobbled by an arrow to the ankle, by the Weeping River. Thousands of years ago."

"Hobbled by whom?"

"By a huntsman loyal to the House of Anjan," Zur said, as easily as he could in his sleep. "He sought to protect Eduard's last heir, who fled after the king had his sister-wife and other children slain. Eduard was trying to kill his last child."

"A vile act that broke one kingdom into many, unleashing chaos. Why, then, did the gods raise Eduard to the heavens?"

"To always remind the faithful of Eduard's betrayal, and of my ancestor Elzura, who begot his treachery with a spell."

Drexan reared up from the skyglass. "What else?"

Zur ran through his paces, fretting that he'd forgotten something. "Nothing, lord. That's what they teach hostages, lord." He didn't want to seem insolent.

The chancellor made a curious grunt that half-sounded like a scoff. "Of course they would. Why teach one of Elzura's Children anything else?" He forced the skyglass to collapse on itself with a series of ringing clinks. "If you mean to serve me, I'll need you to be curious. Knowledge I can teach you, Zuran. What I cannot teach you is the *desire* to learn, a thing priests and readers do not want in their legions of sheep."

"What would you have me learn first?"

Drexan smiled approvingly. "Not to learn, but remember, to hold fixed in your mind on your fourteenth birthday." He gazed up at the stars. "The Lame King is sacred to faiths and wise men all around the world . . . even in your native Casaan. Sacred, because one day another constellation will appear, and Anjan's last heir will return."

At least he believes in the prophecy. The faithful stubbornly held that one day the First King's last true heir would reemerge from obscurity, ascend his Silver Throne, and unite the thirteen realms and all the world under a banner of peace. In those days the Twelve Testaments held the Casaanites, his people, would be free of Elzura's Curse.

The King's Crow gestured at the sky. "The Lame King is a harbinger of change when it appears. Those stars *invite* change. Neither good nor ill, but change nonetheless. Just as this is a time of change for you, Zuran." He watched him curiously. "I know what they say about me, here and around the Walls. You needn't fear me."

"You . . . you won't turn me into a toad?"

Drexan smirked. "If only I knew the trick! I might've tried it on your predecessors. Sadly, the Order of Six Sights teaches its students the more tedious magic of letters and statecraft."

Before he could reply, a shadow bolted through the open-air window. Flapping its wings, the brownish blur circled the chamber five times before alighting on the window ledge.

Drexan grinned. "What timing! Zuran, I want you to meet someone very important to me."

Zur eyed the creature with a cat's body and hawk's head and wings, breathing unevenly. *A griff,* he knew beyond doubt. The smaller cousin to griffons looked no less fearsome. Black talons sickled out from four feline paws, scraping the window ledge. White was his furry belly and legs, brownish-gold and spotted black his feathered backside and wings. His wiry tail flicked to and fro, almost sentiently. The griff warmed to the chancellor as he stroked his feathered head.

"Don't be afraid. Griffs can sense fear." Drexan lowered his arm, allowing the king's bird to amble up with catlike grace. "I call him Furos."

"You named him after King Anjan's great battle griffon." Zur tried to hide his nervousness. "I thought these creatures liked to avoid the castle."

"Griffons do." Drexan beckoned Zur closer. "Not griffs."

Zur reached for the griff's feathery neck. One stroke of a feather and the griff hissed. The boy retracted his hand.

"He senses your fear," Drexan said with an admonishing look. "I can't have fearful servants, Zuran."

Zur opened his mouth to speak . . . and heard the blare of a horn. Swiveling, the griff stretched his wings and sprang into flight, leaving the way he came.

The chancellor flew to the window. "That is a horn I haven't heard in two years," he said breathlessly.

"That's the king's horn," Zur said. *Sounded only when the king has fallen.*

CHAPTER 2

The Brother

orana hated the sounds of horns.

No matter the occasion, weddings, feast days, religious observances, or funerals, she'd feel clammy in her hands. Her shoulders would tense involuntarily, and she'd sense the dull ache in her back that only came during bleeding. Cursed with a weak stomach, she often retched.

She couldn't help it, any more than she could the need to breathe. She was three when she saw her father's men gallop into the bailey, horns braying, her stepmother's body jerking about in their cart, black like crisped bacon.

The dislike set in with the stubbornness of a religious conviction when, at nine, she heard the horns blare for her second stepmother. Garrett, her cruel older half-brother, had made sure she'd known that Romara would lose her head.

Things like that had a way of sticking in a girl's head. And as the thinkers of the Awakening held centuries ago, what the eyes saw the body felt twice over.

The horn blared distantly. The princess sat upright, blind in the steaming water of the bathhouses.

Fear was spoiling a moment's fun. Sweat glistened on the buds of her lover's nipples. Splayed below her, dreamy-eyed and achingly beautiful, Anyasha uncoiled her feet from around the princess's ankles. The nether moisture from their thrusting betrayed the moment's seriousness.

Anyasha furrowed her brow. "That's your father's horn."

Pivoting sharply, Lorana vomited. Slivers of egg white, bread crust, and tomato flesh, her breakfast, bobbed in the water like flotsam.

To her horror, she saw not all of the splatter had made it into the bath.

Ignoring her apologies, Anyasha slicked the mess off her breasts as if it were nothing and rose from the floor. The girl collected the steward's chemise from the floor and wordlessly pulled it down over Lorana until wet skin resisted no more.

"My father wasn't supposed to be back this soon," Lorana began. The threat of more bile seared her throat. "Something's wrong. He's in danger."

She didn't want to say *dead*. Couldn't. She burned away the thought that it could be any of her brothers. *Not Jason,* she told the gods she never spoke with. *And not my father.*

Her servant, lover, and friend fitted her with her sandals. Lorana followed the girl's eyes to her own erect pink nipples, clear as day under a soaked chemise, even in sparse torchlight.

"Let me fetch a cloak," Anyasha said. She vanished into a wall of bathhouse steam.

Lorana waited until the next horn blast. Deciding modesty was a privilege she could spare, the leader of her kingdom ran for the door.

For it was enough to lose three mothers in twenty years. Imagining life without her father or half-brother was too much to bear. Too much.

Bracing for the evening chill, she flew up two narrow stairwells and down the Great Hall's red carpets. She was almost to the gatehouse when a cloak closed comfortingly about her shoulders, sopping the moisture in her hair like a sponge. Anyasha kept up with her brisk pace, herself cloaked and sandaled.

They found the king's carriage in the bailey, at the Great Gates. Knights surrounded the carriage, exchanging awkward glances as the stone maiden strode over. Dressed shabbily in travel-stained helms, mail, and tabards, the men resembled the mud-and-clay figures of saints that littered parish windowsills; they looked about as useful.

No one offered up a single word of explanation. They just stared at the princess and her servant.

Lorana sighed irritably. "Oh, *please,* sirs, can I play this game?" she said, hands on her hips. "Is this how you win, just staring at each other and not telling the king's daughter *WHAT THE HELL is going on?*"

The carriage took to shaking violently, as if a boar were trying to get out. Shouts erupted from inside. Lorana shared a look with Anyasha, decompressing with relief.

The king cursed up a storm, browbeating his knights and bemoaning his lot in life. Which was to say, the king was being himself. *A good sign,* she thought, still tasting bile.

". . . goddamned boots and all, this motherfucking piece of—*oh,* just get off already, *DAMN YOU!*" he growled.

Lorana hurled open the carriage door and braced for the reek of gout.

Were it not for the stately carriage, or the knights ringing it, someone might've mistaken the chubby, half-naked man on cushions for a Common beggar. Disheveled gray hair matted the king's rosy cheeks and forehead. Silvers salted his untidy auburn beard, yet the king looked like a boy as he clutched at his knee, gritting his teeth and wincing. Hexar the First, Lord of Loran, was trying to attend to his ulcered leg.

Hexar was also almost at blows with Sir Jeremy Hunt, just as the knight worked to ease him out of the carriage. Which the king was not having. Sir Rogir Levan looked on tiredly.

"Goddamn you, Jeremy, you quibbling wet nurse, off—I said, *off!*" Hunt fell in a clatter of armor, reeling from a meaty royal fist. "And let *that* stay with you the next time you think about blowing the king's rally horn *WITHOUT HIS FUCKING SAY.*"

"Father," Lorana said suddenly.

Startled, the king spun and whacked his gout leg on the carriage's door. His cheeks flushed red as oil lamps. "*GOD! ANA!* Why didn't you tell me you were there?"

"I'm standing right here," the king's daughter said. "Why are you here early? Charles said you'd planned to stay another day with Lord Thorngale. And your leg—how?" She didn't even know how to order her questions.

"Fell off my damn horse yesterday," he grumbled. "You, Rogir"—he latched onto the knight's arm with his free hand—"I want you to kill that damn beast. Do you hear me? I want it fed to the Commons. They'll get more use out of it than me."

Moments later, Drexan and Hanor flew down the steps. With them hobbled Jon Applewood, the king's surgeon and apothecary. Sighting Jon, the king softened like a hurt boy seeing his mother.

"God and gods, Jon, I could kiss you," the king wheezed. "Get me out of this fucking thing! I need your Healing Halls."

With dusk slicing through the ever-present pearl light of the Silver Walls, Hexar's harried knights lifted their king onto a makeshift litter of carriage cushions and trundled him into the Great Hall.

On the outside, the princess was all smiles and courtesy, and a few incredulous headshakes. On the inside, she thanked gods she did not pretend to know or care for.

As she had since thirteen, Lorana Eddenhold assumed control of the situation her father left in his wake. Clad only in a chemise and wool coat, she trudged up and down the lines of their house's returning forces. Rogir Levan reported the count to her as joylessly as the tax-men had.

After two years at war in the wintered north, the king had returned home with a poorly two thousand knights, even fewer barded horses, and a train of loot-laden carriages.

It was a grim scene as the last men hobbled in. *This was not the army you left with, Father,* she thought. Many of them had wounds they'd seen to in Tesos, but she isolated those with worse injuries and had them sent to the apothecary's staff.

That evening, with all the men off unloading the royal caravan or seeking relief in their cups, Lorana returned to the Great Hall with Anyasha. The two women waited for the king on a bench outside the Healing Halls, unblinking as his curses carried through the door.

"I'll probably be here until sunrise, Yasha," Lorana told her. "Why don't you get some rest?"

She lost herself in Anyasha's guileless brown eyes. "I'd rather stay," her lover responded.

She smiled despite herself. "You were with me at court all day. You somehow managed to stay awake during the Tessian's counts. You ran after me, to wrap a cloak around me, before the world saw my tits and all."

She shrugged. "Like father, like daughter, I suppose."

Lorana *tsk-tsk*ed. "Unforgivable. I shall tell my father to return you forthwith to the jungles of Casaan."

She slapped her arm lightly. "You bitch."

The steward raised an eyebrow. "For that, maybe I'll have you sent to the Red Tower."

"And what, pray tell"—Anyasha leaned in with a teasing smile— "would you do without me, Lorana Eddenhold?"

I'd fall apart, Lorana thought.

A few years her junior, the girl's warm smile could thaw Lorana at a moment's notice. Anyasha had grown from a twig into a comely young woman who could, in a world free of her people's curse, attract a wealthy suitor. Everywhere she went she drew the eyes of lords and servants—even those of other hostages, she'd noticed . . .

Lorana had the girl's hands in hers. "I'm more capable than you know, Eden." The princess felt her cheeks stinging from shame. "I said her name, didn't I?"

The hurt in Anyasha's eyes was perceptible. "Two years away, and for you, it's like she left yesterday."

The steward was fumbling out her apology, a rather bad one, when the door flew open, hitting both women with a wall of reek mingled with the scent of rose oil. The king lumbered forward on his favorite cane, the one clutched at the top by marbled griffon's talons. Lorana unlaced her hands from her lover's, folding them in her lap.

Hexar flitted from Lorana to Anyasha. "Why are you still here?" he grumbled with mock displeasure.

Lorana contained her sigh. "Where else would I be?"

"*Humph*. Off finding a suitor, for starters. Where—"

Just as the king finally found his balance, he nearly lost it. Two pale arms looped around his belly from behind. Heather Eddenhold, her half-sister by the king's fourth wife, nearly ran circles around their father.

"*Father!*" Heather said giddily. "Where are you off to now? You aren't leaving again, are you?"

"God and gods, child," Hexar said, exhausted.

Heather was a picture of what a proper princess *should* look like. The twelve-year-old had porcelain skin and smooth lustrous hair that seemed woven from gold thread. These were Lady Romara's gifts to her only offspring with the king, and they'd one day soon make her a fetching match for the son of a powerful rival lord.

Lorana didn't begrudge Heather her flowering beauty. She *did* rather mind the not-so-subtle oinks and screwed-up pig faces her little sister's ladies-in-waiting made when they passed Lorana in the hall.

"I've *missed* you so," Heather went on. "What did you bring me back from Anjoun and Tesos? You told me you were bringing me back silk and toys, and I don't see them."

"Yes, ermine and dolls!" he said. "But away with you for now, child. I have dealings with your older sister."

"But I've missed you, and I want my dolls," Heather pouted. "Where's Jason? Did he come back with you?"

That name gave the king pause, fleeting but there long enough for Lorana to discern something was, indeed, amiss.

Without prompting, Anyasha curled her hand around the girl's hand. "I'd like to play, Heather," she said with an adult's feigned interest. "Come with me to your doll room. I'll play the dragon, and you a lady in her tower, hmm?"

Heather made a face. "I don't want to play," she protested. "I want to see Jason."

So do I, sister, Lorana thought. *So do I.* Eventually, Anyasha succeeded in tearing the younger princess from her father. She left with hurt in the edges of her eyes. *I'll have to show her how a princess apologizes, later . . . without retching on her breasts.*

The king watched Heather go. "She looks just like Romara." He groped for Lorana's arm. "Come. We have business."

The steward stood. "Are you well enough, Father?"

"Now you're sounding like Jon. I only fell off a horse."

The king looped his arm around hers, and father and daughter plodded off. *I've missed you, Father,* she thought, *even the smell of gout and rose oils.* Lorana walked with her father past the hall leading to the throne room, past exquisite dining halls and trophy rooms.

He didn't need to tell her where they were headed. Hexar had made war on barbarians for two years.

He wanted to see his wives again.

"You fell off a horse only *after* you ended the raids from Uzland," Lorana prodded him. She was the steward. She had questions, but drawing answers from her father was often a game.

So he surprised her when he came out with it: "The whole damned campaign was a botch." He made an irritable gesture.

"But the loot you returned with—"

"Copper coins and rusted steel." Hexar looked away from her, as if ashamed. "Any gold and silver we recovered we paid to King Grisholm in Tesos."

For our war debt, Lorana thought grimly. "But you routed Kar Kravack, at least. Put an end to his raids on Tesos."

Hexar worked his jaw. "Kravack sprung a trap on us in the Spearshield Mountains. Five thousand horse and men marched through the mountains one way"—he held out the column of his arm—"and out came less than half that number."

Lorana felt winded, as if she herself had fallen off a horse. *So that's where all the men went. To snow-covered graves. What a calamity. God and gods . . .*

The king had a dark look. "He's clever, Kravack. He hides in his mountains when Ansaran kings come north, showering their armies with arrows from on high. We snuck an assassin into his mountain camp, once, but we only killed his decoy."

So much war, and so little to show for it all. Thanks to their excursions in lands far north and east of Loran, their house had dusty coffers and owed other kingdoms enormous debts. Now, they had even fewer fighting men.

Hexar saw her expression. "But it wasn't all for naught," he said. "The songs they'll sing about Hexar's army! Especially about Darren Thorngale. Thirty-nine Uzmen cornered him, and he killed them on his own." He clenched a fist, laughing like someone who's won a game against his rival. "You know what they're calling him? Now *there's* a suitor for you, Ana."

Lorana swallowed disbelief at her father's glibness.

A sentry knight, Sir Kyle Urron, stood watch at the Hall of Memory. Seeing them, he opened the door and shut it behind them softly.

A hundred lifelike statues presided on either side of a long red carpet. Torchlight awoke a silverstone glitter dormant in every statue. Incense and rose petals spiced the air, and she listened to the whispers of their feet on the carpet.

Statues on the Street of Kings and inside the Red Tower honored kings, but the Hall of Memory honored loves lost by royal families. Lorana lingered on them as they walked past. King Lathros, the king slain by knights and peasants, meditated on the crown in his hands. Her eyes found Queen Barbara, the last woman to wear a crown, serene amid her antlered stags. Still visible was a shorn antler she'd mistakenly snapped as a girl. *We did that, Edenia,* Lorana thought.

Now was the time to speak honestly. "Father, this is dire news you've brought home with you," she said.

Her tone hardened him. He'd expected this from her, no doubt. "I know, Lorana." He called her by her full name only when he was flustered.

"I don't think you do. You've been away for two years."

She brought him up to speed about their kingdom in a way she couldn't have done through easy-to-intercept letters. Loran's war debts were crippling, and the lords and clergy of the king's Worthy Assembly, which had the power of the purse, did everything they could to make someone else pay for them.

"The merchants in the Wing of Knights can't pay for it all, so the onus falls on Commoners," she said, "who can't speak for themselves in the Assembly."

Hexar waved at her like he would a fly buzzing too close. "Now you sound like my dear brother-by-law, agitating for the bloody Wing of the Commons."

"Father, your kingdom is in trouble." She sounded as helpless as she felt. "Half of your kingdom wants to kill the other half, and I don't know what to do about it anymore."

Whether a steward sat the Silver Walls, or a king, no one could make the Assembly do anything it didn't wish to do. No other kingdom had to deal with a body of men so conniving, ill-suited to governing, or brutally self-interested.

Hexar finally acknowledged her frustration with a grim nod. "The lords and priests do as they've always done: suckle the little people like ticks. Jon told me you named the sheriffs justices of the peace. A wise decision, methinks, daughter." He patted her knuckles almost proudly.

He wanted to change subjects. She wouldn't let him. "A cloth bandage over a gushing wound—nothing more," she said with a hand swipe through the air. "The lords are bidding these sheriffs do terrible things. I'm not sure whether paying them from our treasury will stop it."

"Send the sheriffs to Uzland, then," Hexar joked.

Lorana halted so abruptly the king slumped forward on his cane. "*They're parting peasant children from their parents for trifling reasons,*" she said angrily.

For two years, Loran had suffered under laws made in the Worthy Assembly that required the lower classes to pay higher rents and taxes, or lose their children. Fathers regularly wound up in dungeons for hiding their babes. The children themselves were given over to priests, to be raised and educated at temple.

On the surface, these laws made good sense. If peasants were too poor to pay their taxes and rents, they couldn't well raise children, who might prosper in the care of godly men.

But anyone with half a brain knew what the lords really wanted. Loran was a kingdom divided along the fault lines of two major religions. The lords worshipped their twelve gods in temples led by priests; peasants prayed to one god in parishes led by readers. It was an ancient conflict between Elvarenists and Free Believers . . . a conflict one side wanted to win.

Lords and priests, who pined for an Elvarenist Loran, had simply given up on ruling in good faith. They meant to salt the earth of Free Believers by raising their children in temples. To ensure this would happen, they were deliberately refusing to raise peasant wages, and deliberately hiking taxes and rents. Squeezed by the jaws of that terrible vise, families everywhere were fracturing . . . and because peasants lacked seats in their Assembly, they had no voice. No recourse.

And it was no coincidence that all this began when King Hexar and his sons left for war. "You know who's behind this," Lorana said. "The Assembly does nothing that its Speaker of the Wing of Lords doesn't himself command."

Hexar rubbed his jaw, scowling. "Pinkhands," he muttered with contempt.

"Something must be done, Father, and the kingdom won't suffer a woman to do it," Lorana said. "Something must be done about your Worthy Assembly."

Hexar reddened. "My 'Worthy' Assembly," he sneered. "Worthier are the lords and priests who lie dead and buried! I should've killed them all after the Long Summer Rebellion. Wiped my hands of Assemblies . . . then I'd rule alone, the way Drexan says I should. Like a *true* king."

Lorana listened, unspeaking.

If anyone were eavesdropping—if Hexar's empty threat reached anyone in the Worthy Assembly—they'd have more than debt and unrest to worry over. Worthy of contempt as it was, the Assembly *was* Loran—its greatest nobles, clergy, and merchants. No king had ruled without them for thousands of years. Some, like her father, had fought wars against them.

Hexar raked his beard with a hand. "There was a time all I wanted was the Assembly's adoration," he said.

"The Kingstrials were a long time ago, Father."

"The horn gave you fright earlier," he changed the subject abruptly, softening.

"It always does." A note of bile lingered in her throat.

"I'm sorry for that. It was that fool Hunt's mistake. The Lord of Loran scrapes his leg in a fall a mile out, and his knight sounds his king's horn? Without his leave? *Outside his Walls, around the fucking Commons?*" He grimaced. "I'll strip him of honors and have him gaoled. Remind me to speak to the Grand Inquisitor."

Lorana sensed license. She decided to use it. "Come now, Father. We both know you bluff."

Hexar rounded on her. "Bluff? I *bluff?*" he seethed. "Shall I show you Lady Romara's statue? Or Hanorr Wexley's? Or Alyse Jannus's? See how I *bluffed* when I learned of their treasons."

The princess shied away, refusing to take the bait. Men said Hexar's anger was a lightning bolt that broke the clouds with warning but rarely struck.

Sure enough, remorse softened her father in seconds. "Forgive me, daughter. That was beneath me."

"It was, my king."

Something else troubles you, but what, Father? Rare was the occasion that Hexar uttered the name of her traitor mother, Alyse, the Medecian woman whose joyless countenance drove the king into the arms of the beautiful Sarah Sinclair . . . and the kingdom itself to near ruin. A Long Summer Rebellion was the fruit of their affair, as was the head of Alyse Jannus, lobbed off before the Worthy Assembly could lay siege and rescue her.

Lorana had never blamed her father for beheading Alyse; she was his daughter, not hers. But then death had always been a fact of life in her family.

Walking arm-in-arm with her father, she remembered a clever rhyme the Elvarenists had spun for his four dead wives:

Three rings Hexar gave
To Harriet, Alyse, and Romara,
Whom no man could save—
Not from bloody birth, or Lady Sarah,
Or hearts misbehaved.

In fact, Hexar and Sarah *had* exchanged wedding rings. Her father still wore his.

Two of Hexar's wives stood waiting near an empty wing of the Hall, sculpted from stolen silverstone, forever young and beautiful. Her father's first wife, the Lady Harriet, lifted a slender hand heavenward. The third, the one illegitimate wife, the mother of Hexar's bastard prince, occupied a dais opposite hers, the hint of a smile on her lips.

Hexar put his fingers to his mouth and touched Harriet's stone lips. "My beautiful wives," he intoned. "Harriet, who gave her life for Garrett." He turned to Sarah. "And the woman my *Worthy* Assembly slew," he added bitterly.

"With aid from her own brother."

Hexar shook his head. "No, Evan Sinclair took no part."

She arched an eyebrow. "Are you sure you're my father? Not some changeling like Asha-Ra?"

The king smiled. "'Like Asha-Ra'? Are you my daughter?" He slipped from her grasp and hobbled toward Sarah, staring at her likeness. "For a time my wrath knew no greater object than her brother. Had him thrown in the Tower. Removed his titles—nearly his head."

"As you removed his blackpowder," said Lorana, "saving Loran from the destructive power that stole Sarah from you." Her father flashed her an appreciative look. "Why do you speak of Evan Sinclair?"

Hexar plucked a strand of spider silk from Sarah's chest. "Things change as you age, Ana. Bold kings can know regret."

Regret? Now she *was* worried. "And Alyse the Traitor? Have you forgiven her, too?"

"She wasn't so terrible. She and I both made mistakes."

"My mother was a *traitor*, Father. She conspired against you with the Worthy Assembly. And you rightly beheaded her."

"I know what she did," he snapped. "We're all traitors to our own hearts."

She didn't know what to say. Hexar Eddenhold forgave himself often but never the handful of betrayers whose names still had the power to inspire frowns and dark words from him: Alyse Jannus, Shaddon Eddenhold, Hanorr Wexley, and Romara Verascoli. And, until now, Evan Sinclair . . .

"Father, what aren't you telling me?" she asked suddenly.

Hexar turned to her, lips trembling. His vulnerability frightened her. "Sweet child, mourn with me. Your brother Erick is dead."

The king slumped into his daughter's arms like a falling wall. His tears wetted her cheeks. *My brother. A brother I never knew.* Two years ago, they'd traded Edenia back for Erick, on grounds that Hexar's stolen son would return to Loran.

Instead, Erick Eddenhold went to war for a priestking he saw as more his sovereign than his own father. He hadn't gone to war alone.

"And Jason?" Lorana asked in a tremulous voice.

Hexar pulled away, sucking snot back up his nose. "Fine, thank god, though he disobeyed me in leaving for war in the first place. Garrett is fine, too, thank god." He stiffened. "They're both returning. I sent for them when I was in Tesos. I'll not risk any more of my sons in the priestking's wars."

The princess breathed relief. "When do they return?"

"In a matter of weeks, if they boarded their ship and left without delay. *If* the bastard prince hasn't defied me again."

Jason, you're coming home, she thought happily.

She tried to restrain the bounce in her voice, to little avail. She'd just lost a brother, her only full-blooded sibling by Alyse, a boy she barely remembered and a man she knew only by his infrequent letters to court.

"How did my trueblood brother die?" Lorana asked.

"By the black poison arrows of those heathen bastards, the fucking Muhregites and their dragon Vhizadyn," he swore, fist shaking. "I curse god for my gout, for this age! If I was *half* the man I was . . . I'd leave for the Brace and pay my debt. I'd kill my traitorous brother while I was at it."

She comforted the king. He had a father's rage, even for a son he never knew, a son taken from them as lords and priests stole peasant children. Even if he couldn't say it now, she saw the relief lurking in his eyes. The crown prince lived.

"Erick's death has awoken me, child." The king tightened his grip on the griffon's talons of his cane. "It's made me realize that my days are short. I thought about my reign. What statue of mine would wind up in here or on the Street of Kings? Or god forbid, beneath the Red Tower?" He eyed her solemnly. "Many call me Hexar the Bold. But what will they call me after I'm dead? Hexar the Debtor? Hexar the Fool?"

"Father, no," she assuaged him. In her heart, she knew that one of those names could well one day stick.

He shook his head. "No matter. I've already decided. I'll finally make my peace with Evan Sinclair. And I'll need your help to do it, daughter."

CHAPTER 3

The Example

ara trudged up the village main to Thorn's Keep with the rest of Rosbury's peasants. Beside her walked her mother Rose and their neighbor Caleb. She could tell the other Commoners were unhappy by the way they carried themselves. Every face was serious, and the air felt thick with everything they didn't say.

Not that she needed anyone to tell her what was going on. Even a girl of eleven like Sara Sothron understood when a man was about to lose his head.

The march from the village to the castle was long and uncomfortable in the harsh sunlight. The way there wasn't layered with stone like a proper Romarian road but clod with wet clay and treacherously steep holes. If one walked too fast, he risked jamming his foot and falling; the idiot Praise did this, slipping several times, drawing laughter and headshakes from villagers. The risk of falling made them walk slower, which just made the heat more awful. Sara's pits and inmost thighs clung together sticky-like, irritating her.

She caught Bram the butcher's boy loosening his girdle. If he could do it, why couldn't she? Yet when she made the short-lived attempt, her ear took to burning hot as candle flame. Her mother twisted her earlobe between fingers made of iron.

"Finish what you're doing and I'll whip you like your father did the mules—do you hear, girl?" Rose hissed.

She covered her ear, to ease the burning and hide her face from shame. The village girl couldn't tell what stung worse: her mother's public rebuke, or the mention of her vanished father.

Wroth with her mother, Sara tramped through the mud, trying to put distance between them. Her left foot jammed in a hole, and suddenly she was on her hands and knees, slathered in muck like Praise. At the sound of laughter, her eyes welled with tears she couldn't control. She felt a good cry coming.

Two arms swung beneath her belly and freed her from the mud in one clean sweep upward. Caleb hoisted her in his arms, picking off flecks of mud from her wool. "There, there, princess," he soothed her. "I've got you."

She threw her arms around the farmer's neck and buried her face just below his jaw. It was stubbly and slick with sweat there, but she didn't mind. It was shelter.

Rose walked behind them, arms folded. "You ought not, Caleb," she admonished him softly.

Her mother was a beautiful woman, even when Sara got angry with her. Rose Sothron had dimples that perked with her smile, rich brown hair, and a dutiful womanliness that earned respect for their family in Rosbury. Her father had always said he loved her mother's green eyes best.

"Why, Rose, we both know it's a crime for royalty to soil themselves on Common land," Caleb replied in good humor.

She drew even deeper into the safety of his embrace. Only Praise Whoreson could upset her. Covered in mud and his own filthy rags, the idiot tried desperately for her attention, smiling inches from her face as he kept pace with them.

"Round, round it spins," Praise sang his wheel rhyme with a clumsy twirl, arms fanned out, "until off it rolls again!"

The big man's pustule-covered face, yellow teeth, and sheer height frightened her, but he had a childlike innocence that made her and other villagers look after him as if he were a small boy. His mother had passed from pox the year before. No one knew his father, but guessing his identity was a favorite village pastime.

Sara watched the idiot from the perch of Caleb's arms. "Don't you have any other rhymes you like, Praise?" Bad looks from several villagers reminded her that she and her mother were the only peasants who said *don't* properly, and not *donna*.

Praise didn't notice their reactions. He nodded eagerly, grinning. "Round, round it spins," he answered her.

Caleb must've seen her discomfort, because he told Praise there were faeries in weed patches along the main, and would he like to help him find them?

Bram chuckled as the idiot sat on his haunches, scouring the weeds. "Stupid Pebbleface," he muttered. Other boys their age smirked.

"He donna know there are no faeries," laughed Pesh the Prince. The girl pitied the simpleton as he took to rolling in the grass like a dog, repeating the rhyme.

After a half hour of walking, Thorn's Keep rose above the fields and forestland outside Rosbury. Four stout sentry towers guarded a vine-strewn, merloned keep. Outside sprawled Old Sturdyroot, a withered oak tree said to be as old as a hundred lives of men. A tree stump lay in its shade, crowded with knights in black velvet tabards worked with the sigil of a blood-red tree.

The man who'd summoned them stood on the fringes. Tall and grim, Uthron Morley, Lord Warden of Rosbury, had a forbidding look magnified by his flinty brown eyes and thick, wiry eyebrows. His long black beard swayed with his movements. Beside him stood his youthful son Sam, small and awkward-looking in an ill-fitting doublet and cape. Lady Cathreen hovered by her son.

Sara checked for faces she knew. Seth Briarfield, a local bricklayer, looked on darkly with Bram's smithy father Clyde Hobbs and the cooper Cam Suffrey. Two brunettes hovered close by the dais, admiring the dashing young knight Sir Luc Tolos. Parish reader Gary Henley stood in another tree's shade, flanked by the troublemakers Connor Bagman, Ford Rounsey, Luc Almsman, and Alford Hemlock. The boys Bram and Alfrid and Pesh the Prince, friends all, teased Alfrid's frog-faced sister Jenny, who pled with them to stop.

Everyone was here—everyone but the one who mattered most to

Sara Sothron. *Where are you, Father?* She searched the crowd in vain for the priest Uther Brune and his lost men, for Devan, her father's loyal squire. She had no desire to gaze upon Spittlelip—who did?—but she'd embrace him like a friend all the same if he were present.

Then she would know her father was safe. She still held out hope that he'd show up outside their cruck house one day, Little Lady with him, unsold.

Some of the men grumbled about Sam, wondering what his role could be in the execution. Alford Hemlock leaned into Connor Bagman. "Twelve godfaces, will you just look at it," he said just above a whisper. "Not a hair on that chin. Think he'll swing the blade?"

Luc Almsman harrumphed. "His Wardenship's *always* in want of a demonstration for Sam the Small."

Connor crossed his arms. "It's not *who'll* do the deed that concerns me." And he said no more.

Sara followed his gaze to the man she disliked most. The sheriff of Rosbury, Sir Willard Rittman, stood beside his liege like a loyal hound his master. A stocky, unattractive man, the official had a short-muzzled face and squat nose. An overlong black mustachio curled off his thick, wormy lips, and finery did nothing to help him. By his side were his deputies Sweet Tom, who rarely spoke, and Geffrey Chaffer, who opened his mouth too much, flashing pinkbud-stained teeth.

Once the peasants finished gathering, Morley whispered to Sir Bardo Lym, and the fat knight waddled off. Some minutes later, he returned with the condemned.

Hexaar Olmstead trudged uphill in nothing but leather-patched breeches, his hands tied behind his back. He had a hard, sunburnt body stitched with a Common field hand's muscles.

"Not Hexaar," Rose murmured. "Damien was his friend." *But Father isn't here,* Sara thought.

"Commons of Rosbury," cried a herald she couldn't see through the packed bodies, "harken to the Lord Warden of Rosbury, Uthron Morley, bannerman to King Hexar."

Their lord toyed restlessly with the drape of his long cape.

"Commons of Rosbury," he said, "long have I treated you with love as your Lord Warden. Have we not been friends at times? Have I not looked the other way when you loiter at The Golden Dragon? Have I not allowed you to wear fashions above your station, in violation of the law?"

Alford whispered mockingly to Bagman, "Have you not looked the other way while the Sylvanians cast spells on us?"

"Yet you have not treated me with the same love." Morley scanned their faces like a father disappointed with his children. "The temples and parishes teach the same law—do they not?" His beard ruffled as he twisted to look at the priest. "Brother Elfred?"

The priest nodded gravely. "Justly said, my lord," he said. "Even Reader Gary and I agree on the Great Covenant." Several peasants rolled their eyes or sucked at their teeth. Some turned their heads to catch Reader Gary's reaction, but the parish leader remained statue-still, betraying nothing.

"Secondborn men gave up their naked freedoms in the wilderness for the comfort of the king's love and protection," Morley said. "Our wise forebears did this to save us from dragons and wolves—and did so knowing that with a ruler's protection came sacrifices."

"*Sacrifices*," Alford said. "Gaoler's chains, more like."

"I'd rather suffer the dragons and wolves, personally," Luc said a little loudly.

"One such sacrifice is taxation," Morley said, oblivious to the criticism. "Save for clergy, no one is exempt from what we owe our king. Not even lords."

Another Bagman associate, Ford Rounsey, chuckled with disdain. "Save for the bloody priests, eh?"

The pudgy-faced sheriff overheard that time. He searched the crowd with a hawk's precision until he settled on a culprit. "*What was that,* Ford Rounsey?" his voice snapped like a whip.

The peasant straightened. "Nothin', Sir Willard. Sorry."

Morley took the peasant's measure with his gaze. "Priests are not like our readers," he said stiffly. "Their temples are not ours to draw from."

No one liked that, but that was because most of Loran's peasants worshipped in parishes, where men could hear holy men recite verse in their own tongue. Temples belonged to the priestking and his priests.

The Lord Warden exhaled softly, sadly. "Yet words are not enough." Bardo Lym forced Hexaar to kneel, lay his head across the stump.

"Round, round it spins," Praise sang from somewhere in the crowd, "until off it rolls again." No one acknowledged him.

The lord pointed at Hexaar. "This man before you brought shame on us and his kingly namesake. He was unable to pay his taxes and rents. By the laws of our king and his Worthy Assembly, he was instructed to forfeit his children to priests, who could better care for them."

But that's not what he did, Sara knew.

"But that's not what happened," Morley said. "Sir Willard learned that Hexaar Olmstead tried to leave with his wife and children. *They planned to do this under cover of night.*"

No one shared the Lord Warden's horror. Sara was just a child, but she knew as well as anyone about the hiding games that peasants played with their children when authorities came to collect taxes. No one in Rosbury had five sylvens to pay in poll taxes, let alone five sylvens *per head.* Some neighbors had concealed grown children *for years* to avoid paying what was owed. Unable to pay, many, like Hexaar, abandoned house and land to go into hiding with their children.

Yet Commoners lived by fair play, and peasants never betrayed each other's secrets to the highborn. *So how did Sir Willard learn about it?* she pondered, glancing at faces.

"We must, all of us, pay the king's due," Morley said. "If a man cannot pay what he owes king and lord, he cannot afford to raise children. Thankfully, we stopped this plot and rescued Hexaar's children. I will surrender them to the High Bishop in hopes that he will raise them to lead righteous, dignified lives."

Headshakes and appalled looks swept the crowd. "Peshar the Pederast," Ford Rounsey muttered, disgusted.

Passing over their faces, Rittman settled abruptly on Sara. She reached for her mother's hand, clasping it tightly.

The Lord Warden narrowed his eyes. "I have seen *enough* families go missing with their children," he said. "If you cannot afford your own taxes and rents, you *must* love your children enough to give them up."

"They'd be easier to pay if the lords allowed us to bargain for better wages," Alford ventured within earshot.

Connor scowled. "That'd defeat the purpose of the game, Alford."

"Obey the law," Morley said, "or suffer this man's fate." He comported himself. "Hexaar Olmstead, as Lord Warden of this village, I, Uthron Morley, sentence you to die."

The boyish Brother Elfred separated from the crowd. The priest prayed in First Tongue, the language the lords would not teach their peasants.

As the priest prayed, Hexaar peeled his left cheek off the stump. He had the ire of a man about to lose his head and the confusion of someone who knew he didn't deserve it. "*They're my children*," he said adamantly, convulsing all over. "You'd all do the same!" He wrestled in vain with the ropes binding his wrists behind his back. "Why donna anyone *DO* something?" he demanded. "Someone . . . someone please *STOP THIS*."

In the corner of her eye, Sara saw Ford Rounsey lurching forward, fists shaking, as if he meant to come between Hexaar and his headsman. Reader Gary and Connor Bagman seemed to sense his intentions. They clasped his shoulders, rooting Ford in place.

Rittman lost patience. Stepping forward, the sheriff pressured Hexaar's face flat to the stump, as if he were a butcher forcing a chicken to conform. "*Stop it*," the peasant pled.

"In the First Days, Dracar also resisted judgment," Morley responded, aloof.

The comparison only salted wounds. Lords were always keen on the parable of Dracar, the God Who Rebelled and Died. *A prayer for you and a prayer for me,* went the popular peasant rhyme, *except for Dracar, who burns for eternity.*

Fear gnawed at Sara. *Will you burn with Dracar, Hexaar?*

At a gesture from the lord, Cathreen led their son Sam to the stump. The boy glanced about nervously as she instructed one of the knights to lend her son his sword.

"Oh god," Alford Hemlock said, appalled. "He'll botch it."

Her mother reeled her in close, covering her face with her hand. "Don't look, Sara," she said gravely. Rose pressed her face into her itchy dress, as deep as her face could go. "Don't look."

Sara would never forget what followed, not for the rest of her days. Steel whistled through the air. There was a sickening wet *thunk.* People shrieked.

"Oh my god, he *missed.*"

"Maetha save him, *his fucking head,*" another man wept, calling upon the godface of mercy.

Thwack. Thunk, theck, thunk. Men loudened with horror and disapproval. *Thunk, thunk, theck. THWACK.*

By the time it was okay for her to look, Hexaar was gone. Crimson glistened like dark red wine on the tree stump and grass. The body had gone with a group of men, along with—and this was something she overheard the adults whisper—a shaken, weepy-eyed Sam Morley.

The Commons didn't linger. Connor Bagman turned first, and Rounsey and Alford and others followed him. They halted when the lord's herald blew his horn. "Your lord has not given you leave," the herald fumed indignantly.

"Indeed, I have not, for there are gladder tidings," Morley said. Some peasants turned about fearfully; others remained facing the village main. "By the will of Princess Lorana, acting on the authority of King Hexar, the Walls have named for you, Rosbury, a new justice of the peace."

Sara almost groaned with the others as Rittman stepped forward. "Henceforth," the lord declared over the disgruntled noise, "Sir Willard Rittman shall enforce the king's will in the collection of taxes. Such as it is, he may by the king's authority inspect dwellings, question men, and gaol lawbreakers."

As if of one mind, Commoners turned to leave, silent in their fury. Someone wept for Hexaar, Linda, and their sons, who'd soon be in a *priest's* care, twelve-as-one be with them. Sara hastened back up the main with Caleb and her mother, eager to be done of the whole awful, lurid affair.

"Rose?"

Sara tensed. The voice belonged to the new justice, and it issued in their direction, but of course. Willard Rittman had an eye for her mother; everyone knew it. Never mind that her mother was wife to a noble knight, proper wedded like any decent woman.

Rittman approached them. Rose stood a little straighter, smiling through her nervousness. "Sir Willard." She tucked a loose hair up into her wimple, annoyingly.

Sara seethed with resentment. She didn't like Sir Willard, didn't like his forked beard and squinty little eyes, didn't like his slippery voice, didn't like that he approached her mother like a man in courtship. She didn't like this man.

Rittman clasped his hands together at the front. "A word, Rose?"

Something surged up in Sara. Maybe it was all the worry over her father, or maybe the fact that Hexaar had just lost his head in the worst way possible. Whatever it was, she stepped between her mother and the justice.

"Men *mustn't* speak with married women without their husbands present," Sara said sharply. The One True God gave Rose Sothron eyes for scolding, and they scolded her now.

Rittman had the courtesy to at least *seem* chastened. "But of course. Sir Damien's daughter speaks true. I should expect nothing less." He smiled at her as he would a babbling infant.

"Might you have word about Damien Sothron, Sir Will?" Caleb asked abruptly, in a tone that seemed to suggest he knew perfectly well that Rittman did not.

The justice regarded him with flat eyes. "No, I have not, Caleb Bard, though not for lack of inquiring."

"Then I must thank you for inquiring," he replied quickly. "Rose, shouldn't we be on our way? Evening is almost upon us and I believe you still need me to—"

"A moment, Caleb Bard," Rittman said with some sternness. "That's all I ask."

They all looked to her mother. Rose assented with a nod. Sara wanted to kick her in her shin.

"I know it has been difficult since Damien disappeared, along with Brother Uther and Lord Uthron's other men-at-arms," Rittman said. "My lord has been distraught, and knows about your hardship. I have therefore petitioned Lord Uthron to allow you and Sara to go to the Walls and help prepare the king's feast for Remembrance Day."

Rose and Caleb looked stunned. It wasn't a good sign.

"To the Walls?" her mother piped. "Sir Willard, you . . . you do me great honor."

His wormy lips peeled back for a smile that made Sara's skin crawl. "You and your daughter will help prepare supper for the king, his family, and the Worthy Assembly. You'll be paid for your work. I know this isn't what you wished to hear from me, but it's the best I can do for your loss."

Sara made little fists. "There has been *no* loss," she said fiercely. "My father *will* return. You *must* make more inquiries, Sir Willard."

Rittman offered a fleeting nod. Sara thought it mockery.

"Sir Willard, if I may"—Sara's mouth fell open when she saw her mother reach tenderly for the justice's wrist—"Caleb Bard is a dear friend to my husband. If it please you, I know it would please him and me if, well, if he could attend with us. He knows how to skin rabbits. He makes a delicious onion stew."

Rittman weighed the farmer with a look. "I see no reason why not . . . especially if it pleases *you,* Rose. I shall speak with Lord Uthron." He kissed her hand.

Wisely, Caleb restrained Sara by her shoulders.

On the road back, Sara expected her mother to pinch her ear or reprimand her, but she was positively *happy,* like she hadn't been since before her father had left with Little Lady. She didn't like it, but then Caleb was in high spirits, too. They seemed eager to shut away all memory of what'd happened.

"Oh, Caleb, can you imagine?" her mother said as they walked, twisting one of her wimple's strings around her finger. "No more selling onions at market! Not for a while. Not if we're paid well."

Caleb nodded agreeably. "These are glad tidings—*very* glad. They're said to pay their servants well at the Walls. I've heard as much as three gold lorens for one night's service."

"My husband will rejoice when he hears . . ."

Caleb put a hand on her shoulder. Only *he* could do that, no one else. Caleb himself had never taken a wife, and it was known in Rosbury that he was no threat to her father or any married man. "He *will* return, Rose. I know it." He took Sara by her hand. "In the meantime, we need to make our thanks. Glad tidings deserve glad thanks, don't you think?"

Sara thought her mother would refuse, but she pursed her lips for the smallest of smiles. "Yes, I suppose we should."

Later that night, with the air cool and alive with crickets, Sara Sothron left her family's dwelling with her mother. The two of them found Caleb amid the moss-bearded oak trees in Elf's Grove. He sat on his calves, on the ground, naked save for the cloth around his waist. Between his thighs lay a hare, which he held by its ears. The knife by his ankle glinted in the starlight.

This was forbidden practice, she knew. Neither readers nor priests condoned it, and the High Bishop was said to want anyone caught doing it taken to the Red Tower.

But no one had stopped the Commons of Rosbury from practicing their Old Ways. Times were bad. The people were poor, the taxes and rents high. Men were off at war, and lords were giving their children to priests, who did not pray to the peasants' One True God. Those who refused to give up their children, their lords beheaded.

And Sir Damien Sothron, her father, was missing.

"Come here, Sara," their neighbor said softly. She went to her knees beside him. "Let us thank the old gods, the gods who were here before the priests, before even the Romarians. Let us make a Gift."

With a flick of his wrist, Caleb plunged the knife into the hare's neck. Blood as rich and dark as Hexaar's oozed from the wound, blackening its fluff. He stroked the fur almost lovingly.

"Gods of root and stem," he said, "gods that gave us elves and men, gods that gave us the Great Tree: we thank you for Sir Willard's glad tidings. We pray for Hexaar Olmstead's widow Linda, and her lads Brad and Sam. Let Brad and Sam come to no harm under the High Bishop.

"And we beseech you for Sir Damien's safe return."

"And we beseech you for Sir Damien's safe return," Sara and her mother repeated as one.

CHAPTER 4

A Long Time Away

he *Drunken Adventure* sailed into the Shimmering Bay ahead of forbidding black clouds some of the Geghanese men aboard warned would omen ill for their galley. These were a superstitious folk with a sixth sense for treacherous waters, and they didn't much like their passenger, the bastard prince eager to see his father's kingdom again.

Luckily for Jason son of Hexar, the captain he'd hired in Nerimba had a boastful disregard for fickle sea goddesses and bad signs. He was a sight to see on the quarterdeck, laughing as he manned the ship's wheel, raining insults upon sailors. His ink-black skin gleamed in the sunlight as he pointed to the city.

"Do you smell it?" his captain, Merman Jarrod, shouted against the wind. "The smell of land, my friend!"

Jason wrinkled his nose, cringing. *The smell of Shit Street, more like,* he pondered. The rank reached them a mile out from port. Tiny fishermen were about their business up and down the fingers of damp wooden piers. The flotsam of loose planks and city refuse coalesced along the shore. Behind the smoke-strewn city loomed the vast, twelve-sided curtain of the Silver Walls, a castle that shone with pearl light, as if it were a lamp.

"You see? Merman Jarrod show you the way," the captain roared to Jason from his deck. For added effect, he grabbed his crotch and lunged at the nearest Geghanese sailor, howling like a deranged wolf. "Awoooooh! You see? Awooooooh! *Fuck* your bitch goddess, you scabs! I give my seed to her mouth! Merman Jarrod knows no sea goddess, for he does not care."

Jason smiled at his captain. Smiling felt strange. The bastard prince hadn't smiled for two months. He studied the city and kingdom he'd left behind two years ago, tasting the bay's salty air.

The captain handed off the wheel and joined him. "Why are the Walls described as silver?" Merman Jarrod gestured to the unflattering red brick patterns below the Silver Walls's luminous battlements.

"Ever since I first looked upon them, I felt like I'd been sold lies since boyhood."

I suppose we all have. "It's stonelust that tarnishes," Jason said. "Men have always yearned for the stone that shines. Their theft leaves a hole that must be filled. No one knows where the silverstone came from, or how King Anjan brought it to Loran, so builders fortify the curtain wall with stone and brick."

Merman Jarrod toyed with a spry hair on his chin until he plucked it. "The peasants, eh?"

"Not entirely. Peasants can't reach it all."

In fact, the castle's worst defacers had typically been members of whichever noble house had their turn to sit the Walls. Kings stripped the castle of her silverstone as invaders plunder kingdoms, for glittery statues and tombs, or more often to pay off their debts. King Eduard started the tradition, famously, when he had his builders fashion the Silver Throne.

Jason *himself* was guilty of filching from the First King's castle, but he hadn't required an entire silverstone, just a small piece for the Iron Street ringmaker. He turned his moonlight ring about his finger. *And do you still wear yours, my sweet?*

"Is it as you remember it?" the captain asked.

"Yes," Jason replied. *And no.*

He listed on a balustrade, trying to picture his farewell of two years ago at the piers. He'd kissed Lorana on her cheeks, and the stone maiden hadn't wept, not even then. Heather he'd twirled about in the air, promising to return with lifelike dolls from Chi-Say.

His king father hadn't been there on the docks that day. He'd been furious with Jason for defying him and leaving for Parlisis's foreign wars.

Jason gazed forlornly at the vacant piers. *Will you even honor my return with an escort, Father?*

Yet there were fonder memories. Jason had married the love of his youth in this kingdom. No one knew of it beyond husband and wife—not his half-brothers. Not even Lorana.

His last night in Loran had been with her, curled against each other on a fountain's edge. The fountain water lapping on limestone sounded as real to him now as the waves breaking under *The Drunken Adventure*. If he closed his eyes, he could still smell her intoxicating perfume, feel her golden hair on his face, taste beeswax on her lips. Jason tugged on his wedding ring nostalgically.

"I take you as husband, and love you forever," his secret wife had whispered in his ear, coiling her legs around his waist as she'd yielded to his loins. "I give my heart to you and no one else. I love you Jason, always. I love you."

Merman Jarrod jolted him with a hearty slap on his back. "Lucky for you, eh?" Jason looked at the hulking man queerly, wondering his meaning. The captain nodded to the solid gray curtain around sandstone cliffs to the east. "Lucky for you the Geghanese goddess did not piss on us."

"Not lucky." Jason clamped his right hand, his sword hand, around Jarrod's thick bicep. "We had an honorable captain, and I, a faithful friend."

"And yet we could not save your brother," the Casaanite said, almost reading his mind. "I am sorry, my friend."

Erick. His tongue went slack. He could still taste the iron and pus he'd inhaled from trying to suck poison from Erick's wound. Lorana's brother, whom he'd known only as a grown man changed by war, perished clutching a copy of the Twelve Testaments so worn its loose pages had scattered like feathers in a wind. When he closed his eyes at night, Jason unfailingly saw the bright flames of his pyre raging against black smoke.

And the rank. He'd never forget it. The sweet fetor of his half-brother's burning flesh was all he could smell for weeks. It'd even seeped into his clothes, forcing him to discard them.

"My brother's death is something I will carry with me for the rest of my life," he remarked softly. "He died fighting for a cause he believed in. Whether there be one god or twelve, they grant us no higher honor."

The captain regarded him thoughtfully. "It was not the dead of whom I spoke, my prince."

Oh, yes, my other *brother.* "Prince Garrett's decision was his own. There was naught either of us could do."

"Aye, I fear for him," Merman Jarrod went on. "That ship he boarded, I've never seen its sigil before, my prince. And I've never known a man to return from the world's edge."

"He is a seasoned warrior and the crown prince of Loran," Jason returned curtly, to signal he'd had his fill of conversation on this subject. "And I've told you, I'm no prince." *Even if I am the king's trueborn son. His last son . . .*

The ship captain made a grim headshake. "Such a terrible name, especially for a man of such honor as you. In my tribe, we'd slit a child's throat before we'd name him Child of War in any tongue."

Death might be a mercy, thought the bastard prince, for whom startled looks and disapproving expressions had been par for the course since his youth.

The Long Summer Rebellion had ended in a stalemate with his mother's horrid death, just before Stoddard Trambar, Willard Potter, and their Army of the Gods could besiege the Silver Walls. Yet the tragedy hadn't been enough for the lords and priests of the Worthy Assembly. To prevent an invasion by seven other kingdoms, King Hexar had begrudgingly fixed his seal to a parchment that declared his illegitimate third son by his illegitimate third wife would forever bear the surname Warchild, not Eddenhold.

Irony wasn't lost on the war-weary prince. *I'd give all my remaining days to never draw blood again,* he thought, *and yet I'm the one called Warchild.*

Merman Jarrod unscrewed the top of his wineskin and tilted his head back for a gush of red-violet wine. "Now your brother, the crown prince"—he wiped his lips—"*there* was a man who deserved a last name like Warchild."

Jason peered beyond the bow, toward the pearl-slashed sky west of the storm clouds. *Where are you, Prince Garrett?* he pondered. *And was it grief that drove you to madness . . . and to try for a land beyond the sea no one living has ever seen?*

Weeks after the crown heir to the Silver Throne boarded an unfamiliar ship in the middle of a fog-blanketed sea at night, he still had no idea what to make of it—or what even to tell his king. The whole thing was maddening to think on, a bad dream from which he couldn't wake. *Damn you for making me explain it, Garrett,* he thought, *you and your quest.*

It was the prince's scuffed boot he saw last, pushing off into coiling fog, toward the shape of a galley.

"What will your king father make of your silks, do you think?" the Casaanite captain asked.

I wonder if anyone would even recognize me. He gave himself a look up and down. *I hardly recognize myself.* He had on rich silk from Nerimba, sunset-orange pantaloons that rippled in wind, a cape stitched across the back with his house's soaring griffon, leather boots ornamented with tiny decorative gold chains by their toes. Bronze was his sun-kissed skin, long and smooth the raven-black hair that spilled down his chest and backside.

He was a far cry from the boy who had sailed east for the priest-king's Holy Wars. Two years had changed him. The three brothers had had their fill of strange customs. They'd supped on honey-roasted duneboar with sultens in vast desert palaces. They'd blown smoke from the ivory *chu-churoo* pipes beneath the harem tents of sandlords and their moonwives. They'd even once seen a two-legged merman surfacing for air while anchored.

Jason had killed twenty-five men.

And we weren't always at war, were we, my brothers? We laughed. A brighter memory obscured the blacker ones. Once, in the rolling dunes of some wasteland, they'd asked for shelter with an oasis lord. After some quip by Garrett about his "purer" half-brothers, their host, by then slippery drunk, said he had just the answer, and snapped his fingers. In had walked the Sphinx's Daughters, whom the oasis lords of Nerimba prized for their violet hair, olive complexions, and golden eyes.

Jason had refused because he was a husband, and Erick because of vows, but that didn't persuade Garrett. The crown prince called their cocks flaccid excuses for manhood. Jason shrugged off the insult easily. Not so, Erick. Their half-brother had drawn his blade in challenge. As always, the prince named Jason Warchild had scrambled to make peace.

No peace had to be made. Sodden drunk, the crown prince had unsheathed his sword so clumsily that he broke his nose with the pommel on the upswing. Jason had been the first to laugh, followed by a bloody-nosed Garrett and, finally, Erick himself.

Yet he'd understood Erick's indignation. They'd refused the Sphinx's Daughters for their own reasons. Erick had his piety, and Jason a wife . . . and hers was the Most-Sought Hand in the Thirteen Kingdoms.

"I take you as wife," Jason remembered whispering in her ear by Sarah's Fountain, "and love you forever."

Southpoint was so close now he could make out faces in a Common crowd about its business by the piers. There were the familiar black rooftops of Silver Street, and there, the market shanties of Fish Street, and about them all the merchants, bellowing prices.

"Is that your king I see there?" Merman Jarrod gestured at a pier thick with knights in sunlit armor and silver cloaks. Jason saw a red-robed man among them.

As their ship lurched closer, he recognized the Grand Inquisitor Charles Burke, his father's spymaster. "No, not the king," Jason said. "An old friend and my father's advisor." He decided against sharing *which* advisor.

Sad as the truth was, Jason pondered whether his father had dispatched the gaoler for another reason. *Are you come to escort me to the Walls, Lord Charles—or to a cell in your Red Tower?* Hexar's anger was as legendary as the king himself was unpredictable. Jason had gone to war without his approval. He didn't know what to expect.

Merman Jarrod began pacing up and down his main deck, barking orders to scattered crewmembers. Geghanese sailors scaled mast nets; others unwound the snakes of thick chains connected to anchors. Up top, two men unfurled the crimson and silver of his father's banner. The griffon untangled itself in its wind-tossed folds, soaring. Pride mingled with his grief and sadness as Jason stared up at the banner, imagining the strong faces of his half-brothers, Erick with his disheveled mop hair, and Garrett, the spitting image of their father.

The ship anchored beside Charles's pier. The Geghanese seemed eager to be done with him. Needing no prompting from their captain, the sailors vanished under deck and reappeared with their cargo, chests full of loot from conquered villages and the gifts of grateful sandlords rescued from Muhregite control.

Finished with giving orders, the captain strolled back to where Jason stood. "They're ready to be done of this journey," he said of the Geghanese.

"Done of me, you mean." Jason plucked a loose thread from his tunic. "And can you blame them?"

"Bah! They're superstitious women, all of them." Merman Jarrod crossed his arms, watching as two sailors struggled with an ornate chest; Jason realized it had belonged to Erick. "If I'd had a proper *Casaanite* crew, we might've been able to sail in search of the crown prince, alas."

"Prince Garrett made his own decisions. Now I must make mine." Jason extended a gloved hand. "I hired the right captain. Thank you, Merman Jarrod."

The captain's gold teeth showed in his grin. "Pay me with good Loranian coin, my friend. That'll be thanks enough."

"As agreed, I paid you half what was yours in Nerimba," he said. "Remain anchored here and I will see we pay you the rest after I've seen the king."

Jason began to turn when the captain seized his arm. His grip was vise-like. He grinned still, but his eyes bespoke deadly seriousness. "We will not sweat too long here, I hope?"

He understood. This was a seaman accustomed to less-than-honorable dealings. "Of course. Tell your men to leave half of my chests on-board as insurance until you're paid."

Merman Jarrod left the faint impression of a handprint on his arm. "You are a man of honor, Jason son of Hexar," he said, bowing.

After embracing the ship captain, Jason tossed his left leg over the balustrade and climbed down the net. He found Lord Charles Burke at the end of the pier. He had an escort of steel-lobstered knights. Jason slipped off his twinkling wedding band and stuffed it in his pocket.

The Grand Inquisitor bowed. "Lord Jason, it is a pleasure to set eyes upon you once more."

The bastard prince embraced his father's advisor. "It's good to see you again, Lord Charles," he said.

Slender and frail, Charles Burke showed his more than sixty years in his pronounced stoop and liver-spotted hands. The Grand Inquisitor's scarlet robes fell twisting and curling from shoulders that seemed too brittle for the gold and silver chains of office that hung about his neck. New silvers flecked the hook of a black beard under his chin. Commoners called this the torturer's *real* tongue, corrupt and dripping with the tar he smeared on his guests at the Red Tower.

"I've informed your king father of your arrival, and he and his court await you presently," Charles said.

"How did my father know in advance that we would be here? A storm prevented us from sending word at Ramsport."

The Grand Inquisitor smiled knowingly. "Why, I am his spymaster, Jason. I know all things. Or have you forgotten?"

"Then you must know that Prince Garrett is not with me."

The color drained from the old man's face. "Where is King Hexar's heir, Lord Jason?" Charles asked softly.

Damn you for making me explain, Garrett, Jason thought bitterly. *Damn you, and damn your elves.*

CHAPTER 5

Light and Shadow

ou've been staring at that all morning," Evan Sinclair's son-by-law told him, referencing the letter he held.

The traitor nobleman waxed a thumb over the letter, as gingerly as if it were an heirloom of his ancestral house. *As well as I should make it one*, he thought, *passing it down to Rathos and Mina, for their children and theirs. The letter from the man who saved my head . . . offering me the chance to see the king who wanted to strike it off.*

He watched how the flourish of light from their campfire illuminated each crease in the vellum, every deliberate stroke left by the author's quill pen. The only thing the firelight didn't permeate was the letter's wax seal stamped with the grasping-talons sigil of the King's Crow. *But for what reason would they keep it?* he wondered. *For the peace I bought by persuading my fellow traitors to accept this invitation and send us east on their behalf . . . or the cause I killed—along with myself?*

A wind sighed through the limbs of the sentry oaks around their camp. "You might put it away, lest the breeze snatch it up," his ward, Rathos Robswell, added.

Evan smiled quickly, appreciatively. *Of course*, he thought, *I'm a sentimental fool. There are always eyes in a forest.* Folding the letter, he slipped it inside a cloak pocket. He snapped off a haunch from the spitted hare and blew on steaming flesh until it was safe to taste.

Rathos sat cross-legged on the other side of the fire. He watched Evan intently. "You still can't believe it, can you?"

Evan nipped at the flesh, eyes low on the fire. "It's been twenty years," he said softly. "You were young the last time I visited the Silver Walls, and I still sat in the Wing of Lords. The last time I was there in the king's good graces, my sister was alive. And this forest"—he pointed up and circled his finger—"had another name."

"Haymath, named after the first victor of the Kingstrials."

Evan nodded. He wiped the grease from his moustache and gazed around the forest renamed for his late sister.

Spring had come. White-spotted oaks and pines stirred with life. Squirrels chased their mates up trees. A pair of huge carpenter bees hurtled past his ear. High above, sparrows chirped ceaselessly. He smelled wet earth.

To Evan, all of this was familiar and not. A generation ago, he'd navigated these woods with his late sister and a friend for the last time. They'd been on a mission: to court a married king and deliver reforms to keep their kingdom a peaceful one.

Here we are again, Sarah, with nearly the same goals, Evan thought to himself as if he were speaking with his sister, as was his wont. It'd been twenty years since he set foot in the city of Southpoint, twenty-one since he'd been inside the Silver Walls. He tried not to dwell on that *other* building he counted himself lucky to have not seen in all these years.

The one in which he'd nearly opened his own veins. The one he'd undoubtedly see again by day's end.

Yet the occasion for their travel this time was different. Drexan Lorrain had set up an audience with the king, to mend old wounds and hear the Loyal Company's petitions. *Let this not end in bloodshed, too, sister.*

"I should find Karl," Rathos said with a look around.

Evan savored the meat's sticky grease. "You give him too much credit."

"He gives *himself* too much credit. The fool's got a mouth as big as a catfish's."

Evan opened his mouth and closed it suddenly, imitating a catfish. He broke into easy laughter that Rathos resisted.

"You're less worried, then?" Rathos said with a nervous smile. "Should that make me more confident in this mission?"

Evan sampled the hare again, shrugging. "No," he intoned more seriously, "but life is short enough without laughter."

"Aye, and my days longer until I see her again."

"I told her I'd bring you back safe and sound. I told *both* of them." *And not a word of it assuaged any of us,* he thought.

Rathos cast a longing look westward—in the direction of Evan's ancient castle, where they'd left family to worry about them. He lingered affectionately on the ward he loved as one of his own children, and not only because his father, Matthus, had been his best friend, or even because the knight had sacrificed his life for Sarah's. Evan had warded Rathos and his sister Dana since their parents' deaths.

As head of the Loyal Company, Evan mentored Rathos. He was his adoptive father, truthfully, even though Rathos had never called him father, and he'd never called Rathos son.

Evan was proud of him, and took comfort in his presence.

Rathos looked so much like Matthus it was hard not to confuse their names. He had his father's angular cheekbones, hooked nose, and brittle brown hair. Slender and average in height, he had serious, olive-green eyes that hinted at a fierce intelligence.

Yet Evan also saw his daughter's touch in him, a drab man hopelessly indifferent to fashion. As Rathos was his father's son, Mina was her mother's daughter; she'd insisted upon seeing her husband garbed handsomely for his visit to see the king. He watched, amused, as Rathos fussed with the slit sleeves of his emerald doublet.

Rathos noticed his gaze. "I can make do with the doublet and cape, just not this shiny, attention-catching brooch."

"Better that we're unafraid to be seen this close. Burke's spies watch us. Though perhaps you preferred to wed my *other* daughter, who shares your dislike of finery."

Rathos smiled lightly. He started to say something when the sound of hooves caught their attention. Karl Redmore rode into camp astride his horse.

"Come at once," the Reubenite said. "I found something you both need to see."

Karl sped off without another word. Rathos doused the fire with a stream from his waterskin and untethered their garrons; Evan slung their bags over the horses. Mounting, the two men galloped downhill after Redmore and through a sunlit glen, toward the sound of trickling water.

Rounding a tree trunk, Evan discovered Karl kneeling by a brook.

Their mounts snorted and stomped with displeasure.

"It's death's company that makes them nervous," Karl told them. He pointed downstream. "Look."

Evan focused on a shadow half submerged in the shallow water some yards off. Majestic in life, the creature had died in pain from the looks of its four pitifully shrunken legs, crushed like flowers trampled underfoot. *The men who did this had to cripple the legs to avoid those grasping talons,* he thought. No doubt someone had lost something important trying to subdue the king's bird.

"An omen if I ever saw one," Karl said softly.

Rathos dismounted with a flourish of his cape. He knelt on the bank.

"Show care," Evan warned them. "Lord Reuben wrote that an animal's corpse can still pass disease to the handler."

Rathos acknowledged his caution with the flash of a dagger. He flipped over the carcass with a flick of its tip.

"A baby griffon," Karl announced.

"No," Rathos said. "Its smaller cousin. A griff."

Evan drew close. A griff it was, or had been, kin to the far larger griffons of Loran's Great Tree. Its head was hacked away, its plumage plucked, its lion's tail shorn to a whiskery stump. Its valuable talons were missing; its once-handsome paws were swollen bloody abscesses. The king's bird had been slain for profit, the undesirable parts left to rot.

"We're not alone," Karl said under his breath. "This is the work of outlaws. Maybe the Heretics. We know how fond their Mad Lady is of griffon skulls."

"Doubtful," Rathos responded. "The Heretics follow the Old Ways. The rumors about griffon skulls are fishwife gossip."

"You know a Heretic, then, eh, Silvertongue?" Karl teased.

He doesn't know how close he is to the mark. "Outlaws or poachers, this is grotesque work," Evan observed.

Not even those who opposed him in the Loyal Company would disagree. Killing griffons was one thing; griffs, another. These were beautiful animals, harmless when left alone. Cheats and outlaws peddled a griff's feathers, tails, and talons as indulgences they promised could cure the pox or ferry one's soul safely to the Evergreen Isles. The Commons, whose lot in Loran was suffering, made easy prey.

"Best we be on our way," Evan told them. "Lord Drexan promised us safe passage through Southpoint, but neither he nor the king have much authority with outlaws."

Rathos cleaned his dagger in the brook. He hauled himself back into his saddle. "If I believed in omens, I'd say this was a bad one. Thankfully, we're men true to the Awakening"—he paid the Reubenite a look—"and not superstitions."

"I'd wager this is a *good* omen," Karl ventured with a braggart's daring. "The king's bird is dead. Maybe his whole rotten court and the Unworthy Assembly will follow suit, too."

Evan dismounted. He was in his face in two strides.

"You watch those words, Karl," he snarled, jabbing his chest. "You watch them closely. This is Southland. One false word here, anything smacking of treason, and we'll be killed. Take it from one who has been inside the Tower and lived."

Karl wasn't humbled. "Then why *risk* this journey," he implored the noble. "You lead a company of traitors devoted to the king's overthrow."

"Speak for yourself and not Evan or me," Rathos snapped. "Petitioners want peace. You and Rezlan's Reubenites agitate for that treason."

"Until the next election," Karl muttered. "Until the Loyal Company of Loran speaks with one voice, *for* Loran."

Evan grimaced. Rathos spat from his saddle. Karl seemed to shrink, fully aware of the valuable piece of information he'd let slip. *So, this is why the Company sent him with us,* he thought. *To spy, if not to sabotage. Worse for them that they sent us the Reubenite with a mouth as wide as a catfish's.*

He shifted his jowls, weighing what to say next. "We voted on this months ago," the traitor nobleman said firmly. "We all agreed this was our best last chance to air our grievances with the king and restore the Fourth Wing."

"*If* we're allowed to air them."

"*If* you mean to honor our assembly, stay and work with us," Rathos said. "If not, leave now, while you still can with your coward neck. Lord Evan and I will represent the Loyal Company at the Silver Walls on Remembrance Day."

Inside, Evan grinned. Rathos had made a veiled threat.

They could very well leave the Reubenite behind if Karl broke faith. If the Pigeons, the spies and messengers loyal to their band of traitors, came upon him without them, they'd immediately summon the Loyal Company. Karl could face expulsion for defying orders, and expulsion meant that someone would find him dead in an alley somewhere. A ship filled with traitors couldn't suffer leaks, after all.

Karl seemed to understand that he'd led himself onto dangerous ground. "Well, come on then," he said, eyes low.

A half hour went by that Karl spent in silence, a reprieve for the traitor nobleman. It was a few miles before they started to smell the city, and a few more before the luster of the Silver Walls began to catch the leaves like moonlight. The company splashed through another brook and rode up a large hill in the direction of a horizon rippled with otherworldly light.

Unspeaking, Evan slid down from his saddle. He donned his feathered flat cap and strode to the end of a stone ledge that jutted out over green wilderness. Rathos followed, and then Karl.

"Behold the city of light and shadow," the nobleman said with a sweep of his hand.

Above a smoke-strewn city pulsed an aura of pearl-white light, gently, with the rhythm of a dying heartbeat. Daylight punched pockets in the luminescence, showing them patches of a vast, rust-red curtain wall rimmed with silvery battlements.

A wind cleared the smoke, and there it was suddenly, the Silver Walls, looming over the city like a mountain. Priests and readers taught that the First King had wanted a castle to rival all castles, to forever remind the world of his half-elven power. This, his builders had given in excess. Unearthly light fanned out from battlements, last vestiges of a time when silverstone in the Silver Walls had been the rule, not the exception. No other stone could cast light like silverstone, and it was found nowhere else on earth.

Which was why, Evan observed wryly, he saw even *less* silverstone in the battlements than he had decades ago.

He understood his son-by-law's awe as he stared, mouth slightly agape. That awe had been his once, too. "You said there were no words, and you were right," Rathos marveled.

Evan scanned the rest of the city. "No words."

Below the divine castle sprawled Southpoint, a city that fought for space with everyone and everything, including the ancient, wine-colored walls that struggled to contain it. A main road, Silver Street, still known as Shit Street, sliced the city in two. West and north of that road loomed colonnaded temples and lordly manors. From here, Evan could discern curls in the heads of statues on the Street of Kings.

On the opposite side of Silver Street dwelt another city entirely. South and east, the main road decayed into a warren of narrow streets and alleys, segmenting hundreds of hovels, brothels, inns, marketplace stalls, and poorhouses. The ants of peasants and merchants crowded the streets, navigating carts and wagons trundling through. Fires fumed across the south, belching plumes of smoke that swirled through the silverstone aura.

Karl covered his nose. "Has it always smelled so awful?"

"The worst at noon," Evan said. "Southpoint's mayor came into his position almost solely because everyone wanted—"

The nobleman trailed off, feeling as if a hole had been punched through his chest. It was still there, after all of these years. Waiting for him. Why was he surprised?

"Lord Evan?" Rathos watched him, concerned.

He nodded at the hulk of garish stone that presided over the city's eastern ward like a crimson sentry. "The Red Tower."

Karl seemed unimpressed. "How long did the Grand Inquisitor keep you there?"

"One year, three months, nine days, and four hours," Evan said, transfixed. *The worst year of my life,* he pondered, *but not always because I was a prisoner.*

Had he *really* languished there, resigned to his death? From here, he felt foolish. The Red Tower was tiny, almost an afterthought in the presence of the mighty Silver Walls. In his dreams, the prison would loom over him like a mountain. The Grand Inquisitor stood smiling by the portcullis, always, with Gram Sothos to his side, holding Sarah's head by her hair.

Until recently, his sister's disembodied head was just that in his Red Tower dreams. Then she began to speak to him. Her mouth was always agape, bright with orange flame, eyes white like twinkling stars.

He snapped to when Rathos touched his shoulder. *I rolled the dice,* he thought grimly. *Now I must play the game, or look a fool for turning back.*

"Come, the city awaits, and so does our welcoming party," Evan said. He beckoned at the banners checkered orange and green flapping by Southpoint's entrance.

"The Little Worm," Rathos said under his breath.

"Be on your guard," Evan reminded them. He lingered on Karl. "Lord David is a dangerous man, not to be trifled with."

"Same as any king," the Reubenite muttered.

The company descended from their perch and plodded through a runny mud path that sucked at the hooves of their mounts. Half a mile down, they found the mayor of Southpoint with twenty of his city guard outside Elfgate.

David Renworth had aged. Stout and short of limb, he showed the passing of two decades in the silvers of a curling black beard and a belly that spilled over his decorated girdle. He wore a shabby tunic that reached his knees, faded blue hose, and shoes of cloth felt, proof that not even the realm's most powerful peasant could escape strict sumptuary laws. The mayor proudly wore his one allowance, a livery collar with an iron medallion shaped like a portcullis.

Will that portcullis open for us today? Evan wondered as he regarded the closed gate behind Renworth. He couldn't say with certainty, even with a letter from the king's Chancellor of the Chancery in his cloak pocket. *And if this gate does open, and we enter, will we be allowed to leave?*

For Evan, twenty years could've been twenty days; even now, he could barely control his rage. The man whom Worthy Assemblymen contemptuously called the Little King—whom Evan called Little Worm—had a hand in Sarah and Matthus's murders as much as Gram Sothos. The mayor had wavered up until the last hour, until the Army of the Gods had reached their doorstep, before finally permitting Evan, Sarah, and Matthus to flee for safety they never found. Hexar had sworn he'd mount the mayor's head on Traitor's Gate himself . . . until the Little King, never one to slither into a situation he couldn't wriggle out of, thwarted a siege by closing the gates to the approaching army. Renworth had betrayed his faith and saved the king, and with him his own neck.

Evan would not forgive so easily . . . or forget. Renworth served only himself, then as now. Nothing—no one—not the Worthy Assembly, seemingly not even Hexar himself, could open the gates without first granting the Little King what he wanted. Renworth was that very rare thing in Loran, after all—a respected peasant—and who would risk angering the official whom Commoners revered as their only voice in the realm?

The traitor nobleman dismounted. *Let the star of reason guide me, Sarah,* he prayed, *not revenge. We have too much at stake.* He removed his flat cap, bowing. "Lord David."

Renworth seemed to revel in his deference, smiling. "Evan Sinclair, how long has it been?" he asked. "Twenty years?"

Decades, Little Worm, he thought, *and not long enough.*

"Yes, and yet you look like you haven't aged a day," Evan returned with a practiced lilt. "Prospo favors you."

"Truthfully, I wasn't sure whether to expect you from the west or at Traitor's Gate," Renworth remarked dryly. Evan felt himself stir as the mayor regarded his best friend's child. "And if it isn't Sir Matthus Robswell's son."

Rathos shifted uncomfortably. *Yes, what I told you is true, my ward,*

Evan thought. His son-by-law had scoffed at the idea that a peasant had spies, but someone like Renworth couldn't long retain his office without them. It was said the lord mayor's spycraft rivaled that of even Charles Burke.

He looked on proudly, bittersweetly, as Rathos, who knew what Renworth's wavering had cost House Sinclair, maintained composure. "Lord David." His ward bowed solemnly.

"And Karl Redmore," Renworth noted. He regarded the three of them. "Are you all so eager to die for treason?"

"We've come to petition the king," Karl said defensively.

The mayor had a mocking smile. "Of course you have."

"It's a pleasure to meet someone who knew my father," Rathos said coldly.

Renworth gave a hapless shrug. "'Knew' is a strong word. I knew him as one of Southpoint's many orphans, before House Sinclair took him in. He was a different man after his knighting, no longer a thief. A good man with a strong heart, loyal to those he loved"—he glanced fleetingly at Evan—"and a brilliant swordsman. Such a shame, how he died, mere days before the Long Summer Rebellion ended."

"Yes, a shame," Rathos responded curtly. "If only Matthus had known that these gates would remain shut to the enemy, and not fled, he and Sarah Sinclair might still live."

Evan watched for Renworth's response. The Little King tittered. "You *are* your father's son, truly. But tell me, Rathos son of Matthus, why would you follow in Robswell's footsteps by following Evan Sinclair? Do you also wish to die young?"

"Children are like water," Rathos responded coolly, "flowing where they may. He who says they follow their fathers does not know the twelve."

The father-by-law smiled gently. Rathos had rebuked the Little King with verse from his own sacred text, under the gaze of his city guard, no less.

The mayor wagged a finger at Rathos, grinning. "I could never turn away a man who can quote the Twelve Testaments," he said. "But pardon me for my rough edges. I bear you and your late father no ill will. Wounds from the Long Summer run deep—deeper still as our eighteenth Remembrance Day draws close."

"I lost family in that war, as well," Karl added abruptly.

Renworth didn't acknowledge Karl. "Lord Drexan made me aware of your journey here well in advance, and you are welcome." He spoke gregariously, as if by allowing them in he gave them a gift. *And I should receive it as one,* Evan thought. "Just to be sure: do you have the parchment he sent you?"

Evan reached into his cloak and produced Drexan's letter. The mayor studied the contents. Satisfied, and seemingly done with his insults, he lifted his gaze to a dark crenelated window above Elfgate and clapped twice.

The spike-studded portcullis shuddered open. Behind it rose a second iron gate paneled with wood and plastered with nitre, thick rusted chains clacking against each other.

The mayor began to lead them forward. Evan gestured to his son-by-law for their purse. "Forgive me, my lord—what do we pay for the gate tax? I'm not sure of the rate."

Renworth circled with a sly smile. "Come now, Sinclair. You should know someone like King Hexar's brother-by-law—or rather, his former one—wouldn't need to pay such a lowly Common tax."

"I insist." Evan loosened his purse strings for a good jingle of the contents. "What is it, my lord? Half a loren?" He reached inside and withdrew coins pinched between thumb and finger.

"Five sylvens."

Evan slipped him just that, and no more. "To all a piece."

The mayor smiled at the forbidden reference. They began walking into the city with the twenty-man guard on their heels. Rathos and Karl guided their horses behind the power brokers.

"Your relationship with King Hexar offers you privileges, Sinclair," Renworth said as he walked in confident strides. "I shouldn't need to stress that those privileges rest on the king's . . . shall we say, *present* favor for you."

Evan caught a glimpse of the Red Tower's toothy crimson battlements above rooftops. "I need no reminder."

Southpoint bombarded the senses. The city's food market, Westcheap, roared low with a thousand muffled conversations. On nearby Sausage Street, Commoners elbowed each other for space at stalls festooned with meats and pelts. Across the way, a family of swine foraged for food in corners and alleys packed with refuse and entrails. The brothel windows of Whore Road drew lurid stares from passersby.

Renworth seemed to bask in the chaos. He proffered the gentlest of nods to mothers who stopped to curtsy; he shook the hands of merchants who milorded him. Toothy-mouthed beggars ceased their begging in his presence, retreating out of sight. *His city festers in its hunger and poverty like a stew,* he thought, *and he sips happily from the ladle.*

Evan had spent his life working on behalf of the Common and merchant classes, the sheep whom their lords and priests suckled like ticks. Men like David Renworth didn't mind if the sheep fell ill; they just wanted to play shepherd.

A massive crowd blocked Kingsway, the road that led directly to the Walls. A horrid stench alerted him to Traitor's Pit, the well King Tomas had fashioned with the mortar and brick of a thousand skulls. From what Evan could see, heads still tumbled into the well from the chopping block, and the peasants still pissed into it.

"Are they here for an execution?" Evan probed warily.

"No, that took place earlier this morning," the mayor said, laughing-eyed. He seemed to take sick pleasure from Evan's discomfort. "It could be they're here to listen to a prophet . . . or it could be they gather to welcome back the bastard prince."

"Prophet?" Evan heard Karl ask, but it didn't register. A comet could've blazed through the sky just then, and Evan, a dedicated astronomer, wouldn't have known.

Jason. He spun on Renworth. "Lord . . . *Lord Jason is here?*"

Evan didn't realize he was clutching the mayor's wrist until two city guards stirred uneasily. "Do you know another bastard prince?" Renworth pried his wrist free. "Docked one hour ago. He returns from the Holy Wars, unscathed. Or so I was told."

No doubt Renworth had saved this news for just the right moment, to rankle Evan, to throw him off balance. Whatever his motives, he'd succeeded.

Evan began to search for his nephew, his sister's son. *Does he lie to roil me, Sarah,* he asked his sister, *or is Jason here?*

A voice suddenly rang out through Westcheap, quelling the marketplace's noise. A man stood on a statue's plinth. He had an enraptured audience of peasants. Unattractive and poor in raiment, he wasn't easy to forget, with his long brown hair, weasel face, and distinguishing wart on his left cheek. Every time he delivered a rousing line, peasants pumped the air with their fists.

Rathos looked at Evan knowingly; Karl saw their signaling and snorted with contempt. Alas, the firebrand was one of their own, a member of the Loyal Company, a Reubenite like Karl, only more woodenheaded and reckless with his provocations.

But it wasn't the firebrand who drew his attention now.

A stripe of crimson garb slipped through the crowd. Evan stopped cold, unable to move. Scarcely breathing.

The years have aged us, Lord Charles, Evan thought, trying to suppress the panic in the pit of his stomach, *but I have never forgotten your hospitality.* With his onetime gaoler strode men in filigreed plate armor, and with them . . .

Renworth hadn't lied, as it turned out.

Evan rubbed a tear from his cheek. The prince bore an uncanny resemblance to his mother. His skin was sun-kissed where hers had been pale, but he shared his mother's lean face, her high cheekbones, her unruly raven-black hair, her famous widow's peak. His eyes shone crystal-blue like hers, clear like water by the seashore.

He was undoubtedly Sarah Sinclair's son. He was *her.*

Spellbound, Evan began moving in his nephew's direction, maneuvering through the crowd with spread elbows. Rathos called after him, but he couldn't hear anything other than the familiar voice from his dreams.

CHAPTER 6

Nephew

ason shouldered past the crowds outside a fishmonger's stall on the edge of Wool Street, watching and listening to the life of a city he hadn't known for two years. Soot-faced peasant men and women clogged the cobblestone streets, seeming to burst forth from narrow alleyways and tilting houses in every direction. A vendor bellowed prices for onions and leeks, fresh onions and leeks at less than half the price, as a greasy-haired mother haggled an apple seller, women dumped jets of slop from high windows, and an apron-clad man chased after boys naked as their birthdays. Wagons rattled up and down Iron Street, splattering the unlucky with refuse.

Even in old age, the Grand Inquisitor inspired enough terror to clear a path for them that moved with their feet. Their armed guard followed on all sides, hands on their sword hilts.

Jason regretted his choice of wares for the return journey. His bright-colored silks drew curious and envious eyes. *Always have I felt a stranger in this kingdom,* the bastard thought as he felt their stares, *and nothing changes today.*

"Does Southpoint seem the same as you remembered her, my lord?" Charles asked.

Slop gushed down in front of them like a waterfall. Jason side-stepped the mess. *No more than I'm the same as when I left.*

If it were possible, the city seemed worse. Passing Wax Street, he saw a toothless man with a begging bowl sparse with coins. Down an alleyway, a bearded man shamelessly plowed a shirtless whore with raggedy skirts hiked up to her waist. On Coal Street, a haze of flies loitered hungrily above a corpse left to rot in the sun. Fires burned everywhere, filling the air with smoke that made it hard to breathe without coughing.

Jason covered his nose with a sleeve. "It's . . . different," he said, loud enough for Charles to hear.

The Red Tower lord had a knowing look. "Yes, it seems to grow worse every day. The First King built for us a castle that illuminates the night like the moon, and mankind showed its gratitude by building around it a city of killers, whores, and thieves."

Jason grimaced. "If only we showed more concern for the Common plight," he said suggestively. Charles didn't respond.

They're as responsible for their misery as their lords and priests . . . and kings, he pondered. It wasn't surprising to him that Southpoint had declined. No one cared for the Commons. To many in Loran, peasants were below even the Casaanites, there to work their lands, pay rents, and die—hopefully out of sight. When they weren't wearing down their hands and feet, Commoners were paying their lords to marry, give birth, name their children, and bury their dead. A Common saying went that god had fashioned man with two hands—one for him to lower himself into the ground, and the other to pay his last rents and taxes while in the act.

Jason spotted open latrines overflowing with murk that he could smell from a distance. "Has my father at least tried to clear any of the refuse?" he said through his sleeve.

Upon seeing the king's red-robed torturer, a mother gave up on her negotiations with a vendor and shooed her children off their path. "His Majesty delegated obstructions to the mayor when he left to secure our northern borders in Uzland," he said dryly. "It seems Lord David has delegated that to someone else."

"Then maybe Southpoint needs a new mayor," Jason said, but he knew that would do little, if anything. The king and his Worthy Assembly had all the power in the world to change the Common plight, but what was a peasant's life worth? *Nearly as little as a bastard's life,* he thought.

Charles seemed to relish the jab at his rival official. "Much as I concur with you, my lord, it should be said that a drought inflames the Midlands. Wheat is costly even for lords."

"Remembrance Day is this week, is it not? Maybe I'll take the issue to my father's noble lords." Not that his Assemblymen would turn an ear to the bastard prince. To those who marched once with Stoddard Trambar and his Army of the Gods, Jason Warchild was on equal footing with the Commoners.

Halfway up the road to Kingsway, the party encountered a bustling crowd of vendors, seamstresses hanging wool shirts on wooden beams, fortune tellers tempting the unwary, wine sellers hefting caskets. Everyone knew the Grand Inquisitor and gave him wide berth. Only two men recognized Jason in his foreign silks.

Wine sellers both, their eyes grew large when he passed by their stall. The men hastened to catch a closer look at him, brushing up against their armored knights. One was a heavier man with a mustachio, the other a baldheaded youth, likely the former's apprentice.

"*Lord Jason!*" the heavy man cried through cupped hands. "*Jason, son of Hexar and Sarah!*"

"Welcome home Lord Jason!" said the youth, smiling.

No doubt the vendors saw a wealthy patron in the king's son, but he appreciated the gesture. He acknowledged the wine vendors with a respectful nod. This only emboldened the heavy man, who urged his apprentice to find a wine casket. The scene drew the attention of other peasants, who turn by turn knelt, or shouted blessings. *Let it not be said that Jason Warchild is without friends*, he thought, grateful.

Charles seemed much less taken with the display. "It was my intention to escort you on this road to avoid this attention, my lord, I apologize. It's especially congested today."

Jason shrugged off the apology. It was nice to feel like an *actual* prince in the royal succession. His last night with Garrett on the galley made his popularity with peasants a sweet salve for wounds that didn't show.

The ranks of the admiring wine sellers soon swelled to fifty or more, slowing their speed to a crawl. Charles agitatedly told the guards to keep the peasants away, even as the bastard prince himself extended his hands, letting his fingers brush the soot-nailed fingers of Common men. *This is home.*

Turning onto Silver Street, the party encountered a crowded marketplace that all but brought them to a halt. A stern-looking man addressed the gathered peasants from the perch of a statue's plinth. His drab gray wool and the belt of a rope identified him as a reader of the Free Beliefs, no one important. Yet when he opened his lips, the man came alive with the fire of an anger that radiated through his face. He spoke with his hands as he exhorted his listeners to retake what was theirs by the grace of the god of twelve faces.

Charles sneered. "It's Watley," he muttered to his leftmost guard with contempt. "Summon the Lord Mayor. Tell him that Firemouth snuck into his little kingdom. We need armed men with dogs. I won't lose him again, do you understand?"

Jason flickered from the threadbare reader to Charles. "I don't understand. Who is this?" The speaker delivered rousing lines that drew roars of approval from his audience, drowning out his voice.

The Red Tower lord scowled at the reader. "Forgive me, Lord Jason. He's a treasonous vagrant. Jon Watley's his name."

"What's his crime?"

"*Crimes,* more like. He travels across the kingdom looking to incite unrest. The rat eludes every trap we set, and scampers off to hide with his conspirators in Eastland when we loose the hounds. Not this time."

Jason strained to hear Watley over the crowd. An infant squealed hysterically somewhere. "The Eighth Testament tells us that man knew no shame when elves saw their nakedness. Sent by god himself, the elves, our teachers, upheld the law we still observe in our hearts: no thing living is above another."

Some men hooted rowdily; another cried, "*Point us true, Firemouth!*" Watley waited for complete silence to continue. "If no living thing was above another at man's birth, can any man be within his god-given rights to claim mastery over another?" The crowd's response was swift and jarring: "*NO!*"

I can see why Charles would want this man in irons, Jason thought. For the rulers of Loran, the order of things was set in stone. There was a king, and below him his Worthy Assembly of sworn lords, priests and parish readers, and merchants, in that order; peasants came last, if at all. Treason it was for the poor soul who challenged that hierarchy.

Watley's voice rang out through the marketplace. "No, of course not," he assured the crowd. "The elves were as teachers to men, not their rulers. Yet what are the Commons to the lords and priests of this kingdom? No higher than the flea. Priestking Parlisis dispatches more priests to our shores every day just to remind us. Are *they* wiser than the elves?"

"Then what of the First King's Great Covenant?" Jason was surprised to see the challenge came from Charles himself. Men hadn't taken notice of them on Silver Street; they shied away from the Grand Inquisitor almost instantly. "Did we not give up our ancient freedoms for the crown's protection?"

"*We.*" The reader shielded his eyes from the sun with a hand, squinting as he searched the crowd. He whitened visibly when he recognized the challenger. "That we did, Lord Charles, that we did."

"Then why do you preach this treason?" Charles rejoined. On the crowd's fringes, Jason spotted a familiar face in the man some called the Little King. He had with him a handful of men, plus his poor-of-cloth city guard, no hounds. "You say no thing living is above another. You are subject to a lord, and your lord is subject to the king. Is King Hexar not your better, you little rat?"

Watley stiffened indignantly. "The One True King was the only one ever above anyone, and his line is long broken."

Torturer and reader stared knives into each other. Jason turned to the insistent tug on his left sleeve and discovered the mustachioed wine seller, a barrel in his arms.

"Milord, wine milord?" he asked eagerly. He was opening the spigot single-handedly when one of the guards shoved him off, spilling rich purple wine on the man's breeches. Off in the distance somewhere, an admirer shouted Jason's name.

"Would you like to repeat that in my Dread Chamber?" Charles pitched his voice.

Watley looked like a hunted animal on the edge of flight. "*Turel e'sartha, turan e'sparta,*" the reader said defiantly.

Jason knew the forbidden saying well. It was the motto the Worthy Assembly had sewn in its sigils when the body still housed the Wing of the Commons, which sat peasants beside their lords for the making of laws. *To each a chair,* he recalled the Romarian motto, *to all a piece.* A daring statement.

"*JASON, BEHIND YOU!*"

Sunlight flashed on steel. A sword sliced the air by his ear, slashing his silken sleeve. Jason ripped his sword free from his scabbard. He deflected the next thrust from the heavyset wine seller, shorn his casket, now armed with a falchion. His strokes fell too clumsily for the tested warrior. Jason urged the man to desist, but still he came. He shoved his blade through the man's neck. A fount of crimson erupted from the wound, and down the seller went, dying as peasants dispersed like rats from a burning house.

Jason was still turning when the other assassin leapt up from behind. The wine seller's apprentice lifted a sword above his smooth hairless head. "For Lady Alyse, you bastard," he said in a thick accent. Jason raised his blade much too slowly . . .

. . . and flinched as the blur of a dagger whirled into the man's thigh. The assassin slumped to a knee with a pathetic, half-gurgled scream. Charles, still reeling, barked orders to his men-at-arms, who promptly surrounded the king's bastard, swords drawn. Four guards encircled his assailant, inflicting abuse.

Jason spun on the dagger thrower. He was an older man with blond hair that dripped to gray around his ears and about his beard. He had on a lord's finery beneath his travel-stained cape. He doffed his feathered cap, spread his arms in welcome, and bowed as he would for a king.

"Nephew," the man said loudly. "I am pleased to see you at long last, and find you unharmed."

Nephew? Only two men could call him that, and one was in the east, far from these shores.

The Grand Inquisitor narrowed his eyes, grimacing. "Evan Sinclair," he said through his teeth.

CHAPTER 7

Happy Returns

he king's court and household streamed forth into the lower bailey until scarcely anyone could move without first touching someone else. Hundreds of House Eddenhold's sworn knights, servants, and Casaanite hostages stood in wait.

Lorana stood closest to her father. The king slumped in his gout chair, eyes fixed on the Great Gates, as if by staring he thought he could make his sons appear. Feet away, their noble house's silver-and-crimson banners cracked like whips in the wind. Dark storm clouds gathered in the east, bickering.

Hanor was speaking with Drexan about how he hoped those clouds would find their way to the parched Midlands. Lorana glimpsed her former servant Zur by his lord's side, listening attentively to their conversation. She smiled at him, but he didn't seem to notice.

"I like those clouds not," Hexar interrupted his advisors. "Fell skies for a fell day."

She and every advisor in hearing distance understood his grief. The king yearned to look upon Garrett and Jason again, but mourned Erick, the son he never knew, the one his exiled brother had filched for Priestking Parlisis like a pricey bauble.

Lorana herself often wondered what life would've been like with Erick. Yet his memory felt like a dream she always lost upon waking. Jason was real. She'd be glad to see the half-brother she considered her best friend. Almost tearfully glad.

"Today can't be *fell*," Heather blurted suddenly. Her half-sister played with the fringes of her high-waisted gown. "The bastard prince is bringing me dolls back from Chi-Say. He told me so!"

She saw others tense. Heather had no memory of Erick, so there was no grief. Worse, she broke decorum by calling Jason by that hated name, the one the Worthy Assembly had cursed him with at birth.

As always, Hexar suffered from whatever spell of silence her half-sister had cast on him since birth, and it fell to Lorana to help Heather mind her etiquette. She signaled Namoni with that look that said, *Please do something about this.*

The mistress leaned down to whisper into Heather's ear. The princess crossed her arms in a huff. "No, I don't *care* about the crown prince. He likes to pinch me and tell me I'll lose my head one day like my whore mother."

The court bristled. Trance broken, the king screwed up his face with a look at his youngest child. Lorana smoldered with a sister's fury. *I'll throttle his neck,* she vowed to herself, *I'll do it when he's asleep, no matter how many lives he's taken.*

Her half-brother by Harriet had always been cruel, the worst parts of their father, keen on reminding her and Heather of their beheaded mothers. Once, he'd dropped Lorana's cat down a well. He'd often twist her earlobes raw, yank her hair taut like a rope, swat at her breasts and stalk off laughing. He'd done all that to Lorana. At least, until he awoke one night with Jason's dagger at his throat, with her there to negotiate new terms for their relationship.

What will Heather and I do when he succeeds Father one day? she wondered bleakly. Garrett's place in the succession had always loomed over her like a headsman's axe, her father's health the unsteady hand on the handle that kept it aloft.

A hand found hers. Lorana turned and saw Anyasha. She drank in the comfort of her brown eyes.

Another half hour went by. The herald suddenly leaned out from the sentry tower and announced that Charles Burke was headed up Kingsway with the king's sons. That lightened Hexar's mood.

Seconds later, the same herald emerged from the tower, sprinting toward the king. He whispered in his liege's ear. Hexar whipped about at the herald with a fiery look.

"Open the gates," the king told his herald, who ran back to the tower. "They say Lord Jason was attacked on Kingsway," he announced. "By Evan Sinclair."

Gasps filled the courtyard, followed quickly by murmurs.

"Evan the Traitor," someone muttered.

Relief, anger, and confusion ripped through the princess. Her father had once attainted Sinclair for failing to see Sarah to safety. Drexan had prevented the king from beheading him.

Heralds blew on their long trumpets. The drawbridge began to lower, its chains and winches clinking. The Great Gates shuddered open. Everyone gazed ahead into the dark of the gatehouse, searching for movement.

"*Behold, Lord Jason!*" cried the herald.

Her chest fluttered. The thin red candlestick of the Grand Inquisitor emerged beside someone familiar. Heather squealed with glee, and smiles and hugs swept through the crowd like a breeze on a hot summer day.

Jason Warchild had left his half-sister on the docks by the Shimmering Bay, nineteen years old but still a boy. She still remembered bracing his stubbly moustache when he kissed her cheek, promising he'd come back unscathed. The heir and bastard prince had been so unalike: her loathsome older half-brother a lion with his regal reddish-brown mane, her younger one the black-haired runt of their litter.

Two years later, Hexar's son by Sarah Sinclair strode into his father's courtyard a handsome stranger. Sunlight bronzed his skin. Tall and sinewy, he had arms that bulged with muscle. Raven-black hair cascaded down his broad shoulders, rippling in the wind like the foreign silks he wore. His sapphire eyes were all that seemed the most familiar.

Her ladies-in-waiting sucked in their breath; Heather's retinue squirmed with giggles. *My, have you grown, my long-lost brother,* she thought to herself, feeling proud. *Would even Edenia know you now?*

"Father." Jason strode to the seated king. He bent low to hug their father.

Hexar struck him across his face. The bastard prince felt his cheek, stunned.

"What, you think I'd forgotten your crimes against me?" the king growled. Shaken, Lorana touched her father on his shoulder; he shrugged her off irritably.

Jason wore his dignity well under pressure, straightening. That incensed Hexar, who demanded deference. He waved dismissively at his son. "You show up here, in these—these *ninny silks,* too proud to bow before your king?" Hexar glanced around the bailey. "Is Garrett still outside? Where is he? Where is my firstborn?"

Jason kept his eyes on his feet, as if deciding how best to handle this humiliation. With the court watching, he retraced his steps to Charles and his men. Returning, he lined his arms at his sides and bent at his waist for the most formal of bows. "Forgive me, Your Majesty," he said, eyes cast downward. "I did not mean—"

"To make a fool of yourself? Too late."

Lorana felt her face grow hot from anger on her half-brother's behalf. *How can you still take your son for granted after you've lost one son, Father?* Yet she knew he had his reasons. Jason Warchild had not gone to war with his king's permission. Their parting had not been kind.

"Where is Prince Garrett?" Hexar demanded again.

Jason watched his father with dutiful eyes. "He was alive and well when last I saw him," he replied coolly. "I believe this is something Your Majesty would hear privately."

The king sat back, lips curled with disgust. "You're in no place to tell me where and when I'll take counsel."

Lorana knelt before her father, womanly and entreating. "My king, the herald said that Lord Jason escaped an attack on the Kingsway. I'd like to know if he is unharmed."

The king paid her a weary glance. "Are you unharmed, Lord Jason?" he asked his son.

Her half-brother gave her a look of gratitude. "I am, thank you, Your Majesty."

"And what of Evan the Traitor?" Hexar struggled up from his gout chair. "Where is the man who tried to kill his nephew, as he killed *his own sister?*"

Charles dispatched two men-at-arms with a glance. They returned with the attainted nobleman in their arms, his legs dragging. Guards shoved him to the dirt. Sinclair appeared nothing like Sarah or Jason, who took after her. He was average in height, with a fine flaxen beard and loose hair about his ears. The irons on his wrists clinked as he struggled up, kneeling.

Yet when he spoke, everyone, including Lorana, heard a voice as fine as notes from a violin. "Please forgive me, my king, but it was I who *saved* my sister's blood."

Hexar opened his mouth but Jason rushed to speak first. "He speaks it true, Your Majesty," he said. "This man, if he is my uncle, thwarted an assassin who meant to run me through . . . if you care for my safety." He flickered to Lorana. "He swung his blade at me in Alyse Jannus's name."

Lorana reddened at the court's curious glances. Anyasha tightened her hand around hers. No one had done violence in her mother's name since the Long Summer Rebellion.

Her father seemed as stunned. She recalled his words to her in the Hall of Memory. *We're all traitors to our own hearts.*

"Your Majesty, if I may," came a high familiar voice. From the new arrivals emerged David Renworth, out of place in the bailey with his long, moth-eaten tunic and wrinkled hose.

The king receded into his chair, wary-eyed. The king and their house had a complicated relationship with the city mayor. "Go on, David."

David Renworth bowed his neck, his livery chain links clinking against his medallion. "Your Majesty, Lord Charles made a mistake in seizing your brother-by-law." He glanced at the nobleman kneeling in the dirt.

"*Former* brother-by-law," Hexar growled.

"Yes, Your Majesty. Still, it was a dagger throw from Sinclair that saved your son's life today. I can attest."

Hexar knitted his brows, angry from confusion. "If this is true, then why is he in chains? And why was any man even able to harm my son, *Charles?*"

Charles strode forward in earnest. "We were waylaid by the rabble-monger Jon Watley, Your Majesty. He drew a crowd that allowed the attackers to slip through our guard. I took the traitor Evan into custody because he is and has always been a danger to Your Majesty and this kingdom."

The Grand Inquisitor seemed to wish murder on his rival with his wide-eyed stare. "Tell us, Little King, how was it that Watley entered your city in the first place? Did he slip past the guards you let drink and whore on their watch?"

It was no secret that the Little King and Red Tower lord despised each other. Watching her father's troubled reaction as he receded into his cushions, past done with their rivalry and insinuations—and no doubt eager to hear about his firstborn's whereabouts—she understood why tensions like this festered at his court in the first place. *Not a month back from war, and his old bones hunger for the comfort of a sword and a foe he can toss from his horse—not petty rivalries.*

"My lords, your king asked you about Evan Sinclair's guilt, not to squabble like children," Lorana rebuked them. Pivoting to the Grand Inquisitor, she asked, "Charles—did Sinclair save his sister-son's life, or not?"

The Grand Inquisitor gave the slightest nod.

"Then off with those damn chains," the king commanded. "Charles, I want you on the man who tried to take Jason's life, not the fleas in Southpoint. The son of Sarah Sinclair may be a bastard, but he's *my* bastard, and I want him safe."

Let that be some solace to you, brother, meager as it is.

At a nod from Charles, one of the knights inserted a skeleton key into each of the nobleman's manacles, twisting for a clatter of chains. Sinclair rose slowly, rubbing his wrists. The torturer and his men left through the gatehouse.

"Jason, see me at court at once," Hexar said ominously. "Graxhold, show Evan and his men to their quarters." And he sweated the traitor nobleman one last look, adding, "Welcome back . . . *brother.*"

At the king's signal, Casaanite servants hastened down the Great Hall's marbled steps, a palanquin on their shoulders. Once Hexar was inside, it took another four men to bear the litter back into the Great Hall.

Heather leapt into her half-brother's arms, easing the tension. "*JASON JASON!* I've missed you so!"

Jason hugged her tightly. He let her slide off once Lorana started in his direction, clutching the thick folds of her gown as she ran. They met in the center, embracing. Jason smelled of salty ocean breeze and, less happily, the stench of Silver Street, but he was home. He was hers again, hers to protect and walk and laugh with.

"Oh! I've missed you so," Lorana said, clasping his stubbly face. "Is it truly you? Not some apparition from the desert lands you visited?"

Jason smiled. "You're as beautiful as ever, sister," he lied without malice.

She squeezed his biceps affectionately. "These were just little twigs when I last saw them." She glimpsed a thin scar by his elbow. "Is that from the man who attacked you? You should see Jon immediately. He'll have an ointment—"

Jason tugged on his sleeve to cover the cut. "It's nothing, Ana, just a scratch." Drawing her close, he whispered in her ear, "Grieve with me, sister. We are just four now, it'd seem."

Three if Garrett has fled, or died, she thought. Lorana couldn't care about his wellbeing, but Harriet's son was the crown prince, and with Erick dead, the firstborn of Hexar's brood was the only one of them who could succeed the king upon his death. And he was missing.

"Yes, I grieve his loss, too." *As well as I can for the brother I knew only by his letters.* Lorana looked him over. "You look like orange fruit," she said, trying to change the subject. She felt his smooth lustrous silks. "Where are these from?"

"From Nerimba, and Geghan, and the Sand Lands," he told her. "This cape is a gift from the Imir of Aranzia, and the boots from—"

"From Orran, it seems," a voice finished for him.

Jason swung open his arms and embraced Zuran of Tribe Nuur like he would Heather. Lorana swelled with a happiness she hadn't known for what felt like years. *My true brothers.*

"This *can't* be the Zur I left two years ago," the prince said. He mussed the boy's short kinky hair. "You were half my height when I left. What the hell happened?"

Zur grinned. "I drank a strange potion one day, and grew." He studied Jason's mud-caked boots, fascinated. "But tell me, my lord, are they from Orran? From east of Nerimba, west of Muhregeesia, and north of the Sand Lands?" He bent low to lift a golden chain link fastened across the shoe for decoration. "I ask because they're adorned with snakes done in the Orranese style. See?"

Lorana shared her brother's bewilderment. "You couldn't have learned all that when I had you handling chits. What does Lord Drexan have you do in his service, Zur?"

"Lord Drexan is having me read the histories," he replied, looking embarrassed.

She was incredulous. "In the all of *three weeks* since I sent you to him?"

"He's flown with crows, sister," Jason said, turning toward Drexan as the chancellor approached with arms spread. Jason and Drexan embraced warmly. "How are you, old man?"

"Quite well, my lord," the King's Crow returned, smiling. "And happy to see you've returned in one piece, although I am saddened to learn about Lord Erick." *And curious to know the whereabouts of Hexar's heir,* Lorana almost could've finished for the advisor, *almost as much as me.*

Evan Sinclair approached from the side. Jason stopped his banter with Drexan and reached for his uncle's hand to shake it firmly, in gratitude. She was more nervous than she thought she thought possible. Many were the stories about Sinclair at court, about his role as the

Loyal Company's ambassador—and whether he was still loyal to the king who'd once nearly taken his head.

Could he be the monster Father made him out to be, she thought, *if he saved my best brother's life?*

Turning to Lorana, the attainted Lord of Caerdon was all graciousness and courtly courtesy. "I must thank you for your intervention, Your Highness," he said with a formal bow. "I see now why our king named you steward in his absence."

Lorana didn't recoil her hand when he bent low to kiss it. "I see no goat's horns. Are you sure you're Lord of Caerdon?"

Sinclair had a rueful smile. "I haven't been a noble lord for many years, Your Highness." She felt self-conscious under his stare. "You have your lady mother's eyes, if I may say so. It pleases me to look upon them again."

Lorana withdrew her hand. "It brings me no pleasure to think long on traitors," she said curtly. She reached for Jason. "Come, brother, let us see the king."

CHAPTER 8

The Son

duard's Keep had all the warmth of a sepulcher.

From its high vaulted ceilings to its curved walls, the throne room had a vastness that made anyone inside feel small and unworthy, like an ant in the shadow of a boot. This was by design, Jason knew, for King Eduard had wanted his subjects to bask in the glory of the seated king as if he were the sun, and all of Odma depended on his celestial movement.

Not that this chamber had any warm memories to begin with. Eduard's throne room had been privy to wars and other matters of great consequence to Loran, its neighbor kingdoms, and the known world for thousands of years.

It was from here that Anjan Half-Elf's heirs supposedly ruled mankind for three millennia, fulfilling their royal duties as the First King had laid out under his Great Covenant. And here it was that King Eduard, the last true heir, dispatched his assassins to cut the throats of his sleeping wife and children so that he could crown Elzura his queen. With the true king's line spent, Rorin Romaris ascended the Silver Throne a conqueror, and his inbred descendants had cursed the throne room until their destruction by the Barefoot Knights, who themselves laid waste to Ansara with seven fruitless wars. A faded black stain lurked at the foot of the luminous throne, a grisly reminder of the blood spilt when Sir Bradley Durhurst and his Treasonous Twelve beheaded King Lathros two centuries ago.

So much blood has been spilt in this chamber. Jason had long thought there was a cruel irony to the First King's Great Covenant. The only man in whose veins ran the blood of elves and men had persuaded men to cede their naked freedom to a crown for sanctuary from the dragons and wolves. Yet almost every king since had bled oceans from their subjects, always for their own terrible glory.

His gaze presently climbed the Silver Throne, up the steps that ran with ripples of light, to the utmost height, where fresh garlands festooned the Great Arch and the Great Arch loomed like a huge stone crown above his father's head.

Hexar rested his forehead in his hand. "So," he began after a long silence, "your firstborn brother—the crown prince, who is to succeed me when I die—left you in the middle of the sea . . . to find . . . elves?"

Damn you, Garrett, Jason thought.

Lorana took up position not far from her half-brother. She stood tall and proud, his ally, now as ever.

"It is as I said, Your Majesty," Jason said. "Your son left with me for Nerimba after we made a pyre for Erick." He tried not to think about the acrid smell of Erick's flesh as it burned. "Yet Garrett was not the same afterward. He complained of . . . visions."

It hurt to even remember. The episodes left his strong older half-brother secluded in his tent for days. Garrett had refused everything. He took no food, no liquor; he declined even the *chu-churoo* pipe. By the time they had boarded the *Drunken Adventure*, he was an untidy, disheveled mess with bags under his eyes.

"*Visions?*" Hexar said with a raised eyebrow. "Garrett left because he had . . . fucking *visions?*"

"Yes, Your Majesty." His father was reacting precisely as Jason had warned the prince he would. "Aboard an unfamiliar galley with unfamiliar men. We thought them Muhregites."

"Muhregites couldn't sail in good weather," Hexar spat.

"Yes, as you say, Your Majesty." He was alone with his father, but he kept things formal. His pride still stung worse than his cheek.

"Describe the colors you saw."

"The banners weren't yellow and red or written in the flowing Muhregite script, but black, with an open white hand."

Lorana seemed as incredulous as Hexar. Jason didn't blame her. He still had trouble believing any of this himself.

The night the fog arose, turning the sea into rolling white hills, Merman Jarrod had summoned him to his cabin. There, he confided that the Geghanese were fearful Garrett had brought a curse aboard with them. Believing they'd mutiny, he told Jason to empty a jar of sacred dead bees around his half-brother's bed, and let the Geghanese see him do it. So he had.

That night, he'd awoken to a sword lain across his neck. The crown prince had his hand on the hilt. Garrett had loomed over him, sheened with sweat.

"I have to do this," Jason remembered him saying, more to himself than to him. He'd trembled. "Can you forgive me? I can hardly forgive myself . . . and I haven't even done it yet. But you can't see what I see, Jason. You can't possibly know . . ."

He means to kill me, he remembered thinking. *He's gone mad from grief over Erick.* He couldn't think of anything else to say in that awful moment. So he'd said, "Tell me what you see."

"Fine. Fine." Garrett had bared his teeth. "You want to know, Jason Warchild? Flames scorch the Silver Throne. They consume Ansara's thirteen kingdoms. The lesser brother will herald the worse one. The fallen god wields seven swords in his hands. And they laugh as metal forests burn, and oceans run with blood, and we salt our kings and clean our teeth with the points of their crowns." Jason had flinched as the sword's edge drew blood. "And you . . . *you* are the cause of all of it."

"And why the elves?" the king goaded him in the present, sounding half-amused. As if Jason were a court fool. "Why leave for the Evergreen Isles?"

"He said the Nagarthessi will come. He believed only"—he swallowed thickly—"that only the elves could save us from the Great Burning spoken of in the Twelfth Testament."

"'They will come as two brothers, Asha-Ra and Pathazar, with eyes white like snow and the dead who breathe fire,'" he heard Garrett reciting the Twelfth Testament feverishly as his sweat pelted his skin. "'They'll start with the children. One will rise to summon shadowkings, and he will herald the worse of the two. Man will know a Great Burning.'"

He couldn't forget what he'd said last: "Everything will burn . . . unless I end it. I can end it now. I should. I *must . . .*"

"The *Nagarthessi?*" The king eyed him with something between anger and suspicion. "No. *No.* Garrett didn't give a shit about religion. For fuck's sake, he was banned from temple for pissing in the stoup."

"I know, Father." *It made no sense to me, either.*

He felt the kiss of cold steel upon his neck, and Garrett's sweat dribbling off his face. "Then kill me, and be done with it," Jason had defied him. "The whole world despises me. I don't wish to live in a world where my brother despises me, too."

Minutes had passed like hours. Finally, the sword fell to clatter on the floor. Garrett slumped beside his bed, wracked with heaving sobs. Moved by pity and love, Jason held him in his arms, rocking the future king like a babe. Garrett dampened his tunic with tears, begging forgiveness.

The next day, Merman Jarrod said one of his men had spotted a galley close by, black sails with an open white hand. Garrett had said it was there for him. That he would leave for the Evergreen Isles, which no one had ever found.

"I leave to find the elves, little brother, for I am a coward, and we'll need them soon enough," Garrett had hollered over the clack of his rowboat's oars on water. "I leave Loran to you."

Hexar rose, listing on one side of the Silver Throne. "You dishonored me once when you left without my say for war and death. Tell me the truth, Jason, lest you now dishonor your lady mother."

"Father," Lorana began earnestly, to no avail.

Jason ground his teeth. He had so much he'd wanted to say. About how he regretted leaving for war. About the shakes and sweats that befell him when he remembered the terrors of desert battle, the volleys of arrows, the hard men screaming for their mothers.

About how, perhaps, all that misery had finally made him worthy of the succession line from which the king's Assembly had cast him out at birth.

But for the life of him, none of this came out. Not the way he wanted.

"I have told you true, Your Majesty," Jason said fiercely. "For two years, I fought our cause in the Holy Wars—"

"*Your* cause," his father snapped. "And a cause you failed in any case."

"I never—"

"A cause you failed by allowing one brother to die, and the other to apparently flee, according to your own account—"

"Your Majesty—"

"—leaving for a war without my say, turning down an appointment to the court of King Grisholm—"

"I never *wanted* that appointment." Fire was in his veins. Erick had once told Jason it was Hexar's fire, always fuming for war. "Men don't follow emissaries. They follow men with blood on their swords."

His father smiled cruelly. "Ah! It finally comes out. Jason Warchild wishes to be whole like his brothers. To know what it's like when I die, for the Worthy to crown him and call him king."

Is that so terrible to wish? "'My heart for my kingdom.'"

The king scoffed. "My house's words. Not yours. 'My heart for my father's crown,' more like."

Jason stepped in front of his sister, thwarting her heated advance. "I'm not a bastard because you lay with a woman you loved one night; I'm a bastard because you loved a woman the Worthy Assembly hated." *An Assembly you let ruin my name for the sake of a fragile peace.*

"You wish to be a prince in line for the throne I won through my Kingstrials," the king said, "and yet you come here, without the crown heirs we need to prevent the Trials from even happening and from losing these Walls to another house. How should I receive you?"

Jason didn't want the Trials. But he didn't want to be a stranger in his own kingdom anymore, either. Not after giving blood for Loran, not after burning his half-brother on foreign sand. Not after killing those men.

Not after two years without her touch. *I love you, Jason.*

"Your Majesty, if I may," Lorana cut in.

Hexar watched her warily as she approached the Silver Throne. She curtsied to show respect.

"My king, what you say is right: your son *did* disobey you by leaving to fight with Garrett and Erick. You offered him an appointment to a worthy court," she added with an over-the-shoulder glance at her half-brother, "and he did some dishonor by refusing you.

"Yet those times are past," she went on. "No matter what may have driven him to do it, your eldest son is gone—where, not even Jason can say. Your other son, my trueborn brother, is dead. Which leaves us with no legitimate heir to succeed you at this time. As you know—"

"Aye, I bloody well know," their father, the king, muttered like a browbeaten child.

"As you know," Lorana persisted, "will force the Assembly to call the Kingstrials, god forbid we lose Your Majesty. They will be here in a week for Remembrance Day. The priestking's allies will scheme against us when they learn the crown prince is missing."

"And?" Hexar said. "You would have me name Jason to my succession line? Reward his defiance—risk a war?" He grunted. "If I listen to the gossips, he's not *even my own blood.*"

"*FATHER!*" Lorana cried out, but their father stared past her, at Jason, deaf to her protests.

"Tell me you didn't poison Erick's arrow," the king demanded. "Tell me you didn't throw Garrett overboard."

Blood rushed to his face. "You dare," the bastard prince heard himself growl to his king. Lorana's hands were on him; he shrugged her off. "You *dare* accuse me of fratricide?"

Lorana practically pushed him behind her. "Father, this is not kingly," she said. "Your son by Sarah fought in your name for two years—"

"He fought for his own damn name," Hexar rumbled. "Always

seeking to enter my line, to write his name in the Silver Book as King Jason the First, Lord Protector of the Weak. By god, I should've listened to Shaddon when he—"

"*STOP THIS!*" Lorana broke in, with a voice so rent with grief and fury that she finally gave the king pause. "Your words are hasty and stupid. Jason is your son by the wife you loved most. He tries to please you, Father."

Hexar scowled. "Two years ago, you showed me your back," he said. "Do you think I'd forget? Two years ago, I had to learn from Charles Burke that you wrote Parlisis—*PARLISIS*—for his favor, that you might join your brothers in his Holy Wars. It was treason—"

"I wouldn't let Garrett fight alone. He was my brother by Harriet." *He remembered that, in the end.* "And Erick—"

"To hell with your nonsense," he thundered. "You wanted honor for yourself. Glory. But what about what *I* wanted?"

All was lost in the moment, all sanity, all love of his father and joy in seeing his family and home. Only the fire in his blood remained, fuming.

"So I couldn't fight alongside my brothers and do honor by you and our kingdom," Jason blazed. There were Lorana's hands again; again, he wrenched himself free.

"You damn fool," Hexar sputtered, "you don't know my mind and you don't know what your mother wanted! You'll always be a bastard because of it. God made you a curse to me—giving you your mother's face, so I could never forget what happened to her, and mine own worst parts, so I'd have to constantly worry about you."

"Father," Lorana entreated.

The king waved them off. "Leave my presence, both of you! And take the banquet I meant for Garrett as the gift you want from me. It'll be the last you ever receive. Do you hear me, Warchild? DO YOU HEAR—?"

Jason rounded and shoved open the two doors. Lorana rushed after him, touching his shoulder.

"Jason, those were hasty words from father," she said. "He grieves for Erick and worries about Garrett. You *know* he loves you."

"Are you so sure? He doesn't even believe I'm *his*."

"He didn't mean it. He couldn't stand losing you the way he lost your mother—to the Muhregites, or to—"

"The Worthy Assembly?" Jason spat. "Speak it true, sister. Father may hide his fear with anger, but you"—he took her by her arms—"you have only been true with me."

He wiped his eyes, furious with himself over his unmanly tears. But then, Garrett had wept in his arms that night. "I *am* a bastard, and will remain one until he says otherwise . . . or until I prove to him and everyone else that I'm not.

"I shan't appear for Remembrance Day," he added. "I will leave instead to find Garrett. The son he *does* want."

Jason stalked off. As he did, he could've sworn he heard the king sobbing.

CHAPTER 9

The Silver Walls

ara's mother shook her awake to catch rays of pearl light seeping through the canopy passing overhead.

"There," Rose said, pointing. "*Look, Sara! The Walls!*"

Sara rubbed sleep out of her eyes. They'd been traveling from Rosbury to Southpoint in a mule-drawn wagon reeking of onion since sunrise. Still groggy, she fought for purchase with her feet in an unsteady wagonbed. Far above, King Anjan's castle filled the sky like a shining mountain. Tall and wide loomed the long curtain wall, shimmering hypnotically. A jolt to Caleb's wagon, and the freckled red walls encircling Southpoint once more eclipsed the Silver Walls.

"It's Traitor's Gate," Caleb told her mother discreetly.

"Oh god, god, they're *terrible*, Caleb," Rose croaked. "We should've taken East Gate." She twisted around for a grave look at Sara. "Hide your eyes. Don't look up—whatever you do. Do you understand, Sara?"

Sara nodded. She covered her face with her hands. When she caught her mother looking elsewhere, she ventured a peek through her fingers—and soon wished she hadn't. Grisly black melon shapes decorated a row of spikes on Traitor's Gate. The tarred heads had frightening expressions she saw again when she shut her eyes: vacant eye sockets, furrowed brows, lips twisted into snarls. Flies buzzed in dense clouds above their tousled hair. The dead men's faces made her think of Hexaar, and that led her to dwell on her father. *No, you're alive, you're alive, I know it,* she thought. *Caleb made the Gift of a hare.*

Two city guards waved them to a stop outside the gate. They questioned the farmer about where they'd come from and what they were doing in Southpoint. To their unease, the men flipped over the tarp to inspect their cargo. After all that, they said he had to pay to enter the city.

"*Two* lorens?" Caleb balked. "Wasn't it half a loren last time, sirs?"

The jowly guard looked froggish as he scowled. "Gate tax. You don't pay? You don't go in."

"And you try to get past us—" The skinnier guard jabbed his thumb up at Traitor's Gate.

"Course, we're open to . . . *other* ways of paying." The frog-faced guard ogled her mother.

"She's married," Sara blurted. She drew the guard's scowl. "To a knight of House Morley." She was dismayed when Rose warned her with a stern look.

Caleb broke the tension with an awkward laugh. "*Well!* What's a few sylvens, anyway, Rose?" He deposited the coins into the skinnier one's grimy palm.

Snapping the reins, Caleb guided them through Traitor's Gate. Sara glared at the frog man as the wagon rattled past. She breathed easier when the guards and heads slipped behind the roofs of houses.

Rose was beside herself over the tax. "The king must *truly* have need of coin for his wars if he's raising even a gate tax like that," she said when they were out of the guards' earshot.

Caleb smirked. "The king has need of our coin, but I doubt even half of that will reach his coffers. Those guards will have a taste, and then the Little King will have his."

Their conversation drifted out of Sara's hearing as she took in Southpoint. The sights and sounds of Eastcheap swirled around them like a raging river. She had never seen so many faces! Rosbury had always seemed so vast and important with its thousand villagers; Southpoint had to have *millions*, maybe more. Everyone seemed to be about some business or another. Guards in nasal helms and boiled leather patrolled the streets, checking faces and asking questions.

"The mayor's men are out in force today," Caleb noted as he tugged the reins. "Must be the Worthy Assembly's already here."

Their wagon slowed to a snail's pace in the thick of busy Southpointers. Most gave way. Some shouted insults at Caleb for sloshing mud; Sara made faces at those people. Iron Street with all its billowing smoke forked into Silver Street, which fed into the congested sprawl of Kingsway.

That was where Sara realized that the Silver Walls were actually *hideous*. Up close, the twelve-sided curtain wall looked like a frosted cake, with a topmost layer alight with the pretty pearl colors and a bottom half freckled with rust-orange brick. Behind the curtain wall loomed an unsightly tower notched like tree bark. Long fingers of brown crept up the Walls, as if with a desire to steal the battlements' luster and drag it down into the murk of a gray-green moat.

"It's *ugly*," Sara said decisively.

Her mother chided her with that look she had. "Mind your tongue! This is Anjan First King's great castle. Every one of our Lords of Loran has dwelt here. I won't have mine own daughter saying a wrong thing about it."

"Aye, but Sara isn't the only one to say it," Caleb said. "The Walls were once silver all over. It was said the light from their stone was like another moon above Southpoint for years. Now they're more like the Red Walls, at least on the outside."

Sara swelled with gratitude. She loved that about Caleb: how he would sometimes agree with her against her mother.

"What happened to them?" the girl asked.

"Selfishness. Greedy kings and Common thieves. Lords of Loran have always wanted Anjan's mysterious stone for their statues in the Hall of Memory. Peasants have always peddled it for meat and wine."

The day wore on in Southpoint, unbearably hot, humid, and pungent from the reek of fish and refuse. Sara passed the time counting the many peasants. When Rose wasn't watching, she snuck a hand beneath her sweat-sodden wimple to relieve an annoying itch.

Caleb noticed. "Hot, isn't it, sweet one?"

Leaning down, he retrieved a waterskin from under their seat. He uncorked it, splashed water in his mouth, and handed it to her.

She tilted her head back and squeezed the leather.

"Oh, look!" Caleb said. "They're here." He shifted to make room for her upfront. "A lady of your illustrious line shouldn't miss this, Sara Sothron."

She plopped between her mother and their neighbor, and gasped. Past carts stuffed with caskets and wheat bundles, past other Commoners and their beasts of burden, she saw a parade unlike anything she had ever seen. Beautiful stallions pulled a hundred gilded carriages from either side of the Walls, coming to a halt around the lowered drawbridge. Every horse was as elegant as her Little Lady, with lustrous manes and tails alight in the pearl shine spilling down from the Walls.

"Are they the king's princes and princesses?" she asked.

"Well, if they were, *you'd* be up there with them, wouldn't you?" Caleb said. She smiled. "Though the king is said to have as many princes and princesses," he added with a wink for her mother. "No, no, this is the Worthy Assembly."

Sara knew the Assembly by name but understood little and less about it, save for the fact that Free Believers and the Common folk despised it. Anytime the lords and clergy of the Assembly met, men like her father and Connor Bagman would gather in Rosbury's Golden Dragon as if the inn were a parish. Sometimes they'd actually *listen* to readers over cups of mead; the roamer Firemouth had paid visits until their Lord Warden threatened to hang him.

"How many Assemblymen will we see?" she asked.

Caleb wiped his brow with a greasy forearm. "Not sure, my lovely. Maybe a hundred. But not every Assemblyman is eager to remember the Long Summer, and no one ever invites merchants, so maybe fewer."

Sara knew enough to know the king and his Assemblymen got along as well as cats and dogs. Peasants still spoke of wars that lasted for the longest summers, of smoking fields and dead men on trees. Her father had lost his father and two brothers in the rebellion, her mother a brother and five cousins.

Few could agree on why a Long Summer came in the first place.

Brother Elfred told his congregants that Hexar started it when he wanted a third wife; Reader Gary and Firemouth and nearly everyone else blamed Stod, Willard, and *especially* Priestking Parlisis. Her father, who had named her after Sarah Sinclair, said the priestking was to blame the most because he wanted their souls. That was enough for Sara Sothron.

To pass the time, Caleb started a guessing game about which noblemen were present. She had to stand and try for a close look at their rippling banners. The thrice-crowned blue hart on white belonged to the Old Oak, Greg Thorngale, Lord of Thessela, who hobbled out of his carriage on the arms of his sons Gavin, Darren, and Luc. Portly Lord Dumas she knew from his duo of whales on blue, gold, and white. Her mother leaned forward to catch a glimpse of the dashing Lord Tomas Fawkes, known for his love of the Free Beliefs; a banner displayed his griffon over triangles of orange and black.

They spotted some of the kingdom's most important men of cloth. Exiting a gilded carriage, High Bishop Peshar Grathos walked beside a number of plump-faced boys, acolytes all. His rival, Jacob Sulley, Master Reader of the Free Beliefs, trudged ahead of a retinue of boys with funny bowl haircuts.

"Will we see the king arrive, too?" Sara asked.

The farmer snickered. "No, my lovely, the king sits the Silver Walls. He's separate from the Assembly, and we're all the better for it, trust me on that."

"Why did Hexar ever spare the Assembly?" Sara caught her mother's look and swiftly added, "King Hexar, I mean. His Majesty. After the Long Summer, I mean." She felt stupid.

Caleb rubbed his chin. "It's a good question, princess." She smiled. "Hexar needs the Assembly because he needs coin."

"But why does the Assembly need the king?"

The farmer and her mother seemed apprehensive. Rose circled about. "Come now, you should know better than that."

Her mother didn't need to remind her. Kings had ruled on Odma ever since the elves had left on their ships long, long ago. Once, Anjan

First King had reigned over all of Odma. Reader Gary liked to remind her and the other children that they'd still have one kingdom under one king had it not been for Casaanite witchcraft.

Caleb explained that the Worthy Assembly wasn't one but three assemblies. The noble lords had their Wing of Lords, and priests and readers their Wing of Clergy. Beneath them was the Wing of Knights.

Sara stood on her tiptoes. "Where are all the knights?"

He giggled. "Well, the Wing of Knights doesn't really sit knights, just fur traders, spice peddlers, and their like. Really, they ought to call themselves the Wing of Merchants."

She puzzled her expression. "What about the Commons? Don't they get a wing, too?"

Caleb smiled ruefully. "They—*we*—had one, once. Two hundred years ago. But then Commoners helped bring about the Interregnum. The lords and clergy never forgave peasants for helping kill King Lathros and banished them from their Assembly. Lord David is supposed to be a voice, but he cares about the Commons like he would fleas."

"That'll be enough about Fourth Wings and dead kings," Rose broke in curtly. "We've come to make coin, not trouble."

Sara would have rather liked to learn more. She could sit and listen to Caleb talk for hours. He knew a lot for a Common peasant, but that was because he hadn't been born one. Mother once told her that Caleb had belonged to a highborn house in Westland, and that his lord father had stripped him of his title and inheritance when he refused a plain-looking wife. Father had said he was someone best left alone, but the farmer was all they'd had for help at market since his disappearance. Without Caleb's stinky onions, they wouldn't have been able to pay their taxes, and her mother would've had to remarry or give her up.

Caleb angled his head back for another drag. He handed her the waterskin. "Left a little more for you, princess."

She slaked her thirst as Sacreis rode his blazing sun chariot to the sky stables high above, and thought on how hideous the Walls looked.

By the time their turn came to pass through the Great Gates, Sara needed to make water urgently.

Her mother looked deeply annoyed when she whispered it to her. "You gave her too much, Caleb," she complained.

"Just lift your gown and bend the knees, princess," he told her. "It'll pass right through the wood planks."

For some reason, Caleb calling her by that name, here, in the Silver Walls, made anything like that horrifying. Her thighs cramped from all the pressure in her stomach.

A handful of knights greeted them at the first gate. One of them had deep blue eyes that reminded her of her father's. She sank into the back of the cart, unsure if she was weeping from onion or her own mortification.

Sara rested on her side by the onions and curled her knees into her stomach. She tossed to and fro; she ground her teeth; she counted the spikes in the portcullis overhead.

She finally heard the knight instruct Caleb to board his cart and mules in the stables nearest the South Tower. The farmer snapped the reins, and the cart rumbled over the drawbridge and into a vast court-yard. Every bump brought her to the edge of pissing, and by the mercy of the godface Maetha she somehow restrained herself.

She needed to make this fast.

When she heard fewer voices, she stood abruptly and said, "I'm sorry Mother, I'm so sorry," and leapt off the cart. Sara heard Caleb calming her mother as she ran to find some privacy.

The castle towered above her like canyon walls, alight in the waning sunlight. Servants were everywhere, and nowhere seemed safe for her to lift her gown. As she rushed by, a man nearly spilled the logs in his arms. Near the stables, the horses whinnied, and a gruff-looking bearded man appeared. On the other side of a huge tower, she encountered a scowling lord.

A hedge maze seemed the most promising. Sara didn't enter through a proper entrance but through the first space in the leafy wall that seemed roughly her size. She squeezed her small body between briars, realizing seconds later that she'd lost her wimple to prickly shrub.

In a shady space between the hedges, with no one around, she finally bent low. She barely had time to slide her wool hem over her knees before the golden stream surged into the grass. She exhaled and almost lost her balance. By Felos, the godface of celebration, she thought nothing had *ever* felt so good.

The ecstasy didn't last. She heard feet in the grass. Voices followed. Fearing it was the king himself, she pushed her hemlines down and crouched inside the nearest hedge. Unlike the hard clay of Rosbury, the soil here shifted like sand, and she snaked her hands and feet inside it, seeking invisibility.

She glimpsed two men through a hedge opposite hers. One wore a black cloak, and she couldn't see much more than its folds and his sandaled feet. The other she saw more clearly. Frail and very old, he shuffled about in a gray robe that snaked after him.

". . . perfect opportunity, one your men fumbled," said the first man. "I thought your order was known for these things?"

"Sinclair intervened," said the one in the robe. "The Little King knew they would cross paths. He deliberately misled me."

The black cloak barked with laughter. "Misled *you?* You *must* be getting old."

The robed one glared. "That craven is a thorn in my side. Yours, too. Were that you had made good on your end of this and had the king *send Renworth to the Tower* years ago."

The other man drifted out of her vision. "Hexar likes him. He prefers two spymasters these days, one for the lords and one for their Commons. And let's not forget the peasants' love for him."

"Even though he rifles through their pockets and cuts the throats of those who cross him."

"Jealousy never was a good look on you, my friend."

The gray robe gazed after his companion. "Have you made arrangements?" he asked so softly she strained to hear.

The other one must have done or said something, because the one in gray added, "We did right in persuading the king to name her steward. She has Hexar's strength, but her mother's wisdom. A shame her full-blooded brother died in the Brace."

"Yes, a shame. How are they taking the loss of Alyse's only male child?"

The gray robe stroked his papery hands. "They knew the risks. The Lame King is a harbinger for change. The late prince had an ill temperament, anyway."

The black cloak harrumphed. "A funny thing, that. The king's brother suffered exile for his betrayal, and Sir Hanorr gave up his head. And of all the game pieces on his board, the priestking risked *that* one against Vhizadyn?"

Turning, the other man strolled through the grass, hands clutched behind his back. "I've heard funnier things. What do you know of the crown prince?"

"Only that the Southern Vine had nothing to do with it."

"Nor did the Northern. I thought maybe he went mad from war. Do you believe the bastard prince?"

"I believe prophecy is unfolding. I believe the Ascendant King is coming. The Northern Vine may not, but—"

The gray robe spun on his heels. "Who said *that?*"

"—*but* others still do. Things are in motion well beyond your touch or mine. The crown's enemies move against us. Kar Kravack has seized the north. Vhizadyn Skulltowers conquers the Brace. Evan Sinclair still breathes, and his traitors will raze this kingdom to the ground to give the rabble a voice."

"I recall you had a hand in saving his neck the first time."

"Were that I'd had a choice in the matter. But even Evan Sinclair troubles me less than what Lord Uthron shared with me."

Lord Uthron? She inched closer. Sharp twigs grazed her hair, loosing golden bangs.

"Uthron recently lost a company he sent west to appease pagans in his village. They vanished. On Half-Day. *On the road to Graywood.*"

"You're far too superstitious."

The black cloak stiffened. "The swordwood is a place of evil, and nothing good comes from it." He prodded the robed one's chest. "Tell me, where will *you* be when Those Who Eat the Children show themselves again?"

Sara almost made water again. She knew from parish that name was another one for the shadowkings, deadly servants of the Nagarthessi, the bastard sons of Dracar vanquished by King Anjan in the First Days. A spotty brown spider descended on a silk thread to dangle by her cheek, yet she remained still.

The robe pushed the cloaked one's finger away with a mild look of annoyance. "Oh, I know *you're* a believer," he said. "Forgive me if I have a hard time trusting what you say. I hear you've taken on a new servant. Does that explain why my bed has grown cold, of late?"

"Watch yourself."

The gray robe took the other's hand, a gentle touch. "You know I won't pry. That's part of the arrangement we have . . . an arrangement you know I must now end. So consider this my last gift. You speak of Uzmen, Fourth Wings, and shadowkings, but you should watch *yourself*. My colleagues are watching you. Their intentions are not benign."

The black cloak retracted his hand. "Thank you for your *gift*," he said coldly.

"You should take it more kindly," the other warned. "You and I are the last of our kind. I've protected you for as long as I can, but the Northern Vine has no love for you. They watch the stars. They mean to act. And they'll not suffer you or this—"

A songbird trilled twice. The men stirred uneasily.

". . . not alone," she heard the gray robe whisper.

Terror seized Sara. The man in gray sent his eyes here and there . . . and settled on where she huddled beneath the hedge.

The heads on Traitor's Gate flashed through her mind as Sara picked herself up and stumbled out of the hedge, branches creaking and scraping her arms as she fled. Her stomach rolled with disgust as she stepped through grass damp with her own water. She wheeled around a hedge bush and plunged through three leafy spaces, thorny branches pulling insistently at her hair and wool gown. Her feet carried her so fast that her eyes missed the marbled fountain, and she tumbled headfirst into the pool below the seated statue.

She was wet now, dripping everywhere, her hair a soggy mop that clung slickly to her cheeks and neck. She heard feet just beyond the hedge. Her face crumpled at once and her tears mingled with those from the sad-faced statue.

She blamed herself for this. She never should've drank so much water, never should've left the cart or thought the Walls so ugly. It was her fault, and the king would take her head for sure, and Dracar would take her soul for eternity. She wept.

That was when she saw him in the hedge bush. Her father. She couldn't see his face, but *knew* the blue eyes watching from their hollows. He faded into the leaves.

She was in a dream. It was *her father*; he was here, here to save her from the robe and cloak. Wading through the pool, she crawled out of the fountain. She followed the sounds of his fast-moving feet.

"Father," she kept trying to say, but he was always a few yards ahead, and she couldn't run and talk.

Through the hedges and around the tower, she slammed into Rose Sothron.

Her mother stared at her with horror. "*By the twelve-who-are-one,* where—how—*why are you wet?*" She shook her by her arms. "Your hair is showing. *Where is your wimple, Sara?*"

"I saw Father," she stammered. "I saw him, Mother! I—"

She boxed her ear. "Fool girl! I should've told Sir Willard you were too young to leave Rosbury. *Come!*"

Her mother yanked her by the hand. Glancing back, she couldn't find any sign of her father or the gray robe and black cloak. She lingered on the rust-red brick in the Silver Walls.

CHAPTER 10

Evan's Warning

van sat waiting on an uncomfortable marble bench in the Great Hall outside the throne room. It was Remembrance Day, and the king still hadn't made time to hear his petitions. Hanor the Tessian had assured him he would. He told him the king wanted him seated on this specific bench until the hour.

The traitor nobleman wasn't surprised. Hexar Eddenhold was notorious for his delays, and he hadn't seen or spoken to the king since their reunion in the lower bailey.

There was also a long wait. Every member of the Worthy Assembly's most important chambers, the Wing of Lords and Wing of Clergy, had all but finished trickling into the Walls, and each lord, priest, and reader wanted to petition the king about some grievance before the feast that evening. These men had pride of place. Traitors like himself had numerous other places: the Red Tower, Traitor's Pit, and Traitor's Gate, for starters.

The line to the throne room started somewhere in the middle bailey. Evan watched for familiar faces as Assemblymen filed past. Unable to move, lest he risk the king's anger (a thing he knew too well), he endured literally hundreds of encounters with friends and enemies he hadn't seen in years.

Some, like Sam Wuthers, the disheveled Lord of Minor Sunder, treated him with courtesy. Tomas Fawkes, the young Lord of Westerliche, a handsome man with laughing eyes, bantered openly with Evan, as interested in meeting Sarah's brother as he was in breaking ranks. In line with his sons, the legendary Greg Thorngale hobbled over for a handshake, a necessary gesture from the peace broker who ended the Long Summer Rebellion. Master Reader Jacob Sulley paid him the slightest nod.

Passing him, most averted their gazes. More than a few sought to impress upon others how much *more* they reviled the Loyal Company's speaker than their scowling colleagues. Waddling by, Dumas Sunox muttered something about how his dead sister was still whoring in hell. Tom Gelder, Lord of Major Sunder, spat on his chest. Not to be outdone, Sam Gramlore, the Lord of Eddenwood, sprayed Evan in his eyes.

Evan didn't react. He'd been through worse, much worse. He knew how to spot bait. He wiped the spittle with a sleeve, comported himself, and said nothing.

He'd come a long way, traveling from Caerdon through outlaw-infested borderlands, but his journey had begun long before. At seventeen, Evan tasked himself with righting the wrongs these so-called Worthy Assemblymen inflicted upon those unlucky enough to be born outside their castles. That led him to a truth about men. In his search, he lost a sister and his friend, his father's titles, his ancient family's wealth.

Only his sister's killer could provoke him, and he strode in at the tail's end.

Gram Sothos towered over everyone. He was as wooden and regal as Evan remembered, garbed in a maroon-colored doublet over a gray shirt that puffed elegantly at his wrists. A duo of golden lion pendants fastened a rich crimson cape over his shoulders. He looked hawkish as ever with his sharp nose and quick hazel eyes set below a balding head. His pink hands hung at his sides, one near his ruby-riddled sword haft.

Voice of the Worthy Assembly. Hammer of the Commons. Lordsbane. These were the names men called the Speaker of the Wing of Lords. Pinkhands others called him, never to his face. A Medecian by birth, Sothos had been a stalwart ally to the late Stoddard Trambar, a son, even—such that he married the man's eldest daughter, Tess, whom Evan had also loved.

And like Trambar, Gram Sothos despised the Sinclairs. He would've marched on Southpoint with the great rebel lord, had an explosion not scarred his body and left Sothos unable to do more than languish abed as others decided the Long Summer Rebellion.

Neither man locked eyes until the tall lord was close. Evan remained seated. Sothos loomed over him.

"Evan Sinclair, you of all people should know that a man without a title must bow before a nobleman," he said in that sonorous voice that resonated through men's chests.

"Ah, but that's the key, isn't it, Gram?" Evan replied with a pained expression, looking up. "One *must be* noble first."

Sothos's upper lip quivered. "Careful, Sinclair. You're here at the king's pleasure. Be sure to guard that famous tongue, or I'll see to it that it's cut off in the Red Tower." He leaned in so that only Evan could hear him. "Or maybe you'll wind up like that whore you called your sister, black all over like overdone pork."

Evan smiled thinly. "You'll have to tell me what that feels like one day," he said with a nod at his hideous hands. "Maybe I'll ask the king what he thinks when I have my audience with him."

"You won't. I'm here to remind King Hexar of the snake in his kingdom's garden. Flicking its tongue at our fragile peace."

He wagged a finger, smirking. "Those are my words, you know. I told Tess that was House Sothos's *real* sigil, when she told me she had to marry you. A snake, flicking its tongue at a fragile peace. She must say it often, for you to pass that off as your own."

With a look of barely muted rage, Sothos turned to enter the throne room. "One day, Sinclair," he said, "one day I'll see you reunited with your sister."

The Lord of Saxhold surrendered his sword to a sentry knight and walked into the throne room as if it were his. Evan unclenched his teeth. *One day, Pinkhands,* he swore to Sarah as much as himself, *I'll display your head at my castle.*

The double doors closed with a soft thud.

Evan slumped against the marble wall. He dwelled on his bitter history with Sothos, a man so loyal to Priestking Parlisis and their faith that Commoners said he bled cream and violet. Ever had the two men been rivals: first in love, then in politics, and, finally, in war.

He could never prove it, but he knew that Gram Sothos had loosed the arrow that burned his sister and best friend alive. Almost like divine retribution, fiery debris had fumed into the archers' window, likely scalding Sothos. *Yet the king gaoled me in place of my sister's killer— retains him as leader of the Wing of Lords,* he mused cynically. *Because Gram Sothos is rich and powerful, and I was useful as a whipping post made of Hexar's grief and rage.*

He took pleasure at least in his one piece of leverage. It made him a thorn in Lordsbane's side and ensured fairness in the Worthy Assembly, all from the shadows. It was why Evan was here, now, in the Great Hall, waiting on a king who years before had nearly removed his head. *Let's see how it protects me today, Sarah,* he thought.

Evan listened intently to the voices inside as the morning wore on. He often heard the king's deep bear voice trampling over those of his wheedling, entreating, infuriating Assembly.

Petitions mostly concerned petty disputes between lords. Wuthers complained bitterly about how Gelder's sheepherders were tending their flocks on his side of Sunder Way, and how, if it pleased His Majesty, he'd have a declaration that said those fields were his alone. Gramlore argued too forcefully for rights to forestlands inside Trevor Wexley's Cloudlands, and Hexar, still the Bull's friend after years of silence, flatly refused. Sothos had a rapt room when he urged the king to gaol Sinclair.

 Few joined the Free Believers in petitioning Hexar to ease the suffering in the land. Lords agitated about peasants' poll tax evasions and unseemly bargains for higher wages. Evan almost laughed. *The lords pocket Common coin, tear peasant children from their mothers' teats when they can't pay—and so few see the danger.* Sothos objected fiercely to the princess's decision to name sheriffs justices of the peace. That flummoxed Hexar, who unleashed his anger on other, less wealthy lords.

No one brought up the king's heirs. He wondered if word had leaked about Prince Garrett's absence, or the attempt on his nephew's life. *Where are you now, Lord Jason?* He hadn't set eyes on his sister's son since their conversation in the bailey.

The doors swung open sometime after noon. With drawn faces and dull eyes, the Worthy Assemblymen filtered toward their apartments, paying Evan no attention. Sothos left with his cape fluttering behind his heels, avoiding eye contact.

Hexar's voice barreled through the throne room like thunder. "Evan, get in here," he boomed.

Clad from top to bottom in ceremonial armor, whorls of gold on silver, two sentry knights reached for iron handles set in the huge doors and shut them behind Evan. A whoosh of air freshened the back of the traitor nobleman's neck.

The king presided over a vast chamber from the top of the twinkling mountain that was the Silver Throne. Drexan Lorrain and Hanor Graxhold occupied shadows to the throne's left; just to its right, Evan observed grimly, stood the Grand Inquisitor in his unmistakable crimson robes of office. Evan's wrists tingled in memory of the spymaster's chains.

A herald clacked his staff on the floor. "Here enters Evan Sinclair, formerly Lord of Caerdon, leader of the so-called Loyal Company and—"

"God, I damn well know my own brother-by-law, you twat," the king thundered like some child god from far above. He sighed. "I'm tired from dealing with my Worthy Assembly and have a feast to prepare for, so I'll keep this brief, Evan: I owe you my son's life. I want to repay you with a full pardon and hear your petitions."

Evan choked on his words. He hadn't even bowed. "M-my king," he stammered.

"Before you respond, you need to know that I have conditions," Hexar added. "I will return your titles and seat you again in the Worthy Assembly. I will listen to your petitions. In return, I want the men in your Loyal Company to come here. I want them to show me their faces, give me their names, and declare themselves my loyal subjects—if they *are* truly loyal. I demand this especially from those in your Company who also sit in the Assembly."

Precisely as I expected. "That will take time, Your Majesty, but I'm sure the Company will come forward once you restore the Wing of the Commons."

The king slumped in his seat. He stroked his wiry auburn beard. "I understood you sought for me to tax the lords and priests. No, I will not resurrect the Fourth Wing."

Ah, but of course, Sarah, Evan thought. *I felt hope too soon.*

"Well, that is my judgment. What say you, Sinclair? Are you ready to be Lord Evan once more?"

Evan drew on the gifts for which he was known, the ones that had once helped him survive the Red Tower. "I am deeply honored and grateful, Your Majesty. Long have I wanted us to be kin by law again, united at least in the love we share for my sister. As for your son, he is my nephew and all that I have left of her. What I did for him I would do again, a thousand times over, and with mine own body as his shield if I could."

Hexar nodded agreeably.

"Yet I must not pretend with you, Your Majesty," he went on. "My Companymen will not come forward and forsake their anonymity for making lords pay their due. They want the Wing of the Commons." He eyed Drexan curiously. "And they sent me here on the impression that Your Majesty might use sword and scroll to seat the peasants again."

Covered half by shadow and half by sunlight, the king looked like a scowling gargoyle. "Lorrain, you said nothing about this," he barked to his left.

Drexan paced forward, wrapped in his cloak, torchlight reflected in his steel skullcap. "I believe Lady Sarah Sinclair's brother is mistaken, my king," he said measuredly. "I shared the impression that we'd hear only about Evan's wishes to tax the temples. Not consider a treacherous chamber."

A plain lie. Drexan Lorrain had sent his invitation with assurances that Hexar would consider the Company's most controversial demand. *The king seeks a peace,* the chancellor had written. *Return to the First King's Walls ere Remembrance Day, and he shall consider your greatest demand.*

Are we not still friends, Crow? To call Drexan a friend was charitable, to say nothing of dangerous in the wrong company. Yet the enigmatic advisor had done nothing less than convince a grieving Hexar to spare his life. Why, he still wasn't sure. The gossips whispered that Drexan was a sorcerer; others believed him one of the only men capable of making the wily king listen to reason. The real Drexan Lorrain lay somewhere in-between those caricatures, and only the King's Crow knew where.

Evan decided against producing the letter as evidence. He was here, and that was what mattered. The king wouldn't have agreed to hear his petitions if he knew that one concerned the Worthy Assembly's missing chamber, and the Loyal Company would've scoffed at an invitation that forbade its consideration.

"I can grant your pardon and the tax reforms, nothing else," Hexar said resolutely.

"Then you will merely return my titles and seat me in the Worthy Assembly," Evan said, "and nothing else."

The king stirred on his throne. "*Merely?*"

Evan had known Hexar when he was younger, stronger, strikingly handsome, and still flush from victory in his Trials. Then, as now, he was a bull that men risked their lives trying to tame and only fools goaded willingly. Many would say Evan was the fool . . . but he knew this king like his own castle.

"You risk the king's goodwill, Sinclair," his former gaoler said, his voice rising imperiously. "If not another year in your old cell."

Evan steeled himself against fear. "I'm grateful to Your Majesty for your pardon. For my title, my Assembly seat. But your kindness to me will not keep the peace. Not for long."

Hexar gripped the silverstone arms of his throne. "Is that a threat?"

"Not from me, Your Majesty," he answered. "In my Loyal Company

I am a Petitioner, as are my two companions." Evan was tempted to out Karl Redmore as a Reubenite and remove one of his rival's allies, but word would leak, and he could face a worse fate when he saw the Company again. He liked to think of himself as a decent man, anyway. "Yet there are many who have lost faith in the Worthy who rule this kingdom."

"The king among them," Hexar said to chuckles.

Evan waited for silence. "We fought together, you and I," he said. "We lost Sarah together, you and I. Yet some of my Companymen are not like me. They are losing patience. They do not see a difference between the king and his Assemblymen. And soon, if nothing changes, they will take up arms."

The king threw his hands in the air. "Good! Then you've just made a case for me to cut off the head of the snake." One hand wavered in the air, outstretched, as if he were deciding whether to remand Evan to his old cell that instant.

"Then you will sign our death warrants," Evan returned gravely. "I am your ally, as I was during the Long Summer. I'm also the cork in the poison vial. Remove me, and you will spill an openly *Disloyal* Company onto our heads . . . and bring about another Interregnum."

The word *Interregnum* echoed through the throne room like a stone clacking down some long dark chasm, with the last syllable slowly fading, *num, num, num*. Plate armor clinked as sentry knights reached for their sword hilts.

Burke flew before the Silver Throne, his face almost as red as his robes. "Say the word, my king, and I'll have this traitor on the rack," he said.

With a stern gesture Hexar silenced his torturer. A grim chuckle started low in the king's throat, loudening into a belly laugh that rocked his entire frame. "You see, Charles? You see? *This* is why I'm glad I listened to Drexan the day I wanted his head. You've always had balls, Evan, I'll give you that. Who else would utter that word"—he spread his arms—"in *this* room?"

Evan let his gaze wander to the patch of discolored stone at the foot of the throne. "Forgive me, Your Majesty. I would not mention that black event here unless—"

"It is *because* of the Interregnum that I would not restore your Wing of the Commons," Hexar said forcefully. "Peasants are beneath our feet for a reason, Sinclair. Give them a taste of power, and they'll pick the table clean. Just as Lathros learned."

He'd almost forgotten that beneath all the bluster was a nobleman raised on the histories. Then again, what king who valued his neck *wouldn't* remember the tale of King Lathros? He eyed the centuries-old bloodstain, imagining a king curled up there, ringed by panting men with crimson swords.

"What you say is not untrue, Your Majesty," Evan replied calmly, to soothe rattled nerves. "No one will ever forget the infamy the Wing of the Commons brought upon itself when it helped the Treasonous Twelve behead King Lathros."

Actually, there was more to that story, but who in their kingdom wished to hear it? Not kings who valued their necks. Certainly not lords like Sothos, or priests, who felt a peasant's place was at their feet. Yet Evan knew the truth, as had Sarah and Matthus. The Treasonous Twelve had been Free Believers in need of land and timber for their parishes. When the Fourth Wing asked this of the king, Lathros led petitioners from the throne room to his garderobe, and told them to make the seat inside their altar.

Their anger had been justified. Yet Evan couldn't defend the kingkilling, or what followed.

Hexar pointed at the stain. "Aye, you'll get a Fourth Wing, and I'll add a coat of mine blood to the floor. Why should I risk my neck—*my line*—for your rabble?"

"Because we need a Wing of the Commons again," he said, unwavering. "Not a wing of kingkillers, but subjects loyal to the Walls who can tilt the Worthy Assembly away from the lords and priests. Without one, any petition of mine you grant will have as much salt with the Wings of Lords and Clergy as mine own name. The steward's naming of justices was clever, but Gram Sothos and his lords will pay their sheriffs more or have them replaced over trifling offenses. He'll bid them *do nothing,* and you'll continue squeezing peasants until a village stands up and says no more."

The king rose haltingly. "Sothos will damn well enforce my will if I send catapults to his fucking castles," he growled. He must have nicked his gout leg, because he plopped back into his cushions, red-faced and wincing.

And I suppose nothing backfired when you beheaded Lady Alyse, either, he thought morosely.

"Why do you care, Evan?" asked Drexan, listing on his staff. "What have the Commons ever done for you?"

Why indeed? His passion for reform on their behalf had cost him so much. Evan could've defended the Fourth Wing's legacy of peace and plenty for all.

If it could help his case, he would've elaborated a truth. Rulers sat not upon glittering thrones but bowed shoulders. Those born into wealth and power assumed their positions came naturally, confusing privilege with providence, silence with consent. They forgot that sometimes, shoulders shrugged.

Evan's battle lay in persuading the powerful that refusing their peasants a voice wouldn't prevent a second kingkilling.

To the contrary.

Evan gave them the abridged version. "Little and less," he said at last. "For my own preservation. Because the Common life is brutish and short, and we ignore their pain at our peril. How long do you think they'll let us grind them to dust and rip their children from them?"

"That's Sothos's doing, not mine—"

"Aye," Evan spoke over his king, "and lords like Sothos control the Assembly. A restored Wing of the Commons will check him and end the injustice. With one, there shall be peace. Without one . . ." He trailed off ominously.

Drexan grimaced. "The peasants need only their king."

Hexar mopped his forehead, sighing. "I'm old, Evan. Soon, someone else may sit these Walls. I want peace in Loran. But I tell you, I won't suffer a Wing of the Commons that takes my head . . . or my sons'." His voice croaked when he said *sons.*

"Look for my pardon tonight at the feast," he added. "Tell your Loyal Company I'll do more if they come here and swear their allegiance. Now go with the love I still bear for Sarah."

Evan stopped before the doors. "My king, I would ask one final thing." He circled about. "You've pardoned me. I thank you for that. Tell me, would you return what belongs to my house?"

The king chuckled grimly. "The blackpowder? Don't try my patience."

"Does any of it still remain, Your Majesty?"

Hexar scowled. "Gone. All of it."

"You sold it, then?"

With his cool stare, Burke pierced something vulnerable in Evan. "You will address your king with respect, Sinclair."

"No, Charles, he'll leave." Hexar gestured impatiently. "Get out of my fucking court before I change my mind, *Lord* Evan."

CHAPTER 11

Broken Lines and Thirteen Crowns

ur felt uneasy in the kitchens.

Danger was everywhere. Inside hearths, spits overflowed with greasy spittle that fell to explode in the fires. Long sharp knives slashed and hacked through slabs of beef and pork, through rabbit and tender quail, sounding much like a hundred boots stomping in concert. Milled flour dust and grease smoke pervaded the brick chambers, drawing coughs and grunts from the servants, Commoners, and Casaanites there to prepare the feast.

Yet no one complained. Butchers and bakers, scullions and sauciers, they all toiled at their wooden tables, brimming with excitement. The king hadn't held a proper Remembrance Day feast like this in two years, not since he and his sons left for war and Prieslenne Edenia returned to the Lonely Isle. The evening promised a new pace at the Silver Walls.

Everyone labored at some task or several all at once, he saw. Apron-clad men barked orders to apprentices, dashed strings of white fat from meat, and unhooked spits with a finesse that somehow left them unscathed. Women kneaded mounds of dough, whipped colorful sauces in mortars, and stuffed the mouths of roasted pigs with bright red apples.

Zur stayed close to a corner in the furthest archway. He missed his books. Mistress Namoni had pulled him away from Drexan, who was busy with one thing or another at court. Yet he was at a loss for how to help. He watched as one Common woman seasoned her rabbit stew, churning it with a ladle.

Watching her, he reflected on his uselessness. He could recite the names of the spices she used. He could follow the recipe if she shared it with him. He wasn't sure if he could ladle her stew without scalding his wrists.

He caught a glimpse of Namoni inspecting the work of the cooks. Seeing him, too, the Casaanite head mistress navigated a sea of servants to reach him. Vanishing in the smoke, the stout woman reappeared so suddenly she startled him.

"Zuran, I did not take you out of the South Tower so you watch and do nothing, eh?" she piped in that accent that often made her sound as if she were asking a question.

"I'm sorry, my lady," he said. "I'm just not sure what to do. I've never worked in the kitchens before."

Shorter and less lithe than Anyasha, the woman wore a forest-green dress that brought out her brown eyes and the rolls of her stomach. Her skin was darker than his, her palms tan and leathery from hard-won calluses.

"That's because they reared you here, in the tall towers of Ansara, eh," she said, hands on her hips. "Maybe had you known Casaan, you would be more like me, eh? Used to doing and not idling?"

A sadness tugged at his heart. Unlike Namoni and Hexar's other Casaanite hostages, Zur had no memory of his homeland that didn't feel like a fleeting dream. His mother had given him up after Hexar's knights had laid low Tribe Nuur. All he'd ever known was Loran, and even then the strictures of life behind the Silver Walls. Anyasha was the only other Casaanite to grow up rudderless in that fog.

"I'm not familiar with the kitchens," he said. "Can I return to the South Tower? Honestly, I feel useless here."

Namoni made a baffling nod. She was famous around the Walls for her perplexing and indecipherable facial tics; the king himself would often bemoan how her nods could mean no, her headshakes yes.

Zur decided to pretend he didn't know this. "So, I can go?"

The woman responded as if she hadn't heard him. "You come and work, eh?"

What more was there to do? Zur followed her dutifully through the smoke and tables. He tried to shake off the gazes he, Namoni, and other Casaanites attracted from castle hands and Commoners. The peasants he liked least. Their eyes were dark with mistrust.

Namoni led him to a corner table piled high with yellow flaky onions. A pale-skinned man with short oily brown hair *thunked* the table with his knife, cleaving an onion in two.

"Sir, excuse me, eh?" she said. "Your name again, eh?"

The man promptly set down his knife, cleaned his hands on his apron, gave a loud sniff, and introduced himself. "Caleb Bard, of Rosbury, my lady, at your service."

Zur knew Rosbury, a small village just east of Southpoint and north of South Farcombe. Yet the man had a Westlander's accent and high-born manners, and a kindness that nudged Zur to lower his defenses.

"Ah, Caleb, eh, would you like help here?" Namoni piped.

"Yes, actually, if it please you. My little princess here and I are doing our best, but we still have a few hundred onions and I'm told they're in high demand."

"Very good, eh." Namoni escorted Zuran by his shoulders to a bench opposite Caleb and made him plant himself, as if he needed her guidance. "You help them, eh? I will be back, eh."

She disappeared once more into a haze of kitchen smoke.

The onions were overwhelmingly pungent. Zur tried not to gag. He rarely even ate onion; to sit amid so many all at once bordered on intolerable.

Caleb warmed with a smile that could thaw frost. "And who are you, sir knight?"

Zur stroked his arm nervously. "I'm no knight. My name is Zuran, of Tribe Nuur."

"Oh, I know, I just like to give all my friends highborn titles, Zuran," he said with a grin. "Except for Sara. She *is* a princess, don't let her or anyone else tell you any differently."

He hadn't noticed the little girl sitting beside Caleb. She wore a humorless gray wool gown and a starchy white wimple rimmed by strands of dirty blonde hair. She had pale skin and pink cheeks typical of Ansarans, and curious amber eyes that didn't make him feel unwelcome.

"Zuran, do you know how to slice an onion?" Caleb asked. When he shook his head, he added, happily, "Well, let me show you then! I promise you, it's easy, but you must take care. One wrong slice and—" He showed his right palm. A long scar ran from his thumb to his pinkie. "You don't want one of these, or you may never become a knight, little sir."

Zur didn't like his knight references. He *did* want to be a knight, and every lighthearted mention salted his wounds. Drexan knew too well by this point. He'd recently lectured Zur for cleaning inkpots poorly, given how lost he was in watching melees from his South Tower window.

"I can't become a knight," he said morosely, eyes in his lap. "I'm a Casaanite and the king's hostage."

"What does that mean, hostage?" Sara asked. He sensed mere curiosity in the peasant girl, nothing malicious. Her eyes hadn't left him since he sat down.

"A hostage is someone a highborn takes to make sure someone else does what it is agreed," Caleb explained, with surprisingly little awkwardness.

"Like Prieslenne Edenia?" Sara asked.

"Exactly." Caleb grabbed a fresh onion, planting it in front of Zur. "Now, watch closely."

Seizing his knife with a sleight of hand, he went to work on the onion, slicing off root and stem before making a groove in the side. Off came the flesh, and then he flipped it on its side and reduced it to a stack of flimsy ribbons.

"See? Not so bad." Caleb scooped up the ribbons, heaped them into a large bowl by Sara, and set another onion in front of Zur, along with a short knife. "And if you want to, you can cut this in the water basin we have. That's what Sara has been doing to keep from crying."

"I don't cry over onions," she protested.

Zur placed his onion in the basin and went to work. The water wasn't enough to keep his eyes from stinging with tears; he wiped them frequently with his arms.

He also struggled with his cutting, and it was obvious. Caleb found onion peels that still had the remains of roots and stems; others flaked with waxy flesh. He was showing him how to improve when a Common woman approached. She was the same one he'd seen ladling stew earlier. Pretty for a peasant, she had a slender oval face, gold-flecked green eyes, and brown hair visible about her wimple.

She lingered on Zur in a way that made him forget all that.

"Caleb, I'm not sure what I've done wrong, I need your help," she moaned. "I'm not sure if there is too much salt or pepper, or if the rabbit is overcooked. It's a meal for the lords and it must be right."

"Mother, can I help?" Sara squeaked.

"No, you stay here," her mother responded curtly.

Caleb placated Sara's mother and assured her he would see to her stew. "Princess, I leave you in charge. Show Zuran what I've taught you."

The two departed into the haze. As soon as she couldn't see them anymore, Sara loosened the knots in her wimple and ran her hands through her matted hair.

She looked up at him, as if she had forgotten he were there. "Shh, I'm not supposed to show the men my hair," she said in a strained voice. "You won't tell anyone, will you?"

He shook his head.

"*Ooh!* Is that a silver thread on your tunic? Men aren't allowed to wear things like that in Rosbury. Can I touch it?"

Sara reached for his tunic, her fingernails black in their quicks. Zur swatted her hand. She withdrew with a hurt look.

"I just wanted to touch it," Sara said, wounded.

"I'd rather you didn't."

The noise of the kitchens made the silence between them a little more bearable. "Do you want me to show you how to cut the onion?"

she asked at last. Without waiting for his response, she snatched his, took her knife, severed stem and root, peeled ribbons again. "See? It's not hard."

He disliked her tone. She was a Commoner, after all. Not that a hostage like himself had much to be up-jumped about, but peasants were beneath the feet of even merchants, and anyone below *that* surly lot typically had ticks and fleas. With fingernails that dirty, she had to have fleas. He watched her hair to see if any might pop out.

Soon he tried his hand at another onion, shearing top and bottom before tearing at the flesh with his fingers. "No, no," she interjected. "You're doing it wrong again. Here, let me see—"

He steered the onion away from her. "I can do it just fine."

"Nuh uh, I've seen you try to peel the flesh. *That's* what you're doing wrong. And your slices are too thick. Much too thick. They need to be thin, like blades of grass."

"I don't need a filthy peasant to tell me how to cut an onion."

She screwed up her face. "Don't be mean! I am trying to *help you*"—she spaced out *help* and *you*—"and I'm a *princess*."

Zur crossed his arms, chuckling. "Is *that* what your father tells you?"

Sara slammed the table with her fists; water sloshed over the basin's sides and through the table's planks. Thinking she might cry, he considered apologizing. The girl straightened up, trying for a look of offended dignity that only annoyed him more.

"Fine," she said with a sigh. "Caleb will have to show you how to cut onions again. But I have questions." She looked at him. "If you're a hostage like the priestking's daughter, do your folk pray toward the Lonely Isle, like she would?"

He made a dismissive gesture. "Don't you know? I thought you were royalty."

She gritted her teeth. "*STOP IT!* Stop being so mean!"

Her shout turned heads across the kitchen.

Leery of Namoni's attention, he shushed her with a finger and motioned for her to sit back down. "Okay, I'm sorry. Okay? No, Casaanites are not Elvarenists."

Seemingly satisfied, the girl eased back onto her bench with the exaggerated decorum of a highborn. "Good," she said. "The priest-king brought the Long Summer Rebellion upon us, Father told me so. Where is Casaan?"

"Casaan is across the sea."

"Who is king there?"

He suppressed a sigh. "Casaan isn't a kingdom; it's many different realms."

Yet he wasn't confident about his comparison. The tribes weren't realms, not like those in Ansara. Casaanites lacked high towers and walls, and any kind of king or knight, they said. He wasn't even aware of where his tribe of Nuur was on the maps; Namoni said Casaanites never stayed in one place but migrated with the seasons like birds.

"Kings take hostages to make them . . . keep faith?" she probed uncertainly. "Right?"

Zur nodded.

Sara sat forward with eager eyes. Questions no one but a peasant would ask gushed out of her like water from a faucet: "Why would the kingdoms of Casaan need to keep faith? Is it because you're Elzura's Child and Elzura broke the king's line when she cast that spell that made King Eduard kill his children?" She sucked in her breath, barely able to contain her excitement. "Can *you* cast spells?"

Zur was appalled. He wanted to shake the fool girl by her arms. Did she *know* what the priests did to accused sorcerers? Priestkings of yore had burned the Barefoot Knights into ruin on such accusations. Such lies had rendered Drexan an outcast with all but the king and his council, yet he was Chancellor of the Chancery. He couldn't imagine what eavesdroppers might do to a Casaanite hostage and Common girl.

Looking around to make sure no one had heard, he leaned close and hissed, "*Are you an idiot?*"

Sara bristled. "I am *not* an idiot! I am not like Praise. You, you're so *mean!* I hate Elzura's Children, I hate them!"

"I am *not* one of Elzura's Children." He hated that name, more than anything the lords and clergy called his people.

"You are too!" She stood and chanted, "*Broken lines and thirteen crowns, that's what Elzura the Witch begot; she cast a spell on old King Eduard, and we love her children not.*"

Zur went to his feet so fast he slammed the table with his thighs. Sara recoiled immediately, eyes wide. Triumphant, he was about to scorn her with a few choice words about her low birth when a hand glanced his shoulder.

"Zuran, I've been searching for you," came a voice.

He spun to find Drexan, wrapped in his cloak and listing on his staff. His green irises glinted in the firelight.

"My lord, I—I've been helping in the kitchen, Namoni told me to," he mustered.

Drexan smiled. "Ah, but these caves are no place for a servant of the King's Crow! Come, I have need of you at the feast. Besides, I've sung your praises to men of the Worthy Assembly, and they'd like to meet you."

Zur blushed fiercely. He didn't know what to say. "My lord, you, you do me too much honor."

"Well, they've heard of your prowess as a handler of the Worthy Assembly's gifts for the king!" Drexan added wryly. "I'll have you wash your face and dress for the occasion."

But of course, he thought to himself. *I am one of Elzura's Children. I must serve and handle gifts, and put up with stupid Common girls.*

Turning, he expected to find Sara exultant. She was gone.

CHAPTER 12

The Worthy

orana winced at what felt like a claw raking her side. Seeming to notice, Lorna let the jewel-studded girdle slacken around the folds of her gown.

The girl appeared from behind her in the mirror. "Are you okay, my lady?"

It was the fifth time in five minutes her younger lady-in-waiting had chafed her skin with the girdle's sharp jewel edges, and she was fast losing patience. *Is the griff okay when the tree cat slowly rends it?* she almost said.

Thankfully, Anyasha intervened before the princess permanently ruined the shy fourteen-year-old's confidence.

"Why don't you see to Princess Heather?" the Casaanite encouraged her sweetly. "I'll see to the girdle."

Lorna looked to the princess for solace. Finding none, the ginger-haired girl slipped quickly through her chamber door. Anyasha went to the door and shut it.

"That girl is a mouse," Lorana muttered. "Remind me to tell Lord Alan that he can take his daughter back to Southfar after the feast."

The servant admonished her with a look. "She's fourteen. And are you so great that you need no friends at court? Lorna *worships* you."

"Then she must be a Sylvanian, and I a heathen god." She snorted. "Worships the chance to meet a lordly husband while in my service, more like. Her father would like nothing more than to broker a marriage with someone like Tomas Fawkes."

"Well, of course. Who wouldn't?"

Lorana sought reassurance in Anyasha's eyes, but she was bent forward, unsnapping the girdle. Its emerald and sapphire shards winked with candlelight as the girl pulled it through her hands. Lorana let her eyes stray to that part of the mirror with her reflected cleavage.

"So you think I'm a bitch?" she asked.

"Only with tax collectors who miscount and ladies-in-waiting too young to understand when you're troubled."

"Troubled?" she scoffed. "By whom? My many adoring suitors, who want nothing more than children with my look?"

Anyasha finished refitting the girdle. She stood, smoothing the folds in Lorana's gown.

"I think you look radiant," her lover said, "and I've known you long enough to know when your father troubles you."

She sighed. "Am I transparent as window glass?"

"You haven't smiled since Jason met with the king."

She *had* been shorter with Lorna and some of her other ladies since Jason's meeting with her father. In his grief and anger, Hexar had made awful accusations. Jason had since gone hunting.

It worried her. Sarah's only son was nothing if not a man of his word. *Have you gone to find Garrett like you promised, my brother? Will you not show tonight?*

"I worry about him," Lorana admitted. "Jason is more my father than even my father realizes, and too hard on himself by half. He faces his bluster like he would a steel sword when he should take it for the rain it is, quick to come and go."

"Yet he *did* disobey the king when he left with Garrett."

"He did. And I suppose my father is Sacreis, and honors his every relation and vow," she muttered.

Anyasha didn't respond. Only Hexar's favorite child could speak about the king that way. Only with her favorite servant.

"You look wonderful," Anyasha told her.

Lorana saw herself in the mirror. From her feet to her chin, she supposed she *did* look like a princess of Loran. The gilded girdle and its jewels nicely complemented her cobalt-blue gown and its thread-of-silver workings.

Lorana glanced fleetingly at her face, the one Heather's ladies mocked behind her back for its scatter of freckles and bulbous nose. She had her traitor mother, Alyse, to thank for her uneven shape, small breasts, and bony hips.

She had stared at herself in this mirror since she was old enough to remember. As a child, she'd often run her hands over her face, as if it were pliable wet clay, as if she could sculpt her thick brow and wide-set nostrils into something more pleasing. Sometimes she'd make play with Edenia that the demon Pathazar had transformed her into a monster, and that only a beautiful virgin could lift the spell with her kiss.

Lorna doesn't like me, any more than my ambitious suitors, she thought to herself. *Do even you, Yasha? Or is it the favor and gifts of the king's daughter that attract you?*

"Do you think me fat?" Lorana poked at the jelly in her sides. "Perhaps I should reconsider Lord Dumas's marriage proposal. I can be the big whale in his sigil and he the small one."

Anyasha smiled with familiar mischief. "Speak you of . . . Lord Gut, he of mythical handsomeness?" She held the back of her hand across her forehead, as if she were swooning.

The women exploded with laughter. "How could I have forgotten?" she said, wheezing from the tightness of her stay. "Lord Gut, who ripped his own tunic wolfing down boar? If I became Lady Gut, do you think he'd try to eat me or fuck me?"

"Lady Thunderarse sounds like a fitting title."

The princess held a pillow to her stomach and swayed ponderously, grunting to imitate the heavyset lord's gravelly baritone. Anyasha staggered into her bed, clutching her belly as she laughed. Lorana abruptly dropped the pillow, stunned, as if she were Sunox, the pillow her stomach, so huge she couldn't contain it. Anyasha broke wind and looked at her, stunned; Lorana fell to her knees, roaring with laughter, tears streaming down her face.

"*Now* who's Lady Thunderarse?" she teased.

A passing look was all it took, a flutter in her stomach. Lorana climbed halfway onto the bed and kissed her lover.

A delicate rapping came at her door, ending the promise of a light petting before the formalities. "My lady?" came the Tessian's faint accent. "I, uh, um, the king—he's ready for you."

Lorana stood, smoothing out wrinkles in her gown. She turned to Anyasha.

"You look stunning," Anyasha mouthed with a smile too genuine to be questioned.

"Then I'll see you downstairs, Lord Hanor," Lorana answered the chancellor. "Along with Lord Gut," she mouthed for Anyasha. *And may he be the only spurned suitor I see again tonight.*

Lorana was to escort the king from the Great Hall to the upper bailey, where the lords and clergymen of the Worthy Assembly would be cavorting. She found her father leaning into Sirs Blake and Rogir by the East Tower's stairs, cursing his gout and imparting sage advice to his knights.

". . . and it's why I never should've bedded that Common wench in the bathhouses," she overheard him grumbling. "Let that be a lesson to you lads."

"But is it a lesson about the Common wench, or filthy water?" she said from a high step.

The knights shifted uncomfortably, glancing away. Caught off guard, Hexar seemed to fight over whether to play angry or embarrassed. He settled on the headshake of a parent trying to set a better example. "Come, daughter, I want to eat and drink, and not think too long on serious matters."

Taking him by his arm, Lorana helped the gouty old king down the stairs. Hexar listed heavily on his griffon's-talon cane.

"Your brother is not coming?" he asked under his breath.

"I'm not sure, my king."

"You blame me for what happened in the throne room?"

"I'm not sure the blame matters," she replied. "Only who shows tonight, and who doesn't."

The pair descended in silence. The night air was cool and fragrant with the smell of incense. Silverstone aura bathed the Walls in light that rippled, water-like, across scenes of battle and intrigue engraved into the mysterious stone.

Looking up, she saw the Lame King aglitter in the night sky. If you believed the ancients, a Huntsman would one day appear by Eduard, yank on an arrow made of stars, and heal his ankle. The Huntsman would herald the rise of Anjan's last heir, who would fly astride Furos, the First King's resurrected battle griffon, and rally the world against the Nagarthessi and their fire-breathing dragonmen.

The dragon will lay down with the lamb, where Elvarenists and Free Believers will already be abed, she mused.

Had she ever believed in religious prophecy, or any of it? Not truly, not if she listened to her heart. She'd never paid any mind to religion, save for the endless amount of destruction it heaped on the world. Lorana Eddenhold believed in only what she understood. And that was—you could always rely on a man to heed his belly, purse, and sex over just about anything else, including kings, priests, and his own reason.

"If I need you, will you address them yourself tonight?" Hexar asked as the pair descended haltingly. "Can you?"

"You may not think it, Father, but I was king when you were gone," she replied. "I'm more comfortable holding court than I am stitching headdresses."

"That's not what I meant." He stopped to hold her in his tired eyes. "I'm talking about the princes. I don't wish to cause you any more grief than you already feel."

She smiled sadly. *Oh, Father, I only ever cared about one of my brothers,* she entertained replying. *You burned him as only you could.* "I will do as you have bidden me," she said.

Turning a corner on the stairs, they found hundreds of Worthy Assemblymen strutting about like peacocks. Multiple conversations carried on at a low pitch. *At last, our Unworthy Assembly, come to smile through their teeth and suckle us like ticks.* She scanned the crowded courtyard for familiar faces.

The most prominent was Gram Sothos, the pink-handed Lord of Saxhold, almost a foot taller than most other noblemen, resplendent in his crimson doublet and gray cape. Around the lion gathered his pride: Petor Ellsby, of Swanshire; the slinker Jon Redoak, of Fordham; and Lord Gut himself. Light-haired and lanky, Sam Gramlore, Lord of Eddenwood, loitered nearby. The High Bishop Peshar Grathos was never far from Sothos. A layer of vassals and zealots cushioned the space between this ring of powerful men and other Assemblymen: lesser lords, bishops, and the like, all seeking favors from Sothos or Grathos, or both.

On the outermost edges gathered the Free Believers, their rivals, a gray sea in their robes. Power here emanated from the dashing Tomas Fawkes, Lord of Westerliche, and Jacob Sulley, a striking contrast to Peshar Grathos in his humble gray robes. About Westerliche milled his vassals, Orrenn Silverspear of Copper Grove, Venn Lamporean of Ethelwood, and Shannen Fowl of Wesswood, all dressed extravagantly.

Only the lord who'd brokered peace between Hexar and his Worthy Assembly could travel freely between these worlds without arousing suspicion. Fittingly, Greg Thorngale chose no side, and sat hunched over a trestle table with his three sons. Like-minded men found refuge with the Thorngales.

Lorana turned her attention to the men furthest from the intrigue. Evan Sinclair gathered close with his companions like a trio of crows. Jason's maternal uncle dressed for the occasion of his pardon in padded doublet and leggings. His ward Rathos lifted his head from his cup, catching her eyes.

Well done, thought the princess. The three men's seating off to the side precluded any guesses about who present sat in both the Worthy Assembly and Evan Sinclair's Loyal Company, a question to which lords and spymasters all wanted answers. She let her gaze wander across the courtyard. *Who else here is loyal to Sinclair?* Only Lady Sarah's brother knew the truth.

Hexar searched the crowd with her. He deflated with a sigh. "Trevor didn't come," he murmured.

Did you expect anything else, Father? The noble lord other men knew as the Bull hadn't been seen at the Walls or in the Worthy Assembly for years. His younger brother, Sir Hanorr, had worked with Shaddon to arrange a moonlight kidnapping of her only trueborn brother, Erick. Hexar had chopped off the knight's head for it.

A formidable warrior, Wexley had backed her father in his Kingstrials and fought for their house during the rebellion, but after that, his affections changed. Wexley hadn't believed a word of his younger brother's confession. He accused Charles Burke of securing a false confession and famously challenged Hexar himself to a trial by sword in his throne room. When her father refused out of love for his friend, the Bull swore never to set foot again in Loran proper. Not until Charles Burke hanged from a gibbet.

The king lost more than a friend the day he took Hanorr's head. The saying went that a Cloudlander's word was stronger than sword-wood. Trevor Wexley gave proof when he forbade his sworn nobles from even *convening* with Loran's other lords in the Worthy Assembly. Hexar had neither the heart nor the coffers to force the issue and spent the next decade pretending as if the schism didn't exist. The Cloudlands became a kingdom within a kingdom in all but name, and their tribute trickled to nothing.

Cloudlanders had a name for their strained relationship with the rest of Loran: the Silent Friendship. Assemblymen like Gram Sothos preferred to call it Hexar's Folly.

Yet no one had the love of so many nobles like the Bull. And her father missed no one as greatly: not his own brother, not his dead wives, and maybe not even the sons who drew breath still.

She comforted her father with a light touch. Too late, she saw the herald off to their side, sucking in air for his trumpet. The ringing continued in her ears minutes after he finished braying the King's Grace.

"All hail King Hexar the First, Lord of Loran, and his eldest daughter, Princess Lorana, by Lady Alyse," he cried.

Her father didn't seem to pay the loud applause any heed, merely waving as he hobbled along on his gout cane, free of her arm.

Just when she thought the herald was done, he sounded the instrument again, shouting an introduction for Heather and her escort. Flying merrily down the stairs came her half-sister, a flurry of pink velvet, white tippets, and gold hair. The Tessian clumsily tried to keep up behind her.

A tide of Assemblymen rushed up to meet the king and his daughters. Peshar Grathos got to Hexar first.

In his cream-colored cassock and flowing indigo cape, the priest-king's emissary looked like a gaudily dressed crone. A fleshy wattle danced about his neck, and his rheumy eyes had an eagerness that made her stomach spin.

The High Bishop bowed solemnly before Hexar. "Your Majesty," he said in that soft, oily voice. "Such a pleasure to see you, *ahem*, unharmed from the campaigns in Uzland. Every day you were gone I, um, *ahem*, prayed Amath would protect you, Justar smite your enemies, and Helsar guide you safely home. As did His Holiness."

And prepared a feast in thanks to Felos in case none of those prayers worked, she thought. Watching her father receive the bishop, it seemed clearer than ever that the bitter rivalry between the Silver Walls and White Citadel had never abated. No amount of Remembrance Days could paper over the king's history with the priestking.

Especially not tonight. For it was Parlisis who had offered the olive branch to Hexar so he would join his Holy Wars and release Edenia. The branch had thorns in hindsight: one prince had died, and the other went mad and vanished.

The king tightened his lips. For a moment, she thought he would bludgeon the old man with his cane and make another Willard Potter on the night they were supposed to honor the Long Summer Rebellion's dead.

"I want wine," the king declared abruptly. He found a lord he liked and headed for a long table lined with wooden caskets.

Everyone felt the slight. Trying to recover, the bishop turned his attention to the princesses. "Princess Heather, my, how you've grown! You look *just* like Lady Romara, *ahem*, the best parts of her, I mean."

He bent low to kiss her hand. Heather shied away, toward her older sibling. "I've heard Father say her best parts were her tits, and I don't have those."

Lorana didn't know whether to laugh or cry. A few lords nearby covered their grins.

The bishop smiled awkwardly. "And Princess Lorana, you are, uh, *ahem*, ravishing. A vision from Venas for noble young men to chase."

As surely as you chase them, *Peshar*. It was no secret that the High Bishop preyed on boys, or that the Assembly allowed it. She'd first encountered this side of the High Bishop at eleven, on the night of another Remembrance Day, when she, Jason, and Edenia went searching for cake in the kitchens and found Grathos alone with a peasant child. She'd told Hexar about the incident, but the king had only shaken his head. "It's true that I have Parlisis's daughter, but he has my son—your brother," the Lord of Loran had replied. "That pederast can touch a thousand peasant boys, as long as we get Erick back."

Lorana curtsied. "You do me honor, Your Grace."

"As you honor Lady Alyse." She suppressed a shudder as he leaned in, brushing her wrist with his papery skin. "And yet," he said, "I do worry about you, Your Highness. Matters of court and coin are, *ahem*, unworthy of your precious self. By our First Testament, the elves told man that silence is a virtue Divna expects in women."

Erick is dead, and Edenia is gone, Lorana reminded herself. She looked at Grathos. "You're right, of course, Your Grace. We should *all* follow the exact letter of the Twelve Testaments—temples especially, no? Does the Eighth Testament not recount how Sacreis told Anjan in a vision that the priests must give up their gold for his ships in times of war? Perhaps I'll instruct my justices to follow the holy text and go to temple. Or maybe I'll follow the Third and hang the men who lie with boys."

Flush with triumph, she took her little sister's hand and left the bishop stuttering his response. *Fuck Parlisis and his pederast priests.* Her sister wriggled like an eel in her grasp, demanding to know when she could eat cake. Spotting Lorna by her father and several noblemen, she padded through the grass in their direction.

Lorana almost didn't recognize Zur until she was upon the group. The boy she considered another brother looked positively regal in a fern-green doublet and silky leggings.

She embraced Zur warmly. "Well, don't you look the lord tonight. Has Yasha seen you like this?" she teased.

Zur seemed to will away his embarrassed smile. "Lord Drexan allowed me to borrow from his wardrobe," he said.

She shook her head with mock dissatisfaction. "Dressing in a chancellor's wares. I suppose you couldn't have dressed in mine! Shall we give you the South Tower as well? What do you think, Drexan?"

That drew chuckles from around the circle. Beside Zur, the King's Crow grinned. "I'm coming to think it's his anyway, Your Highness, given how often he stays each day to watch the knights cross swords beneath my window."

Which was his true birthday gift, Lorana thought, satisfied.

"He can't be a lord, he's one of Elzura's Children," Heather blurted. She pinched her nose. "He smells of onion, anyway."

Well, that's enough of that. Lorana touched Lorna on her shoulder and asked her to help Heather find a slice of cake. The promise of sweets inspired obedience in the younger princess, and she left hand-in-hand with the lady-in-waiting.

Drexan's circle had no shortage of powerful lords. Alan Durros and Uthron Morley presided over villages so close to Southpoint that her father wisely granted them special titles and privileges, not unlike the ones he gave David Renworth. Eric the Tall, of House Sundry, held Giant's Pass, an old trade route that had served as a staging point for invasions of the Free Kingdoms. She wondered if Zur knew the caliber of his lord's company.

Lorana half-expected the men to pile on queries about her

womanhood, suitors, and the like. She was positively delighted when they commended her for naming justices of the peace.

"Willard Rittman has long been my sheriff and will make a fine justice," Morley said. "Hopefully my peasants will respect their king enough to give him what is his."

"Aye, but they grow restless," Durros put in, pulling at his fiery-red beard. "I had to give the king's peace to two men for beating and tarring their own justice. They'd accused the man of defiling one of their wives in her dwelling. Nonsense and beside the point! The husband had been hiding their three children in the other's hovel when the justice came round, to keep from paying what he owed on their heads. Now the mother must remarry or lose the children."

Eric the Tall harrumphed. "That's not even the worst of it. Lord Uthron, didn't you say you lost a band of your men to the Commons on an errand out west? Graywood, wasn't it?"

"Aye, I lost them on Half Day to Summer Solstice."

Durros shuddered. "An ill omen. That forest is cursed."

A strong wind blew through the courtyard. She clutched at her arms, wishing she had brought a wool cloak. Alan Durros offered Lorana his cloak; she declined graciously.

"Why would it be cursed?" Zur broke in. He promptly added, "I—if I may, m-my lords."

The men exchanged glances. "It depends on whom you ask," Drexan answered. "Sylvanians believe a metal elk god died in Graywood, turning the forest lifeless. The Elvarenists hold that it's the very place Anjan slew the last Nagarthessi."

Elk gods. Their superstition annoyed her. "Lord Uthron, was it the Commons who took your men?" Lorana inquired.

Morley had a dull look. "I've only my suspicions, Your Highness. They never returned. One was a beloved knight."

The conversation turned back to Common unrest. She stiffened when she saw one of her suitors materialize on the edge of the circle. Justen Sothos was everything in a suitor that Lorna, Heather, or any other maiden could desire. He was tall, handsome, and, as the son of Gram Sothos, heir to outlandish wealth that neither he nor any future progeny could hope to spend in a single lifetime.

Justen bent low and kissed her hand. "Your Highness, a pleasure to look upon you once more," he said. "May I guide you to the dais? I understand the king wishes you to speak."

When he spoke, he watched her as if he had another pair of eyes behind his pretty blue ones. And those eyes, his actual ones, had irises of silverstone.

She accepted the escort begrudgingly, only because she didn't want gossip to spread about how she'd rejected a suitor on Remembrance Day. Eyes followed her as he looped his arm around hers.

"How long has it been since we walked here? Half a year?"

Not long enough, she thought as they walked. The last time he was here, he'd proposed marriage by Sarah's Fountain.

"Uh, yes, I think so," Lorana said distractedly.

"And have you rethought my proposal?"

She feigned a smile. "My lord, I think you deserve better than me. Venas overlooked me when I was made. I am homely and unattractive, where you are so dashing."

"Any other woman would say yes," Justen insisted. "Other kings have approached me with their daughters' hands—"

"And any of them would be fortunate to have you as her husband."

"Even the *priestking* wrote my father with the idea of marrying his daughter."

No surprise there. Lorana paced through the grass slowly, careful not to betray her feelings. "The prieslenne would make you a worthy wife."

He latched onto her wrist, forcing a stop. "I don't want the prieslenne. I want *you,* Lorana."

She tried to pry herself free of his grip. "Show care, my lord," she said through clenched teeth. "You aren't mishandling some waif you can fuck and send home with a bastard. I don't fear your father, and I don't need my father or half-brothers here to show you your error. Unhand me, or I'll take the hand."

Justen tightened his hold, a wintry smile tugging at his lips. "Then you're a fool." He was so close she could smell the wine on his breath. "*Everyone* fears my father."

"I'd do as she asks," came a voice, short and stern. Evan Sinclair stepped near, garbed in a green doublet embroidered with his eight-pointed star in thread of gold.

Justen scowled. "This has nothing to do with you, *traitor*. Fuck off before my father—"

"My father, my father, my father." Their circle widened as Sinclair's cunning-eyed ward appeared by the nobleman's side. "Only cowards and men with the name Sothos use their fathers as shields."

Justen smirked. "Ah, is this your ward, Evan? The famous Sir Matthus's son. And where's your father?" He had a mocking pout. "Oh. He's a pile of ash blown to the wind."

"I'd release the steward," Sinclair said with a step forward. "Take it from someone who's seen the Dread Chamber. Or don't."

The men sized each other up like circling lions. Lorana resented them all equally. She'd run this kingdom like a king for years, and to them she was nothing more than her honor. She jerked her hand free and popped Justen in his cheek with her fist, drawing sharp looks across the bailey.

Justen rubbed his jaw, grinning. "You're as stupid as you are hideous. You'll regret this, ugly cunt." He pointed a finger in Sinclair's face. "Watch yourself, traitor. House Sinclair is not what it was, not without blackpowder, and *neither are you*." He stormed off, bumping into Robswell as he shouldered past.

Robswell dusted off his shoulder. "A true nobleman."

Sinclair went to examine her arm, a look of concern on his face. "May I—?" he began.

She recoiled from him. "Do not think you can touch me so," the stone maiden growled. "Perhaps you and your men would like to lose your hands instead?"

Unlike Robswell, Sinclair didn't frown or react with anger or displeasure. He inclined his chin regretfully. "Your Highness, forgive me, our other companion saw what was happening. We thought to lend our assistance."

By then Connor was there, the king's peace manifested in his silvery armor. "Is Sinclair troubling you, Your Highness?" he asked with a flinty look at the man everyone, including Lorana, viewed as culpable as Parlisis for the Long Summer Rebellion.

The traitor and his ward both straightened. *I'm the most powerful woman in this kingdom,* Lorana thought grimly, *but I'm still only as worthy as the man beside me.*

"Evan Sinclair lent assistance I did not solicit, but I must forgive him." She turned with an icy air of contempt befitting a slighted royal. "He saved my brother's life, after all. Besides, it's Remembrance Day."

Catching her father's glance, she dispatched Connor and crossed the bailey to reach the dais. Oblivious to everything, the king inhaled what looked like a third cup of dark red wine. Strands of his gray hair clung to his sweat-laced cheeks; wine stains speckled his lips and beard.

"What was that about with Sinclair?" he asked with an arched eyebrow.

"Just a misunderstanding, Father."

He stifled a belch that looked uncomfortable. "Had better be. He's lucky I'm after legacy."

No truer words spoken. "Would you speak, Father, or would you rather me?"

"You tell them." He gazed down into his wine cup. "I'm in my cups . . . and I hate Remembrance Days." He caught a young servant by his sleeve and waved his chalice in his face. "What are you here for, anyway? Bring wine!"

She sighed. *As always, Father, I will do what must be done.*

At a signal, the heralds aired their trumpets. The roar of conversation dwindled to a few murmurs and plates a-clatter. Commoners and Casaanites hastened to set the tables.

With the kingdom's ruling caste watching her, she felt small, uncharacteristically small, perhaps because they'd all seen her refuse and then strike the son of the priestking's man in Loran.

Anyasha emerged from the stairs, aflicker with a proud smile. Feeling tall, Lorana prepared to tell the kingdom's rulers the king had no heir but the Warchild.

CHAPTER 13

Remembrance Day

ssemblymen inclined toward each other, echoing the princess in murmurs. Seated beside Rathos and Karl, Evan processed the news raptly. *The one thing that could inflict war on us again,* he pondered. *A succession crisis.*

"Both princes gone, only the bastard left, and the king like he is," said one affected nobleman. "Maetha have mercy."

"Makes no sense," said another. "Prince Garrett, gone to sail around Casaan?"

"He won't find loot, only krakens and skineaters."

"Where is the bastard?" someone asked.

Where indeed? Evan searched the bailey for his nephew. Hexar slouched over his chalice, too drunk to care about his Assembly's reactions.

Evan had to give Lorana credit. The fiction about Garrett sailing around Casaan didn't seem out of character for Hexar's firstborn. Said to be as brave as he was cruel, the crown prince had the king's penchant for running heedless into danger. He watched Alyse's daughter coolly, unoffended by her earlier chilliness. *But where is the crown prince, truly?*

Karl set down his cup, wiping his lips with a forearm. "Maybe the skineaters will find Garrett first," he muttered.

Rathos glared at Karl. "I'll be sure to share that little comment with our friends when we see them again."

"Good, do so," the Reubenite said derisively. "I imagine *they'll* want to hear about the Fourth Wing, too."

Evan shot him a cross look. Drexan had made pawns of them

for a game only he seemed to see clearly, and in that stroke all but delivered their Loyal Company into the hands of his rival Rezlan Ambrose and the radical Reubenites. *What is your scheme, King's Crow?* he thought as he regarded Drexan. He sat with his servant Zur at the far end of the king's table. *What did you gain by misleading His Majesty and me?*

Servants circled the tables with bowls and platters full of the evening's delights. It was excellent timing. Voices softened to mutters as Assemblymen handled the steamy trenchers and roasted pigs.

Peshar Grathos rose tremulously from his seat, so brittle one had to wonder whether a breeze would threaten his balance. "Your Majesty, ahem, if you think the moment is right, I would say a prayer for your sons."

Hexar wiped his mouth with the back of his hand. "So long as the Master Reader of the Free Beliefs also prays after you finish," he said thickly.

A drunkard, whoremonger, and warmonger you might be, Hexar, thought Evan, *but you're a wise man to safeguard your relationship with Jacob Sulley.* Free Believers in Loran lacked the patronage that gave Elvarenists wealth and power, but the masses rallied to the Master Reader and here, a king without a priestking's protection needed the masses.

Especially when that king also refuses to seat the masses in their Assembly, he thought.

With an unsubtle stab of a look at Sulley, the High Bishop led the king and Worthy Assembly in prayer. Grathos asked the sea god Athos to protect Prince Garrett as he sailed around the southern tips of unexplored Casaan. He asked Helsar to guide Prince Erick's soul on its journey to the Evergreen Isles.

Evan glanced at his ward during their prayers, unfailingly picturing the elder Robswell. *Black all over like overdone pork,* Sothos had taunted him. The Lord of Saxhold's balding dome poked out from a table that also seated Jon Redoak, Dumas Sunox, and Tom Gelder, among dozens of other men loyal to Priestking Parlisis. They gathered around

Sothos like beasts at a waterhole, lapping nervously at the source of their power.

As soon as Grathos seated himself, Jacob Sulley stood. He was starting to pray on behalf of all Free Believers when Gram Sothos rose with an air of entitlement. The tall lord lifted a cup in Greg Thorngale's direction.

Hexar had a dark look as the Master Reader trailed off. "Lord Sothos," the king said in gruff warning.

The only man in Loran who could ignore his king did just that, lips curling faintly. "Let us toast the man who made Remembrance Day possible," Sothos said, undeterred. "Where would our king be without Lord Greg? Lord Stoddard's Army of the Gods had the advantage, a catapult for every silverstone in these Silver Walls. With Lady Alyse dead, we all wanted our vengeance. It was the Old Oak of Thessela whose honor saved us, who stepped between king and Assembly, who helped us all to remember that this castle belonged to Anjan Half-Elf first."

Dumas Sunox listed ponderously on his table, spilling wine from his cup. "To Lord Greg!" he cried.

Half the bailey applauded. The Old Oak accepted the praise with a halfhearted rise from his chair. Rolling his eyes, the king beckoned for Sulley to continue. The Master Reader proceeded solemnly, his dignity fortified by faith. He asked his god of twelve aspects to protect Prince Garrett, guide Erick to the afterlife, and slake the Midlands' thirst with rain.

The Master Reader looked directly at Evan. "And we ask the One True God to grant this Worthy Assembly wisdom," he said, "so they and our king may rule the voiceless with mercy and justice."

Sothos sipped his wine. "Justice will do," he intoned. His lords sniggered like naughty schoolchildren.

Someone had to respond. Evan readied a verbal riposte. "Justice *will* do, Lord Gram," Lorana Eddenhold chimed in from the king's table. "Our justices of the peace will see to that, won't they?" *When the money we pay your sheriffs pressures them into not enforcing your child theft laws,* it went unsaid.

Saying nothing, Sothos drank his wine. Evan smiled.

Except for the sounds of eating, the feast went on largely in peace. A fool mimed the barbarian highlord Kar Kravack by the dais, easing tension with laughter. Hexar nearly choked on boar when the fool abruptly dropped his pantaloons, revealing the dangle of a tiny sausage sewn to his undergarments. He pranced about like a savage, unclothed barbarian, mimicking Uzland's unpleasant-sounding language.

After dismissing him, Hexar quaked to his feet. The king extended an arm toward Evan.

"We hold these Remembrance Days to honor the dead, or so we say," the king said. "More like so we'll remember why we need each other, and so I can remember why I should've killed you sons of whores who backed Stoddard and killed my wife." The bailey fell completely silent. "Anyway," he added, "I never do this, but I've lost a son, Alyse's son, and the other one—he's sailing, yes."

And Jason? Evan pondered.

"I, um . . . I'm not good at this," Hexar said. "I was wrong, Evan." Heads turned to Evan. "Wrong to accuse you in Sarah's death. Lorrain had the right of it when he stopped my quill." He cleared his throat. "I'm pardoning Evan Sinclair. He saved my son Jason's life days ago, but more so, he is a loyal subject, and worthy of the Worthy Assembly. You will seat him in the Wing of Lords, where he belongs. I name him Lord of Caerdon once more."

Gradually, some got to their feet, clapping. Rathos and even Karl rapped their knuckles. Sothos drained his cup; he remained seated. So did many men at many other tables.

Evan strode to the front of the dais. Kneeling, he kissed Hexar's ring, which his sister had given the king in marriage. "You do me honor, Your Majesty," he said. "Thank you."

Hexar snatched a second cup of wine from a passing peasant's platter. "Let us share a cup. In Sarah's memory."

Evan smiled with tears in his eyes. "I feel I've spent enough years grieving for her in my cups," he said. "If you drink, my king, I'd have you drink to a just, happy realm."

The king watched Sothos. "Fuck the realm. This is for your sister." He leaned back, emptying his cup into his throat.

The Lord of Caerdon smiled gratefully as tears broke free, sliding down his cheek. His smile ebbed when he heard her, the sister from his nightmares, white-eyed and screaming . . .

The scattered applause sounded surreal as he seated himself. Rathos reached across the table for his hand. "Mina will be most proud when she hears the news," he told him.

As she'll be proud of you. His son-by-law was the nearest thing he had to an heir. If Jason didn't press his rights, Rathos or a son by Mina would inherit his estates, along with a seat in the Wing of Lords. *May this be some consolation to you, Matthus,* he thought. *You were my knight, and a child of yours will inherit the castle you served to the end.*

"My king, if I may."

Justen Sothos approached the dais. Lorana crossed her arms with disapproval, drawing looks.

"What, another petition?" Hexar asked as he finished chewing his meat.

"Only for your eldest daughter's hand, Your Majesty."

If Gram Sothos wanted his son to enter the Silver Walls, Lorana's womb was the gatehouse. Evan pitied her. Still in her early twenties, she had many lordly suitors pursuing her, not for love.

"A thing you'll have to ask her." The king emptied his cup, gestured for more.

"Might I implore *you*, Your Majesty?" Justen ventured. "As we know from the First Testament, women are but children in matters of state, and—"

"So she refused you," Hexar said, to laughter, Lorana's loudest of all. He flashed Justen's father a wine-stained grin.

Glancing at his father, Justen continued, "Of little importance, it seems to me, Your Majesty, especially with the only legitimate princes gone. I would wed your daughter and give you and this kingdom an heir."

His bluntness was poor form. The ambitious lord was sorely out of place, especially with Prince Erick dead, especially on Remembrance Day. Evan wondered if Gram had coached his son, or if Justen's confidence in his own impunity had sufficed to send him on this errand.

"A bold proposal," said the king, swishing the wine in his cup. "I'm not sure my—my daughter would agree. How would you take an unwilling wife?"

"As the gods bade us in the Second Testament, through a test of skill, not unlike how you crowned the Lady Harriet with laurels in the First Trial of your Kingstrials."

That brought Hexar out of his wine cup. Evan judged it a shrewd move. The king was a god of thunder and lightning, but one could clear the skies by kneeling at the altar of his pride.

"You know your history," Hexar said.

"I know Your Majesty."

The king stole a look at his daughter. After a moment, he banged his cup down on the table. "Done!" he shouted. "I like a man unafraid to prove his skill. We'll have a game here, *right here, yes!* What will it be—wrestling? A melee?"

"Archery."

Evan stood as his nephew swaggered in from the Great Hall, seemingly indifferent to the poisonous stares of the men who'd denied him a place in the succession at birth. Jason had replaced his foreign orange silks with a handsome checkered doublet and regal green cape. He cut a straight line through the tables and chairs, to Justen Sothos.

Lorana clapped excitedly, laughing. Hexar grinned. *How strange to have them both here, within feet of each other,* Evan thought, lingering on his nephew. It'd been surreal to see the siblings together in the lower bailey. *What you be proud, my sister . . . or wroth?*

"You would vie with me for your sister's hand?" Justen balked, grinning as he fished for agreement from the bailey. "Are you a Barefoot Knight, my lord, trying to wed your own sister?"

The Solemn Order didn't arrange incestuous unions between its own members, you dolt, Evan thought, but Justen received a scatter of laughter, anyway.

Jason shed his cape at the dais. "I'm no mystic, and no, my sister needs an equal, not her bastard brother. But I'll play if it means humbling *you,* Justen."

Everyone looked to the king for his blessing. He gave it by pumping the air with a fist. "Yes, yes, *yes!*" Hexar gulped down wine in good spirits. "Humble the Assembly as well, my son!"

"Pardon me, my lords"—and everyone twisted to catch Tomas Fawkes, standing as he planted gambling money on the table—"but I wager the Lord of Westerliche could best *both* of you."

Evan couldn't remember the last time he'd seen Hexar so jovial. He challenged Sunox to match his son with the bow; the fat lord drew sniggers when he complained of injured wrists. Thorngale could be heard urging on his unwed sons, but there was strength in numbers, and Gavin, Darren, and Luc resisted.

"It's good fortune for Lord Jason that Darren Thorngale sits this out," Karl intoned. "Have you heard what the Worthy are calling him?"

"I know what they call you," Rathos said, annoyed.

"And I, *you.* They're calling him Darren Stormsword. Thirty-nine Uzmen cut off Darren and his knights from the king's host. Cornered them. They killed his men, thought to torture the lordling nice and slow. A grievous error. Blake Oxley found Darren engaging the last nine on the piled dead. Said it was like watching a bored cat play with his dinner."

"Blake Oxley is hardly a judge of swordplay," Evan said.

But Karl is right about Jason's good fortune. Seated at his father's table, Darren Stormsword had a leaner, more sinewy build than his brothers, a killer's steely reservedness. Evan didn't like the idea of a man like that handling bow and arrow around his nephew—especially when he'd just thwarted an attempt on Jason's life.

The master-of-arms, Connor Tomas, retrieved a colorful wicker target from the stables and planted it near the hedge maze. Commoners went about moving tables and chairs to make a makeshift lane. Assemblymen swarmed to the closest seats. Encouraged by Fawkes, many cast wagers, to Hexar's amusement. Knights went and came back with longbows and fletched arrows for the contestants.

This was no longer lighthearted revelry, or a contest to win Lorana's hand, Evan realized. Remembrance Day elevated the game to a verdict on the war, with the son of Sarah Sinclair playing for a symbolic victory or humiliation against the son of her likely murderer. This was the Long Summer Rebellion writ small. *How apropos for Remembrance Day,* Evan thought.

Fawkes and his nephew filed behind Justen. The king waved agitatedly for the contest to begin. Justen nocked his arrow, aimed, loosed. *Pfft.* His arrow twanged against a center blue ring. He tensed his bow, let fly the next. *Pfft, pfft,* one in the grass, another in the outermost yellow ring.

Justen left the lane irritably. Grumbling, men scoured their purses and handed off lorens. With easy movement, Jason scooped an arrow, notched his bow, and released with a *thwop,* impaling the yellow. Sothos's table sniggered. A second arrow plunged through the bright red center. Evan leapt up, cheering with the royal family. Coins traded hands.

No one paid Fawkes any mind until he splintered Jason's second arrow on his first try, fragments of wood flying. At once, readers and Fawkes vassals roared their approval. Westerliche tasted red again on his second try and blue on his third.

"It would appear I've won your sister's hand, Jason," Fawkes said airily, "but it's clear she favors you, so—" He dipped with a flourish of his hand, bowing out of contention.

Evan chuckled. Fawkes had handled that well, dissolving any stake in an unattractive woman with a play on Justen's well-received joke. Evan saw why the Free Believers loved the lord so. The Lord of Westerliche was notorious for gambling and whoring, all sins in the Free Beliefs, but he had youth, good looks, and charm—and wealth that gave him latitude to thumb his nose at Sothos and the Elvarenist establishment.

The bailey hushed as Justen headed single-mindedly to the royal table. "Another contest, Your Majesty," he cried out.

"You, you lost," Hexar stammered out. He pushed Drexan away.

"Just went down the wrong throat . . . What now, Justen? Swordplay? Or stitching?"

"Lily's Apple," the nobleman replied coolly.

"A daring game." Hexar stroked his beard. "Who would volunteer? Maybe your father can wear the apple?"

Everyone who wasn't an Elvarenist chuckled. *If only,* Evan mused.

"A Commoner." Gold winked in his hand. "For five lorens." Sothos's son gazed at each of the Commoners with torches and pointed like a god in judgment. "*Her.*"

The girl who stepped forward could've very well been one of Evan's daughters. Hair as violet as the flower hung in ringlets about her pale, soot-stained face. She was young.

Evan and his son-by-law shared the same horror. "She has her *hair*," Rathos whispered, angrily. He clutched Evan's sleeve. "They couldn't . . ."

Evan felt his chest cave in when the king nodded. The master-of-arms seized the girl by her arm and hauled her off to the target as if she were property, like a chair. Someone chucked Connor an apple; he balanced it on the girl's head as she wept quietly. She knew what this game was. What it meant. If a lord shot her with an arrow, mistakenly or intentionally, he'd suffer no consequence. She could die, and no one would be held accountable.

One of the torchbearers, an older man who must've been her father, fought briefly to regain her. Commoners looked on.

"They'll murder her," Rathos said gravely.

"This is Loran," Evan said. Karl downed his wine.

Justen jerked an arrow free of the target, stalked back to position. While he was stringing his bow, Jason was protesting, calling for his father's attention. The king had left to fetch more wine.

Jason was still halfway in the lane when an arrow hissed past his face. The girl shrieked. She clutched the place on her arm the arrow had sliced.

"Move, Lord Jason," Justen said crisply as he notched his bow, "or I'll play Lily's Apple with *you.*"

Wordlessly, the bastard prince stepped between Justen and the violet-haired girl. His mother's blue eyes did not blink.

Justen tensed his bow. "Have it your way."

Evan was off his bench, grasping for something, anything, he could hurl like before in Southpoint. "*Jason, no!*" he cried.

His cry was lost in a sudden rush of feet to the dais. A woman's scream rang through the upper bailey, followed by loudening shouts. "*The king!*" a man yelled. "*King Hexar!*"

As men flocked the dais, Evan dashed in the opposite direction. By the time he was there, between his sister's son and the son of the man who'd murdered that sister, a crowd surrounded the king's table.

Evan stopped Jason in his flight to the king. "*They'll kill you, they'll do it in the confusion,*" he said in his nephew's ear.

Jason stared at his uncle, wide-eyed and panting.

Moments later, the king's apothecary, Jon Applewood, was half-running, half-tripping down the Great Hall's steps. Drexan shouted for everyone to make way; the crowd opened and swallowed Applewood.

Jason shoved Evan off him and flew to the dais. Evan sprinted after him, slowing his speed to navigate through the crowd.

No one breathed inside the inmost circle. The king lay splayed across the grass, one arm over is chest. His eyes had paled. Veins as blue as the sunlit sea streaked up his neck and arms.

Rising shakily, the blind apothecary gazed ahead at nothing and no one. Tears wetted his cheeks, aglimmer in silverstone light. "Mourn, for our king is dead," Applewood said.

The courtyard descended into bedlam. Peshar Grathos began speaking in the First Tongue and signing the diamond. Jacob Sulley and his bowl-haired acolytes knelt in a gray line, praying in vulnerable voices.

Not far, Lorana lay sprawled in the grass, retching, her Casaanite servant by her side. Heather curled up beside her father, screaming. Jason furiously checked the king's vitals, as if to prove Jon wrong.

Men raced to control the situation. Sunox forbade anyone from leaving, lords, clergy, peasants, hostages, anyone. Eric the Tall rounded up the Commons, handing off their torches.

Gram Sothos pointed at Evan. "Gaol him *immediately*," he demanded. "Evan Sinclair slew the king. As he slew his sister. *The traitor refused to take wine with him—we all saw it.*"

"Evan the fucking traitor," Sam Gramlore snarled behind him. He shoved him hard. "I saw him flee. Toward Lord Jason. He *wanted* to escape."

"Take the traitor to Traitor's Pit!" Jon Redoak shouted.

"Gaol him in the Red Tower," Sunox said. "I trust Lord Charles to get the truth from him."

Evan looked to his nephew. The prince listed on the table, shorn of breath. He gazed long at his father's body, unspeaking.

"It gives me no pleasure, uncle," Jason finally said. "Seize Lord Evan and his companions. Do not harm them. They are to be given over to the Grand Inquisitor. They're under suspicion of murdering the king."

CHAPTER 14

The Curse

nights in polished armor and silver cloaks stormed the kitchens. They chased the Commoners to the chamber's center, surrounding them on all sides so that no one could leave. One man read from a list of names that included hers, Caleb's, and her mother's.

First went her mother, weeping and pleading they not separate her from her girl. Shoulders heaving, Sara sniveled and wept uncontrollably like the other wet-voiced children. Caleb hovered by her side, stammering out questions politely but earnestly. She'd never seen such bravery.

"No questions," one enormous knight growled beneath his helm. He grabbed Caleb by his arm and began hauling him away.

"Don't be afraid, princess, don't be afraid," she heard the farmer say. That only made her more afraid.

When her turn came, she flat refused. A knight pinned her between his hard armored arms and breastplate and staggered off with her. She screamed and kicked and flung her arms like a wild thing. Down a stairway, her heel jammed in his crotch. Her captor's grip loosened.

"Little bitch," the man croaked.

They came to a cumbersome wooden door riven with cracks and studded with rusted iron spikes. The door shrieked open on its hinges, and in she was flung like a bag of onions, to the cold stone floor.

Her shame and anger and fear were so strong she didn't feel the blaze in her shins for a few good seconds. She burst into tears when she lifted her hem and discovered long pink gashes laced with blood drops.

But then Caleb put his arms around her, and her mother wet her cheeks with her kisses. She wilted in their embrace, trying to ignore the burn that only seemed to worsen.

"Oh, by Prospo, they hurt her, those fucking cowards," someone swore quietly.

Sara opened moist eyes. A ring of smudged faces hovered over her. She knew them from the kitchens. She counted the butcher and his two boys and apprentice, the baker and his wife and their girl, a saucier from South Farcombe, and many others, all Commoners come to the Walls to earn a loren.

"Here, I've garlic in me folds." A gaunt-cheeked elderly woman rustled through her gown and produced two cloves. Sara yelped from the pain as she began rubbing her shins with the greasy pieces, but the stinging faded little by little until it just felt sore. She handed her the cloves. "Keep doing that when it hurts, child."

Caleb and the butcher carried her to a straw patch in the corner. When she lay down with her mother by her, she saw how cramped the room was, how many their number. Some sat on their knees, others paced before the heavy door outlined with flickering torchlight. Their faces were long and troubled. Children like her buried their faces into their parents' smoke-stained wool.

Before long they overheard armor clinking in the hall outside. Shadows darkened the firelight around the door's edges. The door swung open. In came a withered old man, stumbling to the floor. The others welcomed him into their small, cramped hell. The process repeated itself like that for another two hours, with the door opening only for a new captive. If someone asked a question, the knight would tell them no questions or threaten to hurt them.

By the time it all stopped you could hardly move without brushing someone else. The air was thin and everyone took shallow breaths. The smell of sweat and kitchen grease was overpowering.

Some began to whisper. The hushed voices started in a corner and trickled through tight-knit bodies, murmuring softly like stream water. Sara listened as the Commoners shared where they'd been found, what they'd heard from others or seen themselves. They were mostly Southlanders by their accents.

"I heard a Commoner tried to kill the bastard prince," a man reported.

"Ain't the truth 't'all," a saucier whispered loudly. "Heard it was the Lord o' Saxhold who knifed Lord Jason. 'Cause he hated his mother Sarah so much."

"Then what they want with us?" a woman quivered.

"Makes no sense," said the butcher with the two lads. His apprentice agreed with him.

An older man near her shook like a brittle, windblown leaf. "I done nothin' wrong, I've a calfskin from Reader Fred Songsworth, of the Parish in the Light o' the Twelve, in South Farcombe, I've it right here with me," he kept mumbling, sounding as if he might cry. "Said I could bring my swine here for the feast. Said under no pain. Said I'd get five lorens."

"We all got some permit to come," Caleb told him.

"Shhh," someone said, and everyone began shushing everyone else. A lone voice broke through, sure and steady: "I know what happened. I was there. It's King Hexar. He's dead."

Everyone inhaled sharply. "No, it canna be true—"

"It is," the man repeated. "I sawr it with mine own eyes. My girl, Harriett, she's named after his first wife, Gram Sothos's son asked the king to play Lily's Apple, and he picked her. Lord Jason, he"—his voice trembled—"he got between Lord Justen an' Harriett an' wouldn't let him loose the arrow without hittin' him first."

"The king though," the butcher urged him on. "You said you saw the king—"

"I did, I did. Sawr it happen. All the lords, they went to the dais and Jon Applewood, he's the king's apothecary, he said we should mourn because our king was dead."

Peasants sucked in their breath as if they were coming up from the water for air, hands shaking visibly over their mouths. People began to pray for the king's health, pray that this wasn't so. Sara buried her face in her mother's bosom. She was surprised when she felt tears pelting her forehead. She rarely cried.

Sara peeled away, tangles of hair clinging to her mother's wool. "Mother," she said faintly. "I saw Father in the maze. He's okay. He led me to you."

Orange firelight flecked her mother's wet cheeks, turning the tears to crystal. "Wha . . . what?" Rose looked confused and worried and fearful, all at the same time.

"I tried telling you before," Sara began.

The door broke against the wall. Torchlight flooded the crowded chamber. Between spaces in the crowd she saw two knights take position. The man with the writ from Reader Fred Songsworth angled through to show the left-facing knight his calfskin, only to receive the man's backhand and fall limp into the arms of other peasants.

Footsteps clacked through the hall. Through the doorway slithered a robed man. She fought for space to see. Retreating, she breathed so fast she started feeling lightheaded.

"Lord Charles," someone whispered frightfully.

"The Grand Inquisitor."

For a long moment, no one said anything. She heard a soft, familiar voice. "You're here," he said, "because someone among you did treason tonight. Someone poisoned the king."

The chamber shrank, shaking and weeping bitterly with the truth finally confirmed. Someone cried for the One True God, another for the godface of Maetha.

"Do any among you know the Kingkiller's Curse?" the Grand Inquisitor said as the room wept or sniffled. "It's a curse from the High God himself."

Sara knew the Curse from the other children in Rosbury who risked scorn by acting out the Interregnum. She wouldn't dare answer him, though. She leaned into her mother as much as she could, burying her face in her itchy folds.

"Of course, you peasants are probably Free Believers. You believe that the High God *is* the One True God, the twelve gods merely his faces. Elvarenists think you're misled, of course. In their story, the High God created twelve gods, whom he gave free will over the world. To tell you the truth—and I trust you can keep a secret—I don't lose sleep over the difference. Both faiths hold that the High God intervenes directly in one matter and one matter only: a king's murder.

"No one," Burke added in a hard, rising voice, "not the kingkiller— not his family—not his smallest of friends—no one is safe. Death by plague, by sword, by torture: it matters not. When the Curse comes, it finds the kingkiller—and then anyone who gave him comfort in his flight. Anyone who hid him, fed him, clothed him. Anyone who lied on his behalf to keep him safe."

The torch crackled as Burke swept it through the air. "Tonight, *I* am the Kingkiller's Curse. King Hexar is dead by poison. I want the poisoner, and I'll promise the worse fate to any who mislead me."

Fred Songsworth's parishioner pushed aside peasants to reach the front of the room. "I—n-not me, sire, I mean, m'lord. I killed no king, donna know no kingkiller. Loyal, I'm loyal. I only brought swine."

The Grand Inquisitor shined his torch on the swineherd. "The king was seen eating boar. Question him first."

Knights grabbed the man and hauled him out, slamming the door behind them. His pleas echoed down the hall.

A Father's Love

ason had been to his father's bedchambers only twice in his life. It was considered unseemly even for sons to see where a king slept, for this was where His Majesty rested from labors of the crown, and Loran needed its lord whole.

That ruse worked well on boys fully enamored with their fathers. It lost its hold on Jason when he was young. Over time, in rumors and asides, he learned the truth about why the king preferred to keep family out of his bedchambers, and why the lords rarely ventured to the Walls with their ladies.

Garrett had goaded him into opening the doors. Jason was twelve then, smitten with the story of how King Hexar had wooed his mother, sneaking into Caerdon by moonlight to strum his silver harp beneath her window.

He never forgot what he saw. The king was naked as his birthday, wrapped in the legs of the Lady of Landry, a woman the gossips said shared Sarah's likeness, from her blue eyes to her raven-black hair. Unable to even enunciate his curses, the king tripped in his sheets, bolted up, and chased Jason from his chambers, still naked. The Lady of Landry fumbled for her stay, screaming hysterically. Garrett had fallen down, laughing.

Jason got his father's hand. Yet it was worth it. Prieslenne Edenia later told the boy she thought him atrociously mad . . . and rewarded his madness with his first kiss.

He struggled to connect his father the chubby adulterer to the swollen, vein-streaked corpse in the bedchambers now.

King Hexar the First, Lord of Loran, Master of the Walls, lay on an ice-soaked bier. His bearded face, touched by the lips of four wives and many nameless lovers, bulged with chin fat that made him look ridiculous. Jason had helped Jon Applewood fold the king's stiff fingers around the grip of a sword that His Majesty couldn't have possibly lifted in his last years.

Hexar's three remaining children occupied the room with his body, sleep-deprived and grieving. Pitchers clinked with ice melt. The castle's ever-present silverstone aura gleamed in the edges of window curtains, pulsing radiantly. It was as if heaven itself waited outside, beckoning the slain monarch.

Jason stood near his father's feet, still clothed in his cape, sword sheathed at his waist. Lorana and Heather sat together. The two sisters leaned into each other, eyes hollowed out from tears. The bedchambers were shut to all but trusted servants like Zuran and Anyasha. From time to time, they heard their trusted sentries Connor Tomas, Andrew Windkin, and Rogir Levan shifting in their armor in the hall outside.

Jason and Lorana had spent the early dark making sure no one fled the Walls. Hanor had dispatched Charles Burke to find the kingkiller. And here they were, silent before the dead king, the air pregnant with grief unspoken.

Incense burned everywhere, but wicks did nothing for the stench of Hexar's gout. His tourney infection was monstrous. Pink ulcers mottled his right leg like honeycomb, leaking pus that sheened the raw skin. Jason tugged on the cloth draping the king's body, covering it up.

"Father always said he'd die from the stench first," Lorana said, covering her nose. Jason let the smell clot in his nostrils.

When the moment felt right, Jason summoned Drexan Lorrain, Hanor Graxhold, and Jon Applewood. Lorana asked Anyasha to escort Heather back to her chambers, along with the stalwarts Connor Tomas and Rogir Levan, and stubbornly loyal knights like Erick Seam and Kyle Urron.

The Tessian warned against it. "Your Highness, if I may," Hanor implored, "your father is slain. A kingkiller is loose—"

"And none of us is safe," Lorana said. "Yet Connor and Rogir have been with our noble house since before Father's Kingstrials. Erick and Kyle protected Father in Uzland. Yasha I've known since she was a babe. And more importantly," she added, "I'd trust them all with my own life."

Heather sobbed up a storm, protesting, but the stone maiden had made her decision. The king's oldest children needed counsel from the king's advisors. Anyasha took Hexar's youngest by her hand and led her out.

Jason watched Lorana. She still wore her velvety banquet dress, stained with her dried vomit. Her bejeweled girdle hung from a bedpost.

The three advisors seemed as weary and aggrieved as the children. Grief bags hung below their eyes. Jon looked older, and Hanor, chubbier. Drexan listed heavily on his staff, as if he feared he might fall without it.

"Give me your reports," Lorana told the advisors.

Jason marveled at his half-sister. She was still steward, a queen in all but name. For the first time, he was glad the crown prince had left him at sea. Garrett was as hotheaded as Hexar, where Lorana always acted the stone maiden, cold, calculating. Right now, they needed cold and calculating.

One by one, the men brought them to speed. Hanor said the Assemblymen needed no coercion to stay but volunteered to remain in their chambers until the kingkiller was found. The stone maiden told the Tessian to keep an eye on their doors.

Drexan spoke next. David Renworth hadn't needed telling to shut the gates to Southpoint, he said.

Lorana allowed a bitter smile. "The Little King probably knew about Father's murder even before we sent word. He didn't close the gates earlier because he didn't want to seem suspect."

"Or the filthy peasant conspired with our enemies," Hanor suggested. "Charles should take him in for questioning."

The stone maiden shook her head wearily. "My father is dead, but we will act carefully," she said. "Commoners regard the mayor as their only voice. Seizing him could incite a revolt on our doorstep." She gazed at their father. "We'll question him once someone is in custody."

"Where is Charles, on that?" Jason asked. "Has he found a kingkiller?"

"Or *kingkillers,*" the advisor said thinly, fingering a divot in his staff. "Charles swept the Walls with our men. He rounded up the kitchen help and continues to make inquiries."

"Are they still here or in the Red Tower?" Lorana asked.

"Here, Your Highness."

"Have them taken to the Red Tower. I don't want the Assemblymen to hear his . . . questions."

Hear their screams, more like, Jason pondered bleakly.

"And Lord Evan and his companions?" Jason probed. He'd been eager to learn about his uncle's condition.

"They were gaoled in the Red Tower, on the steward's orders and yours," Drexan answered him.

"And Charles knows not to ask them questions?"

The King's Crow answered with a dutiful nod.

Good, he thought. *I mean to question you personally, uncle.*

Lorana turned to the man who'd declared the king dead. "Which leaves us with your report, Jon. What killed my father?"

Some men, like Hexar, shaped a room around their giant personalities. At the age of seventy-seven, those years were long past for Jon Applewood. Pale and shrunken, he seemed to fade inside the chamber. His apothecary's sash, a white felt cloth embroidered with the twelve sacred shapes of godfaces, seemed almost too much for his pitiful shoulders. Wispy white hair stuck to his head like patches of cotton.

"I believe I have, Your Highness," he said. "Your father's ice-blue veins"—he swept a tremulous hand over the king—"seem to point to the Sphinx's Kiss. It can be ingested by food or drink. It discolors and congeals the blood . . ." He glanced fleetingly at Lorana. "Until the heart beats no more."

Jason studied his father, feeling his father's anger test his composure. But who was he angry with? The king's veins ran like blue streams through his cheeks and beneath the fluff of his beard, down to his swollen hands and feet. *Is it you, Father?*

"How long does it take to kill the victim?" Lorana asked softly. *Did our father suffer?* Jason intuited.

"Minutes," Jon answered. "It's very efficient. Whoever did this did not want the king to suffer."

"How very decent of them," she said venomously. "I'll tell Charles's red hoods to take equal care in disemboweling them."

The apothecary tapped his fingertips together, a nervous tic. "There's something I find telling, Your Highness. As its name suggests, the Sphinx's Kiss is a foreign poison."

"It's a Nerimbaan poison," Jason interjected.

Lorana turned to look at him. Jon's pallid lips crept into his mouth. "Yes, lord. Did you come across it in your travels?"

"Not this poison, no. But the rulers of Nerimba name everything after sphinxes. And Nerimba is almost as well-known for its poison stores as Muhregeesia."

Lorana let her broken gaze fall on their father. "Erick died from poison in the Brace," she murmured.

Would that I could forget he had, Jason thought.

The apothecary folded his papery hands over themselves. He had a stern look. "Jason, did Erick die with blue veins?"

"No. As I've said, the skin grayed around the arrow's point of entry in his leg. Like ash."

Drexan flashed Jon a look. "I told you. It's Flesheater."

Hanor turned to the advisor. "What's Flesheater?"

"Jon and I know it from the Long Summer. Willard Potter liked to dip the spikes of his mace in Flesheater he got through Stod Trambar." Drexan let out something between a grunt and a derisive laugh. "The old bishop called his mace Pathazar, after the Nagarthessi whose fangs turned men into shadowkings."

Lorana readjusted one of her gown straps with an air of annoyance. His half-sister had no use for religion, less so with their father's corpse before them.

"Get to the point, my lords," Jason said before she had to.

"Flesheater comes from Nerimba as well," Jon responded. "I was hesitant to name it Flesheater . . . but the coincidence . . ."

Drexan grimaced. "Two poisons from the same kingdom."

Lorana rested her forehead in her hand, as if the burden of knowledge were as heavy as grief. "For the same family."

The room seemed oppressively dark suddenly. Jon, a Free Believer, whispered prayers to his god of twelve faces. Drexan leaned into his staff, eyes low and meditative on the fallen king.

"*A conspiracy,*" the Tessian muttered. He said something in the native tongue of Tesos that everyone grasped without needing it translated.

A conspiracy, Jason thought, the air knocked out of him. *A conspiracy against House Eddenhold. The house in control of the Silver Walls, castle of the First King and capital of the continent's most strategically valuable kingdom. God and gods . . .*

The king's bedroom was on edge as each advisor took it upon himself to identify the most obvious culprits, to jot out theories, to find out just how far this conspiracy went, quickly. Fear sharpened their tones like whetstones would swords.

"It was the priestking, of course," Drexan said. "He wants an Elvarenist Loran that lasts a thousand years." "If it's Parlisis, and he's attempted a coup de grace on House Eddenhold, then we know his designs," Jon added. "He'd kill every male member of this house except the one who bows before him." "Hexar's zealot brother," Hanor spat. "*Shaddon.*" The Tessian muttered his name like a curse. It hadn't been enough to steal the Prince Erick, his nephew, he said; the villain sought to finish the job.

"Garrett went mad," Jason broke through. Jon focused on the bastard prince. Did Garrett take an arrow like Erick? he asked him. He could've gone mad from poison, the King's Crow said it for everyone, and then they were shooting queries at him like arrows: Was he ever alone with anyone? A whore? Did you see anyone with ruffs and striped uniforms on the ship that Garrett boarded?

"Has Charles determined who tried to kill Jason?"

"It's the Little King. His slimy peasant hand's on this . . ."

"The mayor should join Evan Sinclair in the Tower."

"Are we still certain the men *guarding us* are loyal?"

"We should bring Heather back here. She'll be safe here."

"I'll get her," Jason volunteered.

Hitherto silent, her head in her palm, Lorana shot up like a volcanic blast. "*It's not the knights,*" she growled. "It's Gram Sothos." She singed Drexan with her glare. "And his miserable fucking son. I want Justen Sothos taken to the Tower. *Now!*"

The dizzying exchange fell flat at once. Every man, Jason included, regarded the steward stonily, as if she'd just declared war on the faraway priestking and every one of the seven lands loyal to his religion. In a way, she had. A palpable fear replaced the grief, tension, and fury that had roiled the king's quarters.

Jason read the room as Lorana stared down their father's advisors. *And why not gaol Justen Sothos? A king is dead . . .* Yet Justen was more a prince than Jason, in many ways, his father a throneless king. *Why not gaol Justen? Because we fear the same unspoken thing . . . and I fear it more than anyone.*

Drexan scratched a fingernail against his staff nervously. "It can be done, Your Highness," he began, trotting out the word *can* measuredly.

Lorana hovered over their father, hands on the edges of his bier. "I know what it means," she said at the floor. "I know that House Sothos is powerful."

"And under the priestking's personal protection," Jon said. "Gaoling the son of his most important ally could begin a war."

Jason fought the flashbacks. *We cannot have war. Most of all, because we can't afford to fight one.* He rested his eyes on a dead king, the first Lord of Loran to be murdered in centuries. *Are you worth a continental war, Hexar Eddenhold?*

Lorana slashed the air with her hand as if it were a blade, the priestking himself before her. "THEY KILLED MY FATHER. I want Justen taken in, now. His father, I want isolated from the Worthy Assembly." She sniffled out a scornful sound. "Consign him to the West Tower."

Hanor's cheeks went ruddy as dusk. A timid man he was, even with his king poisoned. "Our nerves are scalded hot," he said. "We need time to think. Why not just think on this—?"

"Because the worm mishandled my sister last night, and pointed an arrow at me," Jason barreled in, catching everyone's eyes. "Because my sister is smart to gaol Gram's son first. We can question Justen. Sothos's Assemblymen won't expect his arrest. It won't provoke a war overnight."

Pride glowed through grief as a smile worked the corners of Lorana's lips. *We're a calvary of griffons,* Jason thought with equal pride for his half-sister, *even though we're only two . . .*

"Charles will question the little shit," Jon said with a blink of his cloudy eyes, "and we'll know what to do next."

Jon pushed Hanor toward the door, instructing him to charge Sir Astiban Hoard with this sensitive collection; that knight was a hard, loyal man. Initially reluctant, the chancellor cooperated when the aging apothecary snarled a second order. The Tessian left so hastily he bumped a table, nearly tipping over a candle that Jason caught and steadied.

The door latched shut.

Drexan looked at Hexar. "A war abroad is almost the least of our worries," he said grimly.

Jason understood the implications. More than anyone, he understood. "A succession war."

Lorana slumped into her chair. She pushed her nut-brown hair over her shoulder. "Why else try to off every male member of our house?" she asked no one in particular.

Every male member. It was why she wasn't as concerned about the knights guarding Heather. Women could stand in for kings and lords as stewards, naught else. Loran hadn't suffered a queen in thousands of years, and it likely never would.

Jason had never understood why men feared the rule of women. Lorana had ruled Loran better than their father.

The elderly apothecary said what was on all their minds. "To pave Shaddon's way to the Silver Throne," he said quietly. "Clear it of

Hexar's only legitimate successors."

"Sidestepping the Kingstrials to enthrone him," Jason said. "Making it impossible to crown a king who isn't our vile uncle, without a succession war."

The Kingstrials. A pig farmer's crown games, devised at a time when the Worthy Assembly sat four classes, all designed to constrain violent succession wars to a sand arena. To make would-be kings bear the cost of their ambition, not the people.

Jason weighed his father's unsightly, puffy face, blue veins and all. *Damn you, Father,* he thought. *Erick is dead, Garrett has left us . . . and I could fight in the Kingstrials to save us all, if you hadn't signed a scroll that officially named me a bastard. Named me Warchild.* But that had been a leaf on Greg Thorngale's olive branch. Hexar had no choice but to sign away his son's rights.

"Were that bastards could vie in the Kingstrials," Jason grunted. *Then I could be of some use tonight.*

Drexan glanced at Jon, and the half-blind apothecary fluttered his eyelids as if he knew. Lorana looked puzzled. "What?" she asked bluntly. Worriedly.

The King's Crow traded looks with the king's children. "Bastards have fought in the Kingstrials before," he said.

"*Drexan.*" Jon hissed the chancellor's name in reprimand, as if he'd just cursed the dead king.

Drexan weathered Jon's rheumy stare, unvexed. "What? The king is dead." He pointed at the royal corpse, as if proof were needed. "Our enemies have orchestrated a violent coup against House Eddenhold to supplant a king unfriendly to the priestking with one who makes love to his feet—*and you'd keep the one blade in our arsenal hidden?* With war staring at us?"

As Jason and Lorana faced each other, Jon fronted toward the chancellor. "It's what the king wanted," he said adamantly.

"Goddamn it, *stop talking around us,*" Lorana said. "What do you mean, a bastard's fought in the Kingstrials?"

The bastard prince wheeled from confusion to anger. It was a terrible joke. "We all grew up on the stories," Jason said. "There's never been a bastard king of Loran."

Jon clenched brittle hands at his sides, as if resigning himself. Drexan fixed Jason with his green eyes. "Yes, there has," the King's Crow said. "His name was King Raelin. Unlike you, Jason, he was a *true* bastard. He had seventy-one brothers, legitimate heirs all, and he killed every one in the Kingstrials to claim these Silver Walls."

The stone maiden eyed Drexan skeptically. "I've read *The Terrible History of the Kingstrials*. There's no mention of King Raelin."

Drexan seemed aloof. "It is because I tore out and burned any pages that referenced the bastard king."

Lorana opened her mouth slightly, as if she were deciding whether to rebuke him. Jason flitted from her to the Chancellor of the Chancery. *That's a thousand-year-old tome.* They'd react the same if Drexan had defaced a silverstone brick in the Walls.

"It was at the king's direction," Jon sighed.

A thousand questions bombarded Jason. Only one eked out. "*Why?*" he asked softly.

The apothecary seemed to pity him with those pale eyes. "The king knew the horrors of the Kingstrials," he said. "After Erick was stolen from us, he placed all hope for a succession in the crown prince, and bade us keep the truth about Raelin our secret, regardless of the succession."

Jason glared at his father as if he expected Hexar to open his eyelids any moment and glare right back. "*Why?*" he snarled again. "Because he was ashamed of me? Because he hated me?"

"No." Drexan had a tenderness that Hexar had lacked in life. "He hid the truth from you for the same reason he forbade you to go to war. He loved you, Jason."

Jason almost laughed out his contempt. *The king who welcomed me home from war with a slap?* His cheek tingled from his remembered embarrassment before the court. *The father who questioned whether I was even his?*

It was a look from his sister that corked his scorn. "They speak the truth," she said in a vulnerable voice. "He loved you more than any of us, Jason. More than Garrett, Heather, Erick. More than me."

The words leapt out of Jason's throat, "*He had an odd way of showing it!*" He sank to his knees, covering his eyes with a shaking hand. Tears, hated tears, wetted his palm. He sobbed like a babe. Like a son denied his father's love, until his father lay cold.

"You were his son by the wife he loved most," he heard Drexan say as Lorana helped him up for a hug. He smelled the vomit still on her gown. "The wife he lost in the worst way imaginable." *And I look just like her,* Sarah's son thought.

As Jason blinked out tears, looking at his father, a chill spread through his spine. Every instinct from his childhood, every memory of Garrett boasting about how he'd one day rule Loran, surged up to deny him a hope he nurtured only in the dreams of dreams. He was the bastard prince, born to Hexar and a wife the Worthy Assembly refused to recognize.

The throne wasn't for him; it was for the crown prince. That'd been his father's plan. That'd always been his plan. *But Garrett left to find elves . . . and you're dead, Father.*

He remembered hearing his father's sobs as he pushed through the throne room's doors. Guilt and grief overwhelmed him as he beheld his father, the late King Hexar, Master of the Walls . . . and one of three kings to win all three contests in the Kingstrials.

Lorana faced the advisors. "Lords, if you would give me a moment with Jason," she said. "Our father is dead. The world is changed. We need time to grieve . . . to process everything."

The apothecary's white sash dangled off his person as he bowed. "Of course, Highness." Even half-blind, he shot the other advisor a less courteous look. "Come, Crow."

Jon lingered by the door as Drexan folded his cloak about himself. "We can continue this later in my South Tower, Jason." Passing the bier, he kissed two fingers and placed them on the king's forehead. "You were as great as Anjan Half-Elf," he told Hexar, as if the king could hear him. "On every god there is, or was, I swear . . . your killers will know the meaning of pain."

Drexan squeezed Jason's arm affectionately and left.

As soon as the door shut, his half-sister checked to make sure it was locked. Jason was staring at their father through a moist blur when she took him by his hands.

"I know what you're thinking, Jason," Lorana said. "Father was right to keep the truth from us. The Trials are plagued by sabotage, deceit, and death." She gripped his arms with fingers as hard as the king's had been in life. "Promise me this matter is closed. We've lost Erick, and now Father, and nearly you . . . *Promise me.*"

Jason stared at Hexar Eddenhold's plump, veiny face. "I'm not concerned about crowns or Trials, sister. Only justice." His hand cupped his sword pommel. "I go to see it done."

CHAPTER 16

Coming and Going

ara watched for her reflection in the water as the River Harriet surged beneath her feet. Daggers of morning gold and muted blue flew past. She curled her toes, relishing the spray that prickled the soles of her bare feet. Owls hooted from their perches in moss-entangled sentinel trees around her. Gazing up, she beheld two crescent moons as blue as her father's eyes.

I'm dreaming. A wind disheveled her hair. The rush of the river was in her ears. And yet Sara understood she was not in the forest clearing villagers called Elf's Grove. She clutched her knees against her chest, rocking herself. *Are you ever coming back, Father?* Her chin crumpled like vellum. *Are you dead?*

She extended her legs, letting her feet dangle just above the swift current. She wondered what would happen if she fell in. Would the river ferry her west, out to sea, all the way to the Evergreen Isles? *Will it take me to you, Father?*

Something grazed her shoulder.

Whirling about, Sara discovered a lean man with his hand outstretched. He was pretty for a man, if a touch pale, with long limber legs and arms. White hair draped his shoulders, smooth as gossamer silk. Warm and guileless were his eyes, blue like the dream moons. She marveled at his long, slender ears.

"You will not die there, child," the elf said softly. His eyes fogged white.

Sara bolted up from where she lay beside her mother, and nearly wept to remember that she was still in hell.

The smell of refuse sat on her tongue and left her feeling nauseous. Peasants sniffled constantly or wept softly into their crossed arms. Crimson-red were their cell walls, rich and dark like blood, as if the ceiling had a wound and the wound oozed down. Precious shafts of sunlight drifted in through the narrow strips of two crenelated windows too far above them for any to reach. By night the glow of torches limned cracks in their iron door—the door through which men and women went, never to return.

The Red Tower, Sara remembered with a dread nearly as suffocating as the stench. *Father, save me. Save us.*

Sara couldn't say how long she'd laid in the cell beneath the Silver Walls with Caleb and her mother. Eventually guards had escorted them and the other peasants suspected of killing King Hexar to a caged wagon, and the wagon led them through Southpoint, to the Red Tower, to here, where hope came to die.

I would enter the River Harriet and let it take me away, if I could, Sara thought with a look around. Everything was as it'd been yesterday and the day before that, only worse. Dozens of peasants huddled together in their cramped cell, sweltering in sparse light. Few ate the moldy bread their captors provided them, and yet many emptied their bowels as if they'd feasted at the Remembrance Day banquet, some in their own breeches, others in the corners, if they could brave the hills of filth. Their guards refused to give them slop buckets, *at least* slop buckets, and if any Commoner got too bold or angry at the smells and moldy bread and sounds of people crying, he or she vanished down the hall like anyone else. Like the stuttering man with a reader's writ. Like the scullion who'd pissed through the door cracks. Like the nice old woman who'd given Sara garlic for her scrapes. Like the butcher's apprentice, who'd pitched screams like a toddler when guards dragged him out by his ankles.

There had been thirty-two peasants on that first day. Now there were twenty-four, and who knew how long it'd be before they were twenty-three? Prisoners went missing, and still the Grand Inquisitor seemed no closer to finding a kingkiller.

Their crimson-vested guards offered no solace, only fists and kicks when anyone became unruly. No one was worse than the Grand Inquisitor's Casaanite. Muscled and towering, he was the one with whom peasants went and never came back, and he accompanied his lord like a shadow. Scores of pink scars riddled his left arm and that side of his face. His touch scared the peasants, who feared Elzura's Curse nearly as much as the Kingkiller's Curse, and he took cruel pleasure in abusing and frightening them. Sometimes he just *stood* over them for long periods of time. The day before he'd unfurled his breeches for a leak on the offended faithful, and *laughed*, as if he'd heard the funniest joke. He was Dracar himself, she thought.

Her only light in the darkness was Caleb. Despite his own thirst and a belly that rumbled as often as anyone's, the farmer remained alert and useful and unfailingly kind. On the first day in captivity, he learned everyone's name and made friends with any who could look past his gentle nature. Day and night he'd taken good care of Sara, who needed garlic for the stinging in her legs, *and* Rose, who alternated between bouts of sniffling and restless sleep. *The mother sleeps like a babe when the child cannot,* Sara thought, crouched against the wall.

She noticed Caleb watching how she looked at her. "Don't hold it against her, sweet one," he told Sara softly.

Sara lingered on Rose where she lay, coiled up and noiseless inches from her. Exhausted and hungry, she couldn't resist the urge, and clapped her hands over her mother's head. Louder than she had expected, the noise drew hollowed-out stares from the others. Rose only frowned in her sleep.

The butcher Sean of Southfar glared at her. "*You stop that racket!*" he hissed from across the cell. His two sons Donley and Gamlen stirred awake, sniffling wetly. "Stop it, or I'll make you stop."

"*Sean!*" Erin, the butcher's wife, whispered hoarsely. "She's a child like Don and Gam. She donna know better."

Sean whipped about to stare at Erin. "I *ought!* She knows better. *They took my apprentice!* They'll take us, an' you too if you're nah quiet, Midlander."

Their exchange woke and rankled other peasants. Some of the children wept. A peasant named Dorian urged silence, lest they draw the Casaanite's attention; the butcher cursed him a fool.

Sara sat forward to scorn Sean with a few choice words, but Caleb spoke first. "Forgive her Sean, the fault was mine. I spoke to her first."

Sean scowled at the farmer. "And *you*. By all the godfaces, if I could see *one* man away from me. I seen you, bugger, *prayin'* to your gods of tree and stone at night." He pointed a trembling finger. "Donna you come *nowhere* near me an' mine, you hear?"

The reek of refuse, the horrid butcher, her mother—all of it was too much. Sara boiled up, clenching her fists, ready to do battle. She opened her mouth, and heard someone else's voice. Shouts echoed down the hall outside. Everyone, even Sean, fell deathly silent.

Whoever he was, he wriggled like caught fish by the looks of the shadows wobbling through the door's cracks. "*UNHAND ME!*" he demanded. He had a highborn's lilt. "I won't be treated this way, do you understand? I am *the son* of a LORD SPEAKER! I sit in the WING OF LORDS! Unhand me, *DO IT*, or I'll, I'll . . ."

His protests faded. Sean shushed Don and Gam, burying their heads in his chest. Others prayed. Sara eased back against the wall, sighing when she saw Rose fast asleep.

Caleb sidled up beside her. "How's your leg, princess?" he rasped into her ear.

She checked beneath her hem. "It's okay," she said.

"Just okay?"

Sara looked up at the farmer. Stubble needled his cheeks and neck. Lost sleep hung below his eyes. Still, Caleb Bard had a sprightliness to him. She loved him for that, for checking on her scrape while her mother wept or slept, and for letting her make a pillow of his chest at night.

"It's better."

He smiled wearily. "I'll take better."

Feet away, Sean bristled. "I said *shut it,* bugger."

Sara found a pebble and flung it at the butcher; it struck his nose.

He purpled like grapeflesh but said nothing.

She thought Caleb would reproach her. He concealed his grin with a hand. "A fine throw, princess," he said for her ears only.

"You don't have to lie to him. To Sean." Sara met his gaze. "It was me. I spoke too loud. You didn't do a thing wrong."

Caleb watched her intently. "You've more heart and sense than most, Sara Sothron. But we are Commoners, are we not? And Commoners make the small sacrifices for each other that make life worth living." He kissed her head. "You should sleep, my lovely."

Sara looked at her mother. "I can't. I had a dream."

"A nightmare?" he pressed her.

She stared at her lap, trying to make sense of it all. "Yes . . . no. I don't know." Her belly rumbled hungrily.

"You can tell me." Caleb offered her the invitation of his arm, and she wilted into his embrace. She never thought she'd love the rank of onion. "You might be able to sleep if you do."

Shutting her eyes, Sara saw the crescent moons again. "I was in Elf's Grove. I was watching the river." She decided *not* to share that she'd wished the dream river would take her away; Caleb wouldn't sleep if she worried him. "I saw." She hesitated. "I saw *him.*"

"Sir Damien?"

"No. I saw an elf."

Caleb pulled away with a strange look.

Fool girl, Sara reproached herself in her mother's voice. *What have you done this time?* The elves themselves weren't forbidden to talk about. Priest and reader alike reminded their faithful to be good and patient and kind, as the elves had been with men in ancient times. But they weren't in a temple pew or parish hall.

They were in a Tower cell. Remembering how the boy Zur had shamed her over an offense she didn't mean to give, Sara began to spiral into worry, fearful that she'd offended her only friend here, anywhere.

She struggled to read his face. "Are you . . . mad?"

Caleb stared at her, almost as if she was silk, and he could see straight through her. He broke into a welcome smile. "I'm not mad. I'm glad. *Quite* glad. That is *wonderful.*"

"Wonderful?"

He leaned against the wall with a relieved smile. "Yes. It's a sign. It means we may yet put this terrible place behind us."

A sign? She pictured the semicircle moons.

A pair of guards shuffled through the hall outside, hoops of keys clinking on their belts. Caleb watched until the shadows slithered off. "It's why we made our Gift in that grove, why they call it that name to begin with," he whispered to her.

"But you said we were making a Gift to spirits."

The butcher glanced darkly in their direction. Smiling, the farmer waited until Sean distracted himself with his boys. "Aye, spirits live there, but over them rules an elf-prince."

"An elf . . . prince?" Sara crossed looks with Sean again. She retrieved a pebble from a crack in the floor.

"An elf-prince was said to make his home in Elf's Grove," Caleb said. "He resided there to be close to men, and do good by them. Our Gifts are summonses."

Sara frowned. "Why didn't we see him there then?"

The farmer shrugged. "Who knows? Elves are mysterious, but you mustn't doubt their goodwill." He came close. "It was said elves could do things we could not. Disguise themselves with leaf and branch as we ourselves wear wool." He plucked playfully at a fold in her gown. "Quicken fires without tinder. Turn stone to water. Summon storm-wind and lightning as our lords call bannermen. Even make animals speak like us. There was nothing they couldn't do. The gods of field and forest gave their firstborn children mighty blessings: life eternal, and the power to mold the earth like wet clay."

"Could they summon someone from the Evergreen Isles?"

Caleb drew her in for a tight embrace. He didn't let go. "That was why we made our Gift. And if you saw an elf—in that grove, of all places—it can only mean that he received it, and heard us."

A joy unlooked-for, an impossible hope, swept the girl up like a funnel cloud. Tears broke in her eyes. *Summon the wind and lightning for us, elf-prince. Return my father. Please.*

"Even better that you saw him in his grove," Caleb said. "It's a magical place. After they killed King Lathros, Sir Bradley Durhurst and his Treasonous Twelve sent men and dogs after loyalists who hid in Elf's Grove. The dogs sniffed around the trees without success, and moved on. Little had they known the trees and willows disguised the king's men."

Her mother rolled from side to side, crossing her arms across her chest, as if craving warmth. Caleb wordlessly took off his ratty tunic and slipped it over Rose. She whispered Sir Damien's name and shuddered as she found sleep again.

"What did he tell you, the grove prince?" Caleb asked Sara.

Sara used the wall to right herself. "That I would not die here." She felt odd telling Caleb, almost guilty, as if the dream-elf's promise had been their secret, not hers to share.

"Then you should believe him, Sara Sothron."

Caleb rubbed his palms together for warmth. Trying to help, Sara massaged his arm up and down. He chuckled at her attempt.

She paused. "Why aren't you afraid, Caleb?"

Caleb watched her with something between sadness and kindness. He stroked her wimple-clad hair in measured strokes that comforted her. "What makes you think I'm not?"

A flatulent peasant squatted in a corner, paying no heed to complaints from others. Sara pressed her sleeve to her nose.

"I'm afraid, as much as you or anyone else here, Sean and the baker, their children," the farmer admitted. "It's just that—I don't know." He looked at the streams of sunlight that poured in from above. "I suppose I took after Lord Gram Reuben and the Awakening's sages. They saw the world not as a disc but a marble. They believed our marble and the brightest stars circle the sun."

That confused Sara. How could Odma be a *marble?* Reader Gary said the Evergreen Isles bordered the furthest ends of the earth, where krakens lurked in the ocean deep and foaming sea drizzled off the world's edge like rain off a roof.

"I think it gave me comfort," Caleb said, more to himself. "If we circle the sun, then how important can we men be? If we are grains of sand, quick to come and go with the tide, why feel afraid when we're swept back out?"

She nuzzled her head against his chest. "You're important to me, Caleb."

The farmer planted another kiss on her forehead. "How can I help you sleep, like your mother?"

She closed her eyes. "Tell me about your home. Your *real* home, before you became a Commoner."

That took some prodding. Caleb slowly opened up about his past. Sara heard him talk about a castle, the castle that was no longer his by rights. He described a keep with three towers, a drawbridge, battlements that overlooked pale beaches and a vast endless sea.

Soon she drifted to sleep. She visited Elf's Grove and River Harriet in her dreams, but never found the elf-prince.

Sara woke sharply to screams, pleading, weeping. Night had fallen. The door was wide open, flooded with torchlight that framed a man's silhouette. A hood covered his head, but Sara could see his ghostly pale eye and the crosshatch of scars on his face. Beside the Casaanite stood the Grand Inquisitor, a scarlet candlestick in his robes.

"I'll say this one more time," Charles Burke said with soft menace. "The apprentice gave up the butcher. Sean of Southfar. Where is Sean of Southfar?"

Men like the baker drew their children close as the dead king's torturer entered with his demonic guard. Don and Gam attached themselves to their father's legs as the butcher rose.

"No no no, *NO,* please," the butcher pled desperately. "I have two sons, they donna have their mother."

The Grand Inquisitor had dead eyes. "Then they'll be sent to the High Bishop. Take him. The steward will be pleased that we found her father's murderer."

The sounds of weeping turned to wailing as the Casaanite forced

Sean up. Don and Gam latched onto their father's hands, refusing to let him go. The guard swatted them off like flies. He backtracked to the door with the Southfar butcher writhing in his grasp. Sara felt ashamed for hurling the pebble earlier.

Sean twisted free. "No! No, wait! *WAIT!*"

"The Kingkiller's Curse waits for no one," the torturer said imperiously. "Come quietly, or I'll have Jhazar take that tongue, *after* you've given up any other kingkillers."

"*I CAN GIVE THEM UP NOW! IF YOU SPARE ME I WILL!*"

"Name them."

No, Sara thought with dread. The butcher's crazed eyes wandered the chamber. He squinted in their direction, and pointed. She didn't hear everything that came out of his lying mouth—only that Caleb was a filthy bugger whom he heard praying to pagan gods, aye, thanking them for the poison that killed the king.

Sara leapt to her feet. Words couldn't come fast enough. "*LIAR!*" she screamed. "The butcher is lying, Caleb never did *any* king wrong, he's good, he's good!" She pivoted to the rest of the peasants. "Won't you say something? Tell them Sean lies! Tell them the truth!" But they were all cowards. No one even acknowledged her.

The Casaanite handed off the butcher to another guard outside. The other peasants gave him wide berth, and he was there in three swift strides, crushing Caleb's arm in his grasp, forcing him up for a stagger toward the door from which no one returned.

Sara leapt onto the guard and dug her nails into his arm, ripping into him like a cat. The Casaanite gave her no reaction, nothing but the white teeth of a grin under his hood. When he seized her by the wrist, there was no prying herself free. Sara squirmed like a hooked worm in his grasp.

"You have spirit, bitch," the man said in his deep baritone, the voice of Dracar. "But it won't help you here."

The guard refused to hear Caleb's protests, how she was just a girl, how there was no need to take them both, just him, *please just him, for gods' sakes!* Everyone was screaming now, including Rose, who pulled at Sara's gown, her foot, anything she could grab to keep her from the door.

"Please, no, no, no—my daughter, you can't," Rose sobbed brokenly, grasping feebly for her. "No no no . . ."

Burke sighed wearily. "Release the girl, Jhazar. We don't need her. Just the butcher and this one."

The Casaanite shoved her hard, and Sara fell listless into her mother's vise-like embrace. Sara reached feebly for Caleb, catching only air.

The farmer had shivering eyes as he smiled. "Follow your dreams, princess. They'll lead you back to your father."

"You promised you'd spare me," the butcher protested as he passed through the doorway. Burke didn't respond.

"*Caleb*," Sara screamed. "*NOOOOOOO!*"

Caleb passed into the hall with the red-robed torturer. The door slammed shut.

The Daughter

 early a thousand souls filled the Silver Walls, and yet the castle Lorana called home had never seemed emptier. Were it not for the knights flanking her, the steward thought she could pass for one of the ghosts lurking around the Silver Walls, lying in wait to haunt unworthy kings.

Indeed, is that not what I am now? she pondered as she climbed the cylindrical stairwell to her sister's chambers. She clutched at the silver thread tying her father's heavy, ermine-trimmed mantle at her neck. *A ghost preying on unworthy men.*

Two days had passed since Charles Burke gaoled Justen on her orders. He hadn't gone quietly to the Red Tower. Now eyes trailed after her. The Assembly was nervous. Sometimes she overheard whispers, only to turn to find no one there.

If she believed in ghosts, she'd have thought they were haunting *her.* They might have cause: she was the first woman to sit the Silver Walls in a thousand years. Some small part of her wanted to believe in the spirits, if only so that Hexar was one of them. So that he hadn't left her after all.

Torchlight flickered by Heather's chamber door at the top of the North Tower. Connor Tomas and Andrew Windkin stood watch outside. Beneath their mail and gambeson, the knights resembled ghosts themselves. She wondered how much sleep they'd had in the past two days, if any.

She had them guard the North Tower entrance. She wanted time alone with her sister, and talking with knights outside the door wouldn't give them privacy. Her knights answered with nods, descending in a rattle of mail.

Still carrying her torch, Lorana gripped the iron handle and pushed gently. The door opened with a squeak. Inside, all was pitch dark. Sheets stirred faintly.

"I said *no*, Lorna," came her half-sister's shaky voice. "I'm not hungry. *Go away!*"

"Not even for raspberry cake?"

A shape took form atop the bed, shifting through sheets. "No," came her sullen reply.

Lorana secured her torch in an iron sconce. In the faint firelight her half-sister almost resembled a mergirl, propped up on the rocks of her pillows, her legs submerged in the waves of her velvety covers. Her golden hair frayed like hay.

Seating herself on the corner of her bed, Lorana unfolded the napkin in her hands and produced a square of spongy pink cake. White powder tickled her nostrils. Hearing her stomach complain, the steward suddenly remembered she, too, hadn't eaten in more than two days.

Lorana picked up the treat and nibbled. "It's still moist," she said as she chewed. "There's something"—she sank her teeth into the tart red middle—"about eating this dessert past midnight. Makes me feel *awfully* naughty."

She expected Heather to give in, take the cake, and inhale it. Such was her lust for sweets. But all she said was, "It's from the feast." Her sister collapsed into her bed with a listlessness that left her feeling hollower inside, if that were possible.

Lorana set the napkin on the floor. On elbows and knees, she sidled up next to her half-sister in darkness that smelled strongly of grief. Lorana wrapped her in her arms and lowered her chin into the nape of her neck.

"He wouldn't want you to starve," she murmured softly.

Heather sucked in snot. "You haven't eaten, either."

Lorana's stomach betrayed her with a muffled moan. "You're very observant. You'll make a fine mother to your lord's children one day."

Her little body stiffened. "Not if you keep gaoling your suitors, I won't."

She almost wanted to ask where she had heard it, but then, Justen's arrest wasn't a secret anywhere. Word spread fast. Every captive Assemblyman feared the Grand Inquisitor's Shadow was never far from his chambers now.

Lorana wasn't very good at playing mother. She couldn't tell stories like Sarah or snuggle like Romara. There was only one other woman who could placate Heather's moods, and she was gone. *And how I need her, now more than ever . . .*

The prieslenne's soft voice drifted into her head. She sang one of her favorite hymns lightly, soothingly.

> *Come now, sweet gentle souls,*
> *Awaken to King Anjan's promise.*
> *Let no one forget his Covenant,*
> *Let your heart like a bell toll.*

Heather shifted in her sheets, turning over so their faces met. Torchlight ambered her hair. "You're not Eden," she said bluntly, in Heather form.

The remark wasn't mean, and Lorana didn't take it as such. It was the truth. Only the porcelain-skinned girl with golden hair could ever soothe Heather. Or Lorana, for that matter . . .

"No, I'm not her. What can I do, my love?"

Tears puddled in a groove between her sister's arm and Lorana's chest. "Bring him back," Heather said wetly.

The half-sisters embraced in the dark. Without meaning to, Lorana imagined Garrett beyond the bed, quiet as a mouse, tall as a dragon. She tightened her hold on Heather.

"He's, he's really gone," she said between shudders.

"Yes," the stone maiden replied.

"What will happen to us now?"

Lorana caressed her soft hair. "Don't worry about that now."

The princess pushed herself off her older sibling. "I *must* know. Lorna says they're saying things. The Assemblymen." She went on, at a hurried pace that strung her words together, "They say without Garrett, without Prince Erick, we'll have the Kingstrials. That we'll be sent to Father's castle, only I've never been to Redmount. Father said he never liked Redmount—said visiting the castle in winter felt like being in an ice tunnel."

Once more, she wanted to play Edenia, to sing a lullaby, to comb her sister's hair and whisk her away with tales about far-off princes and happy endings.

Lorana looked on grimly, feeling the stirrings of a plan. "It won't come to that."

An hour later, Lorana pried herself from her half-sister's clinging arms, careful not to wake her. She left the cake on the dresser and softly latched the door shut behind her.

Adjusting her father's mantle about her shoulders, Lorana descended down the North Tower's cracked steps and headed for the one place with answers. The knights Andrew Windkin and Jeremy Hunt shadowed her through the Great Hall's forest of columns. Above them, the castle's pearl aura rolled through the sky like waves of light, as it had for thousands of years.

Lorana arrived at the South Tower. Looming over her, it looked like a pearl lance at night, aglimmer with the traces of silverstone packed into its walls.

She posted her knights outside the gate. They disagreed with her going inside alone this late, but she insisted. "I need time alone," she said. Lorana crossed the threshold, ascending spiraled steps to reach the land's largest library.

Time away from eyes that might see the steward flipping through ancient tomes the day after her father's murder, she thought, *with the succession uncertain, and her family's hold on this glorious castle tenuous . . .*

The silverstone aura made torchlight irrelevant, lighting the building through unshut windows. In the rookery upstairs, ravens squawked up a storm. *If an assassin lurks here,* mused the princess, *the ravens have certainly alerted him.*

A comforting smell of old parchment drew her through an oval door. She walked into a maze of bookcases that reached the ceiling. The spines of richly ornamented tomes glimmered in the silverstone light.

Turning a bookcase's corner, she found a broken circle of desks lined with the dross of used candles and parchments. She threw her mantle on a table, lit a candle in the fire of a sconce, and surrendered to the one thing she did well when she was uncertain: research.

Research calmed her distempers. Angry when she learned that women in Loran could not rule as queens, she'd buried her nose in a book about Queen Barbara and learned about all her mistakes. Desperate to prove Romara guiltless in her adultery, she'd pored over stories about famous trials by sword.

Her feelings for Edenia had driven her here. Histories and religious texts left no doubt about what befell sinners like her. After that, Lorana began to keep secrets from her family. From the world. From everyone. She built walls around herself as tall as these bookcases. And she made Edenia promise. *Just as you made me promise to keep secrets, Father,* she thought. *As I have.*

Candle aflicker, she followed the name plates nailed into bookcases until she reached the histories. She scanned a shelf of neatly arrayed spines. Nothing was organized alphabetically. Walking past, she came across everything—*The History of the Worthy Assembly, A Squire's Account of Sir Bradley's Final Days, On the Symbolism of Solstices for Pagan Folk,* even the annals of Casaan's tribes—everything but the tome she sought.

Her frustration mounted. Was the book misplaced, like the others, or had Drexan just burned the entire damn thing?

She heard footsteps. Rubbing out flame between finger and thumb, she set the candleholder on a bookshelf. Lorana hadn't gone indoors unarmed. She drew Andrew's dagger from her girdle. Hiding behind shelves thick with books, she waited as the footsteps came closer, closer, closer . . .

A shadow shuffled into sight, silhouetted by silverstone light. A book toppled from his hands, and the dagger from hers, clattering on the floor.

Zur pumped his palms at her for calm. "Ana, it's me—*it's me*," he kept repeating.

Lorana lay a hand over her chest, her fright fading. "Zur, what on earth—why're you—" She sighed. "Little brother . . ."

Her dearest friend had traded his fine banquet attire for a tunic and breeches. His rich brown eyes caught fragments of silverstone. Heather and her bullies-in-waiting had dubbed him "Sir Elephant," on account of his ears, which flared out a little to the sides. He was quite handsome, actually.

And loyal. Above all, Zur was loyal. She needed loyal.

"I almost cut you just then." Lorana recovered her dagger guiltily. "Why're you in the library so late?" The tremor in her voice brought out sympathy in his eyes; she tried to disguise it with humor. "Did Drexan send you here to learn a spell?"

"Why, he's a sorcerer, after all," Zur said, playing along.

"Good. I could use a good spell. Something to turn every Assemblyman here into a toad." She bent down and picked up his ponderous tome. Turning it over in her hands, she saw a richly ornamented leather cover edged with metal clamps.

It was the book she'd sought. *The Terrible History of the Kingstrials of Loran* circled a raised medallion in flowing script.

Lorana shot him a look. "So I wasn't far off the mark when I said Drexan sent you here to find a spell." *A spell that my other brother tasked the King's Crow with finding,* she thought.

Zur looked as if he feared he'd given offense. "No. Not him. Jason sent me here, actually."

In the king's bedchambers, Jason had said he wanted to see justice done. He'd left for the Red Tower for that purpose, to learn as much as the Grand Inquisitor knew about who'd murdered their father. *You promised me, dear brother,* Lorana thought, *and yet it's all either of us can think about . . .*

Jason had always burned to prove himself worthy of their father's throne. Hexar had the right of it in the throne room—*that* was why he'd left for war. What better way to do it than by following their father in his footsteps?

The steward couched the tome's thick spine in her arm, flipping through its pages. *If anyone can make it through the Kingstrials at all,* she pondered bleakly. Illuminations sprang to life around the borders, depicting atrocities in cheerful color. Men, cleaving off other lords' heads with swords in an arena ringed with smiling spectators. Rival lords running each other through with lances. A green dragon torching would-be kings. Opposite that, a black griffon dismembered men with its talons. Little legs squirmed in the griffon's beak like worms.

One luminous section enumerated the rules. There were three contests. The leader of the Worthy Assembly's Wing of Lords called the Kingstrials when the sitting king died without an heir apparent. The Worthy Assembly decided the nature of two contests, which ranged from tourneys to dragon hunts and staged naval battles. The Third Trial was reserved for a griffon mounting. Not that anyone had ever flown upon a griffon since the First Days, but a king still had to prove a blood connection to the First King, even symbolically.

If he won all three of his Trials, a claimant would ascend directly to the Silver Throne. Only three men in Loran's history, including Hexar the Bold, had ever achieved that feat. If no one won all three Trials, the Assembly held a direct election. *Three Trials, three Wings,* she read. *Only the Worthy crown kings.*

She licked a finger and turned another page. The thorns of torn paper cluttered the inmost seam. "Anything about Raelin the Red?" She assumed Zur knew everything about the king's deception.

"None," Zur said. "Drexan was thorough. But I found some things of . . . interest. Hold on."

He left and returned with a newly lit candle. Standing by her, he flipped through pages until he settled on a passage with large red initials. One illumination depicted a family leaving the Silver Walls with arrows showering them like rain.

The passage was long, Zur said, so he paraphrased: "The Kingstrials have worked to protect Loran from war, but they've never shielded outgoing royal families."

"The most famous being Queen Barbara." Lorana lingered on the illumination pane. It showed a carriage bolting from the arrows, a queen's face in the window. She looked terrified.

"The incoming king, Peredur Fawkes, spread rumors the queen bedded mules in her chambers," Zur said. "He had men chase her and her five children into Temron's Gorge—"

"Which they named Barbara's Gorge, after they found the bloodbath his men left there," Lorana said grimly. *Ever has this kingdom hated women ruling them,* she thought. *It's why I can't succeed you, Father. Why we're now even contemplating these terrible Trials.*

Zur turned the page. "But"—he said *but* with a note of fascination—"there have been kings who claimed the Silver Throne by . . . other means. Your ancestor, Hexron Eddenhold, was one of them."

He turned the page to an illumination that featured her reviled ancestor, the killer of Assemblies. He clenched a scroll in his hands tightly, as if it were an Assemblyman's neck. With his thick brow and pronounced nose, Hexron Eddenhold bore an uncanny resemblance to her and her father.

Of course, she thought. *This is what I was seeking.*

Lorana smiled a meant smile. "Thank you, little brother. For finding this. Perhaps there's a knighthood in your future."

Zur perked with a fleeting smile, then looked away. It was a distant look.

Lorana clasped his shoulder. "I know I can't grant it," she said. "I know you would've preferred to serve Sir Connor over Drexan. It'll take a king. And the king . . ." She trailed off.

Zur met her watery gaze. "Oh, Ana."

That was all it took. Suddenly Lorana Eddenhold, Hexar's stone maiden, was crying. *Sobbing.* How long had it been? Not since Jason and Edenia had left her, and only then in solitude, in her chamber, where no one could see how much uglier she became when she cried. Tears poured down the banks of her cheeks like water from a rain-gorged river.

She sank into her little brother's embrace, shuddering. He wasn't a knight, but he comforted her as any of her men would. "I'm so sorry, Ana," he kept repeating. "I'm so sorry."

And I'm sorry, Zur, she thought. *I'm sorry I have to keep things from you. But I'm my father's daughter.*

The Message

ason waded through a stream of filth in reeking darkness underground. His torch ruddied creviced wall and knee-length, brackish water. He buried his nose in the bend of his arm, trying not to inhale fumes curling off the water's surface.

These were Southpoint's catacombs, still the city's best-kept secret, even after millennia. No one had ever fully mapped King Rorin's excavated chalk mines, and none knew where all the winding, labyrinthine tunnels led. Through the catacombs, rumor had it you could access any city dwelling, including the Red Tower, even a door that opened in the castle gatehouse . . . if you didn't lose your way and vanish.

Jason took this way to the Tower at his sister's direction. One foiled assassination attempt on her half-brother's life had been enough. It was safer to travel underground. *Yet someone could easily kill me here, in the reeking dark, if they wished,* he mused grimly.

His torchlight seared through the underworld's darkness. Bone-pale roots twisted out of earthen walls like skeletal arms, grasping for him. Brick columns resembled assassins lurking in the dark, ready to strike. A dull sloshing around the corner sent his free hand to his sword hilt. Seconds later, a black rat as thick as his thigh paddled past his leg, fanning ripples.

He shook his head wryly. *Silly bastard,* he chided himself. *How can you hope to see justice done for your father if mere rats startle you?*

Yet it *was* a rat he was after. Or several. They had names like Gram Sothos, Justen Sothos, Shaddon Eddenhold. All loyal friends of Priestking Parlisis, who had cause to kill the king for his dream of a thousand-year Elvarenist Loran. *Maybe you're a rat, too, Evan Sinclair.*

Only one man could tell him which were the real vermin, and he resided in a crimson tower.

The ringing of bells carried faintly through the tunnels. It likely came from the skull-lined well of Traitor's Pit. He wished to avoid the bottom of the well entirely.

The bells toll for you, Father, Jason pondered, melancholy mingling with bitterness. They pealed at the top of every hour. *Does the city miss you, truly? And when the bells are done, and you're buried in the manner of the Free Beliefs . . . will I miss you?*

Doubt invited guilt as thick as the syrupy murk festering about his knees. Yes, he mourned his father, in his own way. He lamented the father he never knew. Yet Lorana said Hexar had loved him most. He couldn't see how that was possible—after all the fights, the words neither father nor son could take back.

Up ahead, flickering torchlight oranged the catacombs. Rounding a brick column, Jason found himself at a wall.

Not a wall. He rattled his sword free.

"Don't strike, milord, I'm your faithful servant," came a baritone voice.

Jason waded forward, sword ready. "If you're a friend, step into the light," he commanded him.

Shadows melted in torchlight but remained thick about the bald-headed Casaanite who loomed before him. Muscular and tall, he wore a leather jerkin and breeches that would've made him an ideal assassin, the way they helped him blend in. Scars layered his left bicep like roads intersecting a city map. A jagged scar partitioned his left eyebrow, fizzling out beneath a ghostly pale eye.

"You're Jhazar," Jason said. Lorana had told him to expect the Inquisitor's Shadow.

"Jhazar of Groth, here to serve, milord. Forgive me, I didn't mean to startle." His practiced bow felt out of place in the sewers. "Follow me. I'll see you safely to Lord Charles."

Unhooking his torch from a sconce, the Casaanite forged ahead through murk, down a flooded brick hall that closed in tight. Jason followed him with sword drawn, from a distance.

He didn't know this man. The Inquisitor's Shadow was new to Charles Burke's service. He was fast becoming a legend among Commoners and lower gentry who feared the touch of a Child of Elzura, especially the one in service to Charles.

"Gods be with you, for the loss of your father, milord," the man's deep voice echoed over their sloshing.

Your father. In the days after Hexar's murder, every castle servant he met had offered condolences for the death of a king. *Yes, Hexar the Bold was my father.*

"You said 'gods,'" Jason said. "Are you an Elvarenist?"

He discerned Jhazar's bald head shaking. "A religion that teaches my people are why Ansara is a mess, with its thirteen kingdoms?" He barked out laughter. "A traitor's religion."

Not all Elvarenists are traitors, Jason thought. He glanced at what looked like a skull bobbing past his knee. They had to be near Traitor's Pit. "Sylvanian, then?" That'd be as shocking as a Casaanite who followed priestkings.

Jhazar circled about, his blind eye as orange as his torch. "Forgive me, milord, it's just an expression." He jabbed his fire into a hall to their right that Jason hadn't known was there. "A little further, and then a ladder."

The hall enlarged into a chamber noisy with the churn of water. Torchlight sketched the swell of ceiling vaults, corridors in the wall, and a flooded floor that seemed a pool and flowed in one direction. Jhazar told him to follow him closely. "A false step here can drown you," he said over the splashing currents.

Jason observed a dark corridor slashed with sunlight. He thought Jhazar planned to turn there and sloshed that way.

The Casaanite snatched his wrist. "Not that way, milord."

"Sorry." Jason gazed down the hall. "Where does it lead?"

"I have no idea, but men have gone in and not come out."

They entered a mercifully dry corridor hemmed in by chalky white walls. The tunnel zigzagged this way and that, often sharply. Occasionally, Jason heard the noise of business in the city above: the march of feet, wheels clunking cobbles, people haggling vendors, and, distantly, bells. *I think we know whether the people miss you, Father,* he thought.

After a half-hour's walking, they arrived at an iron ladder bolted to the wall. Rusted steps fed into the dark of a climbing hole. Cool, welcome air breathed down.

The Casaanite inserted his torch into a rusted sconce on the wall and climbed first. Jason doused his torch in the water and followed him up the shaking ladder, ignoring roots that yanked on his clothes.

They didn't climb long. Stopping, Jhazar pawed about, then lifted a wooden board with screaming hinges. He hauled himself up before helping Jason out of the hole.

Leaving the earth, Jason dusted himself off, waiting for his eyes to adjust. He was in a mudstone undercroft crowded with barrels. The Grand Inquisitor stood with his Shadow, dressed in the scarlet robes of his office.

Jason had never seen such pity from his father's torturer. "Jason." His voice radiated with sensitivity that'd been lacking at the piers. He drew him into the pillowy drapes of his loose-sleeved arms, then peeled away.

Charles rooted Jason in place with his stare. "I swear on my soul," he said severely, "we will turn over every stone in this kingdom, on this continent, to avenge your king father."

The words came out before Jason could stop them: "Why didn't you turn over every stone to protect him?"

The king's spymaster looked humbled. He should've fallen to his knees to beg forgiveness. "You're right, my lord," he said, voice soft with grief. "I failed your family. I failed my king. *I will not fail you again.*"

"Have you learned anything from the man who tried to kill me?" Jason asked him.

A subtle look of satisfaction entered the old man's face. "Let us speak inside."

They left the undercroft for the small outer ward. Even with the smells of nearby Fish Street, the air was sweet relief for Jason, who felt suddenly all too aware of his sewer reek. He balled up his filth-caked cloak, which Jhazar offered to clean.

As the Little King had made Southpoint his kingdom, so Charles Burke made the Red Tower his own. He walked across his grassy bailey with the confidence that here, he was king.

"I regret that you needed to soil yourself in the sewers, Jason," Charles said. *Better that we not risk Hexar's surviving son,* it went unsaid.

"How's my uncle?" Jason watched him for his reaction.

If having Evan Sinclair for a prisoner again gave him any perverse pleasure, he didn't show it. "Unharmed, in a cell. His two companions have their own cells, too."

"And food and water?"

"You asked me to keep them safe, Jason, and so I have."

Contrary to what peasants held, there were no cadavers lying about the bailey, no crucifixions, only daisies and poppies along the vine-strewn curtain wall. The Red Tower reached for a pearl-hazed sky, its battlements a sprawled palm, its merlons the fingers. The palace had a perceptible tilt that made people wonder if it'd one day come tumbling down—a reminder of the colossal stones the Army of the Gods's catapults had flung at it to accomplish that. Some of those stones dotted the courtyard, fringed with willow grass, memories of a cataclysm averted.

Two red hoods opened hickory doors inlaid with polished silver figurines, and in they went. The keep was still the palace that'd hosted emissaries. Colorful tapestries draped the tower's walls, casting shadows across the exquisitely checkered marble floor. They ascended corkscrew stairs ringed with statues of Loran's most exalted kings.

At each step they were greeted by marble kings bearing aloft swords and trophies, Haymath Ironkeep, the first Tomas Fawkes, Jacen Bearslayer, and the like, all men who'd won the Silver Throne through the Kingstrials. Lathros Dejoy stared at the crown in his hands, his expression troubled.

The royal procession paused at a barren plinth. *Was there a bastard king here, Father,* Jason wondered, *and did you have it removed to keep me in the dark?*

Charles saw him looking at the plinth. "King Eddenfogh once stood here," he shared. "When the time is right, I'll have your bold father's likeness erected in his place."

Jason had rushed to judgment. Charles Burke wouldn't care for a Cloudlands king like Eddenfogh in his palace. He had no love for that land's current lord, who'd accused Charles of torturing his brother into confessing in Erick's kidnapping. Time's passing had healed no wounds: Charles still scorned Trevor Wexley, who refused to rejoin Loran proper until the Grand Inquisitor hanged from a gibbet.

"Hexar was one of three men to win all three contests in his Kingstrials," Jason remarked. "He deserves that much."

"He also fathered you and your siblings. For me, that is sufficient reason to honor him."

By the eighth floor, Charles labored visibly up the steps, sweating beads and listing on his Shadow for support. He told Jhazar to leave; he meant to show Jason to the Dread Chamber. The flush in the old man's face seemed to worry the Casaanite.

"He can lean on me," Jason reassured the servant. Charles took his offered arm with a liver-spotted hand. "Thank you for guiding me, Jhazar."

The big man bowed at the waist, milorded them, and left. They headed down a circular corridor filled with cell bars and iron doors. Gaolers in red hoods and vests stood at attention, pikes in hand.

Charles chuckled like a man contemptuous of aging and all that it brings. "These old knees," he complained. "When you were young, I could spring to the Silver Walls and back with a rabbit's speed. Now . . ." He made an irritable gesture.

"Jhazar seems to serve you loyally," Jason observed. "I didn't know my father had resumed hostage-taking."

"He didn't," Charles said. "Jhazar of Groth is a free man. He was a huntsman. Now my Shadow is more feared than me."

Their stroll past cells tested that theory. Prisoners in a cell scrambled off like terrified game, the whites of their eyes following every movement of their scarlet-robed host. In his haste, one man clanged a bucket of slop over on himself, eyes fixed on Charles.

Drexan had been too modest about Charles's sweep of the serving peasants. It was as if they'd rounded up Westcheap on its busiest day. More open-air cells spilled into view, and more prisoners, packed close in their squalid crimson chambers like caged chickens.

Their misery was hard to unsee, the smell as stomach-turning as the catacombs' stench. Unwashed faces on top of faces. Men, his age and older than Jon Applewood. Women. Children younger than Heather.

"*Children?*" Jason hissed under his breath.

The old man stiffened on his arm. He smoothed the hook of his black beard with two fingers. "Innocence makes an ideal catspaw," he said.

Jason realized he was sweating. A cold, familiar sweat that began shortly after he killed his first man. His chest hammered. His vision blurred. And he remembered . . .

He remembered the bodies, porcupined with arrows. The children in the village, wailing like the world had ended. They'd begged for food scraps as the fires of war engulfed their homes. Jason and his brothers had passed them on camelback with the other alliance soldiers, Garrett making insensitive jokes, Erick bearing the world's weight on his shoulders as he took in hell.

Prince Erick, he thought, smelling the sweet fetor of his flesh, as if his pyre burned in the Red Tower.

"*Prince Jason,*" cried a prisoner, using the wrong title.

"Mercy, Lord Jason, *mercy mercy mercy,*" a woman sobbed gauzily.

"We done nothin', m'lord. We loved our king."

"Lord, you protected the Common girl. *Protect us.*"

"Jason," more voices twined together, and suddenly the corridor writhed with outstretched hands. Red-hooded gaolers growled warnings or went straight to jabbing spears through cell bars. The people quailed at once, withdrawing to safety.

Regaining an almost-youthful vigor, Charles led Jason away from the corridor in quick strides. They passed several iron doors before finally reaching the huge, unmissable, spike-studded one. Ensconced torches crackled on the wall.

"My apologies, lord," Charles said with an irate look for the hall. "The rats usually only squeak when . . ." He observed Jason, his concern obvious. "Jason, you're shaking. Are you—?"

Jason shivered as if he were cold. He closed his eyes, breathed, tried to steady himself. Garrett had mocked him for the shakes and sweats. "Did those people kill my father?"

"No. They were suspects."

"Then I want them released. I want the children freed."

Charles had a faraway look. "There's something you should know." He drew a toothy iron key from his robes. He inserted it into the keyhole, opened the door, and beckoned him inside the room men dreaded most in all of Loran.

The Dread Chamber was the real Red Tower. There were no windows, no straw, only blood-red walls patched with nitre. Chains dangled from the ceiling like tentacles. Instruments of torture cluttered a table like spoons and forks a kitchen table. To his right stood something between a horse saddle and a rib cage littered with hair-thin steel needles . . .

. . . and to the left was his unconscious assassin, bound by tweedy ropes to the spokes of a wheel. His body was a map of pain. A sodden red bandage on his leg marked where Sinclair's dagger had landed. Rope burns encircled his wrists like pink archipelagoes, and cloudy purple marks told Jason that gaolers had been at his sides with clubs. A tattoo crisscrossed his bare chest: three black roses budding on a thorny vine.

"I know that marking," Jason said.

Charles observed his captive with a note of satisfaction, as if he were proud of his work. "As fearful people should," he told him. "Black roses are the mark of the Rose Guild."

The Rose Guild was headquartered far east of Loran, in Medecia, where the king's brother festered in exile, safe from Hexar's assassins.

"So they killed Father," Jason muttered.

"They may have been involved." Charles studied him. "But the assassins came for *you*. And they brought a message."

Charles drew something else from his robes. He extended his fist and plopped the cold round thing in Jason's palm. Pearl light glimmered off the band like water reflecting moonlight.

"What . . ." His heartbeat raced anew. He felt the shakes and sweats return, but they weren't from memories of war. "What . . . *what is this?*" Jason demanded angrily.

But he knew what it was. And so did the Grand Inquisitor, knower of secrets, by the way he stared at the ring . . . the one identical to the ring Jason had hidden in a drawer and wore at night while he slept.

I take you as husband, and love you forever.

"We found it on this man when we took him into custody," Charles said in a cold, knowing voice.

It was all a blur, the gnarled club finding its way into his hands, banging the iron wheel dully. The assassin jolted awake. Unclenching a purpled eye, he searched the chamber. "Maetha," he whimpered.

Jason showed him the silverstone ring. "WHAT IS THIS?"

The tortured Rose Guildsman did what a wiser man would've refrained from doing. He flashed him a defiant, smirking eye. "What . . . is it . . . to you . . . Warchild?"

Jason threw all his weight behind his club and made the man's knee twist unnaturally. Were it not for his bindings, the assassin's spasms would've thrown him clear off the wheel. He screamed soundlessly, and then loudly, gutturally.

"Tell me who gave this to you," Jason Warchild seethed by his face, "or you can squirm with both your knees broken. TELL ME NOW!"

The man whimpered. He beckoned Jason close. When he was done whispering, the bastard prince gathered himself up, free of shakes but sweating. "Charles, I'd have you tell me what you know," he demanded. "*Everything.* Then you'll show me to Evan Sinclair. I'll question him myself."

CHAPTER 19

A Devil's Bargain

van heard a girl crying down the hall. Low and muffled, her wet voice carried through his door. *Could Burke torture a child? But what am I saying?* he told himself. *The king is dead . . . and I am no stranger here.*

Still clothed in his banquet wear, the nobleman crouched low in a corner of his cell, a squat, red-bricked cube of hell he knew all too well. He curled up, trying to stave off despair. He was failing at that.

The first evening was a nightmare. On Jason's orders, men-at-arms had isolated him from Rathos and Karl. A burlap bag reeking of onions had been thrown over his head. After a carriage ride through Southpoint, the bag came off, and a hard shove sent him staggering back into a nightmare he left behind decades ago.

There had been no reasoning with his gaoler, a hulking brute of a Casaanite. His one good eye radiated with sick pleasure at the lord's obvious terror. When Evan asked for Rathos and Karl, the man of a hundred scars had grinned.

"They are the Grand Inquisitor's guests now, as are you," the servant had rumbled. He'd bowed mockingly. "*Milord.*"

The iron door had slammed shut before Evan could reach it. On that first, awful day, he'd pounded his fists on the door relentlessly. Hands sore and trembling, his knuckles raw, Evan eventually succumbed to his straw matte. How he wept when he looked and saw the markings on the wall. Markings made by fingernails. His younger self's fingernails.

There was no word the next day. Nothing about Rathos or Karl, not even any questions related to the king. For a while, he held out hope that Hexar had survived after all. Then he heard the Great Temple's twelve bells pealing, and his world folded in on him.

Tears ran like a river undammed. Sarah's husband was dead. But Evan didn't weep for himself or the king.

He wept for the cause he'd once again failed. He wept bitterly for his own blindness. *Once more, sister, I've led my loved ones into hell with me . . . for a cause this kingdom will never see as critical to its own survival.*

Two days went by with scarcely any food and only a jug that stank of urine. On the second day, during a lull in the bells, he heard shrieks carry down the hall. The voices belonged to Commoners, by the telltale sounds of their accents. A guard's low baritone resonated through the wall. Then came pleas and wailing. Begging. A girl shouted for someone named Caleb, the poor soul.

Do not weep, child, Evan wanted to tell her. *Tears will not avail you in a kingdom of wolves . . .*

Day and night, he saw their faces float before him, the faces of the Worthy Assembly. Jon Redoak, Sam Gramlore, Peshar Grathos, Justen Sothos, and—above all—Pinkhands. They were the wolves who preyed on the people and gorged themselves on misery.

Evan hated himself. He hated himself for failing to see things as they were. For years, he'd tried to convince wolves that a seat for Commoners in their Assembly would benefit them. The king had refused to seat the Wing of the Commons. Now the wolves had eaten their alpha, and Evan, Rathos, and another Companyman stood accused of regicide.

Never again, if I somehow make it out of here alive, he thought bitterly, ragefully. *Never. Never. Never . . .*

On his third day, he sat, delirious, his arms on his knees, his face in his arms. Despair felt like worn clothes, as palpable and uncomfortable as his oily skin and unwashed beard.

When Evan slept, for however long he could, memories came to him dressed as dreams.

A younger Evan weathered his father's disapproval. August Sinclair sat behind his desk, signing and stamping scrolls. He had Evan's flaxen hair, a healthy weight he lost toward the end of his life.

"You'll see to King Crook, I expect, Evan," the lord told his son as he worked. "Once a thief, always a thief. *Remember that.*"

The mists swept over his father even as Evan reached out to touch him.

"You know he hates that name," Sarah admonished him.

You're alive, Evan thought desperately as the mists rolled back. *God and gods, you're alive . . . and still yourself.*

"King Crook is what I'll call him if he fucks this up," a younger, leaner Evan told his sister, pacing back and forth. "He'll have stolen the greatest hope we've had in centuries to seat peasants in the Assembly again. It's not very often that a king decides to divorce his wife. This is our chance! You can persuade Hexar, but only if—" He stopped suddenly, annoyed that her attention was elsewhere. "*Sarah.*"

Seated at the table, Sarah Sinclair lowered the book she held in her hands. Sunlight streamed through a crenel behind her, catching in the raven-black hair that pooled about her shoulders. She regarded him with clear blue eyes that could wed kings to unpopular causes.

"He'll understand," Sarah told him. Wetness softened the edge in her voice.

But do you understand, sister? Evan remembered thinking.

She vanished in the mist. When it dispersed, he saw his sister again, devilishly beautiful for her first official meeting with the king. She sashayed out of the carriage in a frost-blue gown that accentuated the curves of her lithe, youthful body. Evan had encouraged her to wear that one. Hexar liked blue.

"Ask him to play his harp," Evan told her as they treaded into the Silver Walls's gatehouse. "Hexar lives for adoration."

The dreams continued. By the third night, he didn't relive his moments with his father or Sarah. Instead, Evan dreamed he fought with King Crook himself. Their friend. *His* friend.

Matthus looked lean as a wolf in his jet-black woolen vest. He wore his ring, a wreath of leaves inlaid with ruby. Crimson blood glistened in its silver leaves.

"You made a devil's bargain," the knight said as he shook his head. "You risked her life. Our lives. What has it earned us?"

As he'd done then, Evan wiped his mouth and surged back up. But unlike then, when he boasted the lies of a wounded ego, he admitted, "I made an error. Get Sarah out. *Now!*"

That's what he wanted to say, anyway. But the words clung to his palate like dough hot out of the oven and scalded just the same.

The mists shrouded everything. "Black all over like overdone pork," he heard Gram Sothos mutter outside the throne room.

Evan felt the softness of a carriage's cushions against his skin, felt himself pitch about amid sounds of hooves. To his left Sarah sat with Matthus, the curve of her belly pronounced against sunlight filtering in through their window. She sopped up the comfort of the arm around her shoulders like a sponge. She was tired. They were all tired.

No, Evan thought, panicking as his hand pushed open the door. But he was too late. He was always too late . . .

When Evan flung open his door, he tumbled out. He fell flailing, head over heels, tumbling through stacks of smoke, through a sky ablaze. The world was a disc, not the marble considered by sages of the Awakening . . . and he'd shatter like glass on its surface. He fell toward Loran. No, toward a city of light and shadow. No, toward a gleaming castle . . .

Something caught him suddenly, stopping his freefall into the fires. He swung to and fro like a clock's pendulum. *No,* Evan thought. A giant pinched him by his ankles like a treat, and that was what he was—a treat—as he was dipped into a cavernous mouth. The creature's tongue slipped about his lips hungrily, and in the dark of his throat hovered his sister's face, white-eyed and screaming.

"NO!"

At the sound of his own voice, Evan sprang awake, drenched in sweat. His heart palpitations came so fast he thought he'd vomit. Afternoon light spilled into his cell.

And he remembered the nightmare was real.

The king was dead. He was here, once more a prisoner of the Red Tower. *Where are your children, Matthus?* he thought, anguished by worry and guilt. *Are they safe?*

Sandaled feet padded swiftly by his iron door. He listened to the exchange of voices. A key jiggled in the lock, and the door flew open, and was softly shut.

The young man with his mother's looks had a foul odor. The terrible smell contrasted with his gracefulness, his tussled black hair, flecks of whiskers, and clear blue eyes. Gone were his mirthful banquet colors. He mourned in a gray doublet, dark gray cape, and soiled black boots that smelled of foulness.

A sword hilt protruded from his nephew's scabbard.

"Uncle." Jason Warchild glanced down at the plate with a heel of crusty bread on it. "You haven't eaten."

Evan watched him warily. He vaguely remembered his pudgy thumb curling about his. "My lord," he said, trying to find his voice. "I am . . . grief-stricken over the king's death."

Jason watched him with something less than love in his eyes. "Are you?" He circled the chamber, eyes fixed on Evan. "Has Charles told you why you're here?"

"Apparently, I killed the king."

His nephew shot him a hot-tempered look. It reminded him of Hexar. "You couldn't pick a worse time to be glib, Lord Evan. My father, the king, is dead. The steward and I hold all the Assemblymen captive."

No better decision has ever been made. "As you should."

"As we hold you and your men captive," Jason snapped. "My would-be assassin—the man you serendipitously knew where to find on the day of your arrival—says my uncle is the kingkiller."

Three days of grief, of nightmares, cost Evan composure. "I saved your life on the Kingsway," he muttered.

"I'd like to know why. We've never met before. You have every reason to revile my father."

"Wrong on both counts." Evan rose weakly. "My hands brought

you into this world. And I didn't hate the king. His grace alone protected me from the Assembly, from Burke, for years."

Jason watched him with Sarah's blue eyes. "So I've heard." He stepped closer. "But you know me not. You, I know only as the man my father blamed for my mother's death, as the leader of a band of traitors that provisions its own army. You want to seat the Wing of the Commons, the chamber that killed *another* king two centuries ago."

"If you believed me guilty in this, why meet me?" Evan parted his wrists, as if clinking manacles should've kept them together. "I'm a traitor unchained. You're alone with me."

Jason grazed the pommel of his sword with a hand. A warning.

"Let us see this through the lens of reason," Evan began fresh. "Your father's protection has kept me alive. Why would I kill him?"

"For revenge," Jason offered. "For imprisoning you. As I have."

Evan shook his head, feeling the bangs of his hair dance across his forehead. "We'd forgiven each other. Your father pardoned me at the feast." He took a step forward, watching his nephew's reaction. "I took you aside to protect you while the Assemblymen rushed the dais. But who else was there?" he prodded gently. "Who else had cause to kill the king—and on Remembrance Day, of all days—if not the men he fought for your mother's hand?"

His nephew thawed enough for Evan to see him through the ice. "I've loved you from afar, Jason. This 'army' you speak of, they are my eyes and ears. And they have told me that you are a man of reason. A man of peace. There's a shortage of that in Loran."

"Then you've heard wrong, uncle. I went to war for a fool cause. Is that reason?" He pointed at the window, as if his reach were long and he could collar a killer. "I am no man of reason or peace now. Someone is laying waste to my house . . . to the people I love. He'll climb our bones to reach the Silver Throne."

Evan ventured closer, hands outstretched. "Then let me help you, nephew."

Jason retreated, wary-eyed, the heel of his hand glancing his pommel. "Answer me this first: did you play a part in killing my father, the king?"

"None," Evan answered without hesitation.

"Swear it on my mother—your sister."

Evan humbled himself on a knee. "I swear it on my sister, the Lady Sarah, whom I miss more than you'll ever know."

Jason watched him for a long moment, unspeaking. He kicked the plate aside with a clatter. "This is a foul place, my lord. Would you like to leave?" He turned and squeaked the door open invitingly.

Evan stood. He regimented his feet, walking slowly, so he wouldn't seem overeager. Everything in him urged him to bolt through the door, to run. He stopped at the threshold.

"Lord Jason, you gaoled my two companions," he said softly. "Can you assure me of their safety?" *Rathos. Tell me Rathos is safe.*

"They're quite safe, though they also share your dislike of dungeon food. I promise, no harm will come to them."

Evan left his cell, and he dared not look back.

The Red Tower hall outside was sumptuously decorated. Orbs of torchlight floated like fireflies in the hall below. Coming to an ivory balustrade, they climbed a ring of marbled stairs.

Evan grew fearful when Jason led him in the Dread Chamber's direction. *Does your son torture me with hope, Sarah?* He had his answer, and relief, when they passed by the spike-studded iron door. A cold sweat moistened his skin.

After ascending another flight of stairs, they came to a thick ceiling door, which Jason opened. Evan followed him through, to wind and blinding sunlight.

We're on the roof. Evan scanned the sky, overwhelmed by the pulsing radiance of pearl light that veiled the sky. Crowned with minarets, the Red Tower's roof was as spacious as thirty cell chambers set side by side. Farther out, the Shimmering Bay glimmered under silverstone light and the afternoon sun like some beautiful broken mirror, cracked with golden, silver, and sapphire shards.

Jason's cape snapped in the wind. "Now that we are truly alone, let me apologize," he said over the bluster. "I know you didn't kill my father, uncle. You saved me on Kingsway and at the feast. I owed you a debt. *Still* owe you."

"And you sent my companions and me to the Red Tower for our protection," Evan said with sudden clarity. He viewed the sky above from a place of nightmares, remembering the giant that had tried to swallow him. He shook off a memory of Sarah's face in the giant's throat.

He smiled. "You're as wise as they say. I couldn't risk your safety inside the Walls. Assemblymen might've killed you in the confusion, as you worried they'd do to me at the feast."

He does us proud, sister. "I couldn't be more thankful. Even if I had to relish a few days in my old cell."

Jason frowned. "Your old cell? That wasn't what I wanted. I'll discuss this with Charles. Are you unharmed, truly?"

Burke, you bastard. Of course you'd do that. "Physically, yes." Evan paused to collect himself, to let it sink in that he needn't fear for Rathos or himself—at least not here. "Now how may I be of service, Lord Jason?"

"Help me seat the Fourth Wing."

Evan wondered briefly if he was still dreaming. "Forgive me, my lord—"

"You're my blood. Call me Jason."

"Tell me how to be worthy of your generosity, Jason."

"Help me defend House Eddenhold," Jason said with steel in his voice. "I know now beyond all doubt that the king's death was an act of fratricide."

The king's exiled brother. He kidnapped Erick, but would he kill Hexar? "Hexar's brother is half the world away. Why do you think it'd be him?"

Jason retrieved something from his pocket. He placed it in his uncle's hand. In his palm lay the spectacle of a singular ring, traced with the same dazzle of pearl light in the sky above.

"This was found on the surviving assassin," Jason said.

"What does a silverstone ring mean to you?"

"It's a threat." He turned his eyes east, as if he could see the one making the threat. "A threat against someone close to me. To warn me in case the assassin failed. To warn me against trying to seek my father's crown."

A damn wedding band, Evan realized with a start. "Lest your wife suffer?" he asked.

A half-lidded look was all Evan needed to understand that he'd overstepped. "I married a foreign noblewoman while at war," Jason told him.

And how did you procure silverstone from so far away? "Is she safe?"

Jason ran a hand through his raven hair, flustered. "I can't say. Shaddon Eddenhold is in Medecia, which the Rose Guild calls home. It all fits. You were the wrong uncle for Hexar to accuse of treason."

Evan handed him the ring. "Shaddon resented the king almost as much as he does me. He never forgave his brother for beheading your sister's mother, Alyse Jannus." He watched him skeptically. *I think you're lying to me, nephew.* "If it is Shaddon, he didn't act alone, you realize."

Jason grimaced. "Gram Sothos." A poisonous smile curled his lips. "His son is already here, in a cell of his own. Gram will join his son soon enough."

Evan swelled with a grim satisfaction that comes from justice long overdue, justice finally done. He'd heard someone crying and cursing his captors on the second day, and he hadn't trusted to hope that it'd been Justen Sothos.

Jason watched him intently. "I thought you'd rejoice."

"I do rejoice, in my own way," Evan said. "Gram murdered your mother, along with my knight. But there was a reason why Hexar hesitated to deal with him. Gram is the wealthiest lord in the land. A priestking protects him. To strike off his head would be satisfying . . . for you, for me, for your sister. But it'd start a war. Loran is but one of thirteen realms, and seven others follow the priestking's orders like unquestioning little soldiers."

"Who said we'll strike off Lordsbane's head?" Jason asked with more cavalierness than he should've had on this subject. "Let Sothos rot, kingkiller that he is. And while the lion wallows in his cage, we'll unite this kingdom against the foreign powers that protect him. The lords, the clergy, the merchants . . . and the peasants." He curled four fingers together, as if each one were a class, and made a fist.

Evan read between the lines. He knew without needing to hear it. Even tired, thirsty, and hungry, he understood why Jason wished to speak with him alone on a windy rooftop. "You mean to enter the Kingstrials." Jason confirmed his suspicions with a look. "You'd seat yourself on the Silver Throne, and then the Wing of the Commons in its Assembly."

Jason smirked with mild embarrassment. "Am I *that* easy to read?"

Evan shrugged. "If what Lorana said is true, the crown prince is gone. You're officially a bastard, but the laws against you aren't impossible to override. You'd need a reputable lord to champion you. And I'm not him."

"No, you're not," Jason said without malice. "But it may take more than a champion to make me king through Willard's games."

"'Three Trials, three Wings,'" Evan said softly, almost ruefully. *You would not want this . . . I know you wouldn't . . .*

"My father became king by winning all three of his Trials."

"Which has happened only three times in thousands of years."

"I think I can follow in his footsteps," Jason said with a young man's confidence. "But if I fall short—if I win one or two contests, and the outcome is disputed—I'll need Assemblymen to crown me directly. That's how the Kingstrials work. Do they not?"

It all fell into place before he finished speaking. Evan felt his bearded chin. "And you believe the Assemblymen in my Company could tip the balance in your favor." Laughter came unprompted, bone-weary laughter he felt from his head to his feet.

Jason tightened the line of his lips. "I'm serious, uncle."

"And so am I when I tell you it's folly," Evan returned. "Listen to me. My Company is made up of two factions. One believes in making petitions to seat the Wing of the Commons. The other faction thinks only a war will bring justice to this country. A war on greedy lords and servile priests, and all those who prefer that Commoners stay a stool for their feet."

"Are you not a man of peace?"

Am I, still? the nobleman wondered. "Loran is a kingdom of wolves, Jason," he said tiredly. "I've tried the peaceful way for all your life. I approached the king seeking that peace. He pardoned me—and the wolves killed him the same night."

A hoarse wind blustered across the Red Tower's rooftop. "Then tell me the way," Jason demanded in an iron-hard voice that startled. He sounded just like him. "It can't be war. I've had enough of it, uncle. I've seen things I still see in my nightmares. With my waking eyes. My men, burning like torches. My half-brother's body, reeking of death. I think Garrett himself went mad from war. *I don't want that madness here.* Not again. Not by the hand of the man called Warchild."

I can relate to your trauma, nephew, Evan pondered.

Jason jabbed a finger at the rooftop, pointing at earth. "I won't drag this kingdom through a war. But we need this realm whole so that we can defend ourselves if other kingdoms bring war to us. What better way to unite the realm than by seating all its people in their Worthy Assembly? What other way can we prevent Shaddon from climbing the Silver Throne?"

Evan wanted to say yes. Nothing more could please him. The offer was even presented like a birthday gift, with Jason the gift box and the Wing of the Commons inside. And the idea of his nephew as king was something he'd envisioned even at his birth . . .

Yet no one rose to the Loyal Company's speakership on the steps of favors. Rezlan had once likened Evan to a cat, too agile, too cunning to be caught unawares. He summoned those instincts now, evaluating his nephew carefully.

"I'd give my life for you, a thousand times over," Evan said. "I loved you from the moment I saw you, boy. I hate that we've been kept apart."

A knowing smile crept into his nephew's face. "But."

"But would-be kings die in the Trials. That is their purpose. Willard invented them to contain the blood of thirty succession wars, and contain them he did—to the Colossus, where the Assembly meets and applauds as ambitious lords die like flies. Your mother would not have you in that viper's pit, and your father—"

"My father didn't want to die from poisoned wine, either, but he did," Jason interjected. "From what I've heard, my mother was as passionate as you are for the Common cause. Would she not look down on us with pride, as I ascend my father's throne, as we finally return peasants to their Assembly after two centuries gone?"

If you ascend the throne, Evan nearly said. *If they don't kill you first, as they've already tried to do.*

He sighed lightly through his nostrils. Hands on his hips, he turned to look at the Shimmering Bay. A lone ship set off from the harbor, and he could see its small crew scrambling to unfurl the sails. Much closer, on Harbor Way and Fish Street, peasants pushed carts full of fish and onions. Children near them played in the mud. Far above, on the edge of night, there twinkled a lone star, as lonely as the sigil of House Sinclair.

Evan looked him up and down. "You'll need to dress with more dignity if you mean to be king," he said.

Jason smiled his father's smile, unmistakably.

They embraced. Even with the king dead, even ahead of a debate with the Loyal Company, and then the Kingstrials, Evan soaked in the moment, cherishing it. A long road snaked ahead of them, but for the first time in a long time, he felt . . .

Hopeful. Yes, hopeful. For himself. For his house. For a realm of people crying out for a good king and a voice in their own rule.

Evan heard him then, vividly, as if he were still dreaming. "You made a devil's bargain," his knight said gravely.

CHAPTER 20

Conspiracy

hat the Silver Walls lacked in silverstone, it was said, the castle more than made up for in rooms. More than three thousand chambers on the castle grounds tested the limits of royal imagination, furnishing space thrice over for grand halls, galleries, apartments, garderobes, kitchens, armories, larders, guardrooms, and—when a king allowed it—chapels.

Lorana meditated on this surfeit as she trudged up the West Tower's stairs, the ring of her men's armor loud in her ears. They passed doors she'd never opened—and a few she and Edenia had opened often during the prieslenne's time as Hexar's most valuable hostage.

Three thousand rooms, a number of them in this Tower, she thought, *and my father gave you one chapel, Eden. A dusty room at the top of a high tower. You stopped using it, after a time.*

And yet, as the steward and her men reached the top of the stairs, she observed that someone was using this chapel now. Voices whispered on the other side of a door edged in candlelight.

They prayed anxiously.

At Lorana's nod, Sir Connor Tomas kicked the door open. Inside Edenia's small chapel stood the High Bishop, garbed in embroidered cassock and miter, as if he were holding services for thousands. Peshar Grathos steadied himself on the altar as Lorana entered in a flourish of her gown. Incense smoked from candelabra arrayed about the stained-glass window.

So much pageantry. All for one man. The only man in the kingdom with the arrogance to remain kneeling on his velvety cushions, back turned to his steward. She regretted sending Gram Sothos to the West Tower. *No coincidence, this chamber. Men will see him as righteous as Edenia, set upon by a woman as mercurial as the king.*

Sighting the knights behind her, Peshar Grathos went as pale as his candlesticks. "Princess Lorana, your late king father, bless his soul, would choose wisdom right now," he said with a fearful expression.

"My king father is dead by poison." Lorana pointed at Gram Sothos. "There kneels his killer."

Sothos kept his back turned.

Grathos flitted to the only other woman present, his eyes widening. "*Elzura's Children mustn't enter a place of prayer!*"

Anyasha kept her dignity, immovable, hands clasped at the front.

Lorana feigned puzzlement. "Why, Anyasha is a woman, and my servant besides. She wouldn't harm you." She glanced over her shoulder. "This one I can't speak for."

Jhazar of Groth, the Inquisitor's Shadow, swept past her. He shoved the High Bishop. Grathos fell into candelabra, losing his miter amid the clatter.

Finally, Sothos moved. He cradled the High Bishop's head with a pink hand, as if he were near death. "First, my son," he rumbled. "Now you injure the Lonely Isle's envoy to Loran. As he leads prayer. *Where does this godlessness end?*"

With impeccable timing, the Grand Inquisitor appeared at her side, clutching a scroll. "The gods regard treason as a worse crime than godlessness, Lord Gram," he said gravely.

"Treason." Rising, Sothos towered over everyone. He strode toward Lorana. Connor Tomas and his knights flanked the princess, baring swords aflicker with candlelight. "Go and arrest the guilty, then!"

"*You* are guilty." Lorana stared up witheringly at her father's killer. "Lord Charles, read us a story."

The Grand Inquisitor crinkled open his parchment. "Gram Sothos, Lord of Saxhold, Lorana Eddenhold, steward of these Walls, charges you with conspiring to kill the king. You acted in league with the king's brother, who procured the poison." He folded the scroll. "The three of you conspired to destroy King Hexar's line and enthrone Shaddon Eddenhold."

An incredulous smile, a mark of impunity, passed over the nobleman's lips. "Conspiracy? What a story, indeed. Your plan is plain. You'd falsely charge my son and me, all to discredit an honorable man half a world away."

The stone maiden remained still, arching one eyebrow.

"Peasants confessed to killing King Hexar," Charles said. "Six of them confessed that your son instructed them to poison our king's wine before the feast. And that Justen got the poison from you."

"*Peasants!*" Sothos sneered. "You base these charges on the words of treasonous farmhands and swineherds."

"Just one was a swineherd, actually," Anyasha chimed.

He glared past Lorana, at her lover, and it taxed the last of the steward's resolve. Were that she could strike off his balding head . . . but that would spark a war Loran couldn't win.

"I understand your grief, Your Highness, but I fear you've lost your way," Sothos said. "Sharing counsel with Casaanites. Taking the word of a rabble that killed your father against that of a lord who fought for your mother. I thank the gods Alyse Jannus isn't here to witness her daughter's fall from grace."

"You should've stopped at the part about grief." Lorana flicked her fingers at the Inquisitor's Shadow. "Take Gram to his son. See that he has a copy of the Twelve Testaments. He'll need his gods."

The Inquisitor's Shadow nodded with grinning eyes.

It was a thing Lorana would treasure for the rest of her days, watching a Casaanite smile as he clamped manacles on Lord Sothos's scalded wrists. Out went Jhazar with his captive. Her guard followed after him, the noise of their armor echoing in the stairwell. Charles and Anyasha remained with her.

Lorana rounded on a shaking, red-cheeked Grathos. She recovered his miter and laid it upon his head, straightening it. "Keep at your prayers, Your Grace," she said as she turned to go. "Lord Gram will need them. And because a prieslenne once prayed here, one of your gods just might hear you."

On most days, the princess alternated between a handful of rooms. Tonight she retreated to her favorite, a chamber halfway up the North Tower, neither too high nor too close to the ground. Here, she felt safe. A balcony space granted her an uncontested view of the bailey outside, and a spacious tower foyer amplified the sounds of footsteps, keeping her apprised of comings and goings below.

Heat from the hearth fire beaded her with sweat as she clutched her lover's curls, thighs spasming at every delicate swirl of her tongue. She found her pleasure. Heaving, she cupped her lover's face, drew her up, and tasted their sin on her lips. She needed this distraction. This love.

Anyasha spooned her on the floor, in a puddle of their sweat. "I'd give anything to have seen you gaol Peshar," she said.

"The way he spoke to you, I wanted to." Lorana ran a hand through her hair. "But gaoling one Assembly speaker is enough provocation tonight. Parlisis will respond."

"Let him." Anyasha rolled onto her side. "By then your half-brother will be king, and the realm behind him."

I tell her too much. So it was with Edenia. She eased into a seated position, donning her chemise. "You weakened my hand by mentioning the swineherd," she said. Anyasha tensed at the rebuke. "Get dressed. Someone's in the foyer with Sir Connor."

Anyasha was on her way out, apologies in her eyes, when knuckles rapped on the door. The master-of-arms opened the door, making way for her half-brother.

Jason smiled warmly at Anyasha. "Yasha, what a beauty you've become. You were this tall"—he held his hand at his chest, measuring—"when I left for the Brace."

"You're too kind, my lord." She charmed with her smile. Lorana disregarded the jealousy coiling in her chest.

Anyasha curtsied and left. Jason secured the door behind him. In his tunic, cloak, and breeches, he lacked a future king's airs. He even looked rather Common.

"The Assemblymen cower in their apartments," Jason said as he neared, floor creaking, "fearful they'll follow Gram Sothos and his son to the Red Tower, or suffer an attack from Charles's Shadow."

Lorana let out a short, caustic laugh. "'Twas a nudge."

"You're bold, sister. By gaoling Lordsbane, you give us an opening this kingdom hasn't had in a generation." Jason held her with his gaze. "Yet we must tread carefully. If I'm to be king, I must win Trials, or votes. I'm under no illusions about Peshar's loyalties, but other Assemblymen will remember this outrage."

"Our enemies conspired against Erick, Garrett, you, and Father—and you worry about *votes?*"

Jason gave her a look. "It's the Kingstrials, Ana. Sinclair's Loyal Company will help tilt the contests for me, but we need as much support as we can get."

She steeled herself for what she had to say next. "Brother, there is no doubt in my mind that you must succeed Father, if we mean to keep the Walls. That you would make a good—no, a *great* king, better than Father. But there's no need for Trials."

Jason regarded her skeptically. She went to her desk, retrieved the writ, and laid it in his hands. "I found this in Father's chambers," she said.

He unfurled the writ. "Father named me . . . his heir?"

Forgive me, Father. "He signed it before Remembrance Day. Without Garrett and Erick, he had no choice."

Jason pinched the letter by a corner, holding it away from himself, as if it were cursed. "The Worthy wouldn't accept this," he said faintly. "Even if Father had signed it with witnesses."

No, you must believe. She wrapped her hands around his. "Don't you see? This is Father's gift. Yes, it may mean trouble with the Worthy Assembly, at first—"

"It'll mean *war* with them, Ana. A second Long Summer. Which would undoubtedly follow, now that the priestking's favorite lord is in the Red Tower."

She wouldn't give up so easily. "We could fight that war from behind the Walls. We have allies. King Grisholm would aid us. There's no need to risk your life in the Kingstrials."

He registered a knowing look. "Charles drafted this. Not Father."

Jason was likely her only brother still living, and certainly the one she loved best. Try as she might, she couldn't play him false. At least, not over this.

"No one needs to be the wiser," she said softly.

Men said the bastard prince was the last vestige of Sarah Sinclair. He had her comely face, her blue eyes and raven hair. In this moment their father percolated to the surface.

"This writ"—he held outstretched the letter, as if it had disease—"is drenched in Loranian blood. You just can't see it."

"I see something different." *I see you alive, unharmed.*

"It means war. The Commons, suffering. Men bloodying the field. Catapults raining hellfire. I've seen enough men die, Ana. And it's treason."

"Treason against whom, Jason, son of Hexar?"

He strode to the hearth. "*King Lathros lost his head,*" he recited the Common refrain, "*and tyranny evermore lay dead. Or so they surely said until the Worthy chose anew.*" He turned to her. "The king doesn't rule this kingdom alone, sister."

"But the Assembly killed Father," Lorana struck back, losing patience.

"Not the entire Assembly."

"Gram Sothos *is* the Assembly. He may sit in the Tower tonight, but I can't behead him, lest I start a war. Charles said Pinkhands aided our uncle's flight from Loran, even as he lay abed, burned. Have you forgotten that?"

A shadow passed over her brother's face. "You didn't chap your lips sucking poison from his flesh. Yours wasn't the hand that lit Erick's pyre. You don't know what burning flesh smells like. *I'll never forget our brother*. Or what Shaddon and Gram did to us when they seized him." He glossed over the forgery. "It even looks like Father's writing."

"He wanted you safe—"

"But he didn't want another Long Summer. And neither do I." Creasing the letter, Jason tossed it into the hearth. Vellum shriveled as flames folded and blackened its edges, devouring it hungrily. "You tell me I'd make a fine king, but you'd have me give proof of my surname."

"You don't understand," Lorana said, hating herself as she heard the pleading in her voice. Only Jason could make a proud griffon like her beg . . . "The Kingstrials aren't all spectacle and glory."

"Hexar won his, and the crowds cheered. Father won his crown *honorably*. Without a succession war."

"But that was Father. Should I share with you what I've been reading of late?" Lorana hastened to her bookshelf and yanked out Zur's tome. "This is a history of the Kingstrials. A history neither Father nor Drexan could erase, no matter how many pages they tore out and burned."

Lorana couched the massive, unyielding spine in her arm so she could flip to a page. "Ah, here. Seventy-nine lords killed each other, and not a single one of them became king. Instead, the Worthy chose someone else not in the Kingstrials, because there *was* no one else. It was mocked as the Kingless Trials."

"That was a thousand years ago—"

"And more recently," she said, turning to another bent page, "Jeffrey the Gentle won the First Trial but was crisped black during the Second, a dragon-slaying contest. His rivals had broken the dragon's muzzle after a lord like Sothos agreed to pay them their worth in gold and grant them chancellorships on the king's council."

There were countless stories in which men of high birth, claimants like the Warchild, had died violently, usually after a wealthier rival had bribed other lords with treasure, promises of land, or the hands of their daughters. On some occasions a man was so reviled that no payment was needed, and his wife and men-at-arms simply discovered his corpse on the day of the First Trial. Other times, a claimant never even reached the Colossus in Northland but perished in an ambush on the road.

This was the ruthless bloodsport that Willard the Wise had hailed as a cure for the affliction of succession wars—the cure other kingdoms mocked. She read that Gram Reuben had once derided Loran's Kingstrials as a moot that chose a king by killing everyone else. She had to agree.

Lorana closed the book and set it down. "The Kingstrials are three circles of hell. Sabotage. Savagery. Death."

Jason watched the fire, stone-faced. "You forget the great kings who came from lower houses. Carl the Clever, Jacen the Bearslayer, Simon the Pure. Father. They called him Hexar the Bold after he crowned Garrett's mother the Virgin of Venas with tourney laurels. Harriet, whose father had wanted him dead, and then gave his daughter to Hexar in marriage."

"And gave us Garrett," she added, knowing she didn't need to elaborate. A sudden understanding washed over her like cold water. "Jason . . . are you doing this for Eden?"

He stared at her as if she'd just read his mind. "How do you mean?" He feigned confusion, but she knew him too well.

Of course she knew about his moonlight marriage to the priest-king's daughter. Edenia herself had shared it with her.

Jason shifted with discomfort. "Did Lord Charles tell you?"

"*She* did. After you sailed to the Brace."

He smiled halfheartedly. "I suppose congratulations are two years too late."

Lorana wanted to hit him, the lovestruck fool. "You realize that Parlisis could've sent that assassin to kill you over your marriage to his only daughter?"

"Edenia would never tell him."

"It's been two years since we last saw her. She's never responded to our letters, Jason. How would you know?"

"Because I queried the only surviving assassin myself." He made a fist. "The man admitted to Shaddon's own involvement, Ana. Shaddon paid the Rose Guild to send two assassins for me. He did it so that he could seize the Silver Throne for himself."

She clutched at her arms, suddenly vulnerable, feeling like a fawn that finds itself alone in some vast quiet clearing. The plot to destroy her house seemed to widen every day. If the famous assassin's guild had men in this, none of them was safe. *The Body Is Proof,* went the Guild's ominous motto. Read one way, it referred to the god Sacreis's declaration that life was a miracle and proof of the gods' existence. Read another way: No corpse, no gold. And the Rose Guild so loved its gold.

Lorana took his hands. "Jason, you *must* let Charles draft another writ," she insisted. "We can defend ourselves here, you, me, Heather. *Please do not endanger yourself just so you can be king and have Edenia as your consort.* It's a fool's quest, and you'd incite a revolt trying to complete it."

He watched the crackling fire. "You really think this is about her? About my wife?" Firelight glinted in his blue eyes. "Twenty-six, Lorana."

She made a face, uncomprehending.

"I've killed twenty-six men." Jason flexed his fingers, examining his hand, as if he saw splotches of blood. "Twenty-six. Including the Rose Guild's man I slew. I can't say how many I felled with bow and arrow in the Brace. I . . . I hate it."

"Of *course* you do. You're not Garrett. *You* should be king."

"But Father signed away my rights. The Warchild name has been my burden to bear my entire life." He gazed at her. "I won't prove the Assembly right about me, sister. The Warchild will not be known for causing two wars in his lifetime."

"But you'll risk your life all the same?" Lorana demanded.

"And spare this kingdom enormous suffering."

She heard her father when she spoke. "Such an *honorable* fool you are. And if you fall, as thousands have before you?"

"I won't." Straightening, Jason seemed the king he already wanted to be, regal and handsome, lacking only a crown. "I'll have sage counsel. Sinclair has vowed to see me through."

"Aye, and your alliance with him complicates everything."

"He promises to deliver the Loyal Company for me. Three Trials, three Wings . . . but if I can't win all three, the Assembly will have to vote. With his Company, they'd vote for me."

"You'd seat Commoners in the Assembly again, after six of them killed Father? They kill our king, and you'd reward them with power?"

Jason shook his head. "Father's killers don't represent the peasants at large. They're Elvarenists who followed Sothos and his son's orders. They're the exception, not the rule. If we seat peasants in the Assembly, we'll seat Free Believers. They'd be loyal to us, Ana—*loyal to Loran*—as so few Worthy men are."

He grimaced. "Besides, my uncle is right. These peasants have been set upon by wolves for two centuries too long. They need their voice in the Assembly again. And when they have it, they'll stand with us against the priestking and his followers."

The words she heard were her half-brother's, and yet not. Charles Burke had always called Sarah Sinclair's brother slick as an eel, with a tongue even slicker. Lorana saw that tongue flicking in her half-brother's mouth. "And you trust Evan the Traitor?" *The man whose ambitions led to Mother's beheading.*

"He saved my life on Kingsway."

There is that. "He also endangers you. Drexan persuaded Father to pardon him and protect him from the Assembly. With Father gone, so is the king's protection. If you ally yourself with Sinclair, you'll be with him when the swords come."

"The swords already *came*. I *need* Evan and his men in the Assembly. As much as I need you to remain here, Ana, until it is time for you to come north. You'll stay on as steward."

Lorana folded her arms. "Oh, I will?"

Jason smiled. "You enjoy ruling. You know you do."

"I do," she admitted. "And I'll move heaven and earth for you. But power has its limits, Jason."

"*You* don't." Jason kissed her brow. "Call the Trials, sister. Summon the Assembly to the Colossus in the Golden Meadows. Move heaven and earth for our house. For our kingdom. For me."

He uncurled his fingers over her palm, and out fell Eden's silverstone ring, aswirl in pearl light. "Her wedding ring. Keep it. I want you to look at it anytime you question my motives."

If only you knew, Lorana thought, ashamed.

Jason started toward the door. Before he could twist the latch, she said, "Fine, then. Be an honorable fool, but heed me. Raelin the Red entered the Trials with a champion. You'll need a friend with a reputation beyond reproach . . . a man with an army that will protect you at the Golden Meadows."

Her half-brother lost his smile when she told him whose friendship she had in mind.

CHAPTER 21

Penance

Hexar Eddenhold's last march began in the lower bailey.

The Great Gates groaned open, and out trudged a regal procession under quivering fingers of silverstone light. From a place in the rear, Zur struggled for a glimpse of His Majesty's heraldic achievements, all bobbing in a sea of crimson banners.

As the king's only legitimate children, Lorana and Heather led the funeral procession alongside an escort of mounted men. On their heels trotted a horse-drawn bier with the king inside. Hundreds of castle servants walked behind the bier. Men of the Wings of Lords and Clergy flanked the servants, arms crossed over their chests. *Does the Assembly grieve for their poisoned king,* he wondered, *or for the humiliation of Gram Sothos, Red Tower resident?*

Zur and the rest of Elzura's Children marched behind the Assemblymen. At half an arm's length from each other, the southern hostages carried themselves down Kingsway with dignity, despite what lay ahead of them. As penance for their ancestor's role in sundering the line of kings, for plunging the world into chaos, they wore wool robes dyed the darkest black.

He spied Jason on the edges of the crowd. His wool made the heat intolerable, but Zur felt worse for the bastard prince. Subjects of all ranks saw bastards as dishonest creatures, and many Assemblymen walking with them had denied Jason his father's surname. That denied him a place of honor with his sisters. *They made him a bastard, and they wonder why he may be spiteful,* Zur thought.

Zur's two nearest companions were less solemn. Musa and Saan, twin brothers from Tribe Maabia, picked incessantly at their robes and complained in their rolling dialects. From what little he knew of their language, he understood the boys were not looking forward to kneeling in the street. Who did?

He did his best to emulate Jason, noble in his velvety blue doublet and silver-lined gray cape. This was his first, hopefully his only funeral for a king. He wanted to do right by what was, in truth, his real family.

Their procession wended over the lowered drawbridge and east on the Kingsway's cobbles. Behind them, the castle loomed like a red mountain capped with twinkling snow. The city guard lined the streets, hemming in countless Commoners with the points of their spears. Zur tensed at the unfriendly gazes of soot-faced men, women, and children.

Broken lines and thirteen crowns, he thought, *but at least we didn't kill Hexar. That was the doing of House Sothos and a priestking.*

And yet the priestking's representatives still had a place of honor here today. Ghostly caretakers awaited them at the first intersection, covered head to toe in linen shrouds dyed blue as clear sky. Mesh screens concealed their eyes.

The Daughters of Divna, Zuran knew, shuddering. These were women who had forsaken house and husband for lives of chastity and piety . . . and who didn't feel bothered by veils that made them look like cerulean specters.

Today, the Daughters of Divna would escort the dead king to the Sons of Sacreis, who'd in turn accompany his bier to the Free Parish of God. This was Lorana's olive branch to hardcore Elvarenists who denied involvement by their faith in the king's death and lobbied hard for a funeral at the Great Temple. The royal family would never have consented to a pyre burning for the king who'd fought a war with the Army of the Gods. For the sake of a *pro forma* unity, to quiet rumors of war, Lorana had permitted the Sons and Daughters to accompany the slain king.

Peshar Grathos strode forward from the crowd.

"Into your hands we commend a king," the High Bishop addressed the gathered Daughters. "Are the skies fair?"

"They are most fair," a Daughter answered, muffled but audible, "and the elves await his coming."

A Common man shoved past the city guard. "*Boyfucker!*" he cried at Grathos, startling him. "*Give us back our children, pederast!*"

Two city guardsmen snatched the Commoner and made a paste of him with the flats of their swords. Eager to move on, the High Bishop said, "The Head speaks," to scattered replies of "The Hands serve."

Knights circled Lorana and Grathos protectively as the procession forged on, with the Daughters of Divna out front, wailing as intensely as if Hexar had been *their* father. Gazing about, Zur had trouble finding anyone else showing the same grief. Ever the stone maiden, Lorana kept her cheeks dry. The bastard prince had eyes cold as iron.

Who loved you, Hexar? Zur thought. Only Heather bawled as inconsolably as the women in cerulean sheets.

Veering right, the procession made it up the Street of Kings. Here, white marble statues stood tall and proud on plinths, beckoning the meek to renown.

On a rearing horse sat Rorin Romaris, the conqueror who built the Colossus and gave all four classes seats in his Worthy Assembly. Jacen Bearslayer arced his sword above his head, as if a beast charged him. Beside Jacen was Willard the Wise, half-hidden in the swirls of his cloak, a scroll clutched in one hand. The Assemblyman was the only Commoner on the Street of Kings, so honored because he'd pioneered the Kingstrials.

They were men who inspired Zur. In his daydreams he liked to imagine himself a knight sworn to a king. But it was a silly fantasy. Ansaran knights were like their kings, pale of skin, their hair wavy or straight. Save maybe for when Eduard ruled Loran, no one with his accursed bloodline had history here.

And we love her children not, he thought bitterly. Zur had searched god's twelve faces for answers about his life. He'd always felt incomplete, like a puzzleboard in want of a single missing piece. He was perpetually on the outside looking in. It was no way to live.

Hexar's death promised only more uncertainty. If Jason couldn't enter the Kingstrials, someone else would. He feared some zealot like Shaddon ruling over him and his people. The king's brother had a terrible reputation. He was said to order the hands of unruly Casaanites stricken off. *God and gods,* he thought, *please don't let Shaddon succeed his brother. I'm rather fond of my hands.*

Up ahead, the Daughters of Divna met the Sons of Sacreis, men with shaven heads, bare chests and feet, and silken cream-colored trousers. Hands in the air, the Daughters wilted to their knees, begging forgiveness for their gender's crimes. When the Sons finished forgiving all women, the entire procession parted to clear a path that led straight to Zur and his countrymen.

Suddenly it was their turn.

This was the last stop before the Free Parish of God. Elzura's Children had to make a public display of contrition. It was a tradition every Casaanite was said to know everywhere in the thirteen kingdoms.

As the eldest, Namoni emerged to lead their kinsmen to the Sons of Sacreis. Zur followed with many of the other boys he knew, including Musa and Saan. Anyasha came on their heels with the women and girls. Passing by the king's bier, he caught a lingering look from Drexan.

Namoni knelt, and they followed suit, forming a sea of black cloth before the baldheaded monks.

This time, the High Bishop took his place with the Sons. Grathos checked for any Commoners before settling his eyes on Namoni.

"A king has fallen," he said. "Although we mourn for King Hexar, *ahem,* greater still is our misery that we must search at all for his successor. In their wisdom, the twelve sent us Anjan Half-Elf, the only one among us fit to rule. From the House of Anjan came three hundred kings. Each of their long lives lasted for six of our own, and their reigns gave us a long peace."

Broken lines and thirteen crowns, Zur thought.

"But it was Elzura the Witch who broke that line when she crossed from Casaan into Ansara. Bewitched by Elzura, King Eduard had his sister-wife and half-elven children slain, and his noble line ended.

Without their rightful monarch, men fell into disarray. Ansara, until then a single kingdom, became thirteen kingdoms." Grathos stared at Lorana. "For without our One True King to unite us, we are like beasts in the field, eating each other. The wicked set upon the godly."

The princess curled her lip with disdain.

"And who bears the shame of Elzura's sin?"

Elvarenists around them said, as one, "*Elzura's Children.*"

Grathos had a righteous air. "Once, all of Loran joined in condemning Elzura's corrupt remnant every year on Penance Day. Then we had a Long Summer, and Penance Day was made Remembrance Day, in honor of the brave fallen. How tragic—and ironic—that we should lose our king on the same day the whole world lost the half-elven bloodline."

Zur looked away to avoid the High Bishop's passing gaze. "Do you confess Elzura's sins against us all, sins you and yours will justly bear until Anjan's last heir returns to save us?"

Namoni rose to speak on their behalf. "We do confess."

Shrill cries went up from the Daughters, spooking the horses. Knights patted their steeds reassuringly.

The High Bishop shook his head. "The Daughters deny you, the Sons deny you, *all of Odma* denies you. Your blood makes you a wicked, wretched, and evil people."

"Enough, Peshar," Lorana cried out, but the High Bishop's voice trampled over hers.

"On the Lonely Isle, the faithful observe Penance Day by rebuking the Children," Grathos said. "Well, let all faithful men rebuke you now." And he spat on Namoni.

Zur saw men working their jaws. Before anyone could move, spray exploded left and right. Spit showered anyone on the fringe first. Nearby, Anyasha squirmed as spittle reached their column. Spittle needled his eyes. Hostages were crying.

He didn't know how, but he knew the rock was coming. Before it even left the priest's hand, he saw—no, *felt* it. He felt the numb ache in his skull half a second later, smelled the iron of blood on his lips. And he ducked. He watched in slow motion as the rock sailed through the Zur no longer there and struck Saan on his temple. Musa rushed to his brother's side.

"In the name of the priestking, *do you confess?*" Grathos demanded again.

In whimpering starts and fits, Elzura's Children, humiliated, shouted, "*We confess! We confess!*"

Lorana flew to Grathos, growling something to him lost on the crowd. The High Bishop returned her stare witheringly.

Their penance ceased. Culprits receded to the safety of the crowd as Elzura's Children gathered themselves up.

"In Loran, we honor Remembrance Day," she snarled for all to hear. "Now move so we can bury my father, or you can share a cell with the Lord of Saxhold."

Hundreds of mourners circled the Casaanites, tramping in the direction of the Free Parish of God. Master Reader Jacob Sulley marched past Grathos, muttered something angrily, and, with Tomas Fawkes at his side, led the Assembly's gray-robed readers on.

Not everyone left the Casaanites in their grief. Dropping to his knees, Jason toweled Zur's face with his silver-trimmed cape. "Elvarenists are savages," he said with contempt.

"Anyasha, my lord," Zur told Jason. "Help her."

Nodding, he unhooked his cape and began mopping up the girl, and she fell into his arms, crying. Following Jason's example, many castle servants stayed behind with leave from Lorana. Zur joined in, ignoring his own wetness as he dried the other Casaanites with whatever part of his garment was dry.

After a few minutes, his people stood, trying for scraps of their dignity. Some forged ahead in small pairs in a halfhearted bid to catch up to the procession. A daring few muttered aloud about how Hexar wouldn't have allowed that to happen were he alive.

Stiffly, Zur strode behind Jason, Anyasha, and Namoni. Saan used his brother for a crutch, limping ahead. Zur felt his hairs stick up as he suppressed the memory of a pain in his temples that had never happened. He pushed the false memory out of his mind. *That didn't happen,* he thought. *None of it did.*

No one spoke as they passed by a statue of the First King on his battle griffon. Drexan lurked in the shadow of the beast's huge marble wings. The advisor urged on Jason and the others, complaining of bad knees as he listed on his staff.

When they were alone, the chancellor straightened. "A foul religion, Elvarenism," he said through his teeth. "Princess Lorana gaoled Sothos and his son, but they're just the peak of a mountain. The priestking and his Assemblymen will never stop until this kingdom is theirs again, and everyone else a stool for their feet." He cupped a hand behind his head affectionately. "Are you hurt, Zuran?"

Zur gazed past him, at the statue of the First King, at the loose locks of hair the holy books said had shined like gold in life. "I am Elzura's Child," he replied wearily.

Drexan had a sad, pensive look. "You're much more than that, Zuran."

CHAPTER 22

Elf's Grove

s Willard Rittman liked to remind Sara and her mother, it was he who had secured their release from the Red Tower, and not Lord Uthron.

A week had passed in their chamber since Caleb Bard's disappearance. And then it was over. Their gaoler opened their door, and out they went with the Lord Warden of Rosbury, who carried Sara in his arms, under a toothy portcullis, through a grassy bailey, all the way to Traitor's Gate, to freedom. Daylight had never seemed so blinding. She had asked about Caleb, only to draw a rebuke from her mother. She was too weak to react, too overwhelmed by what was happening.

On any other day, the sight of Willard Rittman would've drawn a fuss from her. Clad in a handsome indigo doublet and cape, he sat atop a mule-drawn wagon with two other men.

Once they had climbed up, the justice saw to them like a mother hen, making sure Sara and her mother had their share of his waterskin. One of his deputies, Sweet Tom, unwrapped a loaf of bread. Sara stuffed herself with dough and devoured a crisp red apple that Geffrey retrieved for her. Nothing had ever tasted so sweet . . . or bittersweet.

Sleep fell over her like a heavy blanket. She was still groggy when a bounce of the wagon shook her awake sometime later. Poking her head over the side, she glimpsed only the blur of spotted tree trunks and a mud-slathered road flowing beneath the wagon. In a corner of the bed across from hers, Sweet Tom worked at a piece of wood with his knife, shaping it into a little merwoman. Geffrey occupied the other corner, munching on chewleaf.

Rose sat beside Rittman at the front.

Everything was dreamlike. Sunlight burst through the forest canopy, warming her face. Blue jays zipped through the spring air; others practiced their melodies. The Silver Walls, hideous from the outside and beautiful within, had long since vanished behind the trees. There was no Red Tower, no red hoods, no Commoners to huddle with in reeking darkness.

And no Caleb. Caleb is gone. My friend is gone.

Listening to Rittman converse with her mother, it was as if the farmer had never even existed. Only Sara seemed to remember that he was real.

Perched on his seat, the justice muttered to her mother in tones that rose and fell, sometimes gruffly, as if he were cross, and other times gently, with compassion. His voice carried over the sounds of hooves slurping through mud.

". . . fortunate that I have my friends," she heard him tell Rose. "What was I to do when I heard that the king had died? Leave you and her to the Grand Inquisitor's queries? No, no."

Her mother nodded stupidly, over and over, like a child scolded. Sara saw that she kneaded her hands in her lap. "So thankful," Rose kept repeating softly, always sounding as if she might erupt into tears at any second. "Twelve bless and keep you, Sir Willard, twelve bless you. I will always light a candle for you at parish, *always.*"

Twelve? Sara festered. *We're Free Believers.* Her father would've been stunned to hear her mother bless the twelve gods, instead of their god of twelve faces.

"Luckily for you and the girl"—he half-tilted his head for a fleeting look at Sara—"I'm well known at Thorn's Keep, even at the Silver Walls. The steward appreciates my gift with coin. Yes she does. The Commons have been malicious in stealing from the king's due, and the Walls need Sir Willard Rittman."

"The Hands serve," Sweet Tom chimed from where he sat cross-legged.

"The Hands serve," Rittman echoed his man with an agreeable *hmm*. "And these hands most *gladly* serve faithful Commoners like yourself, even in dark times. Was I not sheriff, after all?"

"Yes, thank you, Sir Willard, twelve bless and keep you."

The justice massaged his forked black beard. "Now, you needn't worry anymore, Rose." Sara was appalled. Only blood or a husband could call a woman by the name the priests and readers bestowed at birth.

On and on he went, condemning Caleb as a Sylvanian and an effeminate, praising the Lords Uthron and Charles for knowing the value of his word, divulging how he'd beseeched the Princess Lorana for their release. Sara wanted to roll her eyes.

"But it was not without cost, Rose, oh no," Rittman said. "Lord Charles demanded ransom as the price for giving up you and Sir Damien's daughter. Do you know how much it was?"

"Twenty gold lorens," Geffrey piped up from the rear, unbidden. He pursed his lips to hurtle a sickening bullet of pink chewleaf over the wagonside.

Her mother dabbed her eyes, sniffling. "Sir Willard, you are so generous, I thank you, I pray for you," she whimpered. "How could we ever repay you? Maybe when my husband returns . . . if he returns . . ."

The justice snapped his reins, and the mules hastened their pace. "No need. As I said, the fault was mine. I should *never* have sent you and Sara with that vile effeminate."

Sara could sit and listen to their lies no longer. The justice claimed he was to thank for their release, but the scabbed-over gashes in her legs hadn't been sore for days, and she owed that to Caleb. Just like she and her mother owed him so much else.

"Why aren't you saying his name?" she demanded. "His name is Caleb Bard."

Rittman kept his eyes fixed ahead. Sweet Tom stared at her. Geffrey plopped slivers of apple into his mouth.

Half turned in her seat, her mother transformed into the godface Helsar, eyes ablaze with fire and lips twisted in a snarl. "You are not to mention him *ever again*," she snapped. "He is a traitor—forever gone, forever dead, do you understand? Fool girl, how many times must I warn you in a day?"

Her vision blurred with tears. "But he didn't do anything wrong! You *know* he was innocent. Sean the butcher did it, tell him Mother. He hated Caleb, just like Sir Willard does, and—"

Fire lanced through half her face as her mother crushed her earlobe between two fingers. Squirming free, Sara thought briefly about leaping over the wagon, but the ground rushing beneath scared her into staying.

Her mother apologized profusely to Willard Rittman, prattled on about how grateful she was and then, gallingly, about how Sara was a spoilt girl, long in need of her father's hand.

"A child needs a father as the land needs a king," he said smugly. "That is from the First Testament, yes it is, though you Free Believers may not know it. Perhaps it would do the child good to hear from Brother Elfred at temple?"

Sara did her best to ignore them both. Across from her, Geffrey sliced an apple into halves with his dagger and tossed her one. She caught it with both her hands, turning her palms sticky.

"Wouldn't worry about that bugger anymore, girl," he said. "Odds are his head's on a spike now."

Sara chucked her piece of apple into the forest. Geffrey returned to slicing apples, smiling to himself.

Familiar fallow fields swept into view shortly before evenfall, and Sara knew Rosbury was near. Past the vine-encumbered lookout tower, over the brittle planks of Griff's Bridge, they rode into a village that did not seem to love them.

Everywhere, townsmen streamed out of their houses with half-lidded stares. Outside their cowshed, friendly Farmer Grey and his chubby wife, who usually told her hullo, stared at her as they rolled by, as if she were a Casaanite. A girl her age she sometimes played with, Lara, retreated into her dwelling at her father's insistence.

Sara spotted Connor Bagman and his companions Devan, Alford, and Ford by The Golden Dragon. They all wore tunics and breeches, save for Ford, who sported a leather jerkin with buttons that winked copper in the sunset. Their stares made her uncomfortable until she realized they were watching the justice and his deputies.

Rittman slowed their approach and leaned in the group's direction. "It is almost evenfall, and a curfew is in place. You should be in your huts or at temple praying for our kingdom."

Connor folded his arms across his chest. "Bell hasn't rung yet, Sir Will. I think we're fine here."

"We're nah Elvar'nists," Ford muttered.

"For the sakes of your souls, you should be."

Geffrey leaned over the wagonside. "Awful nice jerkin you got there, Ford Rounsey."

Rittman sneered. "A jerkin isn't yours to wear. Where did you come across it?"

Ford jabbed his chest with a thumb. "*Bought it.* With me own wages. Like it, d'you?"

"Stole it, more like," Geffrey said.

The justice shook his head grievously. "Sumptuary laws forbid it. Unless you've married up"—that drew snickers from Geffrey—"you must dress according to your station, in a tunic and breeches. Yes you must."

Ford spat to his side. "What's mine is mine."

"I could have you *gaoled,* Rounsey."

"You could try."

The air was electric. Rose stayed quiet, a coward. Beside Sara, Sweet Tom ruffled through his travelsack to unveil a morning star threaded with cruel slender spikes. He draped one leg over the side menacingly, looking like he intended to bash in Ford's head.

With everyone watching Ford, Sara recovered an apple from the basket and lobbed it at Sweet Tom's head. He dropped the morning star, clutching his head. Swift as the wind, Alford snatched the weapon, and all four men bolted for the shade of an alley.

Sara was already halfway over the wagonside when her mother started to shout. Geffrey landed behind her. He gave chase but she was too fast and too familiar with every groove she saw coming in the road. Careening around Lara's father's pigsty and through a grouping of huts, she spied Griff's Bridge, and lost her pursuer in tall feathery weeds that hid the muddy path to Elf's Grove.

Beneath sprawling tree limbs, in the crevice between an unyielding boulder and gray-spotted trunk, Sara clutched her knees against her chest, watching. Waiting. Moonlit leaves fell like floating tears from sentinel trees around her. The forest played night's melodies, sonorous with crickets and owls. She occasionally heard the ferns behind her thrashing, and turned about to find nothing.

The farmer's gentle face floated in her mind as she remembered the story he shared with her in the Tower.

"After they killed King Lathros," he'd said, "Sir Bradley Durhurst and his Treasonous Twelve sent men and dogs after loyalists who hid in Elf's Grove. The dogs sniffed around the trees without success and moved on. Little had they known the trees and willows disguised the king's men."

Had it been the elf-prince? Sara wondered presently. Could it have been anything else? Some said the land could be as loyal to a king as his sworn knights. Yet how could the forest and the river be loyal, and not alive?

She dwelled on things. King Hexar was dead, just like King Lathros, and *she'd* been in the company of kingkillers. Did that mean the land wouldn't disguise her if Sweet Tom came upon her? *Will the elf-prince help me?*

It made no sense, just like everything else. Caleb had done *nothing* wrong, and now her sweet friend was alone in the Red Tower. Picturing his face above Traitor's Gate made her weep in shudders.

Sara crawled to the river on hands and knees. Mushy leaves disintegrated under her palms and clung to her wool dress. She felt the water's spray by the dank, pebble-strewn soil around the boulder.

She'd imagined the river ferrying her off to the Evergreen Isles in her dream. She dipped a hand in water icy to the touch. Her reflection rippled in the moonlight, scattering the girl with the cotton wimple and brownish-gold hair.

Hide me, land, she thought desperately. *Hide me forever.*

Before she could step into the water she saw him, a pale face with white silken hair and blue eyes that watched her. She spun around to find night and trees, crickets and owls.

A trick?

"No trick."

The voice came from above. She rose slowly.

Atop the boulder sat the elf from her dream. He was utterly beautiful, with eyes like sapphires and skin silver from the moon. Gold freckles dappled his cheeks and the bridge of his nose. Lanky goat's ears slanted outward from the curtain of his silver hair. He strummed a six-stringed lyre the color of copper.

"*A trick, a trick, the girl said,*" he sang lightly, "*when she the Gift laid and a-pray'd in her head.*"

Uncurling his legs, he slid down the face of the boulder. He loomed over her, tall as her father and Caleb, maybe taller.

She backed away. "You were in my dream," she breathed, amazed. *You're the elf-prince.* Yet the creature didn't *look* like a prince, at least not a prince of men. Highborn men donned silks and furs and other finery. This elf—if he were one—was nearly naked, in a skirt of crusted leaves twined with reed.

He warmed with a smile. "We are all of us in a dream, Sara, daughter of Damien, daughter of Rose." He came close to her ear, as if to whisper a secret. "The only question is who does the dreaming."

She frowned. Graceful as a fawn, the elf tucked one leg under his thigh and twirled in a circle, thrumming his strings for a woody melody. She found herself itching to dance along.

"*A dream, a dream, the girl had,*" he sang, prancing about, "*locked in a Tower, cowering, sad.*"

Sara tried to catch him, but he was too nimble, and leapt behind a tree. "Shhh!" she said with a finger to her lips. "You mustn't be so loud. Sweet Tom and Geffrey will find me."

He poked his head out from behind the tree like a fawn. "And why do you think I told the trees to hide you?"

Suddenly, she remembered that her pursuers *had* been here. She remembered listening intently as Geffrey plodded around the grove. Sweet Tom had called her name, saying no harm would come, not even for the theft of his morning star. *Magic.*

"*Magic, magic, the girl thought,*" the elf sang, "*what to Dray was breath, no test, for no price bought.*"

Follow your dreams, Caleb had said. "You—you're the elf-prince. Is that how you know what I'm thinking?"

The elf emerged without his lyre. Kneeling before her, he propped his ears up with his fingers so they looked like horns. The ear she felt was warm, supple, and soft, fuzzy with hair at its utmost tip.

"You *are* an elf," she gasped. "What . . . what do you want?"

"Not what *I* want." Rising, he circled the tree again. "What you want, Sara of Rosbury. You made the Gift with your friend, here in this place—in *my* place. You beseeched the old gods. Or have you forgotten, as men are wont to do?"

She pictured the hare slackening under Caleb's knife. "But we beseeched them for Father."

"And Dray heard you—and brought a gift from Father."

A column of hot breath blew past her. She swiveled and gasped. Little Lady pawed at the soil, lustrous in the moonlight. The courser nuzzled her shoulder, nickering. She squealed and snuggled her neck.

"*Little Lady!* I thought you lost!" She squeezed her and giggled when she chomped at her wimple. *Is this real? Am I dreaming?* The horse's hair seemed real. "Father sent her?"

The elf smiled warmly. "Sir Damien left her for Dray to find. I forget what short memories your kind possesses. But that is why we loved you."

"Where is Father?" She searched the grove eagerly for any hint of his blue eyes. "Did you bring him, too?"

Dray watched her intently. "That, I could not do. Sir Damien is far away, and my power is not what it was in the First Days."

Tears blurred her eyes. Her father's horse—*their* horse—nudged her arm with her cold nose. "Then . . . Father . . . Caleb's Gift . . ." Her voice shook. "Is Damien Sothron . . . is he—?"

Dray wiped off the tear that slid down her cheek. "Worry not, Sara. Evil men took your father from this world. He walks now in the

Evergreen Isles." He lifted her chin with his finger. "But Sir Damien Sothron is not lost—not to my people." The elf rose from his knee. Moonlight imbued his skin and hair with a radiance that made him seem regal. "We can summon a vessel that will speed Sir Damien back to this river."

Her tears fell freely. "We can? You mean your leaf-ships?"

The elf shook his head. "No, those are long gone, but we can bear him back on swifter winds another way."

She sniffled. "But . . . Reader Gary says no soul can come back from the Evergreen Isles." She recalled the girl Jenny once asking at parish whether they could sail to paradise and return with undying fruits; Bram and the other Rosbury boys had laughed her down. Could a reader be wrong?

Could her father come back from death? As if in response, Little Lady nudged her shoulder playfully.

Dray pursed his pale blue lips for a smile. "Is Reader Gary an elf?" He reached for low-hanging leaves, caressing one as gently as he would something precious. "Think you that men can know all there is? Your ancestors thought not, little one. They came to us as children, knowing nothing. It was my people, firstborn of the gods, who taught them the Song of Souls."

To her amazement, the leaf seemed to *come alive*, twisting and brushing against his outstretched finger like a loyal hound that savors its master's touch. He closed his hand around the leaf so tightly he crushed it. Unclenching his fist, he revealed a stunning white rose that sighed as the petals stretched.

Dray plucked the miracle flower and offered it to her. She inhaled its heady musk. All it took was her fleeting touch, and the rose withered instantly, shedding its petals, as if winter had come and gone in that time. Little Lady snorted behind her.

Without a word, the elf scooped up the petals, reached up again, and withdrew the cup of his hands. The brittle leaf was there again, green and pristine, as if nothing had happened at all. Sara couldn't believe her eyes.

Dray observed her with a sidelong look. "Do you wish to see your father again, Sara of Rosbury?"

She couldn't nod quickly enough. "Yes, yes. *Yes!* Of course! What must we do, Dray? Do your old gods want another Gift?" She didn't like the idea of killing another fluffy hare, but she'd catch a thousand if the elf asked. *For you, Father.*

"Yes, a Gift. But this time we'll need more than a blade of steel. Will you retrieve what we need to make a Gift, daughter of Damien, daughter of Rose?"

"*Yes!* Yes, I will." Her relief and excitement surrendered to guilt. "Dray . . . what about Caleb? Can he sail across the sea?"

Dray softened. "Your friend made the Gift, little girl, but it was for your father. Intent matters. This is the law of gods and elves. Dray will honor it, and see that Damien crosses the sea. But first, *you* must return to your mother."

Oh, Caleb. Please forgive me. She nudged a foot against the other. "My mother will be wroth with me about Tom's mace."

He smiled. "She'll be wroth with you until she sees the horse. Return to Elf's Grove by the next moon, and Dray will tell you what to do next. And ere long, Sara will see her father once more. Now go with the blessings of my people, little one."

Sara decided not to question the elf-prince any longer. Kissing the horse on her nose, she took her reins and guided her away from the moonlit clearing. When she found the set of shallow footprints that would lead back to Griff's Bridge, she turned, and saw the elf had vanished.

As he'd promised, Rose's surprise and worry overcame her wrath. Unable to sleep that night, Sara listened to Little Lady nickering outside.

CHAPTER 23

A Father's Charge

athos walked among ghosts.

Their stern countenances took shape in the darkness as he passed by, torch in hand. Half lit, the ridges and hollows of their faces melted into sinister shapes that followed him, fluid-like. His ears sometimes played tricks, turning the soft slips of his footsteps into menacing whispers.

Were he a superstitious man, Rathos might have avoided this cobwebbed area of the dank cellar, or waited patiently by the door until Evan appeared. He might have prayed to gods or godfaces for protection against the spirits said to haunt the Red Tower and the Silver Walls.

Thankfully, Rathos was a man of the Awakening, and that meant trusting in reason.

Indeed, there was much to admire in this dusty statue crypt. Many of its infamous residents had languished here since before King Lathros's reign, judging by the thickness of their silken veils.

Their neglect would've been a crime were it not for their lifelike subjects. *A fitting crypt,* he pondered grimly.

These were statues that had outlived their popularity on the Street of Kings. Beneath an archway huddled Temron the Fifth, the king who anointed himself a god and fed his rivals to captive dragons, dignified with his hand lain across his chest. Bardo the Mad, who'd hunted peasants like boar, rose beside him, scowling appropriately. Behind a column loomed King Hexron, the only ruler to kill his entire Worthy Assembly, his beard curling to his waist.

Another tyrant lurked in the corner, almost as if he didn't wish to be seen. Swathed in spider's silk, he wore an ennobling hauberk and coif, nothing more—neither crown, nor scepter, nor extravagant armor. Unlike other tyrants, this one, a knight, had never hunted peasants, or fed his enemies to dragons.

No, he'd committed a far more monstrous crime.

Leaning in, Rathos spat on the statue.

Dull footsteps echoed through the cellar. A swirl of fire danced in the darkness, a firefly from this distance, rapidly approaching. Rathos snuck a hand around his sword hilt.

"Would you strike down your own father-by-law?"

Rathos unhanded his sword. Evan materialized by a brick column, ruddied by torchlight. He'd traded worn banquet attire for patchy brown breeches and a frayed green tunic.

Warder and ward clapped their arms around each other. A week of stress melted off Rathos as he embraced Evan. He'd missed this man.

He'd worried about him desperately. Evan feared the Red Tower in his bones. He wasn't sure he could forgive Warchild for stowing him away here, even if it was to protect him, as the Grand Inquisitor had eventually relayed to him and Karl.

"My boy, my poor boy." He gave Rathos a look over. "How do you find your quarters?" he asked as he inspected his face, then his arms, searching for signs of mistreatment.

"I was afraid at first, but I've received bread, water, even clean slop buckets." Rathos drew him in for another solid hug. "I've had to remind myself I'm in the Red Tower."

Evan pulled away, devoid of levity. "Karl?"

"Let's say I'd rather return to Caerdon than stay a second longer around Karl." Rathos had made a truce with these bleak surroundings. Less so, his usually glib roommate. Karl dreaded being left alone, and yet resented his company. It'd made him even more unpleasant to be around, if that were possible. "But I imagine he's still a sight better than the Red Tower's two new guests."

His warder seemed as if he were looking far off. "Would that you could see him, my boy," Evan said. "A lion caged with his cub, pacing to and fro. Finally, my father and your sister have justice."

"They'll have justice when Gram Sothos's head rots on a spike, and not sooner. A lion caged is still a lion."

"It's the best we can hope for. The daughter is bolder than her father—I'll give her that. She also has her mother's caution. She knows that killing Gram would provoke Parlisis into open war—a war she can't win, indebted as the king left Loran."

"But did they act alone?"

Evan gave a slow headshake. "The deaths or absence of all Hexar's legitimate heirs played perfectly into Parlisis's hands. It's an entire religion's work."

Rathos could almost read his mind. The priestking had always sought to reclaim Loran for more than just the Silver Walls. He wanted to stage an invasion of her three neighbors, the Free Kingdoms, which he could backdoor through Loran. Centuries after the Awakening, the lands, which had fathered the movement, worked to spread free thought across Ansara. This threatened Parlisis's iron grip.

"And without the princes," Rathos said, "Parlisis's allies have an opportunity to enthrone their favorite son in Loran."

"Lorana's gaoling of the Sothos men gives us our own opportunity." Evan clapped a hand on his shoulder. "Smile. You'll soon see your wife again. We leave on the morrow."

Never had he felt such relief. The tyrants seemed to scowl at the news. "Good," Rathos said. "What's the opportunity?"

"I shan't be returning with you," he said. "I leave with Lord Jason for Eddenloxley Castle." A vellum scroll appeared in his hand. "You must leave for Wesswood."

Wesswood was misdirection for Charles's spies; the Loyal Company had no business there. But the castle . . .

"Eddenloxley?" Rathos unraveled the crinkly calfskin and read Evan's handwriting in the sparse light. He glossed over it again, then shot Evan a look. *You'd name me your deputy?*

For years, he'd sought nothing else. To be deputy was to lead the Loyal Company with the speaker's authority in his absence. Apart from the speakership, it was the role Rathos had yearned for since swearing his Company Oath. But it put a bright red target on his back. *Mina won't be pleased.*

"What I'm asking of you is no small thing," Evan warned. He came close to whisper. "I need you to win the Company for our cause."

Rathos raised an eyebrow. "*Our?*"

"My nephew will enter the Kingstrials and seek the Silver Throne," Evan said. "We leave for Eddenloxley. Lord Jason will need Trevor Wexley's friendship to overcome the laws against bastard claimants." He touched his shoulder. "I'll need you to deliver our men in the Assembly for his claim."

The parchment could've well been asking the thirteen kings to forfeit their crowns and unite once more under Loran. Rathos watched his warder uncertainly, as if he expected Evan to break into laughter, to tell him this was a joke.

Deliver the Loyal Company, Rathos understood, *deliver the Assembly, and deliver King Jason to his throne.* "If he can't win outright, Assemblymen would vote for him," Rathos translated. "*Our* Assemblymen."

His father-by-law nodded. "To win outright a man needs three victories. Few kings have ever accomplished this. *'Three Trials, three Wings—'*"

"'*Only the Worthy crown kings,'*" he finished the rhyme. He rolled up the scroll and clenched it tightly, as if one of the kings here might reach down and rip it away. "What promises did he make, your nephew?"

"He promised the Wing of the Commons."

"Which his father refused to seat," he noted sourly. "You believe him?"

"Enough to risk the Company."

Enough to risk everything. Including our lives. Rathos offered back the scroll quickly, as if it were contaminated. "They won't agree. Not least because you'd ally us with the Cloudlands, where peasants are no better than slaves."

"They'll agree if Silvertongue convinces them."

Rathos cringed. Silvertongue was the name his colleagues had given him. He'd never taken to it, disliking its implied guile.

"I'm not confident that I could help. The Company is a cage of feces-throwing monkeys. And you *know* how they'll regard this turn of events."

"As a great failure, given the task they sent us with."

"Worse. They'll think you're misusing your position."

He looked taken aback. "Misusing?"

Evan Sinclair was the closest Rathos had to a father, and like any son, he knew his foibles. His earliest memories were of he and Leah Sinclair sprawled before a hearth fire at Caerdon, listening raptly as the lord recited Gram Reuben's verses on reason. Even then, as a child, he saw how his warder struggled with certain poems, especially those his sister had favored. He didn't need to believe in spirits to know the dead could haunt the living: Evan Sinclair gave proof.

Rathos sighed softly. "Men know the guilt you carry over your sister and my father. They'll say your passion is blinding your reason—that you mean to make it right with your sister by crowning her only child."

Evan watched him. He wandered past the statues. "Yes, I feel guilty," he admitted. "By rights I should've died that day in the carriage. Instead, your father did. Your father," he added bitterly, "who warned me from the start that our ploy to wed Sarah to the king could blow up in our faces."

The nobleman shined his torch on the statues' faces. He chuckled abruptly, astonished. "Do you know who this is?" he asked, almost with childlike wonder.

Rathos went to where he stood. He stared at Sir Bradley Durhurst, the usurper knight who led the Treasonous Twelve to kill King Lathros. "How could I not?"

Reaching up, his warder plucked apart the statue's thick silken veil thread by thread, never grazing the granite, as if he were concerned the slightest ill move would wake the tyrant from eternal slumber.

Evan laid a hand solemnly across his breast. "In another time, we would've probably stood by him, you know. A shame that he should be locked in here with the kings he detested."

His words sucked the wind out of him. "I think you need fresh air. You speak as if you *admire* this madman."

"Not admire," Evan said with faint crossness.

"But he *tarnished* the Wing of the Commons. Were it not for him, the Commons might still have a voice in the Assembly. He killed King Lathros in their name, and then butchered them, the men, women, children." His spittle on the statue caught the torchlight.

In many quarters of Loran and across Ansara, the name Bradley Durhurst could unsettle as easily as Pathazar or Asha-Ra. At first a champion for the Commons and the fast-spreading Free Beliefs, the knight went down in history as a king in all but name, a tyrant as much as a butcher of men, highborn and low. Men of the Awakening like Evan blamed his madness on fever. Wet nurses liked to tell children it was the Kingkiller's Curse that caused his unraveling, or even the specters of dead kings said to guard the Silver Throne and haunt the unworthy.

Rathos had a far simpler answer. "Durhurst was a villain. He went mad from power. He tainted the Fourth Wing with his bloodlust. He is the reason for our struggle."

"He did. He is."

"Were it not for the Treasonous Twelve, Loran could be one of the Free Kingdoms."

Of all his crimes, *that one* towered above the rest for men like Rathos and other Companymen. His bloody legacy offered a gift to future kings and Worthy Assemblies, a shield against the Awakening, which taught men to question, and find truths not told in testaments. To trust their own reason. Thus, more than two centuries after the Interregnum, Loran remained a hopeless backwater that preferred to gaol bookmakers while Free Kingdoms like Tesos rewarded inkpress inventors with patents and riches. Thus was Loran deprived of light, and her Common peasants and merchants left to toil in darkness.

Thus, all the scheming by priestkings and lords like Gram Sothos to treat Loran's *bordering realms* as the real threat.

Evan was unmoved. "We should never forget our history, villains least of all. I wonder where Sir Bradley lost his way." He waxed a hand across the exquisite dimples of the statue's hauberk. "Where reason and high hopes turned to pointless butchery." He turned to Rathos. "If he regretted the dishonor he brought upon himself and the Fourth Wing."

The man he considered a father wasn't hard to read. "As some of us blame ourselves for the Long Summer Rebellion?"

The nobleman glanced up with eyes that shimmered.

"My lord, you can't seriously compare yourself to this . . . this *tyrant*. You may feel guilty, but you did nothing like—"

"Start a war?" His father-by-law's laughter dripped with self-contempt. "Trust me, Rathos, there's nothing you can say to convince me otherwise. Your father accused me of peddling my sister like a whore for our agenda. He told me our dreams would end in bloodshed. He—"

He stopped short with a pained expression. "We make our decisions, and then we live with them"—he tapped on Bradley Durhurst's stone chest—"or don't. Well," he added thickly, "I'm not a statue yet—or ash, or a corpse. Hexar is dead. We have a chance to right Sir Bradley's wrongs. To seat Commoners again in their Worthy Assembly and aid the cause of reason. Sarah's son is that chance."

"Or change it for the worse." Rathos strode to Hexron Eddenhold's side. "You yourself said Hexar showed himself Hexron's true descendant. Is it for the best that we enthrone another Eddenhold?"

Evan gave him a dark look. "We may get one either way. Shaddon is coming. He means to vie for the Silver Throne, with the priestking's might behind him. As may Tom Gelder, or Sam Wuthers."

The Loyal Company could profess love for few of those names. Every one of them was an Elvarenist. Gelder, Wuthers: both men fought only for themselves, land, and riches. The late king's brother was another statue waiting to join this tomb for tyrants. They said the exiled nobleman had a habit of descending from his carriage on the steps of peasants' neatly arrayed necks.

"And what of a King Tomas Fawkes?" Rathos inquired.

Evan stroked his beard. "Aye, he's a problem. I have no doubt he'll enter the Kingstrials. The Loyal Company unites behind no one like Fawkes." Rathos wondered whether that tidbit was for his ears, or Charles Burke's.

"He's a Free Believer who favors the Fourth Wing. Why not let them crown him?"

"Rathos, *please.* You know his reputation. Fawkes's a fool and a whoremonger, out for his own glory."

And the late king wasn't? Rathos saw the wheels turning behind his warder's eyes—the mind of a guilt-ridden brother yearning to set things right. "The Master Reader trusts him."

"Jacob Sulley trusts Fawkes because no other lord will protect him so, and Fawkes protects Sulley because doing so shores up support for his claim. That doesn't mean we should make Fawkes king."

"But say we crown the Warchild—"

"Don't call him that."

Surprised by the snap, Rathos inclined his head apologetically. "Forgive me, my lord. Habit."

Evan lingered on him, as if deciding whether to scold him. A week in the Red Tower had made Rathos forget his warder's paternal instincts for his nephew.

"Jason can unite the land behind the Fourth Wing, as no one else," Evan said. "He has a good and honorable heart, like his mother. You saw how he protected that Common girl."

"Aye, I saw. But what if King Jason isn't so honorable? Or if he fails, as we have? What happens when the Loyal Company refuses to accept another disappointing king?"

Evan looked grim in the torchlight. He gazed up at Sir Bradley Durhurst. "Then we act." He turned to Rathos. "You will need to share with *him* what I've shared with you."

Him. Evan could only mean one person. Rezlan Ambrose, the so-called Lord of Shoaltown, commanded as much respect as Evan in the Loyal Company. Together, Evan and Rezlan had founded a Company for Loran's discontents. Now they were the bitterest of rivals—one a diplomat, another a warmonger. Their rivalry had split their Company down the center between Petitioners, who tried patiently for reform, and Reubenites like Karl, who'd have a Wing of the Commons . . . or war.

What I've shared with you. "You can't possibly be serious."

Evan ventured closer, the seams around his mouth stern. "You know I am," he said. "You know the stakes. He lost sight of the star of reason long ago. The news of our failure here will be like blood in the water to him. He'll want it—what remains of it." He prodded his chest with a finger. "If we fail, you'll give it to him. For my daughter's life. For your sister's. For yours."

He means the blackpowder. The substance that killed his sister . . . and my real father.

Before the rebellion, House Sinclair had been one of the largest curators of blackpowder in all of Ansara. They'd tried and failed to learn the recipe, but their huge stores had made them fantastically wealthy. So it was especially tragic when Evan lost Sarah and Sir Matthus in a blackpowder explosion. With Evan gaoled in the Red Tower, Hexar had all the reason needed to distrain Caerdon and abscond with her blackpowder caches. Tragedy fed tragedy as Evan's powerful house declined in wealth and status.

And then, one crisp autumn day, a servant found a writ in their castle's crypts, stuck to the wall with a dagger. There'd been no signature on the writ, no sign of who'd delivered it—just a sum that would've made sense only to Evan, Hexar, and the Grand Inquisitor.

Evan had shared its contents with Rathos before setting the dangerous writ aflame in a brazier. *Five hundred,* the writ had said. *Barley Tower. They belong to House Sinclair.*

"I told him, once," said Evan, referring to Rezlan Ambrose again. "He never saw what it did. To Sarah. What it did to—" He looked at Rathos and paled suddenly, as if he saw a ghost.

"I was never sure about whether I could believe the note. Then I spoke with the king in his throne room." Evan raked his hand against his stubble, grinning wryly. "A terrible liar, Hexar the Bold."

Evan touched his arm. "Rathos, you're our only hope—truly. I fear for my nephew's life and trust no one else with his safety. Even with Sothos gaoled. Either Jason will win all three outright, or we'll make him king because the Assemblymen in our Company show up and vote.

"And should god make mock of our plans, or should I die, or Jason . . ." He cupped his hands around his. "You'll make a deal for your life, Mina's, and your sister's, and we'll seat the Fourth Wing again." *One way or another,* it went unsaid in the Grand Inquisitor's Red Tower.

Rathos's gaze drifted from Evan to Durhurst. The creases in the statue's mouth seemed to twitch in the firelight.

CHAPTER 24

The Steward's Proposal

Justen Sothos was on his knees, and for once he wasn't proposing marriage.

From the chair on her dais, Lorana watched her former suitor grovel for his life beside a well fashioned from skulls. As she listened to his heaving sobs, she kept a finger to her cheek, almost thoughtfully, as if she were contemplating mercy. In his rags, face obscured by his mop of hair, Sothos's son could've easily been mistaken for one of the thousands of Commoners jeering him. Peasants spilled over barricades and jockeyed for space nearby. She spied children on their parents' shoulders.

Good, Lorana thought. *The more eyes and ears, the better this will go.* She needed witnesses, a city of them. As many as the Lord Mayor could scrounge up.

For the executions of her father's murderers, Lorana had chosen the city plaza at the intersection of Kingsway and Silver Street, against Charles's concerns for safety. This was tradition. Many a head had piled up in Traitor's Pit, over centuries, and many had watched. Stories abounded about the crimson roads Sir Bradley Durhurst's tribunals had left, so slick with human fat that men slipped in it.

She wouldn't kill as many today.

The history and stench of this place didn't appear lost on the faces of the gathered Assemblymen. Lords and clergy, they huddled close together inside the octagon of barricades before her, seeking safety in numbers. Nobles and priests grimaced at her. Not that she'd expected anything else from the priestking's men. Word that Jhazar of Groth—*a*

Casaanite!—had roughed up leaders of the Wings of Lords and Clergy was still fresh on everyone's minds.

But Peshar Grathos had heaped humiliation on Elzura's Children. On Anyasha. On Zur. During her own father's funeral. The vile bastard. She could still hear her lover crying, still see the bleeding hostages.

The tit-for-tat had to end. *And after today, it will,* she thought.

Under a silverstone-rippled sky, the steward sat forward. Lords, clergy, peasants: they waited on her. "Lord Charles," she said with airy dignity.

To her side, her enforcer unfurled a scroll that drooped to his feet. There wasn't much written on it, but she'd wanted him to find the longest calfskin possible. Appearances, after all.

The city was so quiet, you could hear the harbor birds.

"Lord Justen Sothos, you stand accused of high treason," Charles Burke said in a high, crisp voice. "You delivered poison to men of your faith who killed our most beloved king."

Peasants, not merely men of your faith. But the words had been carefully chosen. What mattered was that the Commons sided with the royal family against Elvarenist plots on Loran.

"You instructed them to poison the king's wine for the twelve gods," Charles went on. "On the day we use to honor House Thorngale's great peace." His long parchment rustled in a breeze. "What say you, my lord? Silence will buy you death. But even though you'd deserve it, the steward has instructed me to tell you that honesty could buy you a trial."

How she wished he'd remain silent. Charles could call the headsman, and off Justen's head would fly, into the skull-lined latrine. But Lorana was a realist. She was a woman and a ruler, queen in all but name of a kingdom that cursed queens in the same breath as Casaanites. She'd whitened her face with sheep fat, covered her hair, and dressed in chamblet silks slashed with beaten silver, to model daughter, woman, and sovereign.

She had to seem above herself, and Justen had to live.

Justen kept his face down. Taunts filled the air. *Come on, you murdering cunt. Say it loud so the world hears you.*

His lips twisted. Charles leaned in expectantly. "I, I . . ." Justen began. The rest, whatever it was, he stammered out inaudibly.

Lorana conveyed her wishes to the Grand Inquisitor with a look, and he said, "Louder."

Sothos's son lifted his tremulous gaze. Grief lines twisted his handsome face. She relished this moment, the worst of his life.

The truth surged out all at once: "Okay fine, *I did it I did it I DID IT!*" Her former suitor was bawling. "Please! I'm a coward. The rats, please, my lord, no more . . ."

Justen had confided in her once that he was deathly afraid of rats. She'd shared that with Charles, naturally.

"Rats nest at the bottom of Traitor's Pit," the torturer said. "We need details, Lord Justen. What was 'it' you did? What was your despicable crime?"

Justen locked eyes with Charles. He clenched his teeth, as if he could halt the truth working its way up his throat. "I GAVE THEM THE POISON," he sobbed. "But I had no idea—*I wouldn't tell them to poison . . . to poison . . .*"

"The king," Lorana said it for him. Justen looked at her as if he were just now seeing her.

"Then what did you think you were doing with that vial?"

"I was told to give them a vial, that's all!"

Lorana gritted her teeth. The air swelled with a tempest of shouts and curses. Peasants hurled rotten fruit, lettuce, and fouler things at Justen, splattering a few lords and priests.

"To ensnare Loran in puppet strings pulled by your vile priest-king," Charles responded for him, one hand outstretched and grasping, as if he'd choke the confession out of Justen. "You reek of treason, my lord. I shall cleanse you."

Justen blanched. "YOU PROMISED A TRIAL!"

"A trial, if you're honest." Were it not for her wish to see the head of this plotter parted from his shoulders, the steward would've enjoyed Charles's interrogation. Truly, he had a gift for that, and for theater.

"Who gave you the vial of poison?"

The critical moment. Justen's gaze wobbled to Lorana. He firmed his expression. Resisting, again. "I can't. I won't do it. I'll slander myself. Not him. Take my head, then. I won't do it."

Without delay, Charles beckoned to one of the crimson-hooded brutes hovering nearby, one clutching a humongous axe as tall as himself.

Cheers flew up from peasants. Justen shook like he might piss himself as his executioner lurched up the squeaking stairs. Then he lowered his head, exposing his neck.

Shit. Lorana feared loss of face. The executioner raised his axe. She stirred slightly off her chair, to intervene.

"GRAM SOTHOS," Justen cried out. His voice cracked like a pre-pubescent boy's. "*Father gave me the vial!*"

Charles waved his hand straightaway at the executioner, who at once eased off. *Magnificently done, Charles,* the princess thought. *Squeeze a lemon, and out a bitter juice.*

The jeers were deafening now. The plotter quivered on his knees, tears falling off his cheeks.

With one raised fist, the torturer quelled the bedlam.

"I asked you for truth, Lord Justen, and you spoke it for the realm to hear," he said loftily. "Your father, Gram Sothos, Lord of Saxhold, procured a vial through Shaddon Eddenhold and bade you give it to Elvarenists to poison King Hexar. Like a good son, you did as bidden. Your stupidity buys you mercy today, and a trial to decide whether your head stays."

Shuddering forward, Justen splayed his hands on the dais, as if finally unburdened. *Had you shown this humility in the first place, I might've said yes,* Lorana thought.

"But," added Charles, "you aren't absolved of your other crime. At the feast, you were seen seizing the steward by her wrist. You were heard cursing her." Justen flitted from him to her. "Her Highness threatened to take your hand. I think you owe her two."

The axe cleaved the air, to gasps and her former suitor's hysterical, stomach-churning screams. Handless, he flopped on the dais like a fish out of water. Blood jetted from his wrists, so much of it. One hand dangled on his carpal bone; the headsman severed it with another swing.

Peasants roared lustily. Assemblymen, even readers like Jacob Sulley, covered their mouths. Grathos scowled at Lorana as she choked down her own vomit. *Not now. Not out here.*

The Red Tower's other hooded men hurried onto the dais, torches fluttering, and then a gut-wrenching scream, his bloody flesh cauterized by fire. Off they carried the fainted lord, blood spilling everywhere, to boil the wrists and save his pathetic life. Applewood had assured her it could be done. The apothecary waited to receive Justen in a building nearby that Renworth had reserved for him to stymie blood loss and treat the wrists.

For the realm needed to know that House Sothos was a house of kingkillers. As it spread over the dais, Justen's blood was sealing that letter like red wax.

The Grand Inquisitor stepped to the crimson puddle's edge. He retrieved a severed hand and held it high, its blood pattering the dais.

"THUS TO TRAITORS," he cried out. "Elvarenists say the Head speaks, that the Hands serve. But here, all heads must bow for their king and his Worthy Assembly. All hands must serve the king. But heads or hands, whichever strikes down a king will know the Kingkiller's Curse."

He spared a glance for Lorana, almost to see if she had the stomach for this grotesque display. *Those were my words, Lord Charles, but your love for Father gave them power.*

Silence from the Assembly. Then the High Bishop walked through the crowd, a snake slithering through the garden. "All hands must serve the king." Grathos pointed at her. "But there sits no king."

Is that wisdom you think you speak, boyfucker? Lorana rose unhurriedly, stately in her gown. "Yes, Your Grace, you're right," she said. "We'll never replace my king father, but we must try. I am a woman and cannot wear a crown. Yet Father left no heirs you Worthy men consider worthy. So bloodsport must decide our next king."

Grathos grimaced. Justen hadn't implicated her uncle . . . but

Charles Burke had. Ringed by Commoners who reviled Shaddon—a man said to exit his carriage on the steps of neatly lined peasant necks—the High Bishop wouldn't dare call him a successor. Unless he wanted a riot that ended with the little folk tearing him limb from limb.

"Our steward speaks truly," said Lord Tomas Fawkes. The High Bishop twisted at Fawkes, glaring. "Willard the Wise gave us the Kingstrials to stop Loran's succession wars. Stewards traditionally call the Trials. Traditionally at court." He smiled. "But Your Highness—and I mean this respectfully—the Speaker of the Wing of Lords must *consent* to Kingstrials. By his own son's admission, our current speaker is a kingkiller."

"Aye, a new lord speaker must be chosen. He must be a lord of stature—someone nobles and peasants alike respect, given how Gram Sothos tarnished his office." Her gaze found him where he stood with his sons. "And who among us doesn't revere the man who ended the Long Summer Rebellion?"

After sixty-two years on earth, the Old Oak looked the part, a faded tree bowed by his heavy mantle and mossy beard. Assemblymen regarded him curiously.

As we discussed, Lord Greg. A few nights past, she'd had Greg Thorngale brought to her quarters to hear her proposal. Ever wary of anything that could soil his reputation, Thorngale had refused her, courteously. So, courteously, she'd countered by telling him the one thing that old men with legacies loved hearing most: he was still needed.

"The Speaker of the Wing of Lords has come to lead the Worthy Assembly, and I can think of no one better suited to this vital post than Lord Greg Thorngale," she declared.

Listing on his sons, Thorngale shuddered up to his full height. He laid a papery, beringed hand over his chest. "Your Highness does me great honor," he said, interrupted by a baby's squeal somewhere.

Grathos bowed coolly to him. "And a fine speaker for our Wing of Lords you'd make, my lord." He turned back to Lorana, scorning her with a smile she wished to have red hoods beat off him. "But stewards cannot choose speakers for any wing. Not even kings can usurp the Worthy's gods-given power."

"Nor would I try, Your Grace," Lorana said. "Each wing names its speaker. I was merely making a suggestion." She swept the air with a hand, encompassing her Assemblymen. "Would our Wing of Lords want Greg Thorngale for speaker?"

Draped in fur, garments, and jewels they barred peasants from wearing, lords turned this way and that, nervous as sheep in a vast clearing, suddenly aware of wolves. Sure, the princess had invited her Assembly to witness Justen ruin himself and his father—to watch six kingkillers lose their heads in turn.

But *this* was why she wanted them here. Her trap.

Assemblymen believed the barricades were there to keep them safe from the Commons. She saw the octagon as a sheep pen, outside which wolves would salivate and snarl until the sheep chose the right shepherd.

Her half-brother had asked her to move heaven and earth for his claim. For Jason to have any chance, Greg Thorngale had to supplant Gram Sothos as Speaker of the Wing of Lords. Rules governed the Kingstrials, rules that could bend or remain firm as oak. The nobleman who spoke for the Wing of Lords decided which rules bent . . . and toward whom.

Yet encouragement was needed. Elvarenists dominated the lords' wing. They'd never choose a speaker who wasn't like them, in bed with Parlisis . . . not unless pushed by ill-tempered peasants who'd just seen the son of a hated lord lose his hands.

It was music to her ears as she listened to their chants, "*OAK! OAK! OAK!*"

Do you feel the earth shaking, Jason? she thought. *They do.*

Fawkes raised his hand, then ducked a rock that pelted a lord beside him. "I'll have Speaker Thorngale," he ventured.

I expected no less from you, my lord. Fawkes was a darling of the peasants. He also had an ancestral claim that he wanted to stake. Like Jason, Fawkes would benefit from rules firmed by a lukewarm Elvarenist like Thorngale.

After Fawkes, more lords consented to Thorngale, among them Sam Wuthers, another contender. Yet stubborn holdouts remained. Sam Gramlore rallied lords in a feeble protest vote to name Jon Redoak, Sothos's lap dog, as his successor.

A bad idea, that. Mutterings turned to shouts. Angry cries mounted. A few bold peasants slipped through the fences. Then the dam broke. Red-faced men got in the faces of the lords and clergy, berating them. Gramlore wore a brave face, until thick-armed blacksmiths surrounded him. Screams cut through the air as furious mothers dragged a bishop off by his ankles. After that, Redoak began urging his supporters to lower their arms.

Less than five minutes later, Lorana saw a forest of arms raised for Thorngale. The Wing of Lords had a new speaker, and she, a new friend in the Assembly. Mouth agape, the High Bishop traded looks with the other defeated Assemblymen. He was incredulous. They all were.

For two years, they'd thwarted her rule. No longer.

So, Sinclair, she thought with relish, *this is what it'd look like to seat a Wing of the Commons in the Assembly. I see why you fight for it. The lords and priests would think twice before they made laws unpopular with peasants seated beside them.*

"My congratulations, Lord Greg," Lorana said, her victory teasing out her smile. "The Wing of Lords has elected you its speaker. Now, then—would you consent to these Kingstrials?"

Lorana didn't stay to watch the executions of her father's six killers. With Greg Thorngale perched in Sothos's post, and the bloody Kingstrials set two months from now, the job was done. She needed privacy. Urgently.

She barely had a foot in her carriage before she retched. Waiting for her inside, her lover closed the door and ordered the coachmen go as she gagged in her lap.

The blood. She'd never seen so much, and Justen had so much to give. She tried to stave off unwelcome imaginings of the blood from her mother's traitor neck. She retched all the way back up the Kingsway. Anyasha stroked the mane of her hair soothingly, steadying the bowl for what came up.

Close to evening, Lorana sat in the East Tower's chamber, still queasy. She hunched over a table piled with scrolls, letters from lords, and summonses to the Kingstrials. Staring out her window, she watched as Assemblymen left the city in a train of carriages, no doubt eager to be free of her and the Commons. She spotted the intersection . . . and there, the reddened dais.

A rapping came at the door. The torturer stepped inside, crimson robes rustling. He had the satisfied air of a man who's eaten well. *And perhaps he has, with all the blood he spilled for me today.*

"Your Highness." Charles bowed his neck.

Anyasha saw herself out. Lorana sprinkled a signed scroll with pounce, buttoned it with wax, and handed it to him. "Give that to Drexan when you go. The Mad Lady and her Heretics were sighted in the Rotwood. A lord is petitioning us to end her madness. I'm mustering a small force."

The torturer took it, caressing the tuft of tar-black hair on his chin. "On the condition that this lord support your brother in the Kingstrials, I trust." He paused. "My eyes and ears have told me this Mad Lady is Evan Sinclair's daughter."

"Yes, I've heard this song. If it's true, we'll kill her, burn her, and keep her identity secret." She dripped wax, stamped her griffon die. "And never speak of it to interested parties."

Charles nodded. He hated Evan Sinclair, and he'd made no secret of his qualms about his pact with Jason. The Mad Lady was a thorn on that rose, and Charles had been scratching her with it since before Jason had even left. If it were true, no one could know. *A fine line to walk, our house's alliances with House Sinclair,* she thought, *always.*

"Is he still alive?"

Charles went to the window. "The apothecary has a gift. Young

Sothos will live, maimed, humiliated, and dependent on others till the end of his days."

"Thus to traitors." She resisted picturing all the blood.

"Thus to traitors. You sent a message to the world today. One that meted out justice, but which I think stopped short of starting a war with the priestking and his puppet kings."

"And Lord Greg will keep rules from bending against my brother in the Trials, and his reputation will make the outcome legitimate. If Sinclair's Companymen and the Bull fall into line behind Jason, he'll be king in two months' time." *All to keep the peace, brother.*

"Masterfully done, taming the Assembly in public, Your Highness. Your father would be proud." Charles paced to her side. "His killers died confessing to the smallest sins. Turns out one of them was once nobility. Caleb Bard. Son of a Westland lord. Bard kept that quiet, until we pulled out his entrails. I've never heard such poetry."

Lorana acknowledged his macabre jab. "I trust you made his lineage known to the peasants watching them die."

"I did." Charles toyed with his tuft of hair. "But that city was silent as a crypt while my men did their work."

"Silent how?"

"A solemn silence. A silence of solidarity. I think peasants saw the kingkillers as their own."

"But they confessed to *killing my father*. To killing a king, at the behest of Gram Sothos, Hammer of the Commons. All six confessed in public, you said."

"Aye." Charles registered nonverbal permission before easing into a chair across the table. "Commoners stick together like spoilt fruit. I know you won't want to hear this again, Ana, but—"

"We've discussed this." Lorana unfurled another scroll and began reading, to show she'd had her fill of this subject.

"Out of love for you, I must persist. Peasants killed the king two centuries ago. For their crime they were banished from the Assembly. Six poisoned your father, another king . . . and we'd invite them back into power?"

"My father's killers were Elvarenists. They confessed."

"Yes—"

"But that's not the norm. Peasants are Free Believers. The conspiracy against my house is an Elvarenist one, concocted by a corrupt priest in a pointy hat on an island thousands of miles away. You saw what happened out there. Restoring the Wing of the Commons will temper these lords and priests." She made a fist, baring the whites of her knuckles. "And this kingdom will fight *as one* against the foreign enemy that murdered its king."

He had that mildly frustrated look. "Say Jason wins—"

"He will."

"Say he restores the Fourth Wing. What if the day comes that you stand where lords and priests stood, down below?" He beckoned to the city outside the window. "Your father understood the peril of giving vermin power and denied Sinclair to the day he died."

"But I'm not my father," Lorana said.

Charles concurred with a small, almost proud smile.

"The vermin you refer to are the hands that pick our fruit and work our lands. They are the real power of this kingdom, Charles, because they outnumber us. I want a whole kingdom for my brother when he ascends the Silver Throne. One that stands behind him. Or sits, as the case may be."

Charles rose, resting one hand on the back of his chair as he regarded her. "Were that it stood behind you. Its true king."

The stone maiden resumed reading. "In another world."

CHAPTER 25

The Star of Reason

They traveled from Southpoint out into the kingdom, passing by shires littered with humble hovels, over rickety bridges, through forests alive with the trilling of griffs and other birds of prey.

Riding beside Jason, Evan helped lead their eight-person party, which included, on the steward's orders, six of some of House Eddenhold's most skilled knights.

Glancing over his shoulder, Evan allowed himself a feeling of confidence. Bearded and burly, Rogir Levan, the commander, had led Hexar's men in Uzland. Behind him rode David Bridge and Erick Seam, lithe but deadly archers, and Sam Hornby, who could ride as quickly as the raven flies. The last two, Kyle Urron and Harold Marc, were nearly peerless swordsmen.

Their mission was straightforward. They would ride to the Cloudlands, the utmost corner of Loran's Westland, to win Trevor Wexley's friendship. There, the Bull would either invite their party into Eddenloxley Castle for mead and bread, refuse them . . . or loose arrows from protected heights, killing them.

Such was Lorana Eddenhold's gamble. Jason, every bit a bastard in the Worthy Assembly's eyes, needed a powerful ally to even set foot in the Colossus. Evan couldn't decide whether her ploy was a stroke of brilliance or foolhardy—probably a little of both—but there were few such men who could give Jason his chance. If someone could reverse Hexar's Folly and bring the Cloudlands back into the fold, who *wouldn't* wish to crown that man king, bastard or not?

The lush forests of Southland gave way to the flat, lifeless fields of the Midlands. Here, there was only a vast sea of brown as far as the eye could see. The sun glared down at them from a blue sky patched with cloud.

They sized up the barren landscape from the shade of the forest's canopy. "This way lies Scythe Road, which I'd rather we not travel given the drought," Evan told the party. "If we travel west, on Midway Road, we can shelter at Caerdon." He touched his nephew's shoulder. "It was your mother's castle, once, too."

Astride his courser, the bastard prince scanned the empty horizon, shielding his eyes with a hand. He was dressed like the others, concealing his light mail with a merchant's doublet. He looked ever like his mother, but Evan needed no reminder that Hexar had raised him as well. That was never so clear as when Jason responded.

"This isn't impassable," Jason said. "My half-brothers and I traveled through harsher terrain. Deserts, uncle, not fields."

Evan sensed he wouldn't like where this was heading. "I have mead and salted pork at my castle. We can rest and—"

"Remind me, uncle," he said, a little curtly, "which village does your castle overlook?"

"Peacefield."

Rogir Levan rode up beside them. "Peacefield is just north of Wessex-by-the-Sea," the knight said. "If we take that route, we'll have another week's worth of riding before we reach the Cloudlands."

Evan saw the late king's stubbornness now, unmistakable in Jason's rigid cheekbones. "We can't lose another week to travel," Jason said. "The Trials begin in less than two months, and it'll take nearly a month to get to the Cloudlands. We don't know if Trevor will see us, or if we'll need another champion."

If we can't make the Bull our ally, we're finished before we begin, and you won't be king, Evan thought. *Not through the Kingstrials, anyway . . .*

"We'll risk running through the rest of our rations, to say nothing of water," Evan insisted. He glanced up at the vultures flying in lazy circles over the field. "The Commoners we'll find here are in distress besides. They're desperate."

"Good." Jason urged his horse onward, as if he were king already, and the matter settled. "A king must know his subjects, and I've been away two years."

Evan teased his horse's flanks with his heels and entered sunlight at a trot. "Where can we shelter if we take this way?"

"Hexwaite is thirty miles out. We'll camp if we need to."

"And risk another assassin's blade, in the open?"

Jason slowed his horse. "We have six knights, plus us," he told him. "I need you by my side. If my own uncle questions me, who will support me in the Kingstrials?"

"But what are the Trials for?" Evan asked. "To test a man's fitness for the crown. My men in the Assembly will want a king who welcomes questions and examines himself. But I get your point, my lord. Let us see what the Midlands offer."

The party left the forest behind them for an endless field of dying wheat stalks, once amber, now brittle like strands of hair. Scythe Road coursed through the decay, battling dust and weed. A curtain of flying insects hung so thick over the horizon that the knights initially mistook it for raincloud. The noon sun baked them, soaking their faces and chests and armpits. Their fly-bitten horses thrashed their tails ceaselessly.

The worst lay ahead. Like the towering wave that starts small, the miserable Midland Commons washed toward them. It was worse than Evan had heard. They were heartbreaking in their ghastliness, skeletons in loose-fitting clothes of skin, with hollowed cheeks and sunburnt skin and tousled hair.

Wave after wave they came, men and women, boys and girls, young and old. A naked man sat cross-legged beneath the stalks, rocking to and fro, mumbling to himself. A mother with flaps for breasts nursed her child; as they passed by, they saw maggots in the babe's belly. Round-tummied children munched on tattered stalk leaves.

The dead weren't in short supply; bodies rotted openly in the corridors of stalks. The ones who passed into the next life with dignity lay half-covered under wool blankets that popped like heated corn kernels.

The Wall knights mostly looked away, covering their noses and mouths. Not so, Sarah's son. He stared at all the suffering humanity, as if to sear every face into memory.

Perhaps there was wisdom in coming this way after all, Evan conceded inwardly. *He looks as you did when you saw, Sarah. When my cause became our cause.*

"Madness," Jason said softly. "Where do they come from?"

"All over the Midlands. When harvest is good, these folk till their lands and those of their lords like anywhere else," the nobleman replied. "But with the land in drought, lords turn out Commoners who can't work their lands or pay rents in favor of those who can. I suspect many of them fled their villages when their lords demanded they forfeit their children."

"Why do they crowd this road?"

"None will have them. No lord or mayor, not in Eastland, Westland, Northland, or Southland. Nowhere in Loran."

Jason watched the masses grimly. Not far, a pale woman sobbed hysterically into her hands. "A Wing of the Commons could end their plight."

Evan nodded. "Everyone needs a voice in their own rule, the poor most of all. Peasants will never wear crowns or rule from great castles. But give them a seat among the Worthy, and they can negotiate a suspension of rents, or summon the clergy to build poorhouses. Give them representation, and we'll seed a harvest that feeds Loran—*all* of Loran—for years to come."

"To each a chair," Jason quoted the Assembly's old motto.

"*Turan e'sparta,*" Evan finished in Romarian, a hand over his chest. "Yet, a word. There will be a right time and a wrong time to discuss the Common cause with Lord Trevor. A Fourth Wing will never rule the north, so we must wait until the right time appears."

His nephew looked betrayed. *And why not?* Evan thought as he let his gaze pass over the sick, starving, and dying rabble.

"Lord Trevor isn't too far," Jason said. "He could dispatch

wine and bread for this lot."

"Trevor Wexley hates peasants more than Sothos. He'd sooner loose dogs on them."

"The Midlands would be better for it," Rogir muttered.

A haggard wail pitched over the wheat stalks. Up the path ran a fellow in an eye patch and umber robes, crying for help. "*Brigands!*" he screamed. At once men, women, and children dispersed into stalks, fleet-footed as deer. Some stranded their dying. The woman with her head in her hands remained where she sat, weeping inconsolably, as if her fate didn't matter.

Evan saw the look on his nephew's face. "Jason," he said in earnest, but the bastard prince had already instructed the six knights to ride with him, three on each flank. They kicked their mounts' sides and barreled through the press of crops, leaving Evan no choice but to follow.

How could anyone doubt that he was yours, Hexar?

Wheeling past the bend, the nobleman found the knights thick about his nephew, all of them peering past wheat stalks. Forty yards off, three lanky brigands menaced two men and a boy clothed in robes the same color as the fabric worn by the one-eyed fellow. Bits of bread lay around them. The taller of the brigands jabbed his dagger as he delivered an ultimatum.

"Mumblers," Evan said for his companions' ears.

"Poor fools, get what they deserve," Rogir remarked. "This is no road for men, even almsmen."

When he was younger, Evan had considered joining the ranks of these almsmen. A sect of the Free Beliefs, Mumblers swore off all material possessions, to spend their lives tending to the poor, the lame, the blind, the sick.

"But he's a Mumbler," Evan said. "What would he have for anyone to kill for but lice, old bread, and filthy robes?"

"It doesn't matter." Jason pivoted in his saddle, hand on the hilt of his sword. "The king may be dead, but his laws still rule Loran. As I will rule her."

His heart for his kingdom, Evan thought.

Even in disguise, Jason, Evan, and their knights made a formidable sight on their mounts. The brigands swiveled at *clop-clop*ing hooves. They traded panicked looks, then leapt into the withered wheat.

As they fled, one Mumbler, an elderly man with bowed shoulders and a head of patchy white hair, slipped something off his finger and into his pocket. Only Evan seemed to notice.

"You three," Jason called out on approach, "are you okay?"

The elderly man nodded tiredly. He cradled his head in a hand. "Brigands," he said. "Spotted us giving out bread. Wanted to know where we keep our larders. Desperate men."

The sound of feet alerted them. The Mumbler with the eye patch walked up wearily, sweat-sheened from the run. "Thank you, good sirs," he said, panting. "These horsemen, they came ridin' to help when I cried for help."

The old man removed his hand from the blood streak on his temple. "Thank you for finding help, Will. We thank the One True God for you lot. You saved us. Thank you, sirs."

"We're not sirs," Rogir objected under his breath.

The other Mumbler, a fat man, glanced at the sword hilts protruding from their waists. "Armed like 'em," he said.

"We're linen merchants, on our way to Hexwaite," Evan chimed. "Scythe Road is known to be dangerous. We know to travel prepared."

Harold dismounted. The knight procured a strip of linen from his saddlebag and tied it around the old man's head. "We thank god you did," the Mumbler said. "Elsewise we might've had our throats slit over bread heels." He thanked Harold.

Evan looked at the old man. "What's your name?"

The elder Mumbler introduced himself as Orrin. Will had the eye patch. The fat one was named Tomas; the black-haired boy, Dash. Evan used false names for their party members.

"You should come with us to Hexwaite," Jason told Orrin. "Our horses could bear you."

They'll slow us down, Evan thought. Sam glanced at the heavyset

Mumbler. "With four more riders, we won't reach Hexwaite before sundown," the knight warned.

"The lad's right," Orrin said. "If you might escort us back to our camp, we'd be grateful. We'll leave tomorrow. Giving out alms here has become too dangerous."

Jason had his hands on his hips. "Why don't we camp together tonight?" he asked. "We can protect one another. Twelve pairs of eyes are better than four or eight, and we're armed."

"Eleven-and-a-half pairs," Will said, winking his one eye.

Jason smiled apologetically. "At sunrise, we'll take you to Hexwaite."

Evan and Rogir shared a long look. Before either could interject, the Mumbler steepled his hands, as if in prayer. "I give thanks to god," Orrin said. "Wonderful. Wonderful! We have cheese and bread to spare. Come, it's a half-hour ride."

Ahorse with Rogir, the old Mumbler led them west off Scythe Road, down a worn path rutted by hooves and wheels. Jason followed at his side, chuckling good-naturedly at Orrin's jokes about old age. Evan and the five knights trotted behind them, wary-eyed as hounds.

Orrin's companions were clergymen, but it would've been easy to mistake them for tavern drunks. Will rode with Erick, Tomas with David, annoying the knights with hissing laughter at their own crude jokes. The boy was more serious. Saddled with Sam, Dash stayed quiet as a mouse. Evan couldn't shake the feeling that he was afraid.

Something felt amiss. He trained his eyes on Jason and the old man. *You also enjoyed the company of Commoners, Sarah,* he thought. *And look where that got you . . . and us . . .*

The sun had flattened to a blood streak in the clouds by the time they ascended a grassless hill. At the foot of the slope, large rocks ringed the black stain of a dashed firepit. Within lay wool blankets, empty saddlebags, and a little further off, in the high grass, the Mumblers' larder wagon. The knights swept the area, learning the lay of the land.

"Welcome to our humble abode," Orrin said with a smile and shrug. "It's not much, but it's off the road a-ways. People fear griffons and won't come this far out."

Evan stared at the firepit. "You've been making fires," he said grimly. "This area's in drought. You could start a wildfire."

"Hence the hill and the rocks. They're firewalls."

Jason studied the thick clouds flowing toward them. "Maybe we'll see rain tonight after all."

"God willing," Orrin said. "The Midlanders need it."

Will and Dash kindled a fire while the knights hobbled their horses to leafless trees on the periphery. Night fell, and fell dark. Clouds obscured the stars. Everyone sat around the fire. Seated by Jason, Evan couldn't see anything beyond the ruddied rocks.

If this is a trap . . . he thought fearfully. Evan glanced at the old Mumbler. Orrin's gnarled hand rarely left his pocket.

Thankfully, the crickets sang shrilly. If someone out there had any bright ideas about catching them unawares, the insects would give them up with silence.

Once Orrin broke out heels of bread and salted cheese, everyone's mood lightened. Conversation started off low, the Mumblers and knights keeping to themselves. After eating their fill, Sir Harold and one-eyed Will struck up conversation and learned they'd both been to The Tall Pint, a South Farcombe inn. That led to them swapping stories about the Pint's portly innkeep. They laughed infectiously.

After that, David Bridge uncorked his wineskin to share with Tomas, then offered it smilingly to Dash. The boy took a single sip. He stood quickly, flush in the face, hacking like an old man. Everyone laughed when Tomas likened him to Orrin. Jason saw the boy back to the fire, patting his back. Everyone was smiling, even Rogir. The crickets carried on.

Inevitably, talk turned to Scythe Road.

"Things weren't always this bad," Orrin lamented. He sat hunched over, the weight of the world on his shoulders. "Years ago, gold—everywhere. Golden wheat." He wriggled his fingers through the air, as if they were wheat stalks flowing in a wind. "Sure, the homeless came here, but they were few. Now? Mass misery. Starvation. And *now?* Theft. Murder. Godlessness."

"It's a rare thing," Evan ventured. "Peasants aren't known to prey on each other. They stick together."

Orrin nodded. "They do. *Did.* Up until King Hexar died."

Jason let his clutched hands hang off his knees. He meditated on the popping fire. "The land needs its king."

Evan glanced at Jason, recalling Drexan's words to him in the throne room. *The land needs you, nephew,* he thought.

Firelight flickered in the old Mumbler's hazel eyes. "The land needs god. Its true god."

Erick Seam accepted the wineskin as it changed hands, drank from it, and passed it on. "Spoken like a true reader of the Free Beliefs," he said. "But if god is god, why doesn't he end the peasants' suffering"— he snapped his fingers—"like that?"

A bold question that was, one asked by millions of people every-where, and one that could drain the enjoyment out of an otherwise enjoyable evening so far, if these men took offense. Then again, they'd saved the Mumblers' lives.

"Mind you," Erick added swiftly, to avoid poor form, "I'm a Free Believer, same as you."

Evan waited for Orrin's response. "You're asking why god doesn't make it rain," the elder said at last. "End the drought."

"Or end suffering. All suffering."

Orrin nodded pensively, weighing his response. "God could do it, if he were here. He could—with one snap of his fingers"—he pressed thumb and finger together, but didn't snap—"send this parched region rain. Clothe and nourish the poor souls starving out there. End the war in the Brace. Stop Elvarenists from separating peasant families." He sighed. "But god isn't here. God's been gone for millennia. In his absence from our world, man suffers."

The knights exchanged looks, baffled.

David narrowed his eyes skeptically. "You're talking about King

Anjan's heir. The half-elf who'll reign again."

Orrin simply watched the knight, unspeaking.

"Anjan, Eduard, and all their line had great power, but *gods?*" Erick shook his head. "Remember, they were half-*men.*"

Jason poked at the fire with a stick. He disentangled a log from the pile so that it fell, spraying embers. "I once thought suffering was god's will," he said, eyes low. "But then I lost my brother in the—north, in Uzland," he caught himself.

He almost said the Brace, in reference to Prince Erick, Evan knew. *Lies don't come easily to your son, Sarah.*

Orrin smiled. "Ah, I took you for a warrior." He fronted toward Jason, readjusting his legs. "You fought for Hexar?"

"Aye, and lost my brother."

The Mumbler called Tomas sat forward. "Did you fight alongside the Stormsword?" The fat man seemed eager as a youngling riveted by war stories. "Darren Thorngale's a hero."

Jason didn't answer Tomas. "I searched the heavens for answers. I never felt that god provided them. But the star of reason did." Evan stirred with pride. "I think . . . I think our suffering is *our* doing. Our misery. Usually because we allow kings and lords to rule us as they please. We consent to them ruling us without our consent."

I couldn't have said it better myself, Evan thought.

"I've heard another man speak as you do," the old man said. "Goes by Firemouth. Every lord wants to hang him."

"Someone should," Rogir intoned gruffly.

As Jason ignored Tomas, Orrin ignored Rogir. "He thinks giving everyone a voice will better us all. 'To each a chair.'"

Jason smiled like someone surprised to find common ground with a stranger. "'To all a piece.' Yes, I've heard this Firemouth speak before. He calls for reinstating the Wing of the Commons, to make our Worthy Assembly whole."

"And would you agree with him?" Orrin briefly met Evan's gaze, then switched back to Jason. "If peasants made laws with their lords and kings—if they had a seat at the table—would your brother have died senselessly, far from home, in the ice?"

The Mumbler phrased his question insensitively. It seemed to bother Jason. Knights shifted uncomfortably.

"I think the answer is plain," Evan interjected. "The lords, clergy, and merchants of the Worthy Assembly rule Loran with its king. To make war, the king must raise coin from these men. If peasants sat with the other three classes—"

"Peasants got no money to raise," Tomas blurted out.

Orrin held up a finger, as if he were a teacher about to scold his student for interrupting. "No, Tomas, but peasants often *are* the ones who fight. Aren't they? Just like our friend here"—he nodded at Jason—"and like his brother, they likely wouldn't agree to war, even if their lords happily opened their purses. That's the point of sitting all the classes together for the making of laws. 'From the thorny bush of nature we fled naked, together, and together we must rule ourselves, clothed in law.'"

The line was lost on everyone else. Not Evan. He couldn't resist his grin. "You're quoting *State of Nature*. Written by Lord Gram Reuben of Tesos, three centuries ago. Only a few men in this kingdom would know it. You're a well-read Mumbler."

Orrin dipped as if for applause, smiling, a papery hand flat across his chest. "And you, a well-read merchant. But mistake me not. I'm no supporter of Gram Reuben, his Awakening, or the star of reason. If I had it my way, that treacherous Wing of the Commons would stay dead and buried."

Interesting, Evan thought. Mumblers usually supported the Common cause. *But not this one.*

His nephew didn't seem as fascinated. He looked stunned. Offended, even. "*Why?*" he asked. "If peasants had a say in what their rulers do, you'd shoulder less of a burden. There might be poorhouses out there. Justices and deputies to keep the peace on this road, to stop the theft and violence visited on you."

"I see some value in a Fourth Wing," Orrin conceded with airy contempt, "but we have enough ticks ruling us."

Jason set his jaw rigidly. "Ticks . . . ? You spend your days *feeding* peasants. You're one yourself. Don't you want their lot and yours improved?"

Orrin looked down at his lap. "Let me explain another way," he said, sounding chastened. "What happens when children are left to themselves? They squabble. They bully. They hurt each other, as we saw on Scythe Road. People are children. And children need parents, not scepters."

"And you feel as strongly about the other classes in the Worthy Assembly?" Evan asked.

"Yes. Children." Orrin locked eyes with him. There was something to his glinting gaze that . . . unsettled. Evan brushed off the feeling. "Once, a great king ruled the world. He ruled alone. Life was better, then. Simpler."

David clapped his hands once, as if he'd just won a bet. "So you *were* referring to Anjan Half-Elf's heir, earlier."

Evan spoke over David just as he started saying *earlier*, "'Men and women left the thorns and brambles not because a king was king by blood right. They looked within, and lo, they beheld the shining star of their own reason, and desired law.'"

Orrin leaned forward with an admonishing look. "That text is a bastardization of truth. What's the star of reason? A star of self. A self that thinks itself god. *Heresy.*"

Evan chuckled. "Not quite, Brother Orrin. It's a metaphor for enlightened self-interest—the birthright of men high and low. A light that led man out of fearsome nature, where he first woke. Self-interest persuaded him to form a society. To fashion laws. To work with everyone else for mutual benefit."

"When it suits him."

"Yes, of course. It's the basis of the Great Covenant that man made with his king. Protection in exchange for freedom. But"—he stressed *but*—"to join society means having a say in how it rules you. I'm a merchant. I have representation in the Assembly. I can sympathize with peasants craving a voice."

Orrin glanced away, as someone does when he disagrees but doesn't want to give offense. His companions stared at the flames or smacked on hard cheese.

Jason beat Evan to speaking. "Brother Orrin, did you not follow the star of reason earlier?" He spread his arms to encompass their circle. "Brigands nearly killed you today for a little bread. They could've come back for you tonight. But you realized they wouldn't—not with armed men around you. Not with strength in numbers. It's the Great Covenant writ small."

The Mumbler had smiling eyes. "Was it self-interest that led you to confront the brigands, or compassion?" Before Jason could answer, he jabbed his finger and said, "Empathy. *This* is man's sacred light. Our saving grace. Not grubby self-interest."

"Empathy *is* self-interest," Evan rejoined. "A man finds brigands threatening others on a road. When he rescues them, he's rescuing *himself* in a way. He hopes others would act in his interest if the roles were reversed."

A knight offered Evan the wineskin; he declined with a dismissive gesture. This conversation was as riveting as it was revealing. "Self-interest isn't evil. People *improve* themselves by following self-interest, in every age. A hundred years ago, books had to be painstakingly hand-printed. Then, the star of reason led someone to invent the printing press. Hundreds of years before that, men and women thought they could only see stars with their naked eye. Then—"

"Gram Reuben invented the skyglass," Orrin finished.

"'Find your star of reason, and improve your wellbeing as one sharpens steel,'" Evan said. "Reuben wrote that. What did the Wing of the Commons do, if not follow its star of reason, sharpening other classes—and improving our realm?" He held a hand to the night sky, as if pointing at the star of reason itself.

Orrin smiled, hands folded over each other in his lap. "I'm grateful for your compassion and empathy. For your company. But the star of reason?" He clicked his tongue. "I've never heard a funnier joke. Are those peasants ruled by reason? No more than our attackers were earlier. Their skies are filled with clouds of hunger. Of desire. *That's what self-interest is.* What it is for men and women, high and low. The clouds easily become storms, hiding stars."

A wind picked up, whittling away the snapping fire. The night felt darker, if that were possible. "We must all contend with storms within," Evan said. *I should know.*

"No," Orrin said, almost in rebuke. "Men *are* those storms, the rain, the wind, lightning, thunder. They can't see through or past the fury in themselves. What you call the star of reason, I call the storm-wind. A myth about intelligence that makes man see a god in the mirror. Or a king or lord, if he but climbs over someone, reaches a little higher." He gave a tired headshake.

"But they're not worthy of that power. Men lust. They envy. They steal. And they're vain. They pursue, acquire, and abuse power for petty, self-serving reasons. To avenge some offense given. To make themselves tall as mountains when they're small as ants."

"Bleak," Evan said, his smile somber.

"We're just sets of mouths, bellies, and loins. We don't need hundreds more thirsty, hungry, lustful sets ruling over us." Orrin raised a single finger. "Just one."

"But the First King is long gone, his line broken, his half-elven heirs dead. Which leaves us. Just us, as far as we can tell. And your ideal world looks like . . . what?" Evan no longer hid his disdain. The old man was a hypocrite . . . and worse. "Like Scythe Road? Full of suffering no one should repair?"

The wind blew hoarsely, ruffling the bandage around the Mumbler's head while he sat statue-still. "We're not alone. The gods can end suffering. To think ourselves capable of ruling like the gods . . ." He grunted contemptuously. "King Lathros learned the hard way men couldn't rule themselves—didn't he? When the Fourth Wing's petitioners gave Sir Bradley Durhurst and his knights the ruse they needed to storm the throne room and behead their ruler like a chicken."

He gazed at Jason. "I wonder if Hexar remembered the King Who Lost His Head as he lay cold and dying."

Jason was somewhere between confusion and offense. The knights tensed at what felt like a deliberate provocation. *He knows who Jason is,* the nobleman realized.

Evan had a hard smile. "You know, I studied to become a Mumbler. You swear vows: one to the One True God, another to live a life of poverty. You spoke of gods twice just now—and you've got the most exquisite emerald ring in your pocket."

He stood with his sword in hand. "Which means you're either a brigand, or someone else. That you killed Mumblers, stole their robes and larder wagon. You lied to us. Staged that trouble on the road— brought us here." Evan flitted to Rogir. "Bind their hands."

Rogir nodded the command to his men, and they stood promptly, drawing firelit swords. Jason rose, pulling close to Evan, his blade out.

"But it's been a fascinating conversation," Evan told the old man, meaning it.

Tomas and Will went from eyeing the swords in their faces to exchanging nervous glances, with each other, then with Orrin. Dash trembled like he might piss himself. *If these men are brigands, they're not the real threat,* Evan thought.

"Watch your backs," Evan told Rogir. "The other brigands are close." He listened for a lull in the crickets' chirping.

Orrin's lips curled with a smile. "No, they're not. No one is springing a trap. We mean you no harm, Lord Evan."

The closest knights, Kyle and Sam, veered their swords sharply at the old man as he rose. He brushed bits of dirt and grass off his robes, as if the blades pointed at him were reeds.

"*Who the fuck are you?*" Evan demanded. As he spoke, the unusually strong wind turned ferocious, whipping flame every which way. Even the war-hardened knights seemed rattled.

"You lied to us, too," the old man pitched his voice over the blustery wind. "Worry not. I was . . . curious to meet you. No one will know you were here. I promise you." Wind all but guttered the fire, immersing them in darkness. Evan saw only the pile of orange embers and its reflection in Orrin's eyes. "It's in our self-interest."

Crickets fell silent. In the distance, their horses nickered and stomped. Evan stepped protectively in front of Jason, his sword ready. He struggled to discern movement in darkness.

The gusts softened to a breeze. Seconds later, the fire crackled anew, licking logs and tinder hungrily, lighting the area.

The old man and his companions were gone.

CHAPTER 26

Rendezvous

Five days after their parting outside Elfgate, Evan Sinclair's warning clung to Rathos like soaked clothing. He dwelled on their conversation amid the percussive drumbeat of his horse's hooves.

"Work with Rezlan Ambrose, compromise with him, but show care around him," he'd told him as Jason had bantered with Karl. "He's more dangerous than me, and all he wants is war."

Which he'll have, Rathos thought grimly, *along with your blackpowder in Barley Tower . . . if Jason fails, and not before.*

He glanced at his brooding companion. Karl Redmore swayed ahorse woodenly. He sometimes picked at his tunic and cape or patted his steed, but said and did little else. *What did Rezlan tell you before we left Wessex-by-the-Sea?* Rathos wondered. *And what will you tell him when we speak with him next?*

Rathos hadn't known Karl well before their expedition, but by now he could read the Reubenite like a book. Karl was rehearsing a story, the story he would tell Rezlan and their faction members. A story about Evan Sinclair's ill-fated mission to the Walls, about a foolish old man whose guilt had blinded his reason. A speaker gone rogue, trying to draw Loran's only hope for reform into the snake's pit of the Kingstrials. A man unfit to speak for the Loyal Company any longer.

And I'll have my own story to tell.

The air was tense with things left unsaid as the men rode back to Westland. Ahead stretched Midway Road, a length of grass-choked rubble hemmed in by the mighty oaks and limber birch trees of Southland's Rotwood. Limbs overhead sewed a quilt of leaves that glowed emerald and honey in the sunlight. Griffs occasionally shattered the silence with their calls, almost as a reminder of the awkwardness.

Their first day back in the wilderness had been a shrewd dance, to be sure. If Karl asked him for details about Evan's plan for the Kingstrials, Rathos would answer with what he thought was prudent, careful not to tip his hand. To reveal too much could spell disaster for his mission before it ever began, for he knew Karl would do whatever he could to undermine it. Like other Reubenites, he'd opposed them from the start, and his captivity in the Red Tower had embittered him.

By the third day, even innocuous observations wore thin. A lull in conversation stretched into an hour's quiet. With the sun glaring down on their backs, the men rode several yards apart, saying nothing unless they had to speak. Come nightfall, they made camp, munching on their salted bread and cheese, a comfortable distance from each other.

He felt the first stirrings of an argument on their fifth day in the wild. They approached the swordwood. Trees gave way to gnarled silver lances that reflected sunlight like mirrors. On the nearest shiny tree hung a dead raven, its feet twined to a limb. A message from the Loyal Company's Pigeons.

Karl pressed his fingers to his mouth for a birdcall; Rathos jerked his wrist down. "Outlaws are known to pass through the Rotwood," he cautioned. "Better to wait until this strange area is well behind us, no?"

The Reubenite yanked his hand away, surly-eyed. "That's why we have Pigeons." He nodded at the suspended raven.

"Did you forget the griff we found dead in the brook? In any case, Evan said these lands are infested with outlaws." *And as the father of one,* Rathos thought, *he would know.*

"Oh, he did, did he? And I suppose our Remembrance Day mission went as smoothly as he expected, too, eh?"

His sneer quickened days of tension. Rathos urged his horse close. "Neither of us could've predicted King Hexar's assassination," he said softly. "Now, we must deal with our situation reasonably."

Karl burst with a contemptuous laugh. "*Reasonably?* You call this reason? We leave to petition a king and wind up in the Red Tower, courtesy of our leader's own nephew."

"Lord Jason's ploy was for our own safety. And keep your god-damned voice down."

The Reubenite spat. "*Lord* Jason. *Lord* Evan. Methinks you had another reason for following Sinclair all these years. *Lord* Rathos, Lord of Caerdon—isn't that what it'll be now?"

"Tread carefully."

"Why?" he went on tauntingly. "It's true, isn't it? First you'll make deputy, then lord speaker, then Lord of Caerdon. Isn't that what the ambitious Rathos Robswell wants? From orphan to freeholder to lord. And you'll have Evan's precious cunt to thank—"

Still in his saddle, Rathos laced his fingers around his companion's supple throat. Under their cold embrace, their horses stirred uneasily.

"Insult mine wife ever again," Rathos hissed, "and you'll never be able to prattle to Rezlan like the fucking bugger you are. Do you hear me? I'll *kill* you."

Karl wriggled out of his clutches like a snake, drawing his sword. "You fucking prick. How about I kill you here, and make Rezlan speaker by need? How will you sell Evan's madness to the Company *then*?"

"Lower your sword."

Men untangled themselves from their nests in the boughs above. Hands over feet, the Pigeons of the Loyal Company slid down their tree trunks with catlike grace. They looked like the woods come alive in their forest-green cloaks, gray tunics, and faded brown breeches. Each scout had a longbow slung over his chest and steel of some kind at his waist. There were five.

One of them stepped forward. He had disheveled blond hair and a silver-stubbled face and neck. Rathos didn't know him, and neither did Karl by his lost look. But then, most of the Company didn't know the names of their traveling lookouts and messengers, the men who helped traitors like themselves stay one step ahead of spies in service to Gram Sothos, Charles Burke, and everyone who wanted them dead.

The Pigeon raised the flat of his palm. "Hail, Pilgrims."

From his saddle, Rathos replied, "Hail, Eyes of the World."

This was the exchange that identified Companymen to their Pigeons. To err in reciting it could mean death. To divulge it to anyone outside the Company carried the same price.

"Where does the sun rise and set?" their leader asked coolly.

"It rises in the west and sets in the east," Rathos replied.

"Which star shines the brightest in darkest night?"

"The star of reason, the birthright of men high and low."

"Where are the Evergreen Isles on this disc called Odma?"

"Nowhere, for Odma is round."

"What do we call our sun and star?"

"Quill and blade."

The Pigeons deferentially laid their hands over their hearts, and Rathos and Karl mirrored them. With the needed exchange done, all eyes strayed to Karl, who begrudgingly sheathed his blade.

Rathos dismounted. "Well met, friends."

"Well met," the leader said. "My name is Tom Goodfield. These fellows are my compatriots"—and he pointed at each one in turn—"Varn, Reed, Jacob, Yule. We're the Soothsayers."

False names, all, Rathos knew. "You must have foresight to find us here," he said. "We hesitated to whistle for you so close to Graywood."

"You're far from your posts if you're Soothsayers," Karl butted in from his saddle. "Isn't it the Waterfowl who nest in Rotwood?"

"We were sent," Tom explained. "We thought to find you on Midway Road. Left a raven for you." He arched a questioning eyebrow. "We didn't think to find Companymen at blows."

The Reubenite looked away, annoyed or ashamed.

"Mind us not," Rathos said with a feigned smile. "We've had our fill of misadventure recently. We're both on edge."

Tom relaxed his posture. "So it's true, what they're saying. Hexar the Bold is dead."

"By whom, we cannot say. He was slain on Remembrance Day. We were gaoled in the Red Tower."

The Pigeons all looked to a grimacing Tom. "Is that where our lord speaker is, then?" the leader asked.

Rathos made his face a mask. "He's on an urgent errand. My companion and I were returning to confer with the Loyal Company on my lord's orders."

"And with Rezlan," chimed Karl, as a dig at him.

"You needn't go far," Tom said. "Rezlan Ambrose sent us in the first place. He awaits you presently."

Rathos frowned. "Presently?"

Tom nodded in Graywood's direction. "He traveled with us. He wanted to meet with Evan, but Silvertongue will do."

Karl grunted his disapproval. "You traveled *with* a leader of the Loyal Company? On foot? That is dangerous business."

The Pigeon commander regarded Karl, aloof. "If you truly belong with us, you know we have no say. Just as Companymen act as one bloc in the Worthy Assembly." He turned toward the swordwood. "Come, Rezlan is eager to hear your reports about Remembrance Day."

Rathos thought it odd. Why would Rezlan Ambrose risk himself for a conversation he could've had with Evan by way of the Pigeons? Karl, dotard that he was, had the right of it: any journey on foot was fraught with danger, especially for the Loyal Company's other parent. Jason's alliance with Evan gave them protection, but only a fool would think that Charles Burke had turned a blind eye to their activities.

Yet the king was dead. Their mission to restore the Fourth Wing had failed catastrophically. Rezlan had to be furious.

Moreover, there was no refusing Company summons. Especially when one of its parents was involved.

Reflexively, Rathos began to heave himself into his saddle.

Varn took his horse's reins. "Better to travel on foot from here," he said. "The swordwood is good for privacy, but horses, they startle easy. If yours sees his reflection, he might spook, nick a leg, and kick you and your friend down a jagged slope."

He disliked the Pigeon immediately. Varn, whatever his actual name, had a cavalierness compounded by boyishness, locks of chestnut hair, and smug green eyes.

Irritatingly, Rathos also discerned an accent. That could be a problem for Pigeons, who wore bland colors to blend in with the forest, to remain unseen or be forgotten. This fellow rolled his *r* and doubled his consonants like a Penathoan.

We must be short on men, to recruit from other kingdoms, he thought. He made a mental note to broach this with Rezlan.

"Very well," Rathos told Varn. He patted his horse.

Karl smirked as he led his mount to Varn. "What's wrong, Silvertongue? Afraid you'll need to make a quick escape?"

Rathos ignored him.

Their horses stayed behind with Varn. Forming up in a line, with Tom at the front, they marched toward the strange forest that gave even the hardest men pause. They passed the tree with the dead raven. If Rathos were given to superstition, he'd have thought one of its stale black eyes followed him.

Off Midway Road, the familiar oaks and birches dwindled in number. The sunlit grass thickened into barbed reeds that clawed at their sides. Midges whirred in their ears and bit their arms, leaving itchy pink welts.

Then came the strangest forest in the world.

Graywood swallowed everything, as if there had never been anything but twisted metal trees everywhere. Ferns cracked like glass beneath their boots. Sunlit leaves blazed orange as flame. Disorientingly, their reflections followed in the mirrors of trunks. Everyone struggled in the heat, yet none dared remove any mail or garments, fearful of bark, limbs, and needles sharp as fresh-forged steel.

There is no stranger place on Odma, Rathos pondered as he caught his olive-green eyes in the gnarled mirror of a steel tree. *Yet even the strangest things have an explanation.*

Men of reason like Evan and Rathos and Rezlan, even Karl, saw not the divine in this alien forest but a puzzle piece. Dragons breathed fire. Silverstone shimmered like moonlit water. Merpeople swam underwater like dolphins. And steel coated every groove in every tree of this bizarre forest.

The Awakening taught men that none of this was beyond comprehension. The Free Beliefs that Awakening had inspired posited that Graywood and the Silver Walls and all things were like dead languages men would eventually decipher.

Even so . . . there was a dread feeling to the swordwood that Rathos couldn't rationalize away. That stayed with him for the half hour they spent walking in silence, mopping sweat off their faces, watching their extremities. Rathos tried to think on his wife to pass the time and forget his discomfort.

"How much farther?" he asked.

"Little bit," Tom said hoarsely from the front.

After another mile, the metallic trees gave way to a small clearing festooned with silky moss. A fire was dashed to soot in the middle.

Karl turned, hands on his hips. "Where's Rezlan?"

"In Shoaltown."

Sunlight flashed as Yule's blade nicked Karl's stomach. The Reubenite collapsed to the ground and screamed, half-gurgling. Karl had caked his side in the shrapnel of Graywood's steel ferns.

Rathos spun on the points of four swords. The Pigeons regarded him with dead eyes.

"*But why?*" the Petitioner demanded.

Tom gave a shrug. "Doesn't matter now, lad."

Without another word, Yule lunged forward with a thrust of his crimson-stained sword.

Rathos was surprised, but not defenseless.

In his youth Evan had taught him peace first, always peace, but many were the days warder and ward had crossed swords in Caerdon Castle's lower bailey. "Trust your wits and choose peace if you can," he remembered Evan saying, even as he drew his sword presently, "but if you must kill, kill without pity."

The castle-trained swordsman saw Yule's overconfident thrust, narrowly sidestepped it, knocked him off balance, and drove his blade through the Pigeon's side for a torrent of red. Seizing opportunity, Karl dragged Yule into the pile of bloody needles.

Reed and Jacob circled Rathos like wolves. Reed pitched forward with a downward slash. Rathos stumbled over a log to avoid the stab at his unprotected flank. He evaded a slash here, there, and allowed Jacob's next maneuver.

Jacob swung his steel at Rathos and missed, striking a tree

that chipped the point of the sword. "Stay still you skinny fucker," he snarled.

"I prefer to think of myself as lean, personally," Rathos returned.

Reed lunged. Rathos deflected his downward arc and buried Yule's sword in the Pigeon's chest. The killing stroke cost him: Jacob's sword sent fire coursing through his right arm. Rathos drew off, catching sight of the blood darkening his sleeve.

It was a pommel to the forehead that disarmed Rathos. His world spinning, he found himself kneeling, sword kicked into the steel forest.

Karl hadn't fared well. Yule, even with his flank bleeding, now had a sword to Karl's neck. Tom and Jacob circled the injured Rathos confidently.

"No hard feelings, lad," Tom said as he arched his sword above his head.

A spear burst through Tom's stomach.

War cries echoed through Draywood. Yule spun just in time to deflect a bastard sword, but it was bait, and he left himself vulnerable to the two-sided axe that cleaved him neck to groin. A mountain of a man covered in tattoos retrieved his axe, cleaning its edges on the corpse.

Dozens of motley-armored men streamed through the trees, the walls of their spears, axes, and swords closing in on the one Pigeon left standing.

Jacob's sword shook in his hands. "I'm a Pigeon, a Pigeon of the Loyal Company, you'll regret it if you do anything to me," he said desperately.

"I fucking hate pigeons," came a woman's voice, amused. A voice that Rathos knew immediately. "Filthy little pests. My father taught me they carry disease. Like griffs."

"*Chirp chirp*," said a gangly man, flapping his arms. "*Squeak squeak.*"

A lithe, muscular woman emerged from the gang, clad in furs, boiled leather, and pauldrons. She looked sinister with the helm of a sickle-beaked griffon's skull over her head. Jacob pled for his life, up to the second her morning star caved in his head. The gangly fellow crowed and flapped his arms over the bodies like a rooster, drawing laughter.

The woman approached Rathos. She handed off her bloodstained morning star and removed her skull-helm, freeing hair the color of violet flowers.

Rathos smiled wanly.

CHAPTER 27

A Lord's Favor

ara went to feed Little Lady after morning prayers. She waded through coarse, knee-high grass in the predawn gloom. Ahead rose the stable roof, its outline blotting out stars.

Snorting excitedly, the horse angled her head through the wooden beams. Little Lady nuzzled her neck.

"Good morning, Lady," the girl said. "Did you sleep well? I have an oat for you. Father hid them away."

Little Lady devoured the oat and almost her hand; Sara giggled as teeth sampled her wrist. She squeezed through the wooden beams and stroked her sleek mane, complimenting her. She stayed with her until she heard Rose coming.

This had been her routine for the last few weeks. The stable was their refuge, *hers*, from Rosbury, the world. If she thought long on Caleb or began to weep, she'd hug Little Lady's neck or run her fingers through her mane.

The tiny enclosure was also where she'd counted every day until she saw the elf again. Tonight promised a full moon. She was almost nauseous from how giddy she felt. *We'll be a family again one day soon, Father.*

Of course, she hadn't told her mother anything about her new friend in the grove. She burned to tell Rose, but she knew in her heart that the elf's friendship needed to remain a secret.

She and her mother sat around the firepit to eat breakfast, a pottage of oats and parsley sweetened with honey. Bees flew about their hive atop the ridgepole. One of them landed on her arm, planting its stinger; she swatted at it angrily. The one and only good thing about having been away from their house was not suffering bee stings every day.

"Take the bucket and fetch water at the well," Rose told her in a stuffy tone as she spooned pottage into her mouth. "I'll need it to make leek stew tonight."

Sara sat on her discomfort. She hadn't traveled far outside of their house or stable since their return from the Red Tower. Some of Rosbury's roving boys liked to call her names. Rose had mostly left her to herself since the horse's reappearance. She wondered if this was a punishment overdue for chucking an apple at Sweet Tom.

After breakfast, Sara dutifully went into the shed, where they hung their clothes and kept a bath barrel. She felt like her father clamping on armor as she rolled hose above her knees and slipped into her gown. She tucked strands of hair beneath her wimple and recovered their wooden bucket. A bee chased her out the door.

Sunlight peered through rainclouds on the move. Sara walked down a sloping dirt path choked with weeds, bucket swinging in her hands. She prayed the weather would shift eastward in time for tonight's full moon, or north, so that the parched Midlands would suffer no more. *So long as nothing prevents me from seeing Dray tonight.* The elf-prince's powers seemed to hinge on moonlight.

Pigeons fluttered inside the village dovecote as Sara passed by. She glanced at villagers, who went about their business, ignoring her. She didn't mind. She preferred her invisibility.

The world had changed since King Hexar's murder. Sara and her mother had escaped the Red Tower, but not Caleb, or the Hammer of the Commons. The Worthy men had replaced Gram Sothos with Greg Thorngale, something peasants were quite happy about.

In turn, the Old Oak had called the Kingstrials to find and crown the successor. She often heard peasants walking by her house, chatting excitedly about the first tournament in many years. It was like the old king hadn't existed at all, the way they moved on from him.

Sara spotted three women coming up the road. They were

singlewomen—two widows and a maiden. She admired them. Most women couldn't do the work of men. These three women somehow got away with flouting the laws.

Dessa Gord herded sheep past her, conferring with Ashley Vauld and Jaclyn Webster about going north to the Colossus to sell sheepskin and sheaves of wheat. "Lords'll gather there like flies on a lamb's carcass," she heard Dessa saying, drawing out the word *flies*.

Sara smiled at the three women. They glanced in other directions.

Maybe not everyone's forgotten about Hexar, she thought, *or the accusations against us.* It didn't feel good to be ignored, especially by women she liked and looked up to. But then, few spoke to them anymore, even at parish.

Only Sir Willard checked on them regularly.

Passing by Dessa's house, she mistook the tufts of white hair in her tall grass for mushrooms. Sara took relief. *At least we're not the only Commoners disliked,* she thought.

Someone had placed a curse on Dessa. The rabbit fur left little doubt. Caleb had once said Sylvanians were a jealous folk who dealt out curses and blessings like Winter Solstice gifts. She wondered who else practiced the Old Ways in Rosbury. Whether anyone had ever cursed her or Caleb . . .

Whether anyone else knew about Dray.

She overheard shouts at Twelve Mercies Parish. Rounding the post mill, she found people she didn't want to see. Clyde the baker's son, Bram Hobbs, and Pesh the Prince took turns hurling cow pies and pebbles at a man in the pillory. Frogface Jenny stood on the periphery, looking out of place.

From stake to headboard, the pillory wobbled like a hut in a storm. The man locked between boards wept uncontrollably. With his front secured in boards, the rest of Praise Whoreson erupted backward like too much dough pressed into an oven.

Hinges barely held the boards in place. Yet Praise didn't seem to know it. Flecks of dirt and cow pie mingled with pus spattering his raw, cracked pustules.

The boys chanted Pebbleface, Pebbleface, as dirt and cow pies left their hands. Pesh struck Praise with a cow pie. Alfrid scooped up a clump of soil that flew apart midair, dashing the big man's feet. Bram outdid both boys with a rock the size of his fist that hit the idiot between his eyes, inspiring such a frenzy of resistance that the topmost board nearly jerked free.

The big man sucked in air like he was drowning each time he sobbed. "STOP, stop, *pleeeease*," he wailed. "Mother, make it stop, mooother pleeeeease."

"Hear that lads?" Alfrid goaded them. "He wants his Ma."

"He wants for a new song, is what he wants." Bram picked up a rock. "*Pebbleface, Pebbleface, a dead mother's disgrace.*"

"*Pebbleface, Pebbleface,*" Pesh continued the rhyme with cruel delight, "*pale as whitest lace.*"

"You know what I heard 'bout Pebbleface," Bram told the boys giddily, casting Sara a mischievous glance. "Heard that ol' Pebbleface has a noble father."

"Praise Morley," Alfrid snickered. *Morley?* Sara wondered.

"Aye, but it's not possible. Just look at him." Pesh hurled a pie that made a *splat* sound when it hit Praise. "He donna look like Lord Uthron. He's no nobler than me."

"If he were, he'd be . . . *Lord Pebbles!*"

The boys launched into uproarious laughter, clutching their bellies, as if it were the funniest thing they'd ever heard. Praise begged Sara for help with his glassy eyes.

Finally seeing her, Alfrid started toward Sara. She recoiled out of fear that he would bully her, call her a kingkiller, as Pesh and Bram had done sometimes when they passed by the stable.

"Here, help us punish Lord Pebbles," Alfrid urged her. He offered her a handful of pebbles.

The other boys frowned but said nothing; Alfrid carried weight in their circle as Reader Gary's cousin. Sara shifted the pebbles in her hands, feeling strangely proud. She hadn't gone out in a month, leery of japes from these boys about Caleb, her mother, and herself. Sara

Shadowking, they'd called her. Sara Kingkiller. Traitor Sara.

Now they wanted her to overlook all that.

Alfrid struck Praise in the face with another rock. "Well?" he asked her. "You joinin' in?"

Sara set down her bucket. She took her place at the front of the line. Praise shook with the terror she'd felt inside her Red Tower cell. "What did he do?" she asked meekly.

"Idiot snuck into the parish and cracked the bell when he rang it," Alfrid said.

Sara remembered hearing the bell, briefly. Bram and Pesh shared a fleeting look, smothering their smiles. Alfrid eyed her with suspicion. *Praise didn't crack the bell,* she knew.

She pitied the simpleton. "I don't want to play." She wiped her hands of pebbles. "This is stupid."

Bram had a vicious look. "*You're* stupid, Sara Kingkiller."

Pesh the Prince approached her menacingly. "Sara Friend of Pagans."

They abandoned Praise for her in an instant, circling like wolves. "My father went to Southpoint last week," Alfrid told her. "Know what he saw? Caleb Kingkiller's head on Traitor's Gate. Rotting. Covered in flies."

Tears welled up in her eyes. "You, you shut up!"

Quick as a cat, Pesh the Prince snatched her wimple; her hair tumbled out. He pranced off, giggling. "Look! It's her hair. Tell Sir Willard so he can put her in the pillory, too!"

Devan hid the wimple behind his back as she tried for it. "Why donna you want to play with us, Sara Shadowking?"

"Because she *loves* Pebbleface," Bram taunted her. His eyes grew huge. "Sara Kingkiller wants to *marry Pebbleface!*"

"*Lady . . . Lady Pebbles!*" Pesh struggled to finish, unable to contain his gasping laughter. "Sara wants to be Lady Pebbles!"

Everyone laughed, everyone but Alfrid and his sister. "The lady should give her lord a kiss," Alfrid said, unsmiling.

The boys seized her. She fought, kicking and slapping, but they were older and overpowered her easily. Pesh and Devan pushed from behind, while Bram and Alfrid tugged her forward by her wrists. Frogface Jenny looked on from a distance, bug-eyed and cowardly, pulling on her wimple nervously.

Inches away from Praise, she caught a whiff of his stench and almost gagged. He smelled like a dead animal. The closer she got, the more hideous he became, his pustule clusters shiny with pus, the scabbed-over parts dull with crust and mud. Yet he feared her. His neck bulged with fat as he struggled to pull away, almost like a turtle retreating into his shell.

She shivered and shook. "Get off me, get off."

Devan forced her to lean forward. She thought about all of her missing protectors. Caleb would've intervened and scolded the boys. They wouldn't dare lay a hand on her with her knight father near.

When she didn't budge, Devan shoved her. She staggered into the stake and smacked her forehead. At first she thought she had fallen to her knees, but then she saw a mud-slathered stake hovering in the air, pointed at her face like a spear.

"Holy Anjan," Bram swore.

The pillory was now completely out of the ground. Still braced between the boards, Praise lurched about awkwardly, stooping, looking much like a woodsman with a log across his shoulders. Clumps of dirt slid off the stake like horse manure.

Devan stumbled into Frogface Jenny. "God, that must weigh at least sixty stone," he said. "*Look at him!*"

With his head between the boards, Praise looked like a giant bursting through a house that he couldn't break apart. He spun on the boys, gritting teeth flecked with pus and mud. "*Off it rolls again,*" he growled.

Bram wept like a girl. Alfrid ran to find Reader Gary. The others backed away, wide-eyed and shaking.

Inserting fingers thick as sausages between the boards, Praise began to pry them apart. Wood cracked as one of the hinges loosened.

"Stop him, stop him at once!" Out of nowhere, the Morley knights Sirs Luc Tolos and Bardo Lym marched on Praise.

The flash of steel reduced the giant once more to a child; he wept and said Mother, Mother, Mother. Even in their mail and gambeson, the men-at-arms recoiled timidly.

Reader Gary emerged from the parish, long gray sleeves flapping. He went milk-pale when he saw Praise hefting his own pillory. He began to shout him down when none other than their Lord Warden appeared from behind other men-at-arms, arrayed in mail and a velvety black tabard. Reader Gary bowed his neck immediately, and those of the children with their wits still about them followed suit.

Sunlight flashed in a stunning sapphire pendant at Morley's neck. He gazed at Praise from ahorse. "Why is he in that pillory, Gary?" he barked. "Where is Sir Willard?"

"Pardons, milord," Gary said hesitantly. "He . . . he cracked our parish bell this morning."

Morley stared at Praise for a long moment. "Put him in a heavier pillory," he muttered to Lym and Tolos.

Knights surrounded the wailing Praise, lifting the boards and threatening him with steel to force him to a set of heavier, thicker hinged planks. As they did their work, the Lord Warden turned to face Sara. His was a fatherly gaze, soft with recognition. He told one of his men to retrieve her wimple. Remembering her hair was even visible made the girl blush fiercely.

Morley swung off his horse. He knelt to fasten the fabric around her head. She lost herself in the winking of the sunlit jewel dangling off his neck. She'd never seen something so beautiful.

"In the future, let me know if these boys trouble you," he told Sara. "Speak to Sir Luc or Sir Bardo, and they'll see to their punishments." He glanced at her bucket. "What were you doing here, child?"

"To fetch water, milord," Sara said softly. She hadn't seen Uthron Morley since he'd carried her out of the Red Tower, and it brought back painful memories that left her nervous. "From the well, milord. For Mother's leek stew."

"Leek stew?" He sucked at his teeth for a *tsk-tsk*, shaking his head grievously. "You are my knight's daughter. No child of his will want so long as I am your lord." He gestured at Tolos, who scooped up her bucket and trudged toward the well in the distance.

Morley lifted her chin with a finger so that their gazes met. "Now let's see what we can find for you and your mother at market, shall we?" he said. "Peasants leave on the morrow for the Golden Meadows, and we can't let him take all of their beets and carrots north, can we?"

Uthron Morley accompanied Sara back to her dwelling with gifts to spare. Water sloshed in the bucket that Luc Tolos carried for her. A burlap bag swung across Bardo Lym's back, heavy with beets, carrots, and tasty bread. Morley unhooked a brace of featherless pheasants from his horse's saddlebags for her mother.

Rose burst into tears when she saw them with Sara at the door. She thanked Uthron Morley for his kindness, kissing his hand and curtsying. She offered to work in her lord's kitchens, if it pleased him, if he would have her at the castle again. Sara considered that a fool thing to offer after their work had landed them in the Red Tower, but he said he would, gladly—and only if she accepted two lorens in wages.

That night, Sara and her mother feasted on a sumptuous dinner, sweet bread marbled with nuts and cooked pheasant with liquid black skin that slipped off easily. A fine meal it was, the finest they'd had in months, maybe a year. It was the first night Sara's empty stomach hadn't ached in a while.

Sara pretended to be sleepy afterward, but Rose insisted they give thanks to Divna, godface of moonlight, penance, and faithful women. She happily complied; she needed a full moon tonight, anyway. She listened to her mother as she thanked Divna *especially* for Willard Rittman, without whom they might not have Uthron Morley's favor.

But this was Dray, she wanted to tell her. Just like Little Lady, this was the elf's magic. And that made it Caleb's doing, too.

When she heard her mother snoring softly, Sara crept out from beneath her straw. Silent as a mouse, she covered herself in her wool dress and walked barefoot through the door. Little Lady acknowledged her with a curious snort from her stable.

The moon shone brightly in the night sky, wreathed in silver clouds. She thanked the god with twelve faces and sent prayers to Dray's old Sylvanian gods.

Rosbury was asleep. Wary of stirring Praise, Sara took care to avoid the pillories across from Twelve Mercies and the village main entirely. She trod through high grass behind The Golden Dragon, filtered through Ashley Vauld's tall beet crops, and found Griff's Bridge.

Elf's Grove felt like a familiar friend. Perched atop their branches, spotted owls preened their wings, unconcerned with her presence. She listened to the cricket music; felt the damp leaves turn to mush underfoot. A few feet away, some ferns peeled apart, and out waddled a sluggish bewhiskered creature on four paws. It had an ugly pink snout and a rat's ribbed tail. The creature scurried away at her approach.

Moonlight guided her to the clearing. She halted when she overheard someone speaking softly, slipping behind the trunk of a thick oak.

A tall man stood by River Harriet, a shadow among other shadows amid shafts of moonlight. He curled a helm beneath his arm and wore a long black cape that rippled in a breeze. He spoke to no one but the cool night air, and yet paused at times, as if waiting on responses. She couldn't hear what he said over the gurgling water.

Sara tiptoed behind the trunk of another tree, trying for a closer look at the stranger. A cone of moonlight shot through the limbs over the river, pooling in the rims of his pauldrons. He wore a black tabard worked with Lord Uthron's blood-red tree.

No, he *was* Lord Uthron! She spied the sapphire pendant in his necklace. He spoke to the night in what sounded like First Tongue before switching abruptly to Common.

"... and what of the Crow?" he asked. "He might foresee this." He listened intently for a moment. "I'm prepared to make a gift with mine own life. He will die by my hand, or I will."

Donning his helm, Morley trudged into the river's swift currents. His cape and tabard ballooned on its surface as he vanished.

He'll die, Sara thought worriedly. The river waters were treacherous and frighteningly cold. Her father had warned her against trying to swim, telling her only a merman could. Lord Uthron was no merman.

Minutes passed. Sara could no longer hear owls, crickets, nothing but the sighing of windblown limbs and leaves. Suddenly that spot on the river's surface took to boiling as fiercely as water in a red-hot cauldron. Mist swirled over the water, fogging into a vaguely man-like shape. Fingers misted down from the hands, sickling like claws.

Sara didn't realize she was whimpering until it was too late. At the sound, eyes flared in the head, shining as brightly as little stars. The floating lights found Sara, and *knew* her. Panic made her shake. *No, don't see me, please go, please go, Maetha have mercy.* Shifting away, the shape flew into the forest.

Sara spun and ran away, heedless, stumbling. She tripped on a root and landed flat in a pile of leaves. Looking up, she saw Dray standing over her. She thought he might help her up, but the elf twirled gracefully, one leg outstretched, the other bent at the knee, fanning a chip across his lyre.

"*Come, come, Dray had said,*" he sang, "*and come the girl had, her belly full and fed.*"

Sara rose, shaking uncontrollably. "I saw . . . I thought it was him, and . . ." Tears coursed down her cheeks. All words failed her. All reason failed her. *What did I see?*

A crease wrinkled the elf's pale, perfect brow. "What was it you saw, child?"

"I . . . I can't be sure." She shuddered involuntarily. "It was a man. Mist. Shadow." *A monster.*

Dray narrowed his eyes at the tranquil river. "Elf's Grove doesn't belong just to me, little girl. Just as there is day, there is night. Others come to this grove with their intentions. We must show care." His blue eyes comforted her. "I will let nothing hurt you here, Sara of Rosbury." He paused. "Do you remember that we need to make another Gift?"

Sara wiped snot off her nose, trying for strength, trying to shut out memory of mist and shadow. "Yes. Will it take another hare, like the one Caleb slew?"

The elf-prince smiled. "A hare will do, child, even a dog or pheasant, but no steel forged by the hands of man can make the Gift that will summon your father." He lowered himself to her eye level. "We require a very special knife. This blade will make the second Gift and return Sir Damien from the Evergreen Isles. And his daughter must find it for Dray."

CHAPTER 28

Betrothal

he princess sat at the head of her father's long table in the council room, rereading the scroll with a thrice-crowned hart in the ribbon of its wax seal. Shafts of sunlight slanted through the room's oval windows. Around her sat her father's men, garbed in mantles and doublets for the ceremony that'd welcome a griffon to the castle today.

But it was the prospect of *another* winged beast that left her stunned. "A dragon." She pinched the calfskin by its corner, holding it away, as if Greg Thorngale's letter stank of betrayal. "Is this a fucking joke?" *I'm not laughing.*

Hanor beckoned to Musa, their cup-bearer, who poured him another cup of wine. "Even in Tesos, we've never known Thorngales for their humor," he said drearily. The chancellor drank like a man who'd given up on fiscal sanity. He wiped his purpled lips. "We're to help the Assembly pay for it."

"Pay for a dragon from the Isles of Fire," Lorana said in disbelief, "so that the would-be kings, Assemblymen, and me should all roast like pigs during the Second Trial?"

Three Trials, three Wings, began a Common rhyme for the Kingstrials. *But now it'll be* four *wings—and not the kind we want.* In his letter, Thorngale reassured her that the Assembly voted a joust for the First Trial. All well and good—except that Jason and the other Silver Throne's claimants would also slay a dragon in the Second and tame a griffon in the Third. Whoever survived that crucible—*if* any survived—might succeed Hexar.

Lorana flung the scroll at the pile of other parchments. "Is this how Thorngale would repay me for his speakership?"

"I've known Lord Greg since boyhood," Jon Applewood piped up from the table's other end. "He's a conciliator. He's coming into a position that was Gram Sothos's for almost two decades. The dragon was a concession he made to mollify lords who didn't choose him, same as the Sothos knight he tasked with capturing it."

"A concession." Lorana flashed the apothecary the most incredulous look. "After we had Sothos branded a kingkiller? They call his son the Stormsword. That ferocity and backbone must come from Greg's wife."

Drexan looked like a bored student with his elbows on the table, chin in the heels of his hands. "Even Sothos couldn't herd cats all the time," he said.

Seated clockwise from the steward, Charles screwed up his face, as if he'd just heard an outrageous insult. "*Herd cats?*" he boiled. "Flippant, for a man who led us to hell's gates. The king sought to keep his beloved son out of the Trials. Now his last heir will face swords, a griffon, a fire-breathing lizard. All thanks to the incorrigible King's Crow."

Drexan stirred. "And that forgery you prepared for Jason did us a turn better?" He pointed at Charles. "*You* convinced the king that we should join the Holy Wars. Perhaps Garrett would be king if we hadn't, and there'd be no Kingstrials."

"It was the crown prince's decision to sail to war."

"As it was Jason's to want the Kingstrials," Lorana broke in testily. "He chose the Trials so that we might avoid war. So that we might save the peace." *For all the good it'll do, brother, if a dragon incinerates you.* "If I wanted bickering, I'd invite my sister and her ladies-in-waiting to council. What can we do to stop the Assembly from bringing a bloody dragon to Loran?"

Jon stroked his papery hands. "The trapper arrives today with that griffon." His pale eyes found Charles. "We could add him to our list of . . . permanent guests."

"Methinks that'd provoke the war Jason seeks to avoid," Charles said. "Let the trapper sail to these Isles." He shrugged. "He'll sail across the Mirksea, a challenge for tested seamen. Icy, choppy water and fierce wind, for hundreds of miles, and at the end of it, an island of dragons and savages. And ferrying a fire-breathing beast across sea—on a wooden galley? I'd be shocked if the expedition returned at all."

The steward read between the lines. *And I'd be shocked if you didn't already have a man in mind to make sure this voyage sinks, Charles.* Keeping a dragon and its flammable hutch afloat sounded unimaginably precarious. It'd demand sedative, nets, extra ships, men—*a lot* of men. Sneaking a saboteur aboard in the chaos was a task to which her Lord of the Red Tower was, thankfully, imminently equal.

She asked Drexan what game of death the Worthy would choose if a dragon didn't make it to Loran. His answers weren't reassuring. Past gladiator-kings had battled bears and lions, or each other in vicious sea battles. *Would you still trade your life for peace when you face winged fire in the arena, my brother?*

Lorana declined wine from Musa as he circled the table. "Write Lord Greg and express interest in a Trial by archery," she told Drexan. "King Jason would need a Chancellor of War. Tell him he can imagine no one better than his son Darren."

"That'll motivate Greg, but the Assembly's full of leeches," Drexan said. "They thirst for blood, even if quenching it means killing every man who'd be king."

"If only we could've seen the bloodthirst coming," Charles jabbed him.

The heap of scrolls shrank as Drexan unfurled and read each missive aloud. Ansara's eleven other kings had written the Silver Walls. Of those, the three Free Kingdoms refused Lorana's previous invitations to send observers, their armies specifically. Seven others—Elvarenist and loyal to Parlisis—volunteered to send forces to ensure fairness in Loran's crown games.

Eerily, the letters sent by seven Elvarenist kings sounded almost completely identical, as if the rulers of these realms had met and drafted them together. One after another, seven kings echoed the same phrasing in their sympathies over Hexar ("a towering man taken too soon"), their urging of Lorana to free Sothos and his son ("for House Sothos is revered throughout the thirteen realms"), and their demands ("and it is my greatest wish that Shaddon Eddenhold, as your late king's brother, be granted entry into Loran").

"And this one ends the same as the others," said Drexan, head tilted as he read it out, "'in prayer that the Kingdom of Loran respects the peace.'" He put the letter flat on the table and circulated it to Lorana.

Charles reclined. "His Holiness had his puppets send us the same letter," he said with a deep sigh, "to remind us that he's watching us."

"Watching *me*." Lorana read the letter. "Threatening war, should my sweet uncle find himself in the Tower with Gram." She burst with nervous laughter, startling Charles and Drexan. "You see, my lords? Seven realms rattle the saber, and it's not even over that Wing of the Commons you revile."

The seriousness of their gazes wasn't lost on her. No one was fooled. *If Shaddon enters the Trials and wins, there'll be no Fourth Wing. That's the idea. And Jason will lose his life.*

Hanor reddened in his frumpy cheeks. "Intolerable," he spat in his accent. "*Unacceptable!* This was the First King's castle. This realm once encompassed the damn continent—"

"Ages ago, my dear Tessian." Charles stared after Musa as the Casaanite shuffled by with a bowl of succulent berries and grapes. "'Broken lines and thirteen crowns,' you recall."

Drexan raked the spymaster with a look. "The Casaanites didn't kill our king, Charles. Don't you think it's a little early to spit on the hostages, after their humiliation at the funeral?"

The steward's silence was all that was needed to chastise Charles. Musa comported himself with a little more ease.

It fell upon Hanor to ease the tension. "At least the Free Kingdom of Tesos shows itself Loran's true friend," he said. "Your sister will be in good hands at Grisholm's court, Your Highness. Tesos's capital city would delight any princess, with its canals, food courts, and parakeet markets."

Yes, at least there's that. Though I wish King Grisholm of Tesos had offered to host Heather and *fetch a friendly army to the Colossus.* The Tessian king's invitation gave her peace of mind, something in short supply these days. In two months, Lorana would travel north by carriage, to take her place beside three speakers and preside over the Kingstrials, while Heather would head east for Tesos, beyond mountains and the reach of rivals who'd see a valuable hostage in her, if things fell apart.

Whether Heather would leave home without incident was another matter. The princess could be a twat of a sister, before; now she was acting out her grief, pitching china glass from parapets and scolding castle servants over inconsequence.

"Hanor, you'll accompany Princess Heather to Tesos," she said. "Sir Blake Oxley will accompany you east with a regiment of loyal men. You'll all go disguised as merchants and pass her off as your daughter."

That brought the Tessian out of his stupor. He smiled wistfully. "Nothing would please me more than to escort Her Highness to my country. To hear the lutes from a gondola again, fireflies aflicker in canal rosebushes; the sunset, a splash of orange on rooftops."

"It's nice to hear that poetry survives in at least *one* Tessian," Jon said with a toothy grin.

Hanor shook a teasing finger. "We're victims of our own success! The Awakening made mathematicians of too many of us, and *that's* how the world knows us."

"Yes, as ruthless bean-counters, and yet unserious men when war looms over us and my brother faces winged death," said Lorana, steel in her tone. "Drexan. The letter."

The letter, as if the other ones didn't exist. The letter—*his* letter— protruded from the pile in a most ostentatious leather sheath patterned with silver curlicues, ruffled at its ends with silk. As if his words came from the gods themselves.

He wasn't the priestking, let alone a king. Yet her uncle addressed her as if he were both. For added flair, he wrote in First Tongue, the language of elves, noblemen, and cunts.

"'To my beloved niece,'" Drexan read from the calfskin he gripped, but that was Shaddon's only kindness. He wasted little ink lamenting his brother and pledging justice before he turned to his heart's desire: "'The Silver Throne is ours by blood right and ours alone. The Muhregites took Erick from us'"—and that garnered eyerolls and a volley of scorn from the advisors, most of all Charles, who'd weathered a Bull's anger—"'Prince Garrett has left us'"—and again, contempt from men who wagered that he'd poisoned the crown prince—"'and this leaves us the heir apparent.'"

"*Us.*" Hanor cringed. "The pompous traitor isn't king and he uses the majestic plural."

Deciding she could use some wine, after all, she gestured to Musa. "No, the conspiratorial plural," she said as the hostage filled her cup. "'Us,' as in Parlisis, those seven kings, and Sothos and his wretched son. Everyone who killed my father."

Shaddon made demands. He demanded a cessation to the Trials. He demanded safe entry to Loran, and would sail with a "godly fleet" of fifteen vessels, which would accompany him as befitting Loran's heir apparent.

"Sanctimonious idiot," Hanor said. "That's hardly a fleet."

Charles steepled his index fingers below his chin, staring off. "Call his group of warships whatever you want," he intoned. "They're *Medecian.* One of their galleys is large and fast enough to sink five of ours. Last I checked, we had fewer than thirty."

Hanor glanced down at his lap. Lorana drank her wine, burning over Thorngale's *other* conciliatory gesture to her Worthy Assembly. Even under fair weather conditions, even with Medecian ships, the voyage from eastern Ansara to Loran could take nearly three months. As steward, she'd wanted the Kingstrials set two months out, to crown Jason before Shaddon even sailed within sight of the kingdom. To avoid this crisis.

Thorngale had floated her proposal . . . then caved when the Wing of Lords balked. The speaker set the contests three months from the time of his consent, giving her uncle and his ships a window. *They call you Old Oak, Greg,* she thought, *but you bend like a windblown reed.*

"'If the Assembly wants Kingstrials,'" Drexan went on, translating, "'in violation of our succession rights, we'll play. We shall win Loran for the twelve true gods.'"

There was no ridicule over the last part. Only silence. The steward registered a fear in her advisors' faces that she hadn't seen since the king's death. Shaddon could press ships and the men onboard against Loran's undefended northern shores like a knife to the throat. *A testing of the waters for invasion.*

"That settles it, then." Lorana clutched her hands in her lap, pressing them firm together. "We'll leave a small garrison to hold the castle and post what ships we have in the bay." *A welcoming party for whomever wins the Trials,* she would've added for a mixed audience, but everyone knew she'd arranged a meeting with the Little King about the city walls he held as if they were his alone. "All our other forces shall come with me."

No one seemed impressed. Nor should they've been: her father's distant wars had whittled away their house's fighting men. To replenish their reserves would require lords calling their peasants, but that was the rub about the Kingstrials: it'd take place at the Colossus, the seat of the Worthy Assembly's power. There, royal armies never marched. Ever.

Jon acknowledged the obvious. "We should take care, if we really are trying to thread this needle," he said. "To send royal soldiers to the Colossus would have the same effect as Your Highness declaring war on the Assembly."

"Jon is right," Hanor chimed. "Shaddon's ships are clearly a provocation, but to counter it with an army—"

"Would violate the Blackstaff rule," Lorana sighed.

Blackstaff was both a rule and an office. After centuries of bad blood, the crown and Assembly had long ago agreed to a ritual that permitted His Majesty to come north without really coming north. A knight named Blackstaff went in the king's stead to Assembly gatherings; this allowed the Worthy to make laws without fear of the king killing them if he disagreed. But what good was one knight—a symbol—against warships?

What a sad riddle this kingdom is, Lorana thought. *Lords and priests would prefer the sight of Shaddon's foreign sails to their country's banners, and keep my hands tied.* It wouldn't be so, with a Fourth Wing loyal to land and crown . . .

She shrugged. "Very well. I won't bring a royal army. Call it my own personal escort."

Charles smiled like a man unfooled. "Yours won't be the only force traveling north," he said pointedly. "Tomas Fawkes, Sam Wuthers, and Tom Gelder plan to press their ancestral claims and enter the Trials. Each with a force of thousands to guard their backs, in keeping with tradition."

"Jason will have an army of his own." *We hope.* "Allies are made in these Trials, besides. Lords with men to spare."

"If only we could tame a dragon, as Anjan's champions tamed griffons," Drexan said. "Then that serpent could serve some use and torch Shaddon's galleys."

Sabotage will do, Lorana thought with a look at Charles.

Alas, Hanor wasn't the only poet. It was only fitting that her traitor uncle—who'd only just threatened them—would pine for her traitor mother. He devoted two paragraphs to her with his piety ("an angel among women, perfect in every way"), tiptoeing around *who* sent her to heaven ("I had to love your father from afar after her loss").

"He had to live far from the king because he kidnapped the prince," Jon said in an appalled tone, to no disagreement.

Lorana beckoned for Drexan to continue. He cleared his throat. "'As Alyse was to Hexar a union between the lands of Loran and Medecia, so your hand should forge great alliances. Rejoice, then, for I've done what my brother sought and found for you a groom. A prince who could unite all of Ansara against the Muhregites that slew that saint, your brother Erick.'"

She washed out the taste of his matchmaking with wine.

Jon furrowed his bushy eyebrows. "Prince . . . of what?"

"I think he means to reveal that in person," Charles said. "An uncle's surprise for his niece. But I don't think he wrote us knowing about her last suitor's fate." He smiled wickedly.

"I don't like surprises." Lorana pivoted to him. "I like to know about plots our enemies are hatching, especially when those plots involve me. I assume you've informed your eyes and ears."

The Grand Inquisitor, who rarely disappointed, nodded. *Eyes and ears* meant more than spies. Over the years, her uncle had always stayed one step ahead of their assassins. Now he'd be on Loranian soil. This time, he had to trip.

There was more. The worst, for last. The priestking had warned them through seven kings, and he wrote them through the man he hoped to make his eighth about an envoy who'd sail with him to negotiate Gram Sothos's release.

A very trusted envoy. One they *both* knew.

Hanor received the news well. "I think the prieslenne's coming is good for us," he said. "She's a rose on that prickly vine of our relationship with Elvarenist kingdoms. Who here doesn't love her as if she were one of the royal household?"

"But she's *not* a member of House Eddenhold," Charles snapped. "She's the priestking's daughter, and she's been on the Lonely Isle for two years now."

"Still, Eden was best of friends with our steward and Jason," Jon said. "I daresay a sister. That should count for something. A piece of leverage we could use, in the Trials or after, if we must sue for peace."

Lorana glanced at Charles, who sat forward, interlocking his hands. "I've told the steward what I know, and I'll tell you," he said to the room. "It seems our king's brother has moved on from Alyse. He's in love."

She took the measure of everyone's reaction. If anyone had suspicions about them, they didn't betray awareness.

The Tessian sat forward with a start, as if wine had gone down the wrong way. "With *Edenia*?" he spat. "She could easily be his granddaughter!"

"The priestking likely gave the order to kill our king," the Grand

Inquisitor said with clear annoyance. "Does anyone put it past him to seal a kingship for his man with his daughter, a tidy bow on the neatly wrapped gift of an Elvarenist Loran?"

"A prieslenne for a king's consort." Drexan rolled up the calfskin, looking disgusted. "I can't imagine a worse nightmare for Free Believers and peasants, but it'd be music to the ears of Elvarenist lords and priests who might have to choose a king. She'd reassure believers that Shaddon isn't Hexar."

"But we don't know if she's pledged to him for sure," she said flatly. "All we have is rumor, and this letter from my uncle, a known liar."

Yet it discomforted her. Made her feel vulnerable. Deeply vulnerable, more than even dragons or foreign warships could.

I hope you haven't betrayed the family you considered more yours than Parlisis, the princess thought, her stomach twisting into knots. *Or the promise we made each other.*

CHAPTER 29

The Caged Beast

bserving the thousands of peasants surrounding them forty yards out, Zur noticed little details that stayed with him.

An old man on crutches hobbled as near the grounds as he could without drawing the spears of the mayor's city guard. A knotty-haired fellow boosted a small girl on his shoulders so she could see the royal family. Two women, one a crone, the other a maiden, knelt in the dirt, praying fervently.

For the second time in more than a month, Zur gathered with the house of Hexar for public ceremony, only this time on a barren field north of Southpoint that faded into the shoots of oaks and shrubbery of Sarah's Forest. From here, the rippling aura of the Silver Walls waned like light from a setting sun, catching the ramparts of Rorin's checkered city walls.

Zur stood with the royal family's other servants, clad in a crimson-dyed tunic and leggings. To his side gathered Elzura's Children, including Musa, Saan, and Namoni. Saan had recently done away with the bandages over his head, revealing an angry sore close to his hairline. *What was my part in the pain the priests inflicted on you, Saan?* He glanced away guiltily.

Not far ahead stood Anyasha. Ahead of the Casaanites mustered fifty knights astride muscular destriers, in a line, armed with spears and crossbows. The princesses sat beneath the shade of a canopy, resplendent in gowns of satin. The four advisors flanked them.

All of them waited on the honored guest whose coming heralded the Kingstrials.

None longed for this as much as the peasants. So many of them were on their knees praying, and there *were* so many—even more than he recalled seeing along the Street of Kings for Hexar's funeral procession. Zur couldn't blame them. *How often does one get to see a griffon, without fearing imminent death?*

Yet this lot hadn't come only out of curiosity. Commoners

practically worshipped griffons, the winged mounts King Anjan and his Windriders had ridden through the skies. They prayed for its arrival, for it was said griffons protected those worthy of the First King's mercy and justice.

They'd have to pray harder. The griffon was three hours overdue. Sunlight glared down mercilessly. Zur swabbed sweat off his forehead, glad for once that he wasn't a knight encased in heavy plate armor.

Heather tugged insistently on Lorana's hand. "Where is it?" she pled in a tone that portended a tantrum. "We're here, it's hot, I'm sweaty, and it's not here yet." Anyasha rolled her eyes for Zur to see. He smirked. *She complains of sweating, as we bake like slugs.*

Had this been done behind the Silver Walls, Zur, Anyasha, and their people would've had shade, but the realm wouldn't tolerate comfort for Elzura's Children. Not in the open.

"Patience, my sweet," Lorana coaxed her sister. "Don't you want to see the griffon?"

Standing by Heather, Lorna Durros touched the younger princess's shoulder. They'd become fast friends since Hexar's passing, and it showed in how the lady-of-waiting dressed her hair in the chains of Heather's lace braids. "I'm excited to see the beast that inspired your house's sigil," Lorna told her.

"But it's *not* him," Heather blurted. "Anjan's battle griffon inspired our sigil."

You should be more courtly, princess, Zur thought. *Most people don't have a sigil, let alone a proud, ancient house.*

Lorana met his gaze briefly through the line of horse. Zur knew better than to take her distractedness personally, but he sensed something off about her. The steward had relegated all the ceremony to Sir Blake Oxley, a thing highly unusual. *What troubles you, older sister? You enjoy power.*

A knight ahorse wended through the crowd. It was Oxley. He'd ventured ahead to learn about the griffon's whereabouts. He gave word to Lorana and peeled off twelve mounted men for a gallop down the new path the Commoners cleared. Word trickled back to the Casaanites. "The beast is here," Namoni relayed excitedly, nervously.

Minutes later, a huge cagehouse the height and width of the Silver Walls's gatehouse rolled into view beyond the crowd. A prison it was, striped lengthwise with thick steel bars, roofed with iron sheets, and mounted on spoked wheels. On all sides marched men in the crimson of House Sothos, led triumphantly by Sir Gordon Whitecastle on his elegant white stallion. Twelve destrier horses labored to pull the lurching enclosure, twisting about for panicked looks.

"*MAKE WAY!*" a peasant shouted through cupped hands, and all at once the masses shuffled apart, waves upon waves of men, women, and children kneeling with bowed heads. As the cagehouse crept nearer, one heard the complaints of buckling wood, snapping whips . . . and a throaty, bone-chilling *hissssssss*.

Knights struggled with nickering, frightened horses. Even the stone maiden looked unnerved. Oxley and Whitecastle took turns navigating around the cagehouse, issuing orders, easing the ungainly train to a halt a safe distance from the steward.

In the eyes of every man in the escort, Zur saw something. He recognized it because he felt it, too. *Sheer terror.*

Of course, they'd tried to prepare. The griffon ceremony was a tradition in any Kingstrials. Namoni had gathered all the Casaanites beforehand to remind them to stay their nerves, lest they frighten the creature. The royal house would pay respects by kneeling before the caged griffon. But as Zur glimpsed the black fury stalking behind the bars, the sinewy limbs thick as tree trunks, the vast wings spreading to test the enclosure's integrity, preparation failed him. *How on earth could Casaanites frighten anything like that?*

Whitecastle climbed off his stallion. He swept his hands outward, bowing solemnly. "Your Highness, on behalf of Tess Sothos, lady to my liege, I deliver for the Kingstrials this griffon, trapped and netted near the Great Tree of Loran."

Lorana surged toward the trapper knight. Zur thought she'd strike him in the face. "*What is this?*" she demanded.

Whitecastle watched her with disdain. "It's a griffon in a cage, Your Highness."

"No." The steward pointed at the cage. "This is a *monster*. Who could possibly tame such a thing in the Trials?"

"Fairly said. Two men died to bring this creature here. We expect to lose a few more on the journey north. Thankfully, the peasants will handle the more dangerous tasks, not—"

"How in hell can we crown a king if all the claimants die trying to ride this beast?"

She fears for Jason, Zur understood. *How could she not? I fear for him.* Peering through close-set bars, he saw a mustard beak that could pluck his head from his neck like a grape from its stem. A thick plumed tail nearly as long as the cagehouse itself whacked bars like a whip. Talons tore up timber floor.

"The trappers should use metal for the floor, not wood," Zur warned Drexan as his lord paced near, listing on his staff. He saw Lorana's other advisors gathering around her as the stone maiden pressed Whitecastle.

The chancellor looked on grimly. "Yes, they well should. Sir Gordon is known as much for his bravery as his stupidity. I'll share it with the steward before the griffon leaves north for the Colossus."

"How, lord?" Zur folded his arms, as if his feeble flesh and bone could somehow shield him. He blanched at a *hissssssssss.* "How can Lord Jason mount this beast? How can anyone? It's huge. Untamable."

"*He* is huge," Drexan corrected him. He pointed at the tail. "Only bucks have plumage at the ends of their tails. It's why the prize offends our steward. Female griffons are smaller, more mountable, like the one her father rode about in his Trials."

"Would Jason fly upon him, as Windriders rode griffons?"

Drexan shook his head, smiling. "No one's ridden a griffon in millennia. If Jason manages to climb atop this creature, he'd do it for a second, and then be thrown like a sack of leaves."

The advisor's cavalierness about a griffon hurling Jason off rubbed him wrong. *What can we do for you, Jason? What can I do?* How Zur longed to help Jason somehow. The night before last, he'd dreamed they were in Rorin's amphitheater, swords at the ready, tongues of lightning lashing the sky as the crown's enemies closed ranks.

Drexan laid a hand on his shoulder. "Lord Jason will win his crown, I have no doubt. But what of us, Zuran? How often can you set eyes on the king of the skies?"

The King's Crow started off toward the canopy, throwing Zur a glance over his shoulder that told him yes, he expected him to follow. *Serving Drexan Lorrain doesn't always feel like a birthday gift, Ana.* Steeling himself, he trudged after him. He tried to ignore the mistrustful stares of peasants.

Lorana and Whitecastle were arguing yards off from the cagehouse, with her advisors occasionally interjecting in her defense. Stopping yards off from the cage, Zur found he could walk no further. His feet planted themselves like roots.

The man who befriended griffs continued his approach, seeming entirely unafraid. A knight lost his nerve and grabbed Drexan by his cloak, trying to force him back. He withered under Drexan's green-eyed glare.

"Pardon, my lord," sputtered the knight, "you must watch the bars—its talons, they—"

"The Hands serve," the chancellor said through his teeth. "Touch me like that again, and you'll lose one, like Lord Justen."

The young princess stepped closer, passing the knights and Zur, hauling a reluctant Lorna forward by her hand. She sized up the black beast skeptically.

"I prefer the bird on my house sigil," Heather spat. "I bet a dragon would roast this griffon like a spitted pig."

Drexan eyed Heather with a trifle more disapproval than an advisor should. He walked away, joining Zur by his side. "A mouth like her mother Romara's, that one," the chancellor said for his ears. "The mightiest creature in the world, her own sigil, and the insolent brat insults him."

"Is it—I mean, is he the mightiest?" Zur asked. He wanted to change subjects. Nearby stood the Grand Inquisitor, his eyes following them. "A dragon has the advantage, no?"

"How?"

"Because Princess Heather's right. They breathe fire." He studied the beast that was half lion, half bird of prey, and large as a carriage. *Even a thing as fearsome as you isn't fireproof.*

"Aye, a dragon is bigger. Its scaly hide is tough. It breathes flame. And yet a griffon would kill it." Pointing, he let his finger stray from the beast's forelimbs to his tail. "Look at those four paws. A griffon's talons are as long and sharp as dirks, *and they have four sets of them.* Dragons have but two clawed feet. A dragon's tail is cause for worry, but a griffon's acts like another appendage." As if in proof, the plumed tail coiled about steel bars, squeezing them like a python snake would its prey. Zur retreated a bit. "And then there's his beak, a dagger to puncture scaly hide."

"But against dragonflame?"

"Aye, nothing can withstand it, not even a griffon. But the griffon is intelligent. There's power in numbers, and they know this. Dragons are solitary by nature. Were they to meet, a single dragon would make a fine meal for a cavalry of griffons."

Behind bars, beneath a slanted brow, the disc of a golden eye narrowed at Zur. "They'd never meet. Dragons prefer the cold and wouldn't fly south of Uzland. Griffons roost in Great Trees, in warmer climes."

"I see you've been in the South Tower library longer than your duties demand. Yet a dragon and this griffon *may* meet, as we learned this morning." *May?* Zur puzzled his face. Before he could inquire, the chancellor asked him what else he'd learned about griffons.

"They don't like silverstone." Zur nodded at the swirl of light above Southpoint.

Drexan chuckled. "You didn't read that. It's well known."

It was an odd fact, that the First King's stone repulsed the First King's bird, but the silverstone aura had protected the city from prowling griffons for millennia. Such was why Lorana had chosen a field outside Southpoint, farther from the light, so the griffon wouldn't go berserk and destroy his prison.

Zur scanned the tops of a thousand bowed heads. "The Commoners think griffons will bless them with power, if they prove themselves worthy of King Anjan's mercy and justice."

"Also known." The chancellor had the most contemptuous smirk. "But yes, peasants like to think themselves worthy, don't they?"

The long-simmering argument between Lorana and the Sothos knight boiled over. The steward made a thinly veiled threat to visit his liege lord's son, and Whitecastle rejoined by asking *why* she didn't instead lean on Drexan Lorrain, known for his friendship with that witch at the Great Tree?

"The King's Crow no doubt could've trapped the griffon you wanted," Whitecastle said audibly.

"And perhaps our steward should have you join Justen and his father," Drexan answered testily, treading into their space. "To teach you courtesy, if that you shouldn't lie."

Lorana made a grievous headshake. "The Walls will not accept this. I'll have you release this thing at the Great Tree."

"A griffon was asked for, and a griffon has been delivered. Speaker Greg Thorngale was satisfied with it and will not have it released." The trapper grinned with the impunity of someone leal to Sothos. "Why don't you threaten my liege some more, Your Highness? Our allies in the Assembly will happily see to *his* release."

This is unseemly for the peasants to watch, Zur pondered. Lorana looked less collected, with bangs in her eyes, her arms crossed. *What did you learn at council today that unhinges?*

A hollow *thunk* drew everyone's gazes to the underbelly of the cagehouse. Splintered wood lay in a patch of grass. Out from a hole in the floor snaked a plumed tail, gliding along the soil like a thick black serpent.

"Back, *BACK,*" a knight cried. "Gods, the tail, *WATCH IT!*"

Zur retreated with the knights, but it wasn't a knight the griffon sought. An unforgettable, ear-piercing squeal shattered the field's silence as the tail spiraled rope-like about the barrel of Whitecastle's white stallion. With the strength of a kraken's tentacle, the tail dragged the wailing horse side to side, under the cage and out again. Growling low—and using only muscled tail—the griffon catapulted the flailing horse across the field as if he were pitch, into fleeing, screaming peasants.

Zur fell to land sprawled mere yards from the cage, heart hammering in his throat. The King's Crow watched him from afar, horrified. *I may die today.* The force of the tail whooshing overhead cast him onto his side like a gale wind.

Somewhere, Lorana cried his name.

The men of House Sothos brandished their swords and whips. Again and again, braided whips uncoiled at the thick tail, *thwop, thwop.*

One brave soul went right up to the cage and drove his sword through the bars. He kept stabbing and stabbing, failing to see the pale talons uncurling above him. Zur tried to warn him. The knight fell, reeling as blood pumped from the flesh-entangled orifice in his shoulder where an arm had once been. Shadows flew across the field as the griffon pitched two other men at the city walls.

Under Andrew Windkin's command, House Eddenhold's mounted knights surrounded Lorana, offering the griffon a wall of spears and quarrel-loaded crossbows. Zur lied belly-down as the tail swung to and fro overhead, searching for prey. The griffon's *hisssss* vibrated through his chest. He covered his head with his arms, expecting quarrels. Expecting death.

No quarrels flew.

Lorana barreled past Blake Oxley, but the knight pinned her in his arms. Anyasha helped him restrain her. "*HEATHER!*" the name tore through the steward.

Zur looked up.

The younger princess dangled limply above him in the griffon's grip, tail encircling her waist, her arms outstretched. Her golden tresses draped her face. She'd fainted.

Broken lines and thirteen crowns. Rolling toward the man shorn an arm, Zur recovered his blade where it lied. He'd never handled a sword; it felt heavy, as surreal as the snarled growls coming from the cage.

His arms shook and with them the blade as he aimed for the muscled stretch of tail.

Time seemed to slow in that instant. In the space between the cage's bars, he found his reflection in a dilated eye streaked with amber . . . and sensed no malice.

Only fear. Fear and confusion.

Without any sound, the griffon laid Heather on the ground as gently as her own father would. The tail receded below the cagehouse floor, curling through the hole.

Drexan appeared by his side. Gently, he pried from his hands the blade a Casaanite could not wield by laws of kings and Assemblymen. "You frightened a griffon into submission, Zur," he said. "A knight you are, if ever there was one."

How?

The knights closed ranks about the cage, with Whitecastle warning against harm to the creature on Thorngale's orders. Windkin scooped up Heather and supplied her to Lorana. Wall knights tended to the wounded. Sothos's men-at-arms unfurled a canvass matte from their train and pitched it over the cage, backtracking quickly.

Jon Applewood examined Heather behind a ring of men. After the apothecary assured Lorana she'd fainted and suffered no wounds, the eldest princess rushed to Zur, enfolding him in her arms. She checked his face and arms fastidiously for cuts or bruises. He relished her care. *And we love her children not.*

"Zur, that was so fucking stupid and brave," Lorana said as she embraced him. Her tears wetted his cheeks. The steward was shaking. "But . . . thank you, little brother. *Thank you.*"

Behind Lorana, Drexan listed on his staff, watching.

CHAPTER 30

The Mad Lady

In a forest outside of Graywood, the Heretics made camp for themselves and their new companions. Two hard-looking men huddled over a ring of logs, striking flint for fire. A hulking brute in furs and sealskin, unmistakably the Uzman Murg, laid the four dead Pigeons in a line hand-to-hand, foot-to-foot. After he finished, a crone clothed in bearskin and the shingles of tiny chicken bones rummaged for loot to distribute.

Once the fire was tall, a dwarf nicknamed Jeff the Giant cleaned Rathos's wounds and Karl's with maggots. The dwarf heated his skinning knife in the flames. When the blade glowed bright as the sun, he retrieved it and waddled over to where Rathos and Karl sat against a moss-covered trunk, comatose.

Jeff the Giant thrust a wineskin at Karl. "You'll want this first," he said ominously.

Karl took the wineskin with both hands and squirted the liquor into his mouth like a man dying of thirst. He broke into a fit of hacking that drew laughter from the night.

"Ready, are we?" the dwarf asked with a glint in his eyes.

Karl looked a corpse already, pale as milk and laced with sweat. He nodded. The dwarf wedged a stick between his teeth. Rathos overheard men casting wagers over whether the straw-haired twat would pass out.

The Reubenite's wails, tears, and obscenities persisted for several minutes before he finally fainted. When his time came, Rathos gave suck on the wineskin. He nearly lost yesterday's food at the taste of rotten fruit.

Leah was a mirage in the fire and shadow. "Sorry, Ray. I'm afraid we don't have any of Caerdon's golden ale this time."

He bit down hard on his stick.

Once, when he was young, he'd taken a nasty fall down a long dark stairway at Caerdon scored with sinister edges. He'd been at a game of knights and dragons with Leah in the castle's bowels. The fall had broken his nose, a leg, and a few ribs.

Then, as now, Leah stood watch over his recovery, no longer a lanky girl but a woman grown. The violet-haired lady made for a surreal sight in her tattered breeches and boiled leather. Pauldrons covered her shoulders. A tuft of plaid cloth festooned her waist like some preposterous dress, as if in mock of a lawful woman's modesty. He knew her mother's narrow face, the bony chin and fulsome cheeks, the hazel eyes made for watching.

The pain from that tumble so long ago was nothing next to the fire that scorched his arm. The stick snapped in his teeth, and the night deepened to black. He heard laughter in the dark, and mutters, and a man asking Leah if *this* was Sinclair's ward.

He awoke to the sound of two men bickering. Still bleary-eyed, he discerned their shapes leaning into each other against the campfire's fidgeting light.

"That's my dirk, I sawr 'im, I killed 'im," a weasel voice complained. "Won it fair I did."

Answered a deeper voice: "Fuck off, Goose. It's mine, and I claim it! Come and die for this steel if you want."

"Put it to the Lady, then."

"Donna need no cunt to decide this."

From all sides of the fire came low whistles and grim chuckling. Some urged the men to fight; others clambered for their Mad Lady. Focusing, Rathos saw the shadow of his sister-by-law take form against the wavy fire. She stood before the twig-thin Goose and the meatier outlaw like a lord at court.

Chants for her filled the night air. "*Lady! Lady! Lady!*"

Leah planted her hands on her hips. "Whose cunt are we talking about?" she said over the clamor. "Goose's, or Venn's?"

The outlaws roared with laughter.

The heavier man, Venn, lurched toward her. The dirk in his hand glinted in the firelight. "No one says that about me. 'Specially not some—some *stupid slut* in a man's garments."

The man had a look of unbridled rage. Rathos half-rose to defend his wife's sister, but the fierce throb in his right arm lulled him back to the soil.

Leah stiffened. "I like these garments better than any gown. Maybe you ought to try on a gown, Venn? Half this lot needs a hole, anyway. You might be useful for once."

At the chorus of laughter, the outlaw twisted this way and that, baring his teeth like something wild. "*That's it!* I'll fuck you bloody, slut. This dirk is mine"—a sword appeared in his right hand—"and so are the Heretics."

The man charged at her, steel glinting in both hands. Leah was half his size. Any woman would've screamed and fled. Not Leah Sinclair. As he closed distance, she reached for the small of her back. A fleshy *thunk*, and her rival slammed into the dirt at her feet. When she stepped away, Rathos glimpsed a silver-hilted dagger protruding from his forehead. An eight-pointed star on the crossguard glistened with blood.

With practiced smoothness, Leah cleaned her dagger on her breeches and knelt to recover the weapons. She flung the dirk at Goose, who fumbled to catch it.

"The Lady decides for Goose," she said, to cheers and bellows. "Who else demands judgment?"

The chants resumed, louder now. "*LADY! LADY! LADY!*"

Rathos continued to pass in and out of consciousness through the night. Dreams came and went, dreams of his wife. In one dream, she stood by the window in their bedchambers, her hair richly purple, her belly round against the sunlight. He blinked and found Mina on the floor, a dagger lodged in her head.

Rathos woke to a rooster crowing in his ear.

Not a rooster. Opening his eyes, he found the gangly man curled up beside him, his hair greased together like a rooster's comb. His oily, bewhiskered cheeks spread for a grin as he crowed again. Rathos kicked him in his belly. The madman hissed like a snake and shoved a dagger against his throat.

Men laughed. Lumbering over, a strapping man with long, blond hair forced the madman up, whereupon he loped off, neighing. Rathos took Murg's hand, clambered up.

"Do not mind Creature," the thick-accented Uzman said with a hard clap on his back.

Rathos nodded his thanks, confused. He gazed around the campsite. A finger of smoke curled lazily above their dying fire. Around it gathered Rathos and Karl's unlikely saviors, the most despised outlaws in all Loran, twenty to thirty in number, men in tatters of rags and mismatched armor.

Despised, and with reason. They weren't alone with the Heretics. On the camp's fringes stood men of the cloth, parish readers and Mumblers, nervous-eyed and looking rather eager to depart. Initially, Rathos sweated their allegiance, wondering whether they belonged to the Loyal Company—to Rezlan and his Reubenites, come to finish the Soothsayers' work—but he didn't know their faces. Heretics like Murg took cloth-wrapped goods off their hands.

They're robbing these peasants, Rathos knew, disgusted. It'd be one thing if these were priests, but Free Believers like these men opened their sparse pantries to Commoners. *How far you've fallen, Leah.*

He distracted himself until the readers and Mumblers left, aware of his debt and uneager to give offense. Leah Sinclair, the Mad Lady, emerged from the dispersing crowd. Seeing him, she lit up with a smile and approached in fast strides. He tried not to linger on her long violet hair.

She startled him with a kiss on his cheek, close to his lips. He inhaled a perfume of horsehair and sweat. "Ray! At last, he wakes. I wondered whether we'd lose you in the night."

Rathos probed the rutted scar beneath his bandage, wincing from pain. "Leah, I have . . . so many questions. How did you find us?" *How is it you stand before me after all these years?* He scanned the camp. "My companion, where is he?"

Leah nodded at the wretch he'd mistaken for an outlaw. Sunken-eyed and swaddled in rags, Karl looked like he'd aged five years in the night. The Reubenite paid him a wan look and returned to nursing his wineskin.

"Thank you for our lives," Rathos said. "The Pigeons?"

"You're welcome. And you mean Father's turncoat fowl? Buried. Along with the fool who challenged me last night."

Graywood returned like a half-forgotten nightmare. He recalled their names: Tom, Reed, Jacob, Yule, the names of the bloated bodies strewn about the grass the night before, same as Leah's challenger, here no longer.

Varn, Rathos remembered. *Was he caught?* He spotted Heretics dressed in the remnants of their belongings: frayed cloaks, threadbare tunics, scuffed-up boots, longbows, quivers thick with fletched arrows.

"They tried to kill us," he murmured in disbelief. "You . . . you *killed* that man last night."

Leah had a cold smile and dead eyes. "I kill when I must." She touched his shoulder. "Sit down. You're famished. Eat. I'll answer everything on the road to Caerdon, trust me."

In that instant Rathos wanted to mount a horse and ride, ride for Mina, but he was hungry and in pain. He eased himself down on the log beside Karl. The Reubenite looked at him with something between fear and suspicion.

The Soothsayers wanted Karl dead, too, he realized. *He couldn't have aided their treachery.*

On a log across the way, a minstrel plucked at his harp, singing a ballad that implied Shaddon Eddenhold had killed King Hexar. Outlaws hummed along.

> *Now lads gather close to hear this tale*
> *Of a man who valued silver*
> *At a price you and I would not pay:*
> *Aye, so much that he would kill for—*
> *Even his brother and king he'd slay.*

O Brother, O Brother, said brother
Would you kindly lend me your throne?
I've no gold nor silver to pay now—
Just a little poison on loan.

She was a rose I swore I'd make mine
'Til all her petals you plucked
She was gentle and sweet and brittle
Lovelier than all the others you fucked.

Now listen lads, this concerns you too:
This fiend was a bold king's brother
As much a Lonely Isle son
And together we'll all suffer
When his Trials he hath won.

So forget not this tale I've told you
Of the priestking's loyal friend
For a time may come—it may come—
For brother to see brother again.

Rathos half-expected a snide comment from Karl, but his companion munched in silence, eyes low on the fire's embers.

Before noon, an outlaw named Dustin and twenty others rode into camp astride horses not theirs. Rathos took heart when he saw his mount and Karl's among them. Listening to Dustin's exchange with Leah, he learned the outlaws had tracked the one called Varn. In his flight, the turncloak Pigeon had abandoned the horses.

"We'll find the last Pigeon," Leah told Dustin. "We need to escort these two to Caerdon first."

Dustin sized him up. He scoffed. "When did the Mad Lady trade her griffon skull for a wet nurse's wimple?"

Leah snaked a hand around her father's dagger, drawing glances. "Careful, Dustin. We buried Venn just this morning."

Dustin traded looks with Rathos. He strode off in a huff.

Rathos helped Karl into his saddle and then climbed into his own, patting his horse's neck. He stopped by Jeff the Giant before leaving. "Thank you for attending to my companion and me," he said. "We owe you our health and lives."

The dwarf grinned. "Thank the Mad Lady. If it were up to us, we'd have let those Pigeons have you and cast lots for your gold. You'll remember me if I come to Caerdon, woncha, lad?"

He saw Leah smile roguishly.

The Heretics formed up in a line of twenty horses and started off into the forest. Leah commanded Murg the Uzman and Dustin to guard the rear; she requested Rathos's company at the front. Trotting to her side, Rathos caught an unfriendly look from Dustin.

"That one doesn't seem to like me," Rathos told Leah over the *clop-clop* of hooves.

"Dustin doesn't like anyone who'd steal me from him."

"He can rest easy, then. A suitor?"

Leah chuckled. "'Suitor' is too kind. I like him sometimes under the moon, and he takes it to mean I like him in the sun." She watched for his reaction. "Do I shock you, Rathos Robswell, man of reason?"

Nothing should shock me anymore, he thought.

And yet everything did. Leah Sinclair had been eighteen when he'd last seen her, a noblewoman fluent in the ways of court who preferred the language of combat, to her family's unease. She'd vanished from Caerdon a day after her mother Faye's funeral, along with a prized courser, a bag of gold, and a precious heirloom, a silver-hilted dagger inlaid with the eight-pointed star of her house's sigil.

People who'd known Leah Sinclair would only recognize her violet hair. The lady-turned-outlaw had manly confidence, shoulders thrown back, legs brazenly athwart her mount. The Mad Lady earned her name with her griffon skull, oddments of armor, and motley furs. He stole looks at the scars riddling her tanned arms.

Evan, what have we got ourselves into? he thought. *I leave for your first daughter, and it's your secondborn who saves our skins—and from our own damn Pigeons!*

Rathos wanted answers but knew better than to ask questions

unwarily. They trod a dusty road bound by gnarled roots, disheveled with pebbles. Every time he heard a birdsong, he searched the trees for Pigeons. It didn't seem to bother the Heretics, who bantered in low murmurs, occasionally laughing. An outlaw named Pretty Phillip boasted to Karl about the men and women he'd buried and wanted to know his own count.

After midday, Leah circled around for a trot down the line. Rathos realized she was instructing her men to keep their heads low. "Blackfinger," he heard her say. Moments later, Barley Tower materialized in the leafy spaces between trees, a dark-gray lance jutting through blue sky.

Are your five hundred barrels of blackpowder here, Evan? he thought as their single-file line wended past. *Can we even entrust the Loyal Company with that power, if Jason fails us?*

Leah watched the tower warily from her saddle. "Still as ashy as the day Sir Bradley and his traitor knights laid siege with catapult and burning pitch," she said. "And dangerous still. The castellan's an old friend of Hexar's Bull, and just as unforgiving with outlaws and peasants." She peeled back her glove. Abrasions patterned her wrist. "A mastiff gave me this. The castellan styles himself Bardo the Mad. Sends out hunting parties when they see us, as Hexar's daughter sent out men for us recently." She smiled. "But I'm not so easy to kill."

Rathos looked away, refusing to give her the approval she seemed to seek.

Barley Tower gradually receded. When all seemed safe again, Leah loped off to confer with her Heretics. She returned at a canter beside Rathos.

"The men want to rest," she said. "Let's talk."

She kicked her horse into a hard gallop and vaulted over a bank, vanishing into the forest. Rathos followed her lead, albeit with more effort. Fifty yards out, he located his sister-by-law in a grove pierced by shafts of sunlight, her hair faded to mauve. She stroked her horse's mane as he sucked water from a brook.

Leah noticed his apprehension. "We can speak freely here. We'll hear a crow if anything comes too near."

He dismounted. "Thank you for my life, Leah. I wouldn't be returning to Mina without you."

Her smile had a familiar shyness it lacked around her men. "I can only imagine what you must think of me. I don't think I was wearing this"—she splayed her hands across her tattered skirt and breeches—"last you saw me."

"You wore black."

"Yes, I did." She met his gaze. "I recall what you wore that day, too. You'd dressed in the same garb you'd worn when you proposed to Mina. A satin doublet. You looked handsome."

He ran a hand through hair slick with sweat. Five years. Had it been that long? Sometimes he imagined that he'd asked Mina for her hand in marriage the year before. Five years of love, of happiness—of trying for children that never came. He wouldn't have married anyone else.

"Evan and I heard you'd joined the Heretics. We couldn't believe—"

"That they made me their Lady?" She yanked free Evan's filched dagger, flung it feet over her head, and caught it with a practiced sleight of hand.

"Yes. As we were worried that you'd remind those who've seen you of Evan Sinclair's daughter."

She stiffened. "I *am* his daughter."

"No, Leah, you don't understand. You've made them think of your sister—my wife." He stared at her hair.

The world knew Evan Sinclair for his treason, but it knew his daughters by Faye Halifax for their distinctive hair. From an early age, strangers had come to Caerdon to marvel at hair the color of violet flowers.

Some didn't marvel. Some stared, as if threatened. Some wanted to see the girls' hands and feet. For webbed hands and toes usually accompanied hair that color. Faye had denied it to her last, that one of her grandsires had come from the sea, but Mina and Leah had left little doubt.

Neither girl had webbed fingers or toes, or the lungs to stay underwater for hours. But they had a hair color peculiar to merpeople. No one could tell them apart from a distance, which was what most ever saw of the Mad Lady.

That had consequences. A year ago, a sheriff had stopped Mina ahorse outside their castle and angrily accused her of an association with the Heretics.

Leah threw violet hair over her shoulder. "My sister lives behind high castle walls. She has spilt wine to worry over." He disliked her tone. "Me? I have to *lead* these fools."

"Who forces you?"

Leah smiled. "No one forces me to do anything, Rathos."

"How is it they follow you at all?" War-hardened knights acted on the word of women like Lorana Eddenhold and Mina Robswell, but that was different: they led court.

She arched her dagger behind her head, aiming for a red-and-yellow snake slithering down the side of a tree. Her blade thudded into the trunk, pinning snake to bark. "I have ways of getting my point across." She trudged past Rathos, recovering dagger and dinner. "The Old Ways help."

An outlaw . . . and a pagan. The Heretics were known to harbor Sylvanians and follow their unseemly rituals. If Leah Sinclair had traded her father's star of reason for gods of field and forest, it made sense only because the pagan folk accepted leadership from women.

The words tumbled out before Rathos could stop them. "Do your Old Ways also teach you to steal from poor readers and Mumblers?"

Leah shot him a surly look. She sheathed her dagger. "Is that what you thought you saw today?"

A familiar anger boiled up—an anger for Leah as much as himself and the circumstances. "What *should* I think? Your men didn't pay them."

They'd spent years apart, yet the same script came easily to Leah. She held her arms akimbo, twisting her lips. "You show gratitude in strange ways, Rathos. The readers were giving us bread and wine, if you must know."

"Why? Your men worship more gods than Elvarenists."

"They do, and that doesn't stop readers and Mumblers from accepting money we give them from the carriages we'll rob. Or the protection we'll give them on the road when they escort peasant families late on their taxes and rents to other villages, to keep their children out of the hands of justices and priests."

"But you're *outlaws.*"

"As you and Father are *traitors,*" Leah said mockingly. "Is the chasm between us so great?"

"The Loyal Company fights for the Fourth Wing—"

"No, you *talk.* You talk and vote, talk and vote, all from the shadows, and think yourselves champions of the Commons for it. Saviors we're not, Ray, but at least we're *doing something* for the people of this wretched realm." She had a look of offended dignity. "Jacob Sulley, the Master Reader himself, met with me to thank me. Did Father's Pigeons not tell you that?"

The man on spiritual footing with priestkings, friends with the Mad Lady? Rathos thought. *Even if I believed that . . .* "Is that why you abandoned us, then? To aid the Master Reader and the Common cause?"

Her horse nickered. Smiling impishly, Leah stroked his mane. "Look at us. It's like we never left Caerdon. Well, you didn't survive death just to catch up, obviously. You still want to know how we found you, I take it—unless I disgust you so much that you'd rather take your chances on the road without us?"

Rathos sighed through his nose. "Forgive me. I'm grateful, Leah. And yes, if you'll tell me." He glanced around the clearing.

"Don't worry." Leah stared up, as if she saw something in the sunlit canopy. "Father's Pigeons are loud and clumsy, and their birdcalls are shit. I can hear them from a mile away."

"Is that how you found us?"

"No. I wouldn't have known about the plot to kill you without hearing it from the one called Tom Goodfield first."

Rathos made a face. "Tom. That Pigeon. You *knew* him?"

"Only in the sense that I've known Dustin."

He watched her uneasily.

She sucked at her teeth. "What? It's not a crime for a man to bed a whore, but it is for me to bed one with a cock?"

"It's just . . . What if Lord Evan found out?"

"Those men tried to kill you, so how would Lord Evan find out, anyway?" she mimicked his voice, as she would when they were children. "Gods, you sound like him. Are you more afraid of me fucking, or of the turncloaks trying to kill you?"

Rathos urged her on, his contrition plain.

"My men and I were in Grayport not too long ago," Leah said with some annoyance. "On Remembrance Day, actually. My men, well, you've seen them—ill-bred and stupid, but useful. They've got needs, just as I have needs, so we visited a brothel. What better way to celebrate the rebellion's end than with a face full of tits? Hexar would've been proud."

She goaded him with a mischievous look, then rolled her eyes at his unease. "Oh, when did you become such a wooden Willard? You always told the *worst* jokes. Most concerned tits."

Yes, but those days are past, Leah, Rathos thought. *That's why I chose your sister.* "Time is short, Leah."

"Yes, yes it is. You expected to see one Sinclair girl and wound up with the *other* one." She continued, "We went to The Mermaid. Those Pigeons had removed their cloaks, but one of them gave himself away with a whistle for mead. I knew then who they really were. And once I knew . . . well, I always want to know how my father is doing."

"So you fucked Tom, and he liked you so much he just . . . told you?"

She chuckled. "You're a well-bred man, Rathos son of Matthus. Father's ideas took root in you, so you're beholden to them. Less fortunate men? Give them a warm brew and a wet cunt, and they'll renounce oaths and gods alike. Pigeons are even easier. They spend their days in trees whistling like idiots. What bird doesn't sing when it nests?"

"Who sent them to kill us?"

"*That,* I didn't get out of him—and trust me, I tried. All he shared was that someone offered him land and lordship to take Evan

Sinclair captive and kill his companions."

Land and title. Lightheaded, Rathos fought the urge to sit down. If what Leah said was true, the Company could well be blind, its eyes and ears bought by someone with means. The implications were daunting. He asked her if she knew whether he could trust Karl.

"Trust him to fight? No, but they tried to kill him, too."

"How did you sell helping us to the Heretics?" he asked.

"There was a cost," Leah admitted. "When you join these outlaws, you swear off what came before. A few men didn't like me helping Father, or you. That cunt Venn was one. Thought I went soft. Thought to challenge me in front of my men. Well"—she clenched her fist—"he's the one who's soft, for worms."

"You said Tom was promised land and a lordship. Only a king can grant that." Adrenaline made his wound throb anew, painfully. "*The Kingstrials.* Hexar named Evan to the Worthy Assembly before he died."

"Tom and his men were to seize Father, to prevent him from rallying the Assembly behind a claimant." Leah narrowed her eyes suspiciously. "Father sent you and your companion to rally the Company for . . . who, the bastard prince?"

"For someone who should be king." Rathos left it at that.

"The whole realm will know soon enough. Yet I think it's clear who bought the Pigeons." Leah held up the slack coil of her prize, wriggling it by its head. "'A snake in the kingdom's garden,' Father always said."

Pinkhands. Ever had Evan suspected the Lord of Saxhold's hand in the explosion that killed Rathos's father. He made fists. Had his father's killer sought to finish his work?

"Gram Sothos rots in a Tower cell." He knew immediately how foolish he sounded.

"Are all his vassals and friends rotting with him?"

He took her by the arms. "Leah, Lord Evan—*Father*—he's traveling to Eddenloxley Castle with his sister's son. We don't know how far this betrayal goes—how many other Pigeons are compromised. If he meets with a Pigeon, alone—"

Leah pressed a finger to his lips. "The Mad Lady and her Heretics will see that he won't."

He lowered her hand. "You'll have to take Midland roads. Those are dangerous."

"Who said anything about the Midlands? We'll go through Westland. The Lady at the Tree follows our Old Ways. She can tell us which roads Father might be taking."

"I wish you wouldn't. Griffons roam there. And the things they say about the Oracle . . ."

"About how she dines on the blood of children? Not true. Besides, even if she *did*"—she leaned in—"I live for danger. Griffons, mystics, outlaws—you can't find them at Caerdon, only in the wilderness. That's why they call me mad. But . . . it pleases me to know you still care."

Leah drew near, eyes on his lips. He turned away before she could plant a kiss. She exaggerated her pout. "As I said, a well-bred man. A man of ideas, like Father. She's a lucky girl, my sister."

She stuffed the snake in a saddlebag and heaved herself onto her horse. "I'll return you to your wife, then head north."

He gazed up at the outlaw clad in boiled leather and fur, trying to reconcile her with the frolicsome girl from his youth. "What happened to you, Leah? What made you want to trade Caerdon Castle . . . for this? It wasn't just the peasants."

She watched him, on the verge of saying something.

"Father searched for you," he persisted. "We both did. For months. We worried that Gram Sothos or another enemy of his had seized you for ransom or killed you. He had to learn from a Pigeon that you'd joined the Heretics."

"And luckily for him, I had." The Mad Lady tugged on her horse's reins and plunged back into the forest.

It was another day's ride through Southland's fluted oaks before Westland's elms began feathering the land.

Murg spied the first Commoners on the woodland fringes, an older man driving a wagon with what looked like his two sons. They began to appear more frequently afterward. Rathos stirred gladly. Caerdon Castle and Peacefield were near.

At the sight of Peacefield's sentry tower, Leah held up her hand, drawing the outlaws to an orderly halt. She dismounted with a flourish of violet, leaf-flecked hair. "This is where we say farewell, Rathos," she said.

Rathos slid down from his horse for a familial embrace. "Send her my greetings," she said in his ear.

I won't. "And Lord Evan, mine. Ride with all haste, Leah."

When she slipped away, Rathos found himself face-to-face with her paramour. His fist was a wind that sent the Petitioner reeling to his knees. He tasted fresh blood.

Dustin popped his knuckles. "That's how *I* say farewell."

The Heretics chuckled. Rathos wobbled up, dumbfounded to see that Leah and Dustin were taking *their* horses. Karl made a quick approach, halting as Pretty Phillip reached for a dagger.

"You'd take our *horses?*" Rathos said bitterly.

A smile crept into her face. "We're outlaws, Ray. You said so yourself. Luckily, we know each other. Otherwise, we would have let the Pigeons finish their work and taken your horses after we killed them."

Dustin stuffed a roll of pinkbud into his mouth, grinning. Murg handed Leah her fearsome griffon's skull, and the lady Rathos had known vanished inside, the Mad Lady once more. Inclining her great skull in farewell, she dug her heels into his mount's sides and galloped off. The Heretics circled on their stolen steeds and careened after her, almost of hive mind.

Karl spun on him. "So you *did* know a Heretic."

CHAPTER 31

Atonement

he Cloudlands. That was the ancient name for the vast, remote, northwesterly reaches of the Kingdom of Loran long before King Wess declared it one and the same with Westland, almost as an afterthought. The Cloudlands, the folk here called it still, with a pride as formidable as the snowcapped peaks that punctured their rolling, dreamlike fog.

The fog was what gave this land its name. It touched near everything. From the white summits of the Iron Mountains to the village of Wicktown below the Pass of Eddenloxley, it rolled over the land like a gray sea. Sylvanians held the fog as proof of their faith, worshipping it as the last breath of one of their old gods, an enormous ice dragon that died giving birth to winter.

There was a bleak beauty to the Cloudlands that Jason found deeply satisfying. Unlike in Southland, where Romarian stone battled the earth for dominion, nothing here felt foisted upon. When the fog permitted it, he, Evan, and the rest of their party glimpsed rustic hamlets that seemed to grow out of hills beneath the mountains. Grass patched the roofs of poor hovels; moss climbed up enclosures hewn from rock. Pine trees lined the only road to Eddenloxley Castle, and their spicy fragrance pinched the cold air. The chill was a welcome reprieve from the heat and dust of the Midlands.

I could call this my kingdom, Jason thought with wonder, *and die a contented king.*

Less so, maybe, his exhausted companions. Their column held despite the lash of a cold wind. His uncle stuck one foot in front of the other, marching on determinedly in the drape of his gray, dappled furs. Rogir Levan endured the frost with the defiance of an older man who refuses to yield to his age. David Bridge, Kyle Urron, and Erick Seam, all men closer to Jason in age, led their horses by their reins. Only Sam Hornby dared the wind on his steed, and he seemed a bit more sluggish.

Their party struggled up the great road called Amathorn. Their faithful mounts lurched unsteadily through treacherous clay. The men's breath steamed out in columns. He knew their shins, like his, burned like hell. Up, up went Amathorn, a snake curving through mountains, tilting so steeply at times he feared one man's misstep would send him barreling into the others and pitch them all to their deaths.

Evan attempted to distract from the climb with a telling of Amathorn's history. Long before the Romarians, the mountain folk had called this their own kingdom, he shared with them. The land's closeness to the sea and the Iron Mountains put them under constant threat of invasion from Uzmen, reavers of the Isles of Rienne, and, finally, Rorin and his Romarians. So the Cloudland King Eddemraugh ordered his hardy people up. The ancient Cloudlanders built Eddenloxley near the summits to hold constant vigil, hewing Amathorn above the mountain pass so no army could march unseen or without assailment. To this day, no man had ever taken the castle by force of arms.

Their need for protection wasn't ancient history. Frost-covered corpses occasionally appeared up the path, hung from stakes like grisly scarecrows, Uzmen and Rienners by the looks of their shabby furs and painted armor.

"Amathorn literally means 'Judgment Road,'" Evan added.

Kyle lingered on a crucified man as they passed by. "Little wonder why our late king never sought to collect his due," the knight said.

Yes, and here we are, a party of seven cold men on a road up which my father rarely sent couriers. After it became clear that Wexley had no intention of reconciling, Hexar—for maybe the second time in his life—heeded advice and didn't retaliate. Communication between Loran proper and the Cloudlands ceased with the flow of treasure and men, and this bleak place became a kingdom in all but name. *Hexar's Folly*, a minstrel had long ago named his song, and it stuck. *Yet one more sin of my father's I must account for . . .*

Jason focused on the steep ascent, back bent like a crone. "Judgment Road, indeed." He sidestepped a treacherous hole. "How did Wess Romaris conquer it?" he asked his uncle.

A wind slammed into the men and their horses with the force of a falling brick wall. Evan misplaced his foot, and were it not for Jason's sure grip would've tumbled down a steep snow-covered ridge. After steadying himself, his uncle thanked him.

"Not with an army," Evan said as he watched his feet. "Rorin's thrice-great-grandson promised gold and women to the man who could murder the Cloudland king and open the drawbridge." He grunted. "'Twas a castle servant who betrayed the king here. A disgruntled Commoner. Lords of Eddenloxley who followed never forgot, and never forgave, and forever named their little folk *scrorn-ner-gaith*—'shit beneath my boot.'"

I wonder what the Bull would call Hexar's son, Jason thought. It didn't matter. He'd tolerate any name, and he'd make almost any concession. Jason needed Hexar's Bull to enter the Kingstrials. This was how the bastard Raelin had become king despite his bastardy.

Hamlets dotted the flat sallow tablelands that jutted out of the mountainsides. Everywhere there was a hut, peasants shuffled out to observe the Southlanders and their tired horses. The land's ethereal beauty was in their drab, faded wool and gaunt faces. Some of them conversed in mutters, the musical lilt of their Cloudspeech faintly audible.

High above, the mists parted to reveal Eddenloxley Castle, its five towers splayed like fingers of a hand lifted in warning. Jason sensed the trepidation in his company. At any moment, arrows could shower their exposed shoulders and backsides, ending Jason, Evan, and any hope that House Eddenhold could keep the Silver Walls out of Shaddon and Parlisis's hands . . . and Loran out of war. His protective uncle never strayed far from his side.

This is our gamble, Lorana, he thought to himself. *Let us hope the*

Bull's honor is still what it was . . . and that his anger has faded with time.

After a hundred-foot climb, Amathorn abruptly plateaued and curved between the walls of mountains called the Daggers. Windswept cliffs closed in, vise-like, leaving a narrow, pebble-strewn footpath that forced the party into single file. The air was thin, their breaths shallower. Evan looked like a drenched bear, ashy, blond hair and beard matted against his face, and he and Rogir gasped and swallowed as if they were drowning.

The fog dispersed abruptly, and Eddenloxley emerged between the mountains, almost on top of their heads. Smoke-gray was the fortress hewn from the mountainside, and so too the cliffs of its crenellated curtain wall, the watch towers and outbuildings that jutted out, the grotesques that nested on the massive barbican. Five towers stretched to graze the clouds, peppered with arrow slits, their parapets notched with steep embrasures. Behind them, Judgment Road thinned to a thread of silver, weaving in and out of sight.

"You've come a long way just to turn around."

Jason looked up. Bearded men lined the tops of the cliffs above like gargoyles. Their white surcoats were worked with the bold black mountain of House Wexley. He counted at least two-dozen crossbows loaded with fletched bolts.

He raised his palms slowly. "Hail, men of the Cloudlands. We come seeking the friendship and hearth fire of your noble lord. I am—"

"We know who you are," spat one, a lean man obscured by his nasal helmet. He was unmistakably a Cloudlander with that rhotic accent, rolling his *r* and drawing out his *o*. "Your sister by Lady Alyse sent our lord an invitation." *At least he hasn't taken to calling himself king.* "He made a request. Tell me, does the liar Charles Burke hang from a gibbet?"

Not unless anything's changed. "He does not. I—"

"Then go back whence you came."

"Forgive me, I would seek an audience—"

"You cannot. Don't come back this way."

Deep in the pit of his stomach, he felt his father's wrath boiling up. Hexar had struck off Hanorr's head but spared his brother when another king would've done differently. There was no going back. If he couldn't enter the Kingstrials, war was inevitable.

A hand clasped his shoulder. "Let me try, nephew."

The commander must've overheard his uncle, because he snorted and said, "We know you, too, Evan Sinclair. A traitor's word has even less weight here than the Warchild's."

Evan extended his arms. "Aye, I'm a traitor. Apparently, so was your lord's brother. We were both victims of the late king's blundering stupidity, were we not?"

Jason felt the punch in his gut. It was too soon to speak ill of his father like that. Rogir looked ready to haul Evan back to the Red Tower that instant.

Evan ignored his look. "Tell me, with whom do I speak?"

Silence. And then, begrudgingly, "Sir Halford Ironkeep."

"Sir Halford, tell me—does the Lord of Eddenloxley still keep faith with the ancient laws of these Cloudlands?"

Ironkeep huffed contemptuously. "What would a shoreman know about the laws of the Cloudlands?"

The nobleman gave a hapless shrug. "Little and less. My Caerdon is near the shore, as you say. Yet I once received Sir Hanorr at my castle. A terrible storm had waylaid him and his company. When he came to *my* door, he invoked the right of a nobleman under duress to seek shelter with another of the same rank. Of course I opened our gates, since House Wexley was our friend through the king. Sir Hanorr explained to me that this was a nobleman's right in the north. *Lothlaen regis.*"

Despite the insult to his father, Jason almost smiled. This was what Evan Sinclair was known for, apart from treason—his ability to exploit man's laws. *This is why I need you, uncle.* He watched to see if it'd work.

"Sir Hanorr would've told you right," Ironkeep admitted standoff-ishly. "*Lothlaen regis* is reserved for men of high birth, however. You, Evan Sinclair, were attainted."

"The attainder was removed," Evan said, sounding like he was smiling. "By King Hexar, on Remembrance Day."

The guards traded uncertain glances. Ironkeep shrugged off counsel from another man. He sighed like a man who knew what he was in for with Evan. "What is your duress, my lord?"

"Amathorn herself." Evan produced a flaccid waterskin. "We don't have enough water for the climb down. Night will fall soon, with it a deadly cold. May we enter, for life's sake?"

Ironkeep relaxed his grip on the crossbow. He muttered under his breath to the man next to him. "You will stay here," he said, vanishing from sight. It was nearly an hour in silence beneath the crossbows before the Cloudlander reappeared.

"Your ruse seems to have worked, Lord Evan," he said, clearly annoyed. "Under the ancient laws of our fathers, Lord Trevor hereby grants you and your companions *lothlaen regis*. We'll see whether you still want to exercise it after he treats with you. Amathorn's cold might not seem so terrible."

Jason flashed Evan a grateful smile, but his uncle looked away, as if to remind him that the ordeal was just beginning.

Up ahead, the iron portcullis shuddered awake with the grudging complaint of winches. In accordance with *lothlaen regis*, the eight men relinquished their steel to armored men at the entrance. They went in with their horses, passing beneath seven portcullises with murder holes to spare. Men-at-arms followed so closely behind them that Jason smelled the sweat under their pits.

The barbican opened into a lower bailey crowded with fifty of House Wexley's armored knights . . . and the Lord of Eddenloxley himself.

There was no confusing Trevor Wexley with anyone else. At nearly seven feet, he was easily the biggest man Jason had ever laid eyes on, taller even than Gram Sothos. His arms were thick as tree branches, his chest sprawling. Each of his massive hands could clutch a man's face.

Yet he was—and wasn't—the legend of song. The lord's age showed in his rotund stomach, the copious skin folds about his jowls, the fingers of silver that clutched at his auburn beard. Drifts of hair flowed past his shoulders and backside. The black mountain sewn into his surcoat pointed to flinty eyes that did not like Jason or his companions.

Jason and Evan knelt almost at the same time, followed quickly by their Wall knights. "Hail, my Lord of Eddenloxley," Jason said. "We've traveled many miles to have your counsel, and make amends for the past."

Trevor Wexley stared, unspeaking. It was only then that Jason noticed the caramel-skinned foreigners to his side, the widow and children of Hanorr Wexley. They looked much like Muhregites. Hanorr's widow was in the winter of her life, the pronounced wrinkles under her jaw belying the youth of her rich, oil-black hair. She wore an air of cold dignity about her. The two sons beside her had their father's stocky build. A doe-eyed girl Jason's age, bundled in furs, resembled her mother.

Wexley's lips quivered. "Make . . . amends?" he managed softly, in a voice that carried. "You make a mock of my father's laws and take advantage of my respect for them . . . and you want to *make amends?*" His steely gaze shifted to Evan. "Lord Evan, is this the rotten foundation on which you'd leave your father's house? A legacy of trickery and warmongering?"

Jason pushed himself to his feet briskly. "Forgive me, Lord Trevor. We took the Pass of Eddenloxley believing we might treat with you. My king father is dead. Like him, I have need of your honor and courage."

"*Honor? Courage?*" Leaning to his side, the lord sprayed enough spittle to fill a small cup. "Was it *honor* that drove the king to falsely accuse my brother in Shaddon's plot? Do you call cutting off his head at Traitor's Pit like a Common thief, with onion and cabbage thrown at him, *courage?* And it's in this way you come to me, seeking my name for your claim in the Trials, *with a woman's deceit?*"

He hadn't crossed the Midlands and climbed Amathorn thinking a conversation and some mead would put to bed a generation's worth of ill will. On sleepless nights around the fire, Evan had prepared him to address his father's crime. *And yet,* he wondered, *how do I address a crime if I don't believe it was one?*

"Forgive me, my lord," he began measuredly, "but I have met with

Charles Burke. I cannot speak for Sir Hanorr, and whether he truly *did* send letters to Shaddon that gave him Prince Erick. But I cannot refute the Grand Inquisitor's verdict. He has served our house for many years, and—"

"*LIAR!*" The shout issued from the thin, caramel-skinned woman. She shook free of her son's grasp and strode forward, hands clenched, long bony arms trembling. "*Liar,* I name you! You are a bastard, bastards lie, your father hated us, he wanted Sir Hanorr *dead!* Just say it. SAY IT!"

Wexley slunk one strong arm about her tiny frame, and she slumped against him, wracked with sobs. "Do you know who this woman is?" the nobleman said.

Jason nodded. "The Lady Yosar, of Orran, widow to your late brother." He pitied her as she shook with grief as fresh as if Hexar had beheaded her husband yesterday.

"Aye." Wexley tilted his head at the others. "These are his bereaved children, my wards, Hanorr, Trevor, and Yasmeen."

The children watched Jason guardedly. The tallest son, Hanorr, glared unceasingly. He had a swordsman's lean build.

Wexley said, "I took them in after my brother's death, but that hasn't eased their sorrow. Because of our laws, Lady Yosar can never remarry. My nephews will never share my titles or land. All this came from your father's treachery. What amends can you offer them?"

I can only speak the truth and appeal to his sense of honor, Jason thought. "My lady, I can never make amends to you or your family. What I can do is see to it that Shaddon Eddenhold, my uncle, the man responsible for your misery, never ascends the Silver Throne."

Wexley's whiskers shivered. Hanorr's widow watched him with disgust in her broken eyes.

Evan stepped beside Jason. "Lord Trevor, I, of all people, can understand your anger. The king, my brother-by-law, made me into a villain after my sister and knight died. He gaoled me in the Red Tower, where the Grand Inquisitor tortured me. My slain knight's children became my wards."

Wexley watched Evan as if he were losing patience with every second he spoke.

"Yet you, your brother, and I also fought against Stoddard Trambar and Willard Potter"—he gripped Jason's shoulder—"and for this man's unborn life. Such as it is, I humbly ask that we retreat indoors to discuss these matters privately."

"No. I'll hear the truth now." Wexley flickered to Jason. "Do you believe my brother conspired with Shaddon to seize your half-brother for the priestking?"

Evan and Lorana would've beseeched him to lie. But Jason couldn't. He'd killed men, and truth was worth dying for, worth losing life for. "My late father wronged many, Lord Trevor. He'd an ill temper. Some might say he was a terrible king. My father should've kept your brother a prisoner in the Red Tower, but Sir Hanorr Wexley's confession was ironclad."

The Bull narrowed his eyes. "I've granted you the right to shelter with me, but that's all I'll give you. On the morrow, you will mount your horses with full waterskins and leave."

And just like that, he rounded, leaving with Yosar under his arm and the only chance Jason Warchild had to take his throne peacefully. The entire bailey rustled to return indoors.

His uncle was at a loss. Their knights were crestfallen. *No, I can't return without his friendship,* he thought desperately. *If I do, the Kingstrials are for naught, and Father's killer will ascend.*

"LORD TREVOR!" he shouted. "I will have your alliance and friendship, whatever it takes."

Whirling, the Bull flashed him a look that Jason imagined Stod's cowering siege men beheld in their last moments alive. "*Whatever it takes?*" he seethed. "Very well! I've allowed you here out of respect for our laws and the friendship I had with your father, but I can't overlook an idiot's tongue. Before I left the Walls, I challenged King Hexar to a trial by sword. This is our law. *It* is ironclad—and the only full measure of truth the gods grant us."

Wexley's fingers glanced his sword pommel. "Your father refused me. Wouldn't even name a champion. *Cursed me!* Well," he said thickly, "that challenge remains. What say you, Jason Warchild?"

Jason tasted chapped lips. The air was cold in his lungs. "I accept, Lord Trevor. On two conditions: that you be the friend to me that you were to Hexar if I win . . . and if I lose, that you send my ashes back to the Silver Walls."

Only the wind spoke, ruffling his mother's raven hair. As Wexley opened his mouth, Hanorr's namesake son dropped to a knee before his warder.

"My lord, do me the honor of naming me your champion," the knight's son said. "Let me prove the bastard false."

Wexley looked at Hanorr, then Yosar. "I cannot allow it. If you fell . . ." He shook his head gravely as Yosar pulled at her son, begging him to say no. "Your mother . . ."

Hanorr rushed to his feet, hand on the hilt of the sword at his waist. "He was *my* father," he said in a whip-sharp voice. He pointed a finger up at his uncle's face. "I have the right to settle this the old way. Do you consent, under our laws?"

Yosar pled with her son in a high, grief-strangled voice. Hanorr stared at Wexley as if his mother weren't there.

The Bull gazed at Jason with dead eyes. "I won't refuse your right," he sighed. "We'll know the truth of Charles Burke's deceit at sunrise tomorrow."

True to his word, the Bull gave them shelter at his castle the night before Jason would fight his nephew.

Jason ate breakfast with Evan and the knights in a spartan chamber overlooking the bailey where his trial would take place. He cracked a stone-hard loaf of bread, gnawing on tasteless dough as he studied the lay of the bailey. He disliked the low-hanging stone walls. A push over one of those walls would send a swordsman plunging down the mountainside.

Across from him, Evan sat silent, eating nothing. Missed sleep ringed his eyes. Jason caught a look and remembered their heated conversation the night before.

"This is the king's folly all over again," Evan had told him in his chamber, looking like he wanted to throw himself over the bailey wall. "Either way, you lose. Either Hanorr dies, and you've salted our friendship with the Cloudlands worse than what it was, or he kills you."

"You've led us this far, uncle," Jason had told him. "Trust me to get us to the Kingstrials."

"Your mother wouldn't have wanted this," Evan muttered presently.

"My mother isn't here," Jason said as he swallowed bread. He hated crossing swords on an empty belly. Some men couldn't eat before a fight. Hanorr looked like an eater, like him.

Sunlight glanced off water down below, drawing his eye to the bailey well, to the rope slung around its beam, the rope connected to a wall. "But I am," Jason continued. "I'll not have war in my kingdom. If this is the price I must pay for peace, I will pay it."

Evan got up. "Don't die," he said below his breath. "We haven't even entered the Kingstrials yet."

Sunrise bled like an open wound in the misted sky, faintly red. All of Eddenloxley's castle servants gathered on the fringes of the lower bailey.

Jason stepped out first, harnessed in plate and mail. His cuirass fit snugly over his mail, and a skirt of faulds protected his thighs. Shiny pauldrons shielded his shoulders and pits. He carried his helm under his arm. He inhaled the frosty morning air, relishing a heady rush of adrenaline, as intoxicating as any tavern ale. He flexed his gauntleted hands, feeling like himself again for the first time since leaving Nerimba.

Had he missed this? *Yes*, he heard a voice say. He'd had his fill of politics, an arena fit for Lorana and Evan. He'd tired of it even before leaving for war. At least here, a man could confront his enemy directly, sword in hand. *I wonder if I'll still feel that way in the Kingstrials*, he thought. *If I live past today . . .*

The crowd parted for his opponent. Hanorr the Younger wore his beard bush-thick, like a Cloudlander, but his caramel skin reminded Jason of a Muhregite, and that gave him comfort, strangely.

Hanorr came ready in iron-black armor. Jason traded a look with Evan. *That's Gildebirgean armor,* he registered. Gildebirgean smiths were the continent's best. A war hammer couldn't hope to even dent armor that thick and well-made.

He didn't need a hammer to injure Hanorr. Rings of mail patterned his stomach like fish scales. His sword needed only to find weak spots behind the knees or armpits.

But the continent's strongest armor wasn't what caught Jason off guard.

The hilt of Young Hanorr's longsword protruded right of his waist. *He's lefthanded,* Jason realized with a start. The man had worn his scabbard to the left the day before. *He had every intention of fighting me and wanted to mislead me.* His dark eyes sparkled with mischief, confirming the ruse. *Very clever.*

Lefthanded swordsmen were a rarity anywhere, and a deft left hand was dangerous. Jason had only fought one man with that gift, in the Brace. All his instincts had been wrong. He would've died on the swordsman's blade, were it not for Erick's intervention.

Erick, whom young Hanorr's father helped Shaddon seize, he thought. *I couldn't avenge you in the Brace, brother. Today, I will—and the Bull will champion me because of it.*

The Bull towered over his people as he waded through. He gave Jason a long look, then hugged Hanorr, telling him something in Cloudspeech.

A reader shuffled forward to pray. All bowed their heads. "Elvarenists have twelve gods, and Free Believers one god with twelve faces," he said in his thick accent, "but in the Cloudlands a man's bravery is god. That bravery will show us truth today."

When the reader left, Jason slipped his helm over his head. Hanorr bowed first to Wexley, then to his family, and, finally, to Jason himself.

"You are a nobler man than your father, Lord Jason," he said, muffled through his helm. "But that noble heart will not save you."

It may yet save my kingdom—Jason drew his sword—*and you're in the way, young Hanorr.*

The combatants traded a few clangs of the sword, sizing each other up. They danced around the courtyard, servants and household members ceding space as they came near.

After a few minutes, the blows came with more vigor. Hanorr was younger than him but no sapling. He was quick-footed, a talent with his sword. Courtyard observers gave Hanorr words of encouragement. "Show him the strength of the Cloudlands!" cried a lesser lord. "Your father is with you, Hanorr!" someone else shouted through cupped hands.

Is mine with me? Jason wondered as he parried another stroke from Hanorr's polished sword.

He'd barely returned from overseas when he saw Hexar taken from him. They'd had those bitter words in the throne room, and then he'd fallen dead from their enemies' poison. Jason had known few good memories with the king, except . . .

He remembered it like it was yesterday, his father's laughter in the duel with Garrett.

The trouble between the bastard prince and the crown prince had been brewing long before he'd woken to Garrett's blade on his neck in a ship cabin. His older half-brother had an abusive streak. He liked to swat at Lorana's breasts and stalk off laughing; sometimes he pissed in Jason's soup as well as temple stoups.

Over dinner one night, Garrett went a step too far by likening Edenia to a Common whore. The prieslenne had broken down sobbing. Jason, her defender—even then—had demanded an apology in front of Hexar's court. When Garrett refused, he demanded a trial by sword for her honor.

Hexar had laughed off Jason's demand, rather than deal with the surly crown prince or force a peace. No one seriously expected Garrett, the twenty-one-year-old heir, to lift a sword against his half-brother, a boy of fourteen.

But Jason took no refusal.

The king, apoplectic, came barreling down the South Tower steps, where his sons were crossing swords heatedly. His red-faced shouts did nothing to make them desist. The crown prince bled Jason with cuts on the backs of his thighs. "Yield, Warchild," Garrett kept saying, grinning all the while. "The priestking's little bitch isn't worth your trouble. There's a hundred more sluts like her in Southpoint."

But there was no one like Edenia. Jason wasn't as tall or strong as the crown prince, but he knew the lay of the bailey, and he remembered how the marshal fastened girdles a little too securely to his stable walls. Feigning retreat, Jason baited his half-brother to the stables. Their father and the crowd of his court had followed them anxiously.

It'd been easier than Jason imagined. Once inside, Garrett skidded on horse manure, close to the loop of a hanging girdle. Jason grabbed the girdle, slung it around Garrett's wrist, and disarmed him. The contest ended with the crown prince face-down in horseshit, the point of Jason's sword in his face, and their father red-faced with laughter.

Jason narrowly avoided a vicious swing from Hanorr that aimed for his armpit; the next stroke glanced off his vambrace. Hanorr flashed a smiling eye and plunged forward, hacking with his sword. Jason sidestepped a thrust, then another, then another. Observers were starting to jeer, urging him to stand his ground. He whirled and struck Hanorr Wexley's son with a gauntleted backhand so forceful it threw the helm from his head.

The move was as insulting as it was disorienting. Hanorr wiped blood off his nose, slightly dazed.

"The Assembly named you Warchild," Wexley rumbled in mock. "Looks like I had reason to doubt your father as much as his Assembly. They should've called you Jason Ninnyboy."

Through scattered laughter, he heard Evan say something in retort. Hanorr's son renewed his offense. The clang of their swords echoed across the bailey and in surrounding chasms.

Back and forth they went, close, tantalizingly close to the water well. Jason tried to sidestep him again, watching his left wrist for an opening. His opponent hurled his pauldron-plated shoulder against him, making him lose his balance.

The crowd made way for them as Hanorr slashed at him in swift strokes. In the space of a few seconds, he had Jason where Jason didn't want to be, pinned at the waist against the bailey's low-hanging outer wall. The X of their crossed swords forced him halfway off, over a crevasse sheeted with curling fog. Cold air breathed through the open spaces in Jason's mail and plates.

As he struggled against Hanorr, clenching his teeth, his half-brother's mockery from their duel returned: "Is this what the Long Summer Rebellion was for? Jason Warchild's death, at *my* hands?"

Jason kneed his opponent in his groin. The young knight limped off, clutching at his thigh area. It was a bastard's move, but then, the Assembly *had* deemed him a bastard.

The bastard prince made his sword fly like the wind, a whirlwind that overwhelmed even a lefthanded swordsman. The clash of their steel drove his opponent back from the precipice. They bounded across the bailey, to the water well, swords singing.

Jason winced as Hanorr's blade opened the back of his thigh. He whirled for a stab up, at the crevice between mail and garment covering the right side of Hanorr's chest. He felt the pressure of his sword biting into flesh, saw the flicker of pain in the other man's eyes.

A second's delay gave Jason the space he needed to snatch the well's slack rope. He snaked the rope around his foe's wrist to benumb his sword hand.

Jason disarmed him, sending his sword to clatter on the cobbles. He pinned young Hanorr against the well, forcing him over the edge. He pointed the tip of his sword at the knight's exposed throat.

Yosar's anguished cry ripped through the air.

An over-the-shoulder glance showed him the Bull held Hanorr's mother with one thick arm. He regarded Jason with the eyes of a man making peace with the truth of his brother's treachery . . . and the imminent death of his own blood.

Many called on Jason to show mercy. Wexley shook his head. "This is the law," the Bull said. "The victor in a trial by sword must carry out death."

Jason steadied the point of his sword in Hanorr's neck. "I DIDN'T COME HERE TO KILL YOUR BLOOD," he cried. "I CAME HERE FOR YOUR FRIENDSHIP." He whipped around for a look at the Bull. "Champion me in the Kingstrials, Lord Trevor, and I'll spare Hanorr's life, as my father should have."

Hanorr lay still in his grip, panting. After a long pause, the Bull stepped forward from the crowd. He came within inches of Jason, towering over him. He pried his fingers free of his sword and tossed the blade so that it joined Hanorr's on the stone.

For a split second, Jason wondered if the huge lord would clutch him by his waist and pitch him down the well.

"Then you are Hexar as he should've been," Wexley said. The Bull knelt as Hanorr slipped away from the well's edge. "I will see you through the Kingstrials and seat you on Hexar's throne, gods as my witness. And if this is how you'd rule your kingdom—with honor and courage—I would do more. I would end our strife and return the Cloudlands to Loran once more."

Jason saw Evan smiling incredulously, his relief plain. *My first trial, won,* he thought, *and a taste of things to come.*

CHAPTER 32

Errands and Lies

he accused peasant's name was Ralff. He wore a face as long and solemn as any awaiting judgment. He was a plowman and looked the part, his tunic muddy, fingers visible through his worn mittens. Thorns of hair poked through his holey hood.

Ralff was not alone in his time of need. Other Commoners crowded behind him, huddled beneath the drapes of tapestries spangled with the eight-pointed star. Wary-eyed friends and neighbors kept their distance from the man who clutched Ralff by his arm as if he were a teacher presenting a scolded child.

Leaning against a column, Rathos studied Caerdon Castle's justice of the peace, a highborn Westlander feathered in gaudy clothing. *No wonder villagers despise this idiot,* he thought with disdain. The justice all but flicked his nose at peasants with his fine crimson doublet and pointed shoes, all on the same day he asked to hack off a well-liked peasant's head.

Someone pelted the official with a pebble. At a gesture from the castle steward, the bailiff promptly escorted the rock-thrower from Oliver's Hall. *You're a natural at this, song of my heart,* he thought admiringly of the steward, his wife.

At the front of the hall, Mina Robswell reclined into her father's chair with dignified airs. Th Lady of Caerdon dressed in a sleeveless surcoat, green on white, nothing flashy. Ringlets of violet hair gathered about her pale freckled shoulders. Her pale blue eyes missed nothing in Evan's hall—her hall, now, truthfully.

"Your arguments are hollow, sir," Mina said loftily. "While Ralff's guilt is obvious, given how you found him playing with his children when you kicked in his door, what's not is why you think he should lose his head." The justice started to interrupt; Mina silenced him with a stern finger. "Might I remind you, this is Caerdon Castle, not Thorn's Keep. And I'm a Robswell—not a Morley. We don't kill peasants because they're poor and hide their children to keep from losing them."

Several peasants embraced each other warmly. Someone chanted, "Lady Sinclair! Lady Sinclair!" Ralff doubled over with relief. Rathos couldn't help but remember how the Heretics had chanted for the other Lady Sinclair. *You're Mina Robswell now, song of my heart, but you'll always be Evan's daughter.*

"But Ralff," said Mina, voice cutting through the clamor. "The law is the law. The Worthy make laws for their king and his lords to enforce. You can't pay your rents. In recompense, you owe us three goats." She held up three fingers. "Fat ones, Ralff."

Better than owing his head, Rathos thought, *for his sake as well as ours.* His wife had rendered a fair verdict, and—equally important—the smart one. Caerdon's peasants had regarded their lords Sinclair fondly for centuries, that was known, but unrest was on the rise in Loran.

Never more so now that a king had been slain.

Doffing his hood, the plowman inclined his greasy-haired head and stammered his apologies. Rathos caught the justice rolling his eyes as Mina dismissed court. Peasants emptied the hall, heckling the detested official as he led the plowman out. A few stayed to bless the steward; one kissed Mina's ring finger.

When all the peasants had gone, Rathos Robswell met his wife in the hall's center amid shafts of sunlight. Lithe and very pretty, Evan's firstborn child had her aunt's heart-shaped face, cheeks dusted with freckles, and doe eyes that made his world feel right again. She'd gained weight since his departure with Evan and looked a touch healthier for it, thicker in her bosom and about the waist. Sunlight brought out lavender in her hair.

Rathos longed to whisk her upstairs and make love.

He settled on a long kiss. "Is this what you've been doing while your father and I risked our lives at the Walls?" Rathos teased her. "Thwarting Princess Lorana's justices with acts of mercy? How most untoward for a proper lady."

She pulled free of his lips. "Stop," she said chidingly. "You know how I admire the stone maiden. Were that peasants felt the same about Lorana's justices."

"God and gods, I thought they'd free Ralff themselves. Leave his captor dead and naked in your father's hall."

"Honestly? I would've let them."

"I wouldn't have blamed you."

Mina ducked another kiss to inspect his swaddled arms. "How are your wounds today?" she asked as she peeled off a bandage. She examined his swollen, sutured scar.

"Wounds? Hardly. Cat scratches."

She raised a violet eyebrow to show what she thought of *that*. "Cat scratches. *Huh*. Is that what you told the apothecary from Nocastle when he found you and Karl after the brigands left you for dead? It must be why he took such care in dressing your . . . scratches."

Rathos smiled roguishly, to hide discomfort. *She knows. Of course she sees past my lies. I've never been able to lie to her, not well.* Were that the ruse of a benevolent, traveling apothecary had been Karl's idea: then he could resent someone other than himself for his lie.

A protective lie, but still a lie.

Mina refolded the bandage and held him with her gaze for a long moment, almost expectantly. She looked disappointed when he didn't add anything. "Summon the lovely couple," she sighed. "The cooks prepared herring for supper and I'd like to give the peasants their alms before they return to Peacefield."

"Please don't call them a couple. It masks the betrayal."

"*Betrayal?*" She kissed him. "It's endearing to watch you protect your sister's honor, but I remind you that *she* was the one who started it."

"Mina. She was strumming her harp outside, unawares."

"Rathos," she imitated his voice. "Yes, outside apartments where a mysterious wounded guest laid abed." She tapped his chest playfully.

"Karl looks like a lost pup around her. Admit it, it's sweet."

"I admit that I'm concerned that Dana would take interest in a Reubenite. Not least because word will leak that a stranger is in Evan Sinclair's courtyard."

A look of recognition passed over Mina. She straightened. "Is he still leaving today?"

"After supper."

"Good. Summon them quickly. I'll have no horn blown."

His wife turned and walked over to the castle chaplain, reprising her role as steward.

Rathos lingered on his wife's violet hair, then left Oliver's Hall for the bailey.

Outside, a late morning sun winked on the battlements of curtain walls, scattering light across the most fascinating, man-made castle in Loran. Seen from afar, the seat of House Sinclair resembled any other fortress, boasting high walls, two towers notched with arrow loops, and a proud keep.

Within, it was a castle of curiosities, the handiwork of a mind unfettered and at harmony with itself.

Evan had designed most of the castle's newer trappings, the laboratory, glass workshop, and atelier. Yet his fingerprints showed most in Caerdon Castle's famous towers. Covered by the tortoise shell of a wooden roof, the Moon Tower contained a skyglass built by the lord himself. On clear, cloudless nights, Evan would retract the roof for the Sinclairs and their Robswell wards to gather, sip wine, and take turns stargazing, often with Dana strumming her harp. West of Oliver's Hall rose the Sun Tower, distinguished by the iron triangle of a gnomon that rendered the courtyard a giant functioning sundial. Along the inner castle walls were numerals that told the time.

How he'd looked forward to seeing the Silver Walls on the day they'd left eastward. *Hexar's bastard son can have the First King's castle. I never want to leave this one again.*

Descending a flight of steps, Rathos passed by the nearly vacant stables and smokeless forge, always a reminder of this house's days of glory past. Up ahead rose a marbled pavilion. A faint giggle drifted into earshot.

His only sibling rested against one of the pavilion's fluted columns, oblivious to his approach. Hair as dark and brown as his cascaded down her backside like a waterfall. She plucked at her harp strings with long nimble fingers, singing.

In the grass not two feet away, Karl Redmore rested on his side. He was a shade pale still, a hand against his sutured stomach. He curled a long-stemmed flower about his finger, listening raptly as Lady Robswell sang "The Man and the Maid":

> *Duty is a salty wind in the east*
> *When Dalla is your sea-bride,*
> *And a father's will cold as ice*
> *For the land-groom by her side.*
>
> *Lord Alann wanted a silver-like throne*
> *For Domin his son and heir:*
> *That rare Medecian, no ambition,*
> *His heart a chair for one finned and fair.*
>
> *She was silver moonlight and soft sea wind*
> *Lips warm like the sun and blue of skin*
> *His darling pearl, shining, seaweed-twined:*
> *A salt-sea bride unfit for any lord's line.*
>
> *On that rock she sang and braided her hair*
> *When hissed her huntsmen's snares and swords*
> *And blew the wind, salty and coarse,*
> *Over a seamaid who'd troubled a lord.*
>
> *Grief is a storm-whipped sea, deadly and cruel:*
> *It drowned old Lord Alann,*
> *Then Domin, too, who fell down to stay*
> *Forever there by his bride in Dalla's Bay.*

Karl wiped his cheeks. And he *sniffled!* "That's so sad, Dana," he intoned.

Rathos discerned an artist's satisfaction in his sister. "I think its melancholy lends it beauty," she told him.

"It's not so beautiful as you." Not seeming to see Rathos, Karl plucked the flower, wobbled to a knee, and slid it behind her ear. "Do you know a happier song? One where a man and woman find each other"—he leaned close, eyes flickering from her unseeing eyes to her lips—"and love one another unto gray hair and gray days?"

"I've known Dana to play 'A Husband Never Gone,'" Rathos quipped abruptly.

Karl tensed reflexively, clutching at his belly with a strained expression. The thought that he might've pulled a suture gave Rathos grim satisfaction.

Dana turned about, one milky-white eye fluttering. "'A Husband Never Gone' has to do with a man who dies in war, brother," she said with a wry smile. "You startled me! One might think you were one of Father's Pigeons."

The Companymen shared a look lost on the blind maiden. Karl cleared his throat. "Did you wish to speak of our business matters, Rathos?"

"I came to fetch you for dinner," Rathos answered.

Dana sighed. "I may not be able to see you, brother, but I can hear your scowl," she said. "Much as you and Mina like to gossip, I assure you that I remain a perfectly unspoiled virgin."

As she rose balancing her harp, Rathos spied a gray welt lurking on his sister's pale neck, nearly out of sight. Nearly. "I imagine there must be some other explanation for that bruise you sport, then," he noted.

Flinching, Dana misplaced a foot awkwardly on a marbled step. Karl caught her. The harp fell to clatter on the marble.

Dana gasped. "*My harp!*"

Karl steadied her. He inspected the instrument, tugging gently on the coil of loose string. "Worry not, my lady," said the Reubenite, with unbearable chivalry. "The harp's hurt, but not beyond repair."

"You don't understand." Tears misted her eyes. "*That's my father's harp.*"

Seeing the damaged instrument wounded Rathos almost as deeply as his sister. A ruby ring and gilded harp were all that Matthus Robswell had bequeathed his two children by a castle laundress. Stained black from smoke, his father's salvaged ring felt unwearable, even accursed. But the harp *was* their father. How often had Evan Sinclair told Dana that, glassy-eyed as she strummed?

And yet this wasn't the first time the harp had suffered.

Like a smitten boy, Karl fell over himself trying to placate Dana, offering to repair the harp personally, if he could.

Rathos glanced at Dana. She had the smallest smile. *Sister, would you drop Father's harp on purpose?* He sized up Karl, the gangly, straw-haired fool. *For him?*

Dining in Oliver's Hall felt strange without the lord of the castle, but pleasant company helped fill the hole his absence left. Servants whisked in and out with bread and butter, plates with smoked herring and succulent orchard grapes, and flutes of wine. Thick as thieves, Mina and Dana cornered the supper conversation with inside jokes they had about the castle hands. Every absurd nickname perplexed Karl, which kept the women lapsing into laughter.

Their injuries came up but once, early in the conversation. Karl made a telling slip.

After supper, Rathos led Karl into the crypts below Evan's castle, lecturing him about his stupidity. His torch ruddied the patchworks of stone and jutting braziers along the wall.

"You could've named any other forest we went through," he fumed. "Literally any other forest."

"I know, I know."

"Sarah's Forest. Ravenwood. You know, the Rotwood."

"Fuck's sake, I've apologized."

"But, no. *Graywood.* The one fucking place we agreed—"

"To lie to your wife about, aye." Karl rounded on him with a glibness that tried Rathos's patience. "Which baffles me. You wanted to strangle me when I spoke ill of your wife." A black, pink-tailed rat scampered past their feet, vanishing into unlit corridor. "But secrets aren't a thing foreign to you . . . or to the lord who raised you in this castle."

Inhaling, Rathos filled his lungs with the spicy, sulfurous smell that pervaded the castle's crypts. The corridor plunged ahead, littered with arched doorways to undercrofts only Evan had fully explored.

"So this is where Evan's house kept its envied power." Karl skimmed a crevice in the low-hanging ceiling with his finger, inspecting residue on his nail.

"You'll use respect if you're fond of my sister, Reubenite. Dana is as much Lord Evan's daughter as Mina." He expected Karl to rankle him with a sly jab about Leah, but he behaved. "But . . . yes. Lord Evan's ancestors bought a realm's worth of blackpowder from Chi-Sayan seafarers. It's said there were so many barrels in these rooms, you couldn't step a foot inside."

He extended his torch inside the nearest doorway, casting shadows across a vaulted undercroft. Inside was a lone bench.

Karl ventured a peek. "A crawlspace is below the bench?"

"Along with a tunnel, through which you'll walk until you see light and emerge two miles out from a hill in the middle of woodland. No one should see you. Not even Pigeons know to watch this place. But it's all for naught if you can't find him."

The Reubenite watched him intently. Torchlight's glare sharpened the arch in the bridge of his nose. "I'll find Rezlan. He moves around like a reindeer, but his tastes in shelter are reliable, and he makes them known to traitors he trusts." He noticed Rathos's expression. "What?"

"I'm just surprised anyone would trust you."

"You do."

"Because we need each other."

"Your sister trusts me."

Rathos bared his teeth slightly. "I don't like how you've endangered my sister, Reubenite."

Karl hesitated, as if offending Dana's brother was the last thing he wanted. "Robswell, I think I love—"

He pinned Karl to the wall, his forearm across his chest. "Pigeons tried to kill us. I brought you here so you could heal!"

Karl wriggled out from behind his arm. "I'm grateful—"

"You were to stay in your apartments. And you walk in the courtyard with my sister, bringing her into this madness?"

The Reubenite looked him in his eyes. "Robswell, she's Evan Sinclair's ward. He brought her into this madness first."

Rathos backed off. Sighing, he extended his hand. Karl shook it warily. "Find Rezlan. Have him summon the Loyal Company so we can pledge them for Jason in the Assembly. Prove yourself to me, and we'll discuss these . . . intentions."

Karl held a hand over his breast. It was the most solemn he'd ever seen the fool. "I won't fail, Deputy Speaker." The last Rathos heard as he left was the clap of a wooden door shutting.

Something troubled.

Rathos couldn't shake it that night in their tousled sheets. He suckled his wife's breasts, thrusting inside her. Mina sensed it, too. She was off rhythm, uncurling a knee into his thigh and scraping his forehead with hers when he came near. He eased forward to rekindle the fire with a kiss. She must've wanted to take him into her mouth, because in that moment she wriggled lower and jammed her chin into his stitches.

He clutched at his arm, wincing. Blood ran through his fingers, and in sparse torchlight through the door he saw it speckled her belly and chin like spilt wine. She slipped out of bed, donning a chemise at their wardrobe.

"Don't wake the apothecary," Rathos insisted grumpily.

"Don't be proud, Ray. I hurt you."

"I'm not. You didn't." He pretended he couldn't sense her disapproval as he unfolded the linen, exposing his arm to cold night air. "The sutures look intact. It can wait until morning."

But as he protested her concern, his wife was unrolling fresh linen Evan's apothecary had them store in the wardrobe for just this occasion. With the utmost care, she rewrapped his wound and pinned the fabric. She ignored his thanks and went unspeaking to the mirror, sopping a wad of linen in the water basin. She dabbed at her skin in silence.

He got up. "Mina, let me light a candle—"

She scrubbed her skin in brisk, agitated motions. "I'm fine. Go back to bed, Ray. Sleep. You're like to receive summons any day now. You'll need to leave forthwith."

"Are you so eager to see me go again?" he asked piteously.

"Why would you ask me that?"

Rathos had known his wife since childhood. Usually, he could navigate her moods like a sailor following stars at sea. But her cool tone, her standoffish demeanor, held him at bay tonight, guessing. He disliked guessing about anything. *I can't keep up the charade with her.*

He withdrew to their bed, listening as she rinsed linen, sloshing water over the basin's edges. "Mina, I lied to you."

She kept her back turned. "I know."

"But it was with noble cause," Rathos said softly.

She met his gaze. "I wonder if you know how much you sound like Father sometimes."

A swipe, that was. Growing up at Caerdon hadn't always been easy for the daughters Sinclair . . . or for the Robswells. "When he's deceived us, he's had his own reasons."

"And what were yours these past weeks, husband?"

Rathos sighed. "To protect you, Mina. Your sister . . . she saved us. Karl and me."

Mina froze. She hadn't seen Leah in years. *This was why I wished to protect you, song of my heart.* "You saw Leah?"

"Yes. In Graywood. She escorted us back to Caerdon."

She pivoted abruptly, toward the window. "The Heretics, then.

They saved you. From the brigands?"

"No, my song," said Rathos, guilt-ridden.

Often had Evan spoken to him of Gram Reuben's gleaming star of reason, the birthright of men born high and low, of lords and Commoners alike. To sail after that star required removing the blindfold of half-truths and lies that men too often indulged with wishful thinking.

Following the light of his own reason, he knew that he'd been false with his wife to protect the mission Evan had tasked him with, for Jason and the Wing of the Commons as much as his own ambition.

Everything poured out. Everything he'd withheld from her since returning to Caerdon Castle. The truth about their attackers, the false Pigeons. The truth about what her father had tasked him with doing as deputy speaker. How he sent Leah north with her Heretics to warn Evan about betrayal.

Mina hovered by the window, her figure visible through the veil of her chemise. She was so beautiful, and her distance right now pained him.

"Say something," Rathos implored her. "I can't say when the last time was that we fought."

She uncrossed her arms. "I haven't been honest with you, either, Rathos," she said softly. "I'll need you to leave the Loyal Company. Once you speak to them of Jason and his Kingstrials."

She could've walloped him in the belly, and he would've been as breathless. "Mina—" he began earnestly.

He tried to console her, to ask her forgiveness. *But what she asks of me, I cannot possibly do. Evan needs me.*

Mina wiped her eyes. "You don't understand, Ray," she said thickly, between grief and hurt. "I haven't bled in months. Not since before you and Father went to the Silver Walls."

It was the lightness of a feather. A cool ocean wave rolling into his ankles, washing his sand-filmed feet. Rathos lay on his bed's edge, smiling like an idiot, and then swept Mina into his arms. He cradled her, surrendered to her, pushing himself into the nape of her neck, as deep as he could go.

How long had they'd tried for life? Years.

He was home. Home was here. *Finally, I'm home . . .*

Reality wrapped his shoulders like an icy, sodden mantle. *A child. Born amid the Kingstrials. When the Company's Pigeons have betrayed us. What a kingdom for my child to be born into.*

He located her gaze in the dark. "Why didn't you tell me?"

"I was petty. I knew you weren't being honest with me. But . . . I was afraid, too."

Rathos cupped her hand, kissing the knuckles. "You'll never have to fear for me or us again. *I love you, Mina.*"

She comported herself as if she were at court. "You can't promise me that. My father named you deputy speaker because he trusts you to deliver the Company for my cousin. You alone. I'd never sabotage Father's designs. But Ray." She parted bangs in his line of sight. "You must be safe. I—*we*—can't lose you to Pigeons. And regardless of what the Company decides, for the sake of this life inside me . . . you have to leave. The Common cause is too dangerous for you. For us."

He shook his head. "Mina, I swore an oath—"

"Unswear it," she said gravely. "You're Father's ward. The son he never had. He'll protect you. Or would you rather never meet your child—as you never knew Sir Matthus?"

Sir Matthus. His true father had never felt real to him, only a name in tavern songs. His mother, Anna, never told him more about their courtship—only what he could've learned himself.

Rathos felt dizzy. He stumbled back to their bed, listing on his wife. "Yes," he agreed, wearily. "Yes, I'll part ways with the Company after Karl and I meet with them. I'll promise to keep their secrets. Take no part in their efforts in the Assembly."

He hugged her, relishing the moment as much as he could. A child. God be good, they'd have a child. King Jason or no, the Fourth Wing or no, he'd protect his family from danger.

Mina planted gentle kisses on his hand, and then his thigh,

which led her to tease his shaft with her tongue. She eased him back and mounted him in bed, caressing her belly and pumping until he exploded inside her.

She wilted on top of him, skin slick with their sweat. "I'll wake the apothecary now," she said matter-of-factly.

With an easy smile, Rathos relented. Her lips tasted salty from tears and his pleasure. She left bed, wrestled into a long tunic and surcoat, and went downstairs.

After she shut their door, Rathos sat upright, listening to a parish bell pealing in Peacefield.

CHAPTER 33

A Silent Friendship

In a supping hall carved into the mountainside, minstrels gathered beside a dais, each a spectacle in his sheepskin sash, tartan trews, and ruffled stockings. The skirl of their woodwind pipes echoed through Eddenloxley. It was supposed to be a solemn melody, and was, but for their drunken host's revelry, so loud he drowned out pipes, the roaring fire, and a hundred muttered conversations.

Trevor Wexley was both Loran's most renowned warrior and, perhaps, its most peerless drinker. Lest anyone forget that fact, the Lord of Eddenloxley had a whole barrel of honey-wine mead to himself at his table. He was the god Felos himself, with his potbelly jiggling, a beard striped with rivulets of amber. He hummed and belched rowdy songs in Cloudspeech, and every deafening laugh he loosed was like to threaten an avalanche.

Evan sat behind a stone table some distance away from the storm, in a green padded doublet and girdle. Jason and the Wall knights joined him. He smiled as his nephew winced at the bluster. *It could have been worse,* Evan mulled as he drank from his mead cup, savoring the taste. *It could have been much worse, and you prevented that, Jason. But let's not do that again before your Trials.*

Lorana's gamble had paid off handsomely, thanks to a show of honor, courage, and humility by his nephew in sparing young Hanorr. Jason had a viable path to the Silver Throne and a claim despite his bastardy. Better still, Wexley had pledged to sew up the schism between the Cloudlands and Loran and end Hexar's Folly. Tonight's feast was a *rythnoraim,* or blood feast, held to heal all wounds and seal the Bull's commitment.

Blood feast, indeed. They'd succeeded beyond all doubt, but neither combatant had walked unscathed. Hanorr's side puffed with crimson bandages. Jason now walked with a slight limp, thanks to a cut from Hanorr on his leg, a thing Wexley's apothecary, Eorl, said would abate with sufficient salve, rest, and prayerful meditation.

I'm never sure about the gods, Evan pondered. He needed Jason to be whole. In little more than a fortnight, claimants and their armies would trample into the Golden Meadows for the Meet of First Declaration. They had more time, courtesy of Greg Thorngale's decision to set the Kingstrials three months out from the time of consent, but that sword cut both ways.

Thorngale had given Shaddon time to reach Loran. The king's exiled brother was the real threat. *The princess chose a lamb to replace the lion as leader of the Wing of Lords . . .*

A nudge from his nephew brought him to attention. "I'd like to grant the favors soon," Jason said softly, impatiently.

Evan discouraged him with a slight headshake. "Let Lord Trevor finish. Cloudlanders love their toasts."

Overhearing, Rogir leaned in. "We may have to wait some time," he slurred. "The Bull—he's a legendary drinker. I wager he'll empty a-another barrel before the night's done."

Evan spied Hanorr's widow and children at a stone table furthest from the dais, beneath one of the hall's many hanging tapestries. Jason had spared young Hanorr, but the lad didn't seem keen on forgiving and forgetting. When the family spoke at all, they spoke only to each other. Lady Yosar met his gaze briefly and looked away. *Not everyone here is keen to move on.*

Through the grease smoke of the kitchens came Common serving girls, pretty mountain flowers plucked from Amathorn shires. First they set Wexley's table, around which sat his lady wife and their nine daughters. The Wall knights, so accustomed to salted fare and the company of men on their journey north, brightened visibly upon seeing the women and their bowls of broth, steamy trenchers, and legs of greasy mutton.

The Bull stood suddenly. He thrust his cup into the air. The pipes and chatter quieted at once.

"FRIENDS!" he bellowed. "My lords, my knights. Gods-fearing men of the Cloudlands. It isn't often that I admit my faults. Lady Uthra can attest to that." The chamber chuckled. Beside him, his fat wife beamed. "We are a proud folk, still our own kingdom in many ways. *Arae-tha-ganor.*" Men seconded him loudly, rapping their knuckles.

He paused, lost in his cup. "I was deceived," he intoned. "Deceived by mine heart. A brother's heart. Sir Hanorr"—his voice cracked at his brother's name—"was a decent man for most of his life. Who among you didn't know him?" Evan saw scattered nods.

"But a trial by sword is the final word of Amath, and I know now that it was the traitor Shaddon who persuaded my brother to treason." He spat. *Shaddon won't be king, Pinkhands,* Evan thought, *not with the Bull by our side.* "We know that Amath governs us by the sword. This is the law. This is what separates us from the rest of this kingdom, like wolves from sheep." Noblemen glanced interestedly at Evan and Jason for their reactions. "Young Hanorr, Trevor, and Yasmeen"—he held his cup in their table's direction—"I bid you forgive your father his grievous crime."

Hanorr's widow and children stared dully, unflinchingly, at the Bull. Under the hall's gaze, Hanorr's namesake turned to Jason and gave a solemn nod.

Satisfied with the concession, Wexley pointed at Jason. "And this— this man here! Jason, son of Hexar and Sarah. No man is worthier of his father's throne." Evan found himself smiling genuinely. "They call me the Bull, yet who am I but a mouse compared to Lord Jason? I swore off the late king, and his house wrote me, asking for my aid. I declined, and warned them not to come. Lord Jason came anyway, knowing it could mean his death. He climbed Amathorn, knowing the ease with which we loose our arrows. He prevailed upon Sarah's brother to gain entry, knowing I'd honor *lothlaen regis.*"

I'd wondered if that would work myself, Evan mused.

"I said do not try," Wexley said. "And so he answered my anger with truth . . . and courage. He beat my nephew. He then spared him when by all rights he could've killed him, and asked for my friendship. To do so required bravery . . . and respect for us. Hexar's courage flows in Lord Jason's veins. It was, and is, a king's courage. A courage that *must* return to the Silver Walls."

At his urging, everyone stood, cup in hand. "Lord Jason is the son of Hexar Eddenhold and Sarah Sinclair, and the rightful Lord of Loran. On the blood of my fathers, I pledge that I'll see Jason seated through the Kingstrials, and we'll unite Loran and the Cloudlands once more."

The hall erupted with chants as men held high their cups, spilling froth. "*KING JASON! KING JASON, LORD OF LORAN!*"

The chants dwindled as the Bull continued, "Tonight I call upon every lord sworn to me to summon banners. Knights and horses. *Scrorn-ner-gaith.* Let the mountains tremble under our feet as we march . . . *AND LET LORAN ONCE MORE TREMBLE TO SEE US MARCH!*"

A roar of approval filled the mountain hall as Hexar's Bull drained his cup. Evan clinked cups with Jason, drinking to the power of his mercy as much as his cunning half-sister. For it was Lorana who'd dispatched them north on this wild gambit.

Who would've thought, Sarah? Evan wondered. *The path to the Silver Throne runs through the daughter of the Lady Alyse. Gram Reuben was right: history is not without a sense of irony.*

When he first met her, Evan hadn't known what to make of the king's daughter, offspring of the woman handpicked by the powers in the east for Hexar's second wife—that homely, unloved bird he'd urged the king to supplant with Sarah. The steward had every right to despise Evan, to threaten him with a Tower cell, as she had on Remembrance Day. He begrudged himself a growing admiration for Lorana.

Jason stood after the clamor died down. "Thank you, Lord Trevor, for your words and courage. You were a friend to my father, and now I know we'll win the Kingstrials with you by my side. Yet I bear no ill for

Sir Hanorr. When I am king, I will issue a decree pardoning him fully."

The room applauded. Yet when Evan looked, he saw that Yosar, Hanorr, Trevor, and Yasmeen had left.

The Cloudlands' lords and knights gathered to pay their respects. One by one, they introduced themselves to Jason and Evan.

Some, he knew. Zarold Ulbridge, the stocky-framed Lord of Hapry Springs, had been famous in the Wing of Lords for his eloquence despite the roll of his northern tongue. Other lords were unknown to him. Russell Wexrenn, as Lord of Sheep Hills, had inherited his late father's beak nose and pasty skin. Hailing from the shoreline, Derek Clabbard, Lord of Whitecape, had an oarsman's build. The noblemen wheedled Jason with inquiries into whether he was aware of *this* land dispute, or *that* sordid history, or *these* rumors about their unresolved claims. Jason pled for his uncle's help with a glance.

"*Ahem,* my king, Lord Trevor comes this way," Evan said.

His nephew used the chance to pry himself free, smiling gladly. Wexley cut a path through his vassals, squeezing Jason in his barrel arms. The Cloudlands lord turned to shake Evan's hand firmly.

"We fought for your sister before, my Lord of Caerdon," Wexley said. "Let us draw swords together again for her son."

Evan agreed, happily. He signaled his nephew with a look.

Jason comported himself. "Lord Trevor, as a token of my thanks, I would grant you a gift worthy of your valor," he said. "From here to Rexwood, the forests shall be yours once more. As king, I would name you Lord Paramount of Eddenloxley, the Cloudlands, and Eddenwood. All titles, estates, and incomes therefrom will pass from you to your sons-by-law, and their sons, and theirs, forever."

Wexley dipped for a practiced bow. He'd expected this. "You do me great honor, my king."

Perfect. Just as we rehearsed. Wexley had committed his forces to Jason, but a show of goodwill wouldn't hurt anything. Eddenwood, a forest rich in fishable streams and fallow fields, had been contested by the houses of Wexley and Gramlore and coveted by the mountain people for centuries.

And how could Evan possibly fail to repay Sam Gramlore, Lord of Eddenwood, for his *warm* salutation outside the throne room? *Spit on me again, Sam,* he mused smugly.

"A sound decision, my king," Evan added, to make Jason's offer sound less like his own idea. "Eddenwood was part of the Cloudlands long before King Wess separated the two lands."

Wexley nodded pensively. "Wess Romaris. That's a name unloved here. He and his traitor peasant deceived my fathers into losing Eddenloxley, and then Eddenwood, and with them their kingdom." *It's the reason I mentioned Wess.* Wexley turned to Jason. "My king, I will see you to the Silver Throne, but you must know that my people and I have a long memory. We will never bend to laws made by the *scrorn-ner-gaith.*" He gripped Jason's shoulder in his huge hand. "Can I count on you, my king, to respect our Silent Friendship—to keep your peasants in the Assembly out of what's a lord's right to rule?"

Close by, the Bull's vassals took pains to seem unaware of their exchange, betraying themselves with indiscreet looks and fleeting lulls in conversation.

Jason possessed a steel resolve that reminded Evan of his father. *Speak as we rehearsed, nephew.* "Yes, Lord Trevor. I can see dignity in . . . this silence. Your people know peace because of it." Evan perceived a hesitation in his eyes. *To have integrity when politics requires hypocrisy. Yes, nephew, I know the same bitterness.* "As king, I will continue my father's friendship with the Cloudlands, so long as your lands rejoin Loran."

Wexley nodded. "And if some ragtags in this Fourth Wing wish elsewise?"

"Listening has never hurt a friendship."

Evan bristled. "Aye," Wexley said, loudening his voice. "Listening, *because peasants can't write!*"

Ulbridge and Wexrenn burst into laughter. After a tense moment with Jason, Wexley bowed his head and placed a hand over the black mountain on his tabard. Jason nodded cursorily. *I suppose that's a yes. Under King Jason, peasants will make laws with their lords again—so long as those laws end at the Pass of Eddenloxley. At least the Cloudlands will rejoin Loran in every other meaningful way.*

"And Sam Gramlore can *fuck* himself on that twig he calls his manhood, eh?" Derek Clabbard butted in good-naturedly.

Wexley chortled. "If only I had sons to give Eddenwood, I—" He smiled wide, as if with the most delightful idea.

Swiveling, he made a thunderbolt by clapping his hands for his wife's attention. "*UTHRA!* Bring them here. I want King Jason to have his pick of the pride of Eddenloxley."

Were it not for the politics, Evan would've found Jason's discomfort amusing. The Bull's nine daughters rose from their table in orderly fashion. Half of them reached Wexley's height. They shuffled out and lined up, oldest to youngest. They were all surprisingly lithe and very pretty, for children of Trevor and Uthra Wexley.

Jason refused them all. "You are all lovely, and deserving of husbands and good marriages," he said, "but I am obligated to another."

As you are obligated to finally tell me her identity, nephew.

"What of *her,* my king?" Russell Wexrenn chimed.

The stick of a noble plucked one of the Common serving girls from the crowd, unquestioning in his entitlement. Jason furrowed his brow.

"Ah, they call her the prieslenne," Clabbard chuckled. "As you can see, little wonder why."

Yes, little wonder. Evan had never crossed paths with the priestking's daughter, but he heard what they said of her looks, and the peasant whom Wexrenn mishandled could've been her Common twin. Dressed in the rags of a linen dress, the woman had frost-colored eyes, porcelain skin, and golden hair that swayed at her waist.

Wexrenn sniffed at the nape of her neck as if he were a feral creature, planting soft kisses, eyeing Jason all the while. The vassal navigated the front of her dress with an ungentle hand, fondling her breasts, utterly without shame or decency. It was his right as a lord. The girl flinched at every lecherous provocation, tears filling her eyes.

Evan watched Wexley, his wife, their daughters. His ladies of court shared Evan and Jason's unease. *They're used to such perversions, of course.*

This was the Cloudlands, where peasants were but shit crusted on their lords' boots. The chamber ate, drank, and laughed, as if nothing were happening in its midst.

And the Bull was watching Jason, not Wexrenn or the girl. *This is a test,* Evan understood. *A test to see what we, who'd give peasants power and justice, will tolerate.*

"What say you, my king?" Wexrenn asked with a proud look, as if he were displaying a trophy. "Does she not look like the Most-Sought Hand in the Thirteen Kingdoms?"

Jason smiled coldly. "I must say, she is her spitting image. And you, Lord Russell, look like something I tracked in on my boot. Perhaps I'll call *you* the *scrar-nar-gaith*."

The merrymaking of *rythnoraim* sounded softer notes suddenly, cups and dishes clinking across the chamber. The nearest noblemen, Clabbard, Ulbridge, and others, lost their mirthfulness. Trevor Wexley made a thin line with his lips.

Evan exploded with laughter that drowned out the pipes. He circled about, clutching his belly, forcing out tears. *As well I should be crying.* He gave Jason a hearty backslap his nephew received stonily, unmoving where he stood.

He wiped his eyes. "Oh, oh—forgive me. My king nephew has much to learn when it comes to Cloudspeech. He says 'wife of my boot,' if I'm not mistaken. A jape, is it not, my king?"

Wexrenn saved face with a grin. The noblemen chuckled grimly. Even Edenia's lookalike smiled shakily.

Only the Bull remained as dour as the sheer cliffs of his land. "Yes, we must teach you our language, my king," he said. "Among other things, I hope." Rogir and the other Wall knights watched Wexley like good, protective hounds.

The Cloudlands nobles drew Wexley into conversations elsewhere, to forget the obvious insult and drink. With Jason watching closely, sword hand tensing, Wexrenn slunk off to a hall with the poor serving girl.

"Let us talk," Evan told Jason under his breath. "Now."

Jason regarded him coldly. *If I were my younger self, filled with passion, I'd be distant, too.* The bastard prince followed his uncle with a slight limp. Had the matter not required privacy, Evan would've chosen a table in the feast hall, to spare Jason the pain of walking far.

But this matter *did* require privacy.

Refilling two cups, Evan led him out of the room, through a hall crackling with torches, to a balustraded balcony sculpted from the mountainside, rough-hewn and uneven. Listing on the stone rail, Evan enjoyed a fine view, a rolling sea of mist dotted with the islands of snowcapped peaks. *Such majesty in a brutal land.* Yet he liked better the balcony's solitude, as much as the unchallenged view he had of the long, well-lit hall behind them.

Jason joined him on the balcony.

"Tell me," Evan began crisply, staring off, "did the Worthy Assembly lift the taint of bastardy from you while we slept last night? Are you Jason Eddenhold? Has your half-sister scraped up an army to accompany you east to the Kingstrials? Because if not, we must tolerate these Cloudlanders, or you risked your life against Hanorr's son for naught."

The bastard prince made a scornful sound. "I should ask the same of you. Are you *not* the leader of a group of traitors sworn to serve the peasants this realm rapes?" The quivering in his lip abated. "I know. *I know.* This is . . . politics. Evil though it is. My passions clouded my reason."

"Don't let it happen again—no matter the abuses these 'noble' men parade before you. We need the Bull and his army. I'll work to repair the harm." Evan drank his mead and wiped froth off his beard. "But that isn't why we needed to speak." He took his nephew's measure. "Did you marry Prieslenne Edenia when she was Hexar's hostage?"

Halfway through his cup, Jason lowered it with an unease the father and warder found familiar. His sister's son told him the truth with a flat, blue-eyed look. *He's not ashamed,* he knew. *He's afraid. For her. For the daughter of Loran's foremost enemy.*

Evan stifled a sigh. His gaze wandered to mountaintops. "How many people know of this?"

For a long moment, Jason said nothing. "Only Lorana and Lord Charles."

"You must forget you married her. It never happened."

"I love her. *We* love each other. In spite of the politics."

Where have I heard that before? "Then it must be a chilly love, as cold as the Cloudlands, as silent as its friendship with Loran proper." Evan turned to him. "If you fail to win even one of your Trials, we will need votes. To have them, to crown you king, we must convince this man and that one who each hate the other to forget their differences. The alliances fall apart if it becomes known that you wed Priestking Parlisis's daughter."

Jason set his cup on the rail. "I know how the Kingstrials work, Lord Evan," he said tersely.

"But you *don't* understand how the Company works. The Reubenites in the Assembly would cut out my heart and yours and set themselves ablaze before they see the Silver Walls fall to a king and prieslenne consort."

Jason clenched the balustrade so tightly the whites of his knuckles flared. "*If* your ward delivers this fractious Company."

"He will." *He must. You will, Rathos Silvertongue.* "No one can know, Jason, ever—"

"They won't." Jason slapped his cup off the balustrade for a fading clatter down the mountain. "No one will know."

"*Someone* knows. You told me yourself Burke found her ring on the Rose Guild assassin. Someone paid the Rose Guild for your head. It could've been the priestking. It could've been Gram Sothos or Shaddon. One way or another, that knowledge will come to the Assembly and our enemies will use it to divide us like chaff from wheat."

"I'll deny it. Cast it off as a rumor spread by my enemies."

"But will she?"

"We wed secretly, hoping for sunnier relations between Loran and the Lonely Isle. We grew up together. I trust Edenia." A distance Evan first glimpsed in the Midlands reemerged in his nephew's gaze. "I trust her more than I do you sometimes."

Evan flushed. "Trust goes both ways, nephew. I need honesty from you, and an attentive ear. I can't stress how much I wished you'd disclosed this tryst with the high priestess of our kingdom's most hated foreign power, the daughter of its leader."

He lost his fury when he saw his sister's eyes. They were unnerving. He tried to shake off a memory of her dream-self's luminous gaze, white as virgin snow. "You ask me to be truthful when you yourself are hiding something *from me*," Jason said. "My mother. I want the truth about the Lady Sarah, uncle."

"I'm not sure what you mean."

Footsteps echoed downhall. A lord stumbled drunkenly in the flickering torchlight, lurching toward their balcony. Spying Evan and Jason, he sloshed his head about in what looked like a nod and trudged back to the feast hall.

The man who would be king took his cup before he could drink and set it down on the balustrade. "All my life, I've heard stories about it. Stories about her. Stories about you and your knight. All this time on the road together, and every time I ask you for an account, you use remembered pain as an excuse . . . but I've learned your moods. I know you hide something."

Learned my moods. I believe you said something similar at one point. At their inn in Hexwaite, after the trouble on Scythe Road with that Mumbler, Jason had pressed Evan to finally tell him how Sarah Sinclair died. The real story, that was—not the propaganda spread by their enemies about how Sir Matthus was his true father, or the courtiers' gossip that held Evan had caused the explosion, or any of the odious tavern songs.

A wind whipped Jason's forehead with a strand of raven hair. Evan still remembered how brittle her hair had felt, the hair she'd worn in life like a lion's mane.

"The truth, uncle," Jason insisted. "Elsewise I must assume that my father spoke some truth of you after all."

"The truth," Evan said softly, eyes low on the mountains. *What is truth?* he remembered Matthus saying once. "The truth is, I was like you, Jason." He smiled sadly. "Full of ambition. Out to set the world to rights. Unwilling to bend for cruel realities. So was your mother."

Evan shut his eyes. He was back in the carriage, jostling to and fro on a bumpy road, observing the outside world through a sliver in his window's drapery. Then as now, Sunder Way was a sleepy road, dotted with cruck houses that doubled as market stalls in busy seasons. A younger Evan twisted for a look at his sister. Tresses of her raven hair spilled out from her gray hood, catching sunlight radiantly. She stroked her swollen belly, the belly that held a prince. His knight sat beside her protectively.

As Evan opened his eyes, a single, cold tear raced down his cheek.

"We were fleeing Loran—your mother, Sir Matthus Robswell, and me."

"Matthus Robswell. The knight the Assembly said was my *real* father, to delegitimize me."

Evan discerned his anger. "Sir Matthus was easy prey for the rumors. He accompanied us." He went on, "Applewood said you were due any day. We had no choice but to leave, with the Army of the Gods bearing down upon Southpoint, and so little time, after the Little King had misled us and wavered until the last hour. We hung our hopes on the Free Kingdoms. On Tesos especially. But we had no way of knowing which king, if any, would take us in—not with Priestking Parlisis breathing fire at the realms like a dragon."

Jason's eyes fluttered. *Yes, from far away, the father of your beloved wife was as tangible a threat to your mother and me as the Army of the Gods.* "You took blackpowder with you," his nephew said, "to make it a gift to the king who sheltered you. Against Father's wishes. That part I know."

"Blackpowder was the source of House Sinclair's power. My forebears, who bought it from Chi-Sayan merchants, knew how to sell it, but not how to make it, like the rest of Ansara." He sneered. "I *curse* that blackpowder ever came to my family. As your father cursed me when he learned that I'd smuggled a keg eastward. Hexar was my king, but I didn't want to trust to chance. Our last defenses had failed us in Southland. By then King Hexar had robbed Alyse Jannus of her head, and us of any leverage over Lord Stoddard and Willard Potter. They were coming—and with them thirty thousand Elvarenists. I didn't think . . ." He trailed off. *I didn't think our enemies would use the pride of mine house against us.*

"We were leaving Loran disguised as merchants fleeing the war, with two carriages—the three of us in one, the gift of my blackpowder in another," Evan went on, clutching the stone rail. "We were worried about Sarah. She hadn't eaten anything since Southpoint. I wanted to buy my sister an apple." As he opened his door, flooding the carriage with sunlight, he heard Matthus's voice. "I had the coachmen stop, and I stepped out."

He remembered pacing back and forth outside his door, waiting for a confrontation with Matthus. They'd been arguing all morning. From the dark window of a house, a glint of steel caught his eye. A wood shaft. Bowstrings, tensing. Rising, the archers set their arrowheads alight with a kiss from a brazier smoking indoors.

"Too late I saw the bowmen," Evan said. "Too late, I saw the brazier, and too late the second coachman fleeing, after he drew the keg-boarded carriage near ours. The trap was sprung; I just didn't know it. To light the blackpowder, all it would've taken was one well-placed flaming arrow. But I saw a volley fly. Like me, my enemies wanted nothing left to chance."

Evan felt the blunt impact from the blast shuddering in his ribs, the force that hurled him like a child's doll through a vendor's stall. He heard the shrill ringing that would linger in his ears for weeks. Smoke and the acrid smell of burning flesh irritated his lungs as he navigated a firestorm of debris. Horse parts lay strewn across Sunder Way. He climbed the burning rubble, singeing his hands, catching splinters as he threw aside spears of lumber. His vocal cords strained as he screamed.

"Your mother I found burned but whole," Evan said. "Sir Matthus, I found . . ." He glanced at Jason. "Matthus gave his life for my sister, shielding her with his body. Like few knights, he lived up to his oath. Without his sacrifice, I know Sarah Sinclair would've died instantly, and you with her. Peasants helped me rescue your mother and likely warded off our assassins. And on the floor of a peasant's house in the wilderness, I pulled you from her womb. Lady Sarah, dubbed the Most-Sought Hand in the Thirteen Kingdoms, died beneath a Commoner's roof. She would've found it fitting, had she been conscious.

"Later, at the Tower, Lord Charles tormented me with the information that their killing had been revenge for Lady Alyse's beheading," Evan said thickly. "So Hexar told you true. It was *I* who killed my sister and friend, as if with mine hands. Without my subversions, the Long Summer would've never happened. I would still have Sarah and Matthus, and you, a mother."

So cold before, his nephew softened like snowmelt. He clasped Evan's knuckles. "But I wouldn't be here. Not without you, my mother, and your passions for justice. Besides, it was the enemies of *our house* who killed them. A priestking's men."

Evan smiled bitterly. "Were that you could've convinced the king of that. Hexar blamed me for disobeying him. And so I was gaoled, ousted from the Wing of Lords, relieved of all titles and nearly my head. My house was laid low, her blackpowder plundered. And men who believed I'd started the Long Summer Rebellion called me Evan the Traitor."

"Where were Sir Matthus's children in this?"

"Safe at Caerdon, thankfully. We'd planned to have Rathos and Dana join us by ship once we found refuge. I took solace in two things during my stay at the Red Tower: the survival of my valiant knight's children, and the help I gave Burke in hunting down the coachman who'd betrayed us."

Jason stared at the mountaintops. "But Lord Charles was never able to take *all* my mother's murderers into custody."

"Not until recently," Evan said. "One of my sister's killers languishes in the Red Tower. We'd be fools to think that brick and mortar alone will keep Gram Sothos. Assemblymen fear him even in his cell, but your half-sister made Greg Thorngale his successor, and my Loyal Company counts for half of three wings." He prodded his chest. "And with the Bull at your side—reassured that the peasants we seat will lack power over his Cloudlands—Sothos will not stop us from making a king of you, Jason, son of Hexar and Sarah. Legitimately, for all of Loran and the world to see. Either you'll win three Trials, or the Worthy will crown you." *And if the Worthy cheat you . . . there's another way,* he thought.

"So long as no one takes seriously the marriage rumors."

Evan nodded.

The Agreement

ara was brushing Little Lady's mane when she heard that Sweet Tom had been found dead on the village main, his head bashed in with a rock. Passing by their stable, Bram bragged to Pesh that he'd seen the body, white like milk and carpeted with flies. Probably knowing she could hear, Alfrid teased that Caleb's ghost had slain the justice's deputy. Devan called him stupid and said all of Rosbury knew the killer was Connor Bagman. No one had seen Connor since the theft of Tom's mace, and he and Willard Rittman hated each other.

She never got to investigate for herself. Rose summoned her indoors and forbade her from venturing anywhere near the village main. "Bad enough that we were friend to a kingkiller," her mother told Sara, ignoring her daughter's sharp look.

After a day's pandemonium, the justice paid a visit to Sir Damien's house. He was a sorry sight, Sara decided, with his sagging cheeks, disheveled hair, and crescent moons under his eyes. Cap in hand, he asked if Rose might stand with him at the funeral, to be held in two days in South Farcombe, Sweet Tom's village.

"Your presence would mean a great deal to me," Rittman said, voice quaking. "I'm afraid there are few others to stand with me. The Commons despise us, and Lord Uthron is away, and Geffrey, he's a small comfort." He hesitated. "Tom was my friend. Yes . . . yes he was. My best friend."

Her mother relayed her decision over supper. "We owe our lives and health to Sir Willard and Lord Uthron," she said adamantly, as if preparing for a go. "We will accompany him and give him comfort in his time of need."

So Rose was speechless when Sara said yes, she thought that a fine idea. When they knelt to pray before bed, Sara gave thanks to the old gods . . . and to the elf.

She'd been at wits' end over how to recover Dray's knife.

She'd only been to South Farcombe once, with Father, and the journey there had taken a full day by cart and horse.

"I'm just a Common girl," she'd complained to the elf. "My mother would be wroth with me if I left on my own. How will I get there?"

Dray had answered with music from his lyre. *"And how, and how, the girl wond'red,"* the elf had sung, *"away from the Tower, free of its donjon."*

And here she was, delivered by Dray once more.

Not even Geffrey could dampen her mood on the rumbly ride south. She sat beside the weasel-faced deputy in the justice's wagon bed. Her mother sat with Rittman upfront. The thoroughfare was in shambles, punched with mud pools and strangled with weeds. The cart leapt anytime it banked, hurling Sara about like a sack of potatoes. Geffrey braved the rattling for a stick of pink chewleaf and yelped when he bit his tongue. That pleased Sara.

Rittman left no doubt about whom he blamed for the murder. "Connor Bagman will lose his head, I swear it," he growled. "Lord Uthron will give us satisfaction, Geffrey. Yes, yes he will."

"How do you know it is Connor?" Sara asked.

Rose reprimanded her with a sharp look.

"Maybe if he'd had his mace," Geffrey put in, "Bagman would be dead instead."

His comment made her cheeks burn. Her mother said nothing in her defense, of course.

Rittman checked over his shoulder, lingering on her. To her surprise, he said, "The fault lay with no one but our enemy, Geffrey."

"Who, Bagman, or the Commons?" the deputy asked.

The justice lashed his mules in rapid succession, as if one of them were Connor. "There'll be an investigation," he vowed. "Rosbury will know justice. Yes it will. And there will be no shelter for discontents, Amath help me."

I hope no one helps you, Sara thought.

South Farcombe snuck up on them before sunset. The village hadn't changed at all. A mossy sentry tower guarded the entrance. Cruck houses crowded the village main, leaning on each other like old friends. She saw the parish, a few inns, the idle blades of a post mill. Above the rooftops rose the pearl-white steeples of the Elvarenist temple, reaching for the clouds. Lord Alan Durros's keep lurked low on the horizon.

Geffrey pressed the justice for shelter with Alan Durros. "I don't know Lord Alan well," Rittman responded. "In any case, I'm not sure he would be keen on hosting peasants."

Rittman inspected the first inn, The Tall Pint, and found it to his liking. He negotiated three rooms with the innkeep, a plump man in a grease-stained smock that stretched over his stomach. Initially mistrustful of a justice from out of town, the man brightened considerably after he pocketed two handfuls of sylvens. Sara looked up and saw her mother's eyes were as large as the coins themselves.

Up the rickety stairway, away from the smell of stale ale, Sara followed her mother into their room. She was as surprised as Rose when Rittman insisted she take a room all to herself.

The justice took no refusal. "Let me do at least one good thing on this sad journey," he told her mother as he cupped her hands in his. "I imagine Sir Damien's daughter hasn't known a chamber of her own. Consider it a gift."

Thank you thank you thank you, she said inwardly, to Dray and the old gods and the twelve and the One True God. The elf had come through for her again! Not that she cared two spits for the spacious chamber, or for the feathered bed, or for the coverlets soft as silk (well, maybe she liked all that).

No, it was the privacy. Dray had warned her against trying to filch the knife in daylight. "Don the cloak of night, child," he'd said. His advice had baffled her . . . until now. Rarely did priests shutter their temples.

It was *perfect.*

Night's quiet descended on the inn. The floor's planks squeaked outside her door. In came her mother, bathed in orange from her candle. Sara forgot how pretty her mother could look, a maiden even in drab wool, kind-eyed and petite. Ringlets of brown hair curled about her frilled wimple.

Her mother sized up the room. "This is a fine chamber," she said, exhaling happily. "Oh, do you like it, my sweet?"

My sweet. She *had* to feel pleased. How long had it been since she'd called her that? "Yes, Mother, very much."

She eased herself onto the bed beside Sara, gently, as if she feared wrinkling the coverlets. "I feel pity for Sir Willard," she said. "He has lost a friend, a man who helped rescue us when I thought all hope lost."

Sweet Tom didn't rescue us, she almost said. *It was Lord Uthron.* She remembered the last she saw of her Lord Warden. She shivered visibly, determined not to think on him.

Rose tensed. "Are you cold?"

"I'm ready to see Little Lady again." *With the knife Dray needs for our Gift.*

"Do not think about that half-mad horse on the morrow. Think about Sir Willard and his grief. Pray that Justar will find poor Tom's murderers."

Sara acquiesced with a nod. Rose kissed her on her brow and buried her to her chin in thick covers.

She halted at her door. "Sir Willard is a good man," said Rose, almost admonishingly. "Maetha and Divna have blessed us with his friendship. Please, Sara, be good on the morrow. I'll not have him shamed."

She shut her door. Her candlelight danced in the cracks, ebbing.

Despite her feathered bed, Sara couldn't catch any sleep that night. She was anxious about where she would find Dray's knife at Saint Eric's. The elf-prince told her to seek the chamber with urns, whatever that meant.

The justice himself hadn't helped. To her bewilderment, he'd poked his head through the door not once but *twice*. The first time, she bolted up from under her covers, and he closed the door without a peep, as if embarrassed. The second time frightened her. She could've sworn he stood there, watching her like a cat does his prey. She couldn't say how long it was before his glinting eyes disappeared.

The intrusions were startling and unwelcome. Men were forbidden from seeing a Common woman's hair, let alone one sleeping in her bedchambers.

Even more bewilderingly, Rittman acted as if *she* were the one at fault when they broke their fasts in the table area come sunrise. He was short with her when she and Geffrey both went for the last buttered biscuit on their table.

"Where in the Twelve Testaments does it say the lowborn can deny their betters?" the justice rumbled imperiously.

"Geffrey isn't my better," she retorted.

Her mother rebuked her with a fierce look. Swift as a hawk, Geffrey swiped the biscuit, sopped it in his yoke, and crammed it into his mouth, smiling as he chewed.

Sara kept to herself afterward. They left The Tall Pint for the zigzag of cobblestone streets, passing villagers toting hay and baskets of fruit. Peasants watched the justice and Geffrey with unease. *You might watch my mother and me, Sir Willard,* thought Sara, *but the Commons watch you.*

Saint Eric's wasn't hard to find. All temples were tall and pretty, and the one in Southfar proved no exception. Pale of stone and crowned with steeples, the temple seemed heavenly, as if Sacreis himself had carried it down from the sky. Staring up, Sara lost herself in its winding arches, the tiny figurines at war in its ornamented portal, the shimmer of its stained-glass windows. She tried to ignore the grotesques scowling down at her from the bell tower's ledges.

Mourners massed before Saint Eric's thick hickory doors. Rittman introduced Sweet Tom's mother, Harriet, a jowly old woman in gray veil and worsted gown.

Rittman bent forward to kiss the crone on her cheek. She slapped him. "Bastard, I didna wan' you here," she snapped.

The justice touched his cheek, shaken. "Harriet—"

Sara enjoyed seeing her slap him again. "You donna think I know you're the cause o' this? Tom was never in harm's way 'til he fell in with you." She rounded hotly on Geffrey. "An' *you.* Look a' the two o' you, goin' round, robbin' peasants. An' *other* things. An' on the orders of tha' *whore* steward an' her Tessian! *Shame!* Think the Commons wouldna answer you?"

A priest navigated the crowd to find them. He was young for a man of the cloth, baby-faced and freckled. "Come, Mother. Your son's friend, a justice of the peace no less, comes to help us prepare the ship that will take Tom to the Evergreen Isles."

Harriet's chin trembled. "Bastard can give me no justice," she said wetly, "an' he bring no peace."

Rose comforted Rittman when the crone was gone, telling him she was an old woman in grief. Geffrey spat.

The priest admitted the mourners. Nearest the doors was a stoup filled with holy water, and everyone was expected to dab their fingers and sign the diamond. Sara didn't dab or sign, and had to interrupt the procession to double back and do her mother's bidding.

The pretty temple interior took her breath away. Rays of light fell through the windows, sampling every pew in the long marbled hall. Statues of the twelve gods and goddesses lined the walls. To her right stood Amath with a javelin of lightning, Justar astride his flaming destrier, Sacreis in his sun chariot, big-bellied Felos and well-dressed Prospo, and Athos with his oil lamp held aloft. To her left she saw Maetha with her hands spread in warm welcome, Helsar recording the names of the brave on her long scroll, beautiful Venas, veiled Divna, Gourda stewing a huge pot, and Selyssa caressing the hole in her belly. The God Who Rebelled and Died had no statue or likeness, here or anywhere, of course.

Each statue was lovelier than the last. Sara caught herself dwelling overlong on the chiseled folds in Venas's marble gown and shook off her admiration guiltily. Free Believers weren't fond of idolatry. Parishes like hers prided themselves on a faith that could afford bread for the hungry.

She wondered what her father might say if he saw her at temple. He and Connor Bagman were known for airing their opinions, and that had seen the Sothrons out of Thorn's Keep. Coming home from The Golden Dragon, he often complained bitterly about the lords and clergy who lined their pockets with parish money. "They steal from us like bloody cutpurses," he'd lamented. Sara had liked hearing her father talk, but it always upset her mother, who'd throw something or storm off. She glanced at Rose. *Are you happier now, Mother?*

Shuffling single file down the aisle with mourners, Sara spotted several interior doors. She saw no urns, no clear sign of which might lead to a chamber with Dray's mysterious knife. She wished the elf could've accompanied her, somehow. That would've made the task easier. Safer.

They took their seats, Rittman and Geffrey on one side of her mother, Sara on the other. The priest led a train of acolytes down the aisle, spreading incense and chanting in a rich voice that made Sara feel more awake momentarily.

A dozen men in cream-colored cassocks and hoods took turns reciting from the Twelve Testaments in First Tongue. She wondered if the elf-prince might teach her that language after all this was over and Father was home again. She nodded off a few times, waking at a sharp pinch from her mother.

After recitation came the strangest of Elvarenist rituals, a procession of the Daughters of Divna, veiled and unknowable, and the Sons of Sacreis, so austere with their shaven heads and hairless chests. Twelve in all, the Daughters and Sons bore aloft an oricus, the small skiff that ferried the dead out to sea.

Sara knew what lay inside. She averted her gaze.

The Daughters and Sons propped Sweet Tom's casket on the altar table and left, passing an acolyte with an urn under his arm. Caught unawares, Sara glanced about to see where he'd come from. *The chamber with urns,* she knew. *But where is it?* Each acolyte retrieved flower petals from an urn and dashed them over the oricus. In a pew at the front, Sweet Tom's mum shuddered in someone's arms.

The priest eulogized Rittman's friend in Common Tongue. He spoke highly of the man called Tomas Leer, describing him as the king's faithful servant, just and brave. Sara had trouble reconciling his Sweet Tom with the man she and other villagers had learned to avoid at all costs.

"Like King Anjan, he will sail to the Evergreen Isles, where dwell our firstborn teachers, the noble elves, dressed in cloth of gold and armor of light," the priest said. "The Head speaks."

"The Hands serve," mourners answered as one.

Sara frowned. *Dray doesn't wear armor or cloth of gold.*

Night found Sara ready.

She stood against her door with her ear to the surface, listening. Hearing nothing, she pulled on the iron handle. The hinges shrieked like a pair of dying cats. She froze, waiting for her mother to hurl open her door. But Rose didn't come. Sara sighed softly.

Deciding she shouldn't risk the door again, she tiptoed to the stairs. She slunk against the rail for support, descending as planks bemoaned even the lightest footsteps. Downstairs, she gasped as something sharp embedded itself in her foot. Sara stopped to feel around her sole. *A splinter,* she guessed. All the wood in this smelly old inn was notched rough as tree bark.

Her last obstacle was the front door. She groped for the chain link and rattled it loose. It took a little pushing, but the door finally swung outward, whispering against grass. She shut the door and walked down the dark village main.

Save for the crickets, South Farcombe was fast asleep. A sickle moon slashed a veil of clouds overhead. Stars glimmered like white gems. Her father once told her that the stars were actually heroes the

One True God had raised to the heavens. She saw Old Eduard himself, lamed by his huntsman's arrow.

It was harder to find Saint Eric's at night. When she got lost, or turned around, she looked for the slumbering giant of the castle on the horizon. When she got scared, she reminded herself why she was here in Southfar.

I'll find you, Father, she swore to herself. *Wherever you are now, I'll find you and return you. Dray's knife will do it, and we'll be a family again. We will.*

The temple emerged on the edge of town, nestled in the clutches of trees that by night appeared monstrous. Moonlight and shadow danced across the temple exterior, animating the hundreds of figurines engraved in the portal.

Sara tried to open the hickory doors. Neither budged. She yanked on elaborate handles; the doors resisted stubbornly. Every time she pulled, a chain clinked against the wood from within. Again, again, again, she tried. Tears coursed down her cheeks. Sniffling, she sank to the marble porch and buried her face in her arms.

"Why the tears, child?"

The voice was familiar. She glanced up, expecting Dray through the blur of her tears. Connor Bagman ducked beneath an elm tree's low-hanging branch. The outlaw had on a tattered green tunic and dirt-brown breeches, almost indistinguishable from the surrounding wood. He had long, unruly black hair and a face coarse with manly stubble.

Sara rushed to her feet. Connor squinted down at her in the moonlight. "I know you, Sara Sothron," he said.

She nodded stupidly.

He looked left and right. "It's a strange time of night to be here, Sara. In Southfar, no less. How'd you get to be so far from Rosbury?"

"That's my business." Her curtness surprised her.

Connor seemed to enjoy her. He grinned. "Business? Then I suppose we're here for the same reason." He strode past her.

"What are you doing?" she whispered loudly.

"Business." He wrestled with the doors. "Huh. They seem to be locked. Priests never lock their temples to the faithful. Not unless there's a body inside."

An iron rod flashed in his hands. He slid the rod between the doors and jangled it. In three swift strokes, he butchered the chain, spraying the floor inside with links that clinked like little bells. Connor lifted his boot and kicked the doors inward.

"There we are," he said, sounding pleased with himself. "Now the faithful can pray."

As if on cue, the bushes rustled. Torches wafted through the night, moving fluidly. She recognized the torchbearers, Alford Hemlock, Luc Almsman, and other peasants of Rosbury. Ford Rounsey wore his jerkin still. Several strangers kept pace, among them an ox of a man, tall and brawny, and an older boy with a bowl of black hair. A last companion followed them in a gray hooded cloak, a specter.

Connor stepped aside, granting each man entry into Saint Eric's. "I donna know what business you have here, child, but you should leave," he told her. "This is no place for a Common girl."

"But Dray sent me," Sara said feebly. "I can't go back, not without the knife that will help us find Father." She nudged one foot against the other. "And besides, Sir Willard made us come here. We can't leave 'til the morrow."

Still in earshot, the other men halted and spun on their heels, as if she'd said heresy.

"Sir *Willard* brought you here?"

The weight of their gazes was crushing.

Connor sank to a knee before her. He had kind, reassuring eyes. "Where is Sir Will, Sara? With Lord Alan in his castle?"

"No—at The Tall Pint. With my mother, Geffrey, and the innkeeper."

Alford inhaled sharply. "Oh, it's bloody *perfect*," he said with frightening relish. "Forget Sweet Tom. We got fire. Let's torch the inn."

Her protests leapt out of her throat. "*No no no, NO!*" Tears wetted her cheeks. *Mother, what have I done?*

Connor hushed her. He twisted at Alford, glaring. "No," he said flatly. "You heard her. Willard isn't the only one inside. We donna hurt our own."

"But Sir fuckin' Willard—"

"Rose Sothron isn't extorting the Commons, and the innkeeper isn't raping our women. Not one of them rules the Walls or makes law in the Assembly. It's not the priestking at The Tall Pint."

"Then we can storm it. They won't know we're coming."

"No, Connor is right," the cloaked man interjected. Sara knew that voice, and who wouldn't? "We hurt our own, we've already lost before we've begun."

Sara peered up. Beneath his hood, torchlight caught his wart and filled the stern seams around his lips. *Firemouth*, she knew without a doubt. Despite what Jon Watley said, Sara felt even less safe around a man all the lords wanted to hang.

Connor rose. "We came here to send a message. Tonight is about more than Sir Willard."

"What of the girl?" Luc asked with unusual coldness.

"She's seen us," the bowl-haired lad said softly.

She dropped her gaze to her feet, as if that could prove she'd been blind to them all along. Connor Bagman was silent for a moment. "You said someone sent you here to help you find your missing father," he said finally. "Who?"

She expected them to laugh or accuse her of witchcraft when she named the elf. No one did, though. Connor Bagman had a strange, sad look as he watched her. "And if he returns from the Evergreen Isles, Mother won't need to remarry," she finished.

Ford stepped forward, eyes full of recognition. "*You*. You were there when we took Tom's morning star. You threw the apple at his head."

"Had good aim for a girl," Alford said admiringly.

Connor smiled. "That she did. You're not fond of Willard Rittman and his deputies, are you, Sara?"

She shifted uneasily, remembering how he'd watched her through her door crevice. "He favors my mother," she said. "My mother is married to my father." She thought of nothing to add.

The outlaw seemed pleased. "They donna know you're here, do they?" When she indicated no, they didn't, he added, "I think we can help each other, Sara. I'll help you try to find this thing. If I do, can I trust you to keep our being here a secret?"

She agreed, happily. Alford and another man grumbled their complaint, but after that no one contested Connor.

Sara trailed after the sound of their heels clacking against marbled floor. The air rushed to meet her, heady with leftover incense and decaying flowers. Wafting torchlight transformed the gods and goddesses into scowling grotesques. Too late, she realized she hadn't halted at the stoup or traced the diamond, but neither had anyone else.

Connor swept his torch through the air, letting its light glide from the puzzle of rafters in the ceiling to the exquisite windows and statues and pews. "Too fine a place for Sweet Tom of South Farcombe," he said with certainty.

They gathered before the oricus. Sara kept a distance. An unforgettable stench mingled with the temple's sweet aroma. The men stared down at what lay inside.

"Tell me, Sara Sothron, what did the priest say in eulogy?" Connor asked.

She told them what she could remember. "The priest said he was brave. A true king's servant. He said he would sail to the Evergreen Isles. That he'd walk beside King Anjan."

Connor and Alford shook their heads in disgust, as if she had just spoken fondly of Priestking Parlisis. Ford joked about how the late king's brother was sweet as a maiden, too. Under his hood, Jon Watley looked as grave as any god's statue.

"Did they say who killed him?"

"Sir Willard believes it was, um, um, that it was"—her eyes meandered to Connor—"uh . . ."

Alford snorted with laughter. "Bagman *wishes* he had."

"I'd shake the hand of the rock-thrower," Connor said. "I imagine they left out why the Common folk called him 'Sweet Tom.' You see,

Tom wasn't sweet to the peasants he tortured." His gaze drifted to Ford. "Or to their wives."

Ford leaned over the casket. "Walk beside the First King? Fuck you." He spat on the body. Sara flinched as the others each took turns slinging spittle. "Rot in hell, you piece of shit."

Connor cast her a sidelong look, drawn in torchlight and shadow. "Are you shocked, Sara?"

She averted her gaze. This was sacrilege, she knew . . . almost as terrible as killing a king.

The Rosbury peasant didn't wait for her response. "Your father wouldna be," he said somberly. "Make no mistake, your father wouldna be here, but he'd understand, girl."

"Understand?" Sara echoed him.

"Understand our cause."

"The Common cause," Luc Almsman intoned reverently.

"'To each a chair, to all a piece,'" Connor said. "That used to be the Worthy Assembly's saying. But these days it's more a chair to every priest and lord, and readers and merchants who give them their *own* pieces. The Common folk, people like your father and mother—even you, Sara—we're yoked like oxen."

"Not anymore." Firemouth stiffened. "Not if we do what we came here to do tonight."

"But why *are* you here?" Sara asked.

She felt embarrassed under their gazes, as she had when her mother chastised her for passing the stoup.

Connor softened. Was it pity she saw in his eyes?

Jon Watley threw back his hood, loosing brown hair that cascaded down his shoulders. He stepped closer to the oricus. "To pray, Sara. To pray for a fire that will stir the Commoners awake. Long ago peasants made an agreement with their lords to keep themselves safe, and fell asleep. Now that agreement is broken, and men like Sweet Tom open their doors for the lords and priests to rob them as they slumber unawares. To rob *us*. To steal from us our hearts' desires: a hearth fire to warm our hands after a day's labor, coin to call ours, a voice in our own rule. *Freedom.*"

The peasants honored him with solemn nods. Firemouth had a hard, unsavory look, and his presence sickened Sara with fear. Yet his strong, sure voice stoked a fire in her belly that all at once made her desperate and fiercely proud.

"As they steal our children," Connor added grimly.

"Aye, the children," Watley agreed with a hard look.

Alford raised his torch, illuminating the faces of the gods who watched in silence. "Well, I didna come here to be hanged, lads. We ready to give Sweet Tom a proper farewell?"

"Not yet," Connor said. "I made a promise to Sir Damien's daughter."

The reader lingered on Sara. She shifted uncomfortably, unable to shake the feeling that in this temple Watley's word was law. "Quickly then, my friend," he urged Connor.

Their footsteps echoed off the temple walls as Connor led his men to three chamber doors left of the aisle. Sara followed. Every door was locked tight.

"The urns have to be in one of these chambers, right?" the peasant asked her. She nodded.

Connor gestured for her to stand aside. The brawny man slammed his shoulder into the door like a battering ram, over and over and over. In all her life nothing had seemed so loud. She covered her ears, worrying the temple itself would crash down upon their heads at any moment.

The third try loosened the doorframe. Motioning for the big man to stand aside, Connor inserted his iron piece into the crevice and leaned back as far as he could. The door snapped open, clinging to a hinge. Sara searched inside. In the flickering torchlight she found only cobwebbed pews, no urns.

Connor glistened with sweat, panting. "Well?"

"Dray said it would have urns inside," she said nervously. The other peasants seemed restless.

The second door was shown less patience. Again, the big man

heaved himself into the door, causing frightful clamor. The girl glanced at the entrance for any sign of the young priest, or Rittman, or her mother, whom she feared would barge in and demand to know why, *why* she was with Sweet Tom's killers, and breaking curfew, and desecrating a temple that wasn't hers to worship in but sacred all the same.

Inside the second chamber, decorated ceramic urns lined the floor and several shelves. Sara clapped her hands excitedly, relieved. At a nod from Connor, she flew inside, checking urns.

She glanced at the urns on the shelves. "I can't reach those ones," she told Connor.

Alford watched the temple doors. "Connor, we need to hurry," he said. "This much noise, I'll be amazed if Lord Alan doesna hear it."

Connor saw Jon Watley signal him. "He's right, lass. I'll set these down for you to look. If you canna find what you're after, you'll need to leave at once. No excuses. Do you understand?"

Sara bolted up, frantic. "But what if I can't find it in those urns, either? You *promised*."

"I promised to *help*," he corrected her. "Commoners aren't like their kings and lords. They're honest folk who respect fair play. Your father was fair to us. Will you be fair like him?"

Connor offered her his hand. The men watched her for a response. Sara remembered Caleb speaking to her in the Red Tower. *Commoners make the small sacrifices for each other that make life worth living.*

She sealed her promise with a handshake.

Seemingly satisfied, Connor quickly removed the topmost urns and set them side by side on the floor. After finishing, he trilled like a bird. At once, the temple descended into mayhem. The others scattered quickly, flipping pews, hurling candelabra to the floor, ripping prayer books in half. Someone helped Ford overturn the skiff; she averted her gaze but heard the stomach-churning thud.

I have to find it. I have to leave. Sara flew from urn to urn, heedless as the sounds of their disturbance grew louder. She could see enough in the dim light, the urn holes big enough for her arms to slide through.

She searched through dozens of urns and retrieved only sticky spider silk.

She felt a sob coming on when reflected firelight caught her eye. Something warped and almost stick-like protruded from a gap between two urns, and yet carried light as if it were mirror glass. She knelt on the hard stone floor and pushed the urns apart.

It *was* a stick . . . and it wasn't. Longer than her hand, the narrow object seemed wooden and metallic at the same time. She ran a finger along its notched surface and stopped before its sharp edges drew blood. *Dray's knife*, she knew.

Wrapping her hand in the fabric of her gown, she picked up the stick made of steel, rolled it into her folds, and tied off a makeshift pocket so she wouldn't need to fear the knife poking her.

I found it, Father, Sara thought, dizzy with joy and fear. *Now we'll find you. We'll bring you home.*

She wanted to thank Connor Bagman, but by then flame had spread from the drapery to the beams, as hungrily as if fanned by wind. She fled. Glancing over her shoulder, she saw three men put their backs into heaving Amath's statue off its plinth, to the floor.

Sara bolted from the temple, back to the inn and to safety, stumbling through wet clay. She could still hear the windows crashing in the distance, through the night, when she flew past the post mill.

By the time she reached The Tall Pint, flame needled the dark eastern sky, lighting bags of smoke above the temple. She squeaked up the stairs, shut her door, and snuck back into bed, rolling the sheets to her chin. Outside, the village was waking.

CHAPTER 35

A Meeting of Friends

Zur rode the Kingsway with Drexan, watching silverstone light ripple like water across the predawn sky. He tugged groggily at his wolfskin robe for respite from the morning chill. His donkey stumbled while navigating Southpoint's uneven cobblestone, forcing him to forsake comfort and clasp the reins with both hands.

Beside him, Drexan bobbed astride his horse, a shadow in his black cloak. His helm reflected silverstone light, making the Eye of Guldan look eerier, if that were possible. He rode with his staff balanced across his lap and a sword at his waist, with a travelsack slung over his mount's backside.

They were headed for a meeting in Sarah's Forest—a clandestine meeting. Drexan had been sparse with the details and sworn him to secrecy, but Zur had gotten this much from him: it concerned some danger to Jason in the Kingstrials.

"A lord has information he'd impart to no one but me," Drexan had told him the day before. "This is critical to Jason and the crown, and I need you there as my lookout. Will you accompany me?"

It'd occurred to Zur to ask why Charles Burke wasn't privy to this information, but this made him feel important. Needed. Helpful. He'd been at a loss for how to support the royal family—*his* family. This was his chance.

And if it's useful information, perhaps Princess Lorana will reconsider my chances for squirehood, Zur thought. He'd saved Heather's skin in that scrap with the griffon. *Perhaps I will have proven myself worthy of sword and armor.*

Sunlight had begun to pierce the silverstone aura rolling above them when they passed by Traitor's Pit, and then onto Silver Street. The putrescence was overwhelming.

"A little early to tour Silver Street, isn't it, King's Crow?"

The voice came sharp as a whip, startling his mount and causing a stumble on the cobblestone. A trained rider would know how to soothe a donkey, but Zur had only guided beasts of burden on foot. His world twisted sideways as he plunged into the slop of horse droppings, pig entrails, and god knew what else.

Dismounting, Drexan helped him to his feet. Zur thanked him, embarrassed. He patted himself down . . . and felt gobs of filth caking the fur of his prized wolfskin robe.

"A pity." The mayor of Southpoint ventured closer, so wan in the silverstone light he seemed a ghost. He gazed at Zur, eyes glinting. "A fine robe. Alas, this is not a road for the unwary."

Zur wanted to hit him. A tear stung his eye as he disrobed and threw the princess's birthday gift over his donkey.

Drexan stiffened, looking equal parts annoyed and wary. "Bored, are you, Lord David? Not busy enough ruining this city, so you enjoy throwing scares into the king's servants?"

A smile played about David Renworth's lips. He had on a cloak that rippled around his belly and cloth felt shoes smeared with refuse. He ran his sausage fingers through the chain links of his livery collar.

"You're the *steward's* chancellor now, Lord Drexan," the Little King said. "Maybe King Jason will see fit to retain you if he wins. I doubt King Shaddon will."

"Think on your own sins. I doubt Shaddon Eddenhold's forgiven the mayor who closed the gates to the Army of the Gods, allowing Alyse to die and Sarah to flee." Drexan steadied Zur's donkey so he could mount up. "We take our leave."

"I'll be sure to mention this fortuitous encounter to Her Highness," Renworth said as they passed by. "I hear she is so fond of your servant."

Zur felt the Little King's eyes on his backside until he and Drexan rode their mounts around a street corner, passing out of sight. He tried in vain to pluck specks of mud from his robe, sickened over a dark orange stain prominent on the front.

"Forgive me, my lord," he said sulkily. "I'm not a rider."

"If I'd wanted a rider for a servant, I'd have chosen a stable hand."

Cold as ever, Zur thought, frustrated. *If this lord gives us something that can help Jason, I'll ask Lorana to reassign me to Hanor . . .*

There was no other unsought attention along the way to Southpoint's walls, and they passed through Elfgate without harassment from the mayor's nasal-helmed city guard.

Rather than follow the buckled cobblestone road west, they ventured off-path, up a knoll garrisoned with sentry oak trees. Limbs stretched overhead like fingers, knitting a dense canopy that allowed only a few pockets of sunlight. Crickets sang deafeningly from the tall, unkempt grass lining their path.

A few miles into Sarah's Forest, they came by a winding brook stopped up with pebbles. Drexan dismounted from his horse and helped Zur clamber uneasily off his donkey.

Without asking, the advisor reached for Zur's wolfskin robe. He knelt to rinse the filthy garment in the water.

It was an incredible act of kindness. Elzura's Children were responsible for their duties, in addition to themselves. Even bastard princes were still princes, with Casaanites and castle hands to wash their linens, empty their chamber pots, attend to every need. No one waited on the southern hostages.

Zur was speechless. He felt guilty for wishing for removal from Drexan's service.

After removing what he could, Drexan wrung the water out of his robe and hung it on a branch to dry. "A fine token of love from the late king's daughter," he said. "I'm sorry for your spill on Silver Street. The Little King is a rat I'd hoped to avoid."

"My lord, I—" Zur began, humbled.

Drexan went to seat himself on a rotted log by the brook. He collapsed with legs shaking, and an audible oof. "*God!*" He massaged his lower back sorely. "Never forget, Zur, we return to infancy as we age. Treat your body kindly." He observed him for a moment. "Zuran . . . do you remember your mother?"

My mother? The question scratched at a wound he'd long forgotten was even there. "I remember nothing," he responded. "I was a babe when I left Casaan."

"'Left.'" Drexan wrestled through his travelsack until he located his wineskin. "I have a friend who could tell you about her," he said as he sipped wine.

"A . . . friend?" Zur frowned.

Since he was young, he'd been told that Namoni had been the one who brought him to Loran. Such was custom: a hostage would travel to Casaan in the company of a king's men and find new hostages, tearing them from their mothers like calves.

"So you remember nothing?" Drexan probed.

His curious look kindled a memory. Not a memory. "I dream sometimes that I feel her tears on my forehead," Zur said, surprising even himself. "They fall like summer rain."

Drexan corked his skin with a pensive look. "Would you like to meet this friend of mine who knew her?"

Words stuck in his throat like honeyed bread. Suddenly the nearest bushes rustled apart. A man emerged by the tree bearing the wolfskin. He draped himself in hood and cloak.

Drexan stood with effort, offering the man, his informant, a firm handshake. "Under the stars he comes," he intoned.

"Ever feal and repentant," the lord answered softly.

The exchange puzzled Zur, but he remembered the voice from the night the king died. The man lifted his hood, revealing a familiar face seamed with laughter and framed by fiery-red hair. Eric Sundry acknowledged Zur with a nod. "And glad to ascend."

"And glad to ascend," Drexan repeated.

Zur exchanged looks with the two men. "My Lord of East Sunder," he said. "I thought you had gone to the Trials." *What might Eric the Tall know about Jason?*

The lord had traveled in disguise. Beneath his shroud he wore a wrinkly, travel-worn tunic fit for a peasant. His wooly face desired a shave. Only his boots and the sword cinched at his waist hinted at someone above a Commoner's station.

"I have another . . . pressing matter," Eric Sundry said with a strange look for Drexan.

"You have news about Jason." Zur regretted his poor form. The

King's Crow had asked him to accompany him as a lookout. To his surprise, neither Drexan nor Eric chided him.

Indeed, the Lord of East Sunder didn't seem to register his *faux pas.* "The road here was dangerous, my friend," he said for Drexan's ears. "Rife with conspiracy and the threat of violence."

Drexan listed on his staff like he would a friend. "Aye, our time grows short."

Eric glanced about the surround. "Where is he?"

There's more than one informant? Zur thought, confused.

"Give him time," Drexan said. "He may be dealing with the temple that burned in South Farcombe."

"Do you know who set it to torch?"

"Who else?"

Eric spat in disgust. "Damned peasants. Everywhere, they grow rebellious."

Drexan stared off, almost longingly. "The land must have its king, Eric."

"Lord Drexan," Zur said abruptly. The two men turned to face him. "Who else are you expecting?"

Drexan pursed his lips for a response. An oak limb shook suddenly, startling Zur. Out flew a creature that he mistook at first for a flying squirrel. The spotted griff sailed into another oak, squawking as he flew.

"Furos," Eric said with a warm smile. The two men circled at the sound of leaves wrestling beyond the brook. "*Ah!* Uthron. Your timing is impeccable, old friend."

Zur followed their line of vision to the Lord Warden of Rosbury. Yards off, Uthron Morley advanced in quick strides, passing through underbrush, paying no mind to the fingers of reeds and limbs clawing at his surcoat. He slogged through the brook determinedly. A flawless sapphire pendant swung at his neck, catching sunlight.

Eric went to shake Uthron's hand.

A second later, fluid flew from what had been Eric's face, splattering Zur and Drexan. As the dying nobleman buckled at his knees, as Zur cleared warm blood from his face, he thought he saw Uthron

Morley flexing pebbled gray hands with black claws.

God and gods, Zur thought, shaking involuntarily. *This is a dream. It's not real . . . Wake up, Zuran. Wake up!*

Something terrible was happening. The skin on Uthron's face turned slippery, beading off his exposed cheekbones and jawbone like melted tallow. A mist swept up from behind him, enveloping the lord so that he looked like a shadow of himself, a dark, vaguely manlike shape with claws and the orbs of little white lights instead of eyes.

It's a dream, Zur told himself, *this is a nightmare. I'm still asleep at the Walls.*

Slow, dreamlike, and entirely without sound, the shadow with stars for eyes swirled toward him. The apparition had no feet, *it had no feet,* but as it passed over the soil, blades of grass withered instantly, as if winter had come and gone in seconds. *It's a dream,* Zur assured himself. *God and gods . . .*

The mist rolled over him. Zur fell hard on his back as the pebbled hands came, lacing about his throat, tightening so that he couldn't breathe. The morning sun shone brightly, yet he'd never felt so cold. It felt like dying. Zur attempted to scream, but nothing eked out.

Sunlight winked overhead. Drexan arced his sword down on the shadow's neck . . . and castle-forged steel crumbled like brittle clay. A sound emanated from the mist, a low, faintly human chuckle, harsh and joyless. A tendril of mist snaked out from the shadow creature, wreathing about Drexan, who flew back, gasping, clutching his hand as if he'd been burned by fire.

The claws that had rent Eric Sundry's face to pulp reached for Zur's neck. *This is how I die,* he understood. The creature's eyes were bright like stars . . . hypnotic . . .

Air filled his lungs so suddenly he wondered if he'd been rescued from drowning.

The mist recoiled sharply, swatting at the four-legged bird above its vaporous head. Beating the air with his wings, Furos swiped at the living shadow with his beak and talons.

"*Zuran!*" Drexan's voice snapped him awake. Zur followed his pointing finger to his gnarled staff, discarded on the forest floor. *"Bring it to me! NOW!"*

Still heaving air, Zur flew past the shadow. He lurched up after tripping on Eric Sundry's corpse, snatched the staff, and pitched it awkwardly at Drexan.

Furos bounded off with a cry, and Zur was in the mist's snares again, his skin numbing like it would in a fierce winter wind. *No, please go,* he thought hopelessly. *I want to live. I want to learn about my mother.*

An inhuman shriek pierced his ears. The apparition gathered up and moved like a windblown fog, with single purpose, toward Drexan.

Feet away, Drexan menaced the shadow with a spear—no, his staff! Its top had been removed like a sheath, revealing a steel point misshapen and notched like bark. The King's Crow slashed at the creature almost recklessly, forcing it away from Zur and into the brook.

Yes, YES, Zur thought as his lord lunged again and again, warding off the shadow. A tendril of mist reached out, curled around the staff, and tossed it away. Drexan fell to land hard in shallow water. The mist rolled over him like living pestilence.

Once more the griff flew fearlessly at the mist creature, harassing the enemy. Yet Furos seemed a mere hindrance, and if any of the mist glanced his flank or legs he beat his wings for a haphazard retreat.

Zur did the only thing he thought he could. He reached for Eric the Tall's scabbard and freed his sword. With all his terror and fear he ran at the mist and hacked at the shadow with the sword, only to see his folly as the blade shattered into shards.

The creature rounded on him.

He heard the sound of a tree falling, saw in the periphery of his eyes the blur of limbs and leaves tumbling down, and in a second's passing was flat on the ground again. A birch tree had crashed down onto the mist . . . which trickled through the ruin like water, reconstituting itself into the shadow of a man.

Drexan emerged with his staff in hand, panting. With his neck and cheeks streaked in blood, he looked like a madman. He studied the mist with a lost look. Raising his staff, he drove its jagged steel tip into the part of the shadow where a man's heart belonged.

Zur watched in disbelief as the shadow and its claws evaporated like water on hot stone. Uthron Morley's finely attired body appeared under the downed tree, in parts, as if it were emerging from a fog. His eyes were pale. Sapphire shards gleamed in the dewy grass below his neck, shattered like glass. He was tangled in Zur's wolfskin robe.

Zur fell to retch in the grass. He saw what remained of Eric Sundry's face, pulpy as mashed-up strawberries. When only water came up, he collapsed onto his rump.

He gazed up at the King's Crow, who might as well have been an apparition himself, a dream he couldn't place. Blood oozed out of the claw marks in his chest.

"My lord," Zur began, still tasting bile. "Your chest—"

The King's Crow opened his hand, and out flew a fine mist of powder. Zur coughed and sputtered. Sarah's Forest blurred with the brook. He felt his head loll sideways into grass, felt the dew wet his skin.

Afterward, in the feeling dark, he dreamed he was an infant again. Tears pelted his brow like warm summer rain.

CHAPTER 36

The Mayor

he princess donned her cerulean gown. About her flew other ladies, busy as bees as they cinched her corset, spotted her neck and wrists with lavender, fussed with her hair bun.

Last came her headdress, an awkward thing made more awkward still by its caul of silver net. She hadn't covered her hair in an age, and it felt like a slap to her father, given how only peasants and Elvarenist women practiced the tradition. *Almost all Elvarenist women,* Lorana mused.

Anyasha dismissed the ladies-in-waiting and shut the door. She pulled the princess close by her waist, kissing her.

"For luck," Anyasha said. "Though I doubt you'll need it."

"Renworth looks out only for himself. I'll need to sweeten this pottage I'm asking him to eat." She tapped her lips with her finger. "I need more luck."

Anyasha rolled her eyes. "Something that rhymes with luck, maybe." She allowed a chaste kiss, dabbed beeswax off her mouth with a cloth, and re-rouged the princess's lips. "Or distraction, more like."

"A temple just burned, the first in centuries. Could you blame me for craving distraction?" She peeled Anyasha's strap from her shoulder with her best look of mischief.

"No, I couldn't." Her lover readjusted her strap. "But the distraction I'd give you would make you unkempt . . . and you need to be careful around Lord David. I hear he's a bloodhound for details others overlook." *And we obviously can't have him learning about us,* it went without saying.

Anyasha gathered signed-and-twined scrolls on her desk. "I'll find Zur and give him these for Drexan, as requested," she promised, and left with an air of mild annoyance.

It wasn't her meeting with David Renworth that bothered Anyasha. If she had to guess, she wasn't thrilled with Edenia's impending official visit. *I'd suspect me, too, if I were Anyasha, watching me receive the Most-Sought Hand in the Thirteen Kingdoms. And if I were you, brother . . .*

She buried her shame, buried it as she had for years, and headed downstairs, modest, yes, and ready for a battle of wills.

Descending marbled steps pearled in silverstone light, the steward crossed the middle bailey, Connor Tomas and Andrew Windkin flanking her in plate and gambeson. She navigated the neatly trimmed boxwood maze to the gentle plash of Sarah's Fountain. There, the Little King waited with his hands clasped behind his back. As if *she* should wait on *him.*

Someone who didn't know David Renworth would think him just another flea-bitten Commoner. Where she'd dressed to curry favor, he underwhelmed in a patchy, moth-eaten tunic and faded sable hose. The bush of the mayor's beard cushioned the portcullis in his livery collar. *A door that can close if it must, Jason,* thought the princess, *or remain open . . .*

Upon seeing her, Renworth brightened with an unsightly yellowed smile. Bowing, he brushed his lips against her hand. "Your Highness, you're as reassuring a presence as your father ever was. A welcome sight in uncertain times."

"You remember how to flatter," Lorana said with an easy smile. "Hello, Lord David."

"I'm no lord, Your Highness, no matter what men say to honor my office." Focusing on a spot of her elaborate wimple, he picked something off its surface. A wisp of black hair.

Connor and Andrew tensed at the breach of protocol. The princess polished off her unease. *Bloodhound, indeed.*

The Little King flicked away the hair, smiling. "Forgive me, Your Highness. Old habits. In a city of chaos and filth, one learns to practice cleanliness vigilantly, lest he lose his mind."

"Well, I hope my lack of cleanliness doesn't offend." She beckoned with a nod, eager to start fresh. "Care for a walk?"

Inclining his head, Renworth smiled so genuinely she found herself returning it. "It'd be my great pleasure."

Her knights shadowed the pair as they began a leisurely stroll, passing under a bushed entrance guarded by the stone likenesses of regal griffons. Towering above them like cliffs, the Silver Walls silvered the maze with a rippling luminescence.

There were some pleasantries. Some *pro forma* apologies, too. Charles Burke's red-hooded thugs had paid Renworth an unannounced visit after the king's murder, to question him and sift around his house for mislaid proof of a conspiracy. The city mayor was an Elvarenist, and Elvarenists had slain the king.

No evidence had turned up, of course. And even if it had, Lorana wondered if she might've let it go. She needed this man. *Jason* needed him.

After a lull, their conversation turned to South Farcombe.

"Gods, a travesty," Renworth said with felt dismay. "Saint Eric's was the oldest temple in Southland. Five hundred years old. Its statues were some of Loran's most admired, outside of those in the Great Temple."

"My sympathies, Lord Mayor. Temple or parish, no house of worship should suffer desecration." *Temples, perhaps.* "Have you any word about who burned it?"

In truth, Charles already had his list of suspects, topped by the wandering reader Firemouth. That troubled her, on account of the rabble-rouser's Company affiliations.

"Free Believers, aye. Peasants first and foremost."

Even better. She wouldn't cry over the ashes of ancient temples. The priestking was their enemy, and so, too, all of Parlisis's allies in Loran. If Commoners were smashing open temples on their own volition, trouble would follow for any Elvarenist usurper who won the Kingstrials—fairly or not.

Lorana was planning for contingencies, and she needed Southpoint's mayor to play a part. *If* he'd play it.

"Peasants know it's lords and priests who crush them." Lorana touched Renworth's wrist—a deferential stroke, as if she were seeking wisdom. "Lord David, I believe the peasants around Southpoint need to hear more about how my brother would give them back their ancient seats. What do you think?"

Out of a corner of his mouth, the mayor smiled. "I'll speak this truth to my eyes and ears, and they'll speak it to peasants, who'll rejoice. The Commoners love your brother, more than that dandy Lord Fawkes—more than *me*, if you can believe it!"

Oh, I can believe it, Little King. For every Commoner who adulated the kingdom's most powerful peasant, someone else owed the usurer money, resented his religion, or knew a man found dead in his brothels. David was a hypocrite, spymaster, cold-hearted killer—and, occasionally, a friend to her house.

"But not me," Lorana said as they strolled around a corner, into a quad of immaculate emerald hedges.

Renworth stroked his salt-and-pepper beard. "Peasants are like anyone else anywhere, fearful of strong women. But it's not your sex they hold against you."

"The justices of the peace. They're too heavy-handed."

"Try *hated*. From Hexwaite to Ramsport, from South Farcombe to Westerliche, from shires to villages—"

"You needn't spell it out, Lord Mayor."

"Has Lord Charles spelled it out for you?" She didn't like his insolent tone, but she preferred cold, hard truth to flattery. "They're sheriffs and tax collectors, and because they're paid ten times their worth—and charged by the crown to inspect houses and gaol Commoners—they can squeeze your subjects with impunity." He clenched his hand, as if he held a peasant, the head bursting like a pustule. "But this is by design, and out of your control. Elvarenists in your Assembly mean to salt the earth of Free Believers by raising their children in temples. Without the Fourth Wing, you lack the seats to overrule them."

"I've bidden my justices to stop seizing children."

That was the point of naming sheriffs justices and paying them royal wages: to make the lords' officers hers and stamp out enforcement of the Worthy Assembly's vulgar child-theft laws. Gaoling the Hammer of the Commons had given her hope the family separations would end.

The effort wasn't paying off, as Hanor liked to remind her. "And yet the separations continue," Renworth himself pointed out.

Sinclair's warning in the throne room had come to pass. The lords were overruling their steward, bidding justices first sworn to them to continue the practice. Justices who refused were sacked and replaced. It was happening like clockwork, all over the kingdom. It infuriated her. *My brother, how can I move heaven and earth for you, when the earth's politics is so rotten?*

They stepped into a grassy clearing with a commanding view of the Walls. Freckled rust-red and silver, the curtain wall bore traces of a once-magnificent engraving, a king astride his griffon, belted in place by the creature's tail, soaring through a lightning-forked sky. A clatter of armor reassured her that her men remained near.

Renworth stopped to face her. "It's no coincidence that the body of a slain justice's deputy was in Saint Eric's when it burned. Or that Rosbury's justice was in Southfar the same night."

"Willard Rittman."

"The same. Rosbury has little love for Sir Willard. The peasants see him as cut from the same cloth as Peshar the Pederast. They believe he abuses and kills children he seizes, then buries their remains in the forest. Some call him Willard Shadowking. They say he eats them."

Those Who Eat the Children. "But that's *mad.* Is there any truth to the accusations?"

"Not at all. Rittman can ride the peasants rough, and the deputy he lost was a menace, but the justice himself is a pious temple-goer. My eyes and ears tell me he seems to care about the children taken. Checks on them once they're in a priest's custody. I think it has something to do with his own childhood. Yet if men are willing to smash into a temple and raze it to the ground . . . does the truth matter?"

"It matters to me."

Lorana didn't like Rittman, didn't like his greasy forked beard or how he watched her with something to gain. Uthron Morley's justice was a rank social climber, oily, obsequious, and constant with the excuses he found to simper into court.

Yet he had his uses. He'd proven himself a precocious taxman, rising above other justices by reliably filling coffers her father's foreign wars had emptied. That made their debt collectors less of a threat. Keen to keep them at bay and help finance Jason's Trials, she'd obliged Rittman in the release of a Rosbury woman and her daughter wrongly swept up in the Remembrance Day arrests.

She'd known why he insisted on their release the moment he begged her in court: he was in love. Yesterday, she'd affixed her seal to a petition from the Morleys asking that she declare the woman widowed so Rittman could wed her. *Perhaps I should rescind her widowhood until I can verify these rumors are false.*

"My father named Lord Wardens for the villages around the capital for a reason. Keep an eye on them, Lord David."

"Two." The Little King pointed at his eyes. He glanced about him. "This maze is the most secluded place. Perfect for someone who wishes to elude eavesdroppers, but not eyes. Why'd you ask me to come, Highness? Certainly not to discuss troubles you've discussed with your Inquisitor."

Lorana pretended mild offense. "You used to walk this maze with my mother, my father after her. And I don't know many Commoners who'd sneer at a royal invitation."

"I'd never sneer at Lady Alyse's only daughter. And yet"—Renworth pinched the fabric of her headdress—"you've never been known to cover your hair. Not even when the prieslenne was hostaged here. I'm but a lowly peasant, and yet I suspect you've done more to impress me than I, you."

In her periphery, she saw her men bristle at the mayor's transgression. Were Renworth any other peasant, he'd lose a hand. "Sirs, a little privacy," she told them.

Andrew Windkin started forward with a concerned look, as if he intended to dissuade her. The older, wiser master-of-arms, who knew this willful princess like the castle, obediently led him off by his arm, out of sight but not earshot.

Lorana faced the official. "A peasant you may be, but you're more powerful than many lords. A Fourth Wing unto yourself in many ways."

"And susceptible to flattery, on occasion." Renworth's grin reminded her that, in fact, he wasn't.

Slinking her smaller arm around his thicker one, Lorana escorted him past a row of rosebushes. Her father had come to trust him, she reminded him—lean on him, in fact. If Charles Burke had been the king's griffon, guarding against rival birds of prey, Renworth had been his owl, scouring his city for rats.

"My father loved his five children equally, but none more than the son his Assembly spurned, from the wife he lost," she said as they walked. "He kept silent about the laws of bastardy to keep him out of the Kingstrials."

"That was love, indeed. As someone who won Kingstrials himself, the king knew what they were: scarlet silk the Worthy pull over our eyes, to distract from a verdict agreed in advance. *Expensive* scarlet silk, especially when they import exotic life."

The verdict will be mine. Charles had informed her that Gordon Whitecastle was readying a band of dragon-trappers, among them a saboteur. If all went well, their galleys wouldn't sail within a league of the Isles of Fire. As for that wild griffon, well . . . there were many ways to skin feathered cats. *I'd rather do harm to mine house's living sigil than risk its last living son.*

"Yet my father won Trials presided over by an Assembly that regarded him with contempt."

"Yet here you are, working me like a Silk Street vendor."

Halting, the stone maiden uncoiled her arm from his. "You once closed the six gates to save your king from the host come to kill him. Would you do it again?"

Renworth watched her with distant eyes. He clasped his portcullis medallion, as if he feared she'd rip it off his neck. "I see why you sought privacy," he said with a grim laugh. "What you ask, a mayor of Southpoint has never done."

"And a temple hasn't burned since the Interregnum," she said pointedly, "until last night."

"Closing the gates to a rebel host was one thing. You're asking the unthinkable. If I can close Southpoint to a lawful king lawfully crowned. *If I can keep the king from his throne.*"

"Not the king. A usurper, foisted upon us unlawfully."

"I assume you mean an Elvarenist, like me."

I mean Shaddon, the king Parlisis and Gram Sothos desire, and you know it. "You chose your country over your faith once."

The mayor fingered the lattice grille of his livery collar, calculating his response. "I paid a steep price. You tell me I'm more powerful than lords, yet I haven't been allowed to set foot in a temple for twenty-one years." He sighed. "Your sweet uncle's doing."

Lorana saw her opening. "Do you want a man like that riding through your gates, sitting these Walls? He'd do more than prevent you from praying in pews. Charles tells me he blames you and Sinclair both for my mother's beheading." She came close. "Close the city to him if he wins, David, and you'll have your *own temple* when my brother reigns. I swear it."

"But what good is my own temple, if I lack a head to bow and hands to pray with?" He steepled his sausage fingers, his expression almost mockingly pouty.

Renworth had good reason for concern. Especially if her vile uncle somehow became king. Elvarenist fanatics like the Intercessors had a gruesome habit of cutting off the heads and hands of apostates for public display.

All the more reason for Renworth to side with Jason.

"Twenty-one years ago, you closed all six gates to protect my father."

"No, Your Highness." Renworth had a dignified air. "I closed them to protect you and Erick. Your *true* brother."

She ignored the unsubtle swipe at Jason. "Then protect me again. Protect *yourself.* Shut the gates if lords and priests outmaneuver us. Stop Shaddon from taking the Silver Walls."

The Little King curled his lip. "I think you're made of stuff stronger than Southpoint's walls." He admired the glistening curtain wall. "It wasn't grille or brick that made the Old Oak's peace more palatable to your father's enemies, but the millions in our city. To have besieged the Walls, the Army of the Gods would've had to slaughter us all and push siege towers through the streets. By then the king had beheaded your mother, and Stod Trambar lost his stomach for war. As much as my fellow peasants revile Lord Stod's memory, I do wish they understood that he showed them mercy in a dark hour."

A line seamed his forehead. "You deal with less merciful men, these kingkillers near and far. They wouldn't share Stod's reservations. They *want* these Walls. This kingdom. For all that it signifies, and because an Elvarenist Loran will give Parlisis what he craves: an end to the Free Beliefs here, and with that end, staging grounds to invade the Free Kingdoms. Even if I did as you ask me, as no mayor ever has, Rorin's crumbling brick walls would not stop them."

No, but it'd slow down our enemies. Leave them vulnerable to attack and force them to abandon the Walls. "They killed my father, almost my brother. You needn't remind me." She looked at the mayor. "How'd you like for *Lord* David to actually mean something?"

"I'll agree to think on this." He offered her a tanned arm. "Come, Your Highness. I'd rather see you to your knights ere they suspect me of another *faux pas.*"

And I'll agree to think on other ways to persuade you, she thought.

On the way through the maze's griffon-guarded entrance, her knights reappeared with her other spymaster. Charles had a panicked expression, which twisted into a grimace on seeing Renworth.

"The two of you couldn't guard a buttery," spat the Grand Inquisitor. "Make safe your steward."

Blades drawn, Connor and Andrew hastened her away from the mayor. Marching up behind them, six other men-at-arms formed a circle of spears around Renworth. The mayor raised his hands, staying cool.

Lorana spun on Charles. "What's the meaning of this?"

It was as if he didn't hear her. One spymaster bored holes into the other with his scowl. "You were seen speaking to him this morning," Charles barked. "Why don't you spill what little secrets you and the King's Crow kept?"

Drexan? Lorana was trying to understand. Then she saw what Charles clutched. A wolfskin pelt, caked in mud, refuse, and wine. *No—not wine . . .*

"*Charles*," she said with a ferocity that shook the knights.

Charles fixed Renworth with his icy stare. "The Chancellor of the Chancery absconded with a hostage." He glanced at her, confirming *which* hostage. "There are bodies in Sarah's Forest. Where this was found." He handed the pelt to Lorana, which could've been a battering ram, the way it crashed through her.

"*What . . . bodies?*" Her voice eked out.

"Not his," Charles said. "Nor that of Lord Renworth's co-conspirator."

Renworth snorted. "To think, I was just given a royal apology for the *last* time I was falsely accused of treason."

"You passed the chancellor and his servant this morning."

"I also passed several other people. It happens when you walk through a city."

"You *spoke* to Lord Drexan."

"He insulted me. Much as I'm being insulted now. Had I known anything was amiss, I would've alerted Her Highness immediately." He arched his eyebrows at the spear in his face. "I worry that peasants will hear of this, Your Highness . . ."

A threat. If I didn't have a brother in the Kingstrials, I'd detain him. She waved off the spears. "My sincere apologies, Lord Mayor," she said. She asked her knights to see the mayor out. She strode off hurriedly with the Red Tower lord.

All the way, he objected fiercely to releasing Renworth. "Arresting him could start a revolt," she snapped. "Now isn't the time for some petty feud. Drop it."

She flew with Charles to the sanctity of the throne room, ripping off her silken headdress. Sentry knights shut the doors behind them. Ribboned with the Silver Throne's light, the room had a ghostly aura that heightened her anxiety.

Charles spilled everything.

Two dead nobles, Zur's robe, and a fallen tree. None of it made sense. Yet Drexan had either killed the two lords or fled with whoever did . . . but *why?*

She was shaken to her core. She nearly retched.

She feared for Zur. She almost had trouble breathing. *Why would he kidnap you, little brother?*

"Is Drexan in league with Parlisis?" It was insane to think about. As painful as her father's death. Drexan had been a truer uncle to her than Shaddon—to Jason, to all of them. *As Shaddon kidnapped Erick, Drexan kidnaps Zur.*

"I have no idea, but we must move quickly to find him," Charles said. "Drexan knows hidden paths to which even the Red Tower is blind. He'll vanish like a tick in the forest."

"Ticks can be found. Burst between our fingers. Where would he shelter?"

"At the Great Tree. He's a friend to that witch, the Oracle. Or he could've fled to the Order of Six Sights in Anjoun."

The Oracle. Unsettling rumors abounded about Orella, Lady at the Tree. Rumors that made the ones about Rittman seem bland by comparison.

Rumors that were actually true. *Little brother . . .*

"Scour the South Tower for evidence of conspiracy with Sothos," she said. "Lord Charles, I charge you with finding and gaoling Drexan on counts of murder and treason. You will not harm him before he can confess." She clutched the matted robe to her chest, as if the more tightly she did, the more his frame would fill it. "I charge you with returning Zuran safely. This, above all. *On the blood of my father, can you swear to do this?*"

The Grand Inquisitor curled his tuft of hair about a finger. "I cannot. But I know of someone who can, who *will* find them." He lingered with a lost look that unnerved her. "There's more, Ana."

She listed on her father's throne. "Go on, then."

Finish the Story
in Book Two

Alas, like many an ambitious fantasy author before me, I wrote a mammoth treatment for *A Seat for the Rabble* that exceeded printing standards and forced me to split the book into two volumes. *A Seat for the Rabble* is, as such, the first half of the first book in this epic fantasy series.

Please follow me on social media for updates about the epic conclusion to *A Seat for the Rabble*, which is scheduled for release under the title *An End to Kings* in 2023:

Facebook: @asftrabble
Instagram: @asftrabble
Threads: @schuette.ryan
Twitter: @RyanMarcS
Newsletter: RyanSchuette.com

APPENDIX

A GUIDE TO HISTORICAL EVENTS

THE CONFERRAL

Forty thousand years ago, the First King, Anjan Half-Elf, found himself and his army cornered on a mountain. According to the legends, Anjan's elven priest called down a lightning bolt that broke the mountain, entered the First King, and transmitted his power to twelve human champions.

THE END OF KING ANJAN'S LINE

Ten thousand years ago, King Eduard, a descendant of Anjan Half-Elf and an Ansaran, received a Casaanite queen named Elzura at his court. Religious texts hold that Elzura, a witch, cast a spell on Eduard. He vowed to kill his sister-wife, Tretha, and their half-elven children.

The king gave Tretha and his children a ten-minute start before riding out to kill them. A huntsman loyal to the House of Anjan followed on their heels, killing the wanton king and his party, but he was too late to save Tretha and the children.

This ended the House of Anjan and half-elven dominion. Bereft of a powerful king, ambitious men divided Ansara, hitherto one realm ruled from the Silver Walls, into thirteen kingdoms.

Ever since, Casaanites have been called Elzura's Children.

THE AWAKENING

Three centuries ago, a cultural, intellectual, and philosophical revolution spread through the Free Kingdoms. Started by Lord Gram Reuben of Tesos and other freethinkers, this movement taught men to question tradition and follow reason. This led to a schism in Elvarenism, yielding a new faith called the Free Beliefs.

THE INTERREGNUM

Two centuries ago, Sir Bradley Durhurst, along with twelve other knights, killed Loran's king, Lathros Dejoy. Petitioners from the Wing of the Commons helped them storm the throne room. This led to the Interregnum, a period of chaos in which Loran had no king. After Durhurst's ignoble end, Assemblymen restored the crown and expelled two classes from their ranks. Anointed men were driven from the Wing of Knights; the Wing of the Commons was banished entirely.

THE LONG SUMMER REBELLION

Twenty years ago, a civil war erupted in Loran. King Hexar wanted to divorce his wife, Alyse Jannus, an Elvarenist, and marry Sarah Sinclair, a Free Believer. The Worthy Assembly mustered an Army of the Gods and marched on Southpoint to save Alyse and arrest the Sinclairs. Before they could, Hexar beheaded Alyse, and a blackpowder explosion killed Sarah. Lord Greg Thorngale made a fragile peace between king and Assembly, ending the war.

LORAN'S GOVERNMENT

The Kingdom of Loran is ruled by a king and Worthy Assembly.

THE MONARCHY

The king rules from the Silver Walls, a castle in Southpoint. He executes the laws and wages wars. A queen hasn't ruled Loran since Queen Barbara's reign a thousand years ago.

THE WORTHY ASSEMBLY

The Worthy Assembly is a congress of the kingdom's classes. This body makes laws and raises money for war. Governing from the Colossus in Loran's north, its three chambers include:

- THE WING OF LORDS, which seats Loran's noblemen;
- THE WING OF CLERGY, almost evenly divided between

Elvarenist priests and readers of the Free Beliefs; and

- THE WING OF KNIGHTS, which only seats merchants, despite its name.

The Worthy Assembly once seated peasants in THE WING OF THE COMMONS, also known as the FOURTH WING.

Each wing, or chamber, elects a speaker from its own ranks.

THE KINGSTRIALS

If a king dies without a legitimate heir, his Worthy Assembly must call the Kingstrials, a tournament designed to choose a new monarch. To become king, a lord must win three contests outright, or the Assembly will choose a king by consensus.

LORAN'S RELIGIONS

ELVARENISM

Elvarenists believe in a pantheon of twelve gods. Traditionally, they follow a religious leader called the priestking, who rules from the Lonely Isle off the coast of Eastern Ansara. Of Ansara's thirteen kingdoms, seven are Elvarenist.

THE FREE BELIEFS

Free Believers believe the Elvarenists' twelve gods are faces of One True God. A leader called the Master Reader leads Free Believers in Loran. The Free Beliefs hold sway in Loran and the Free Kingdoms.

THE OLD WAYS

Although Elvarenists and Free Believers dominate Loran, many in the kingdom still follow the Old Ways—pagan beliefs in gods of field and forest. They call themselves Sylvanians, and they're known for practicing blood sacrifice.

HOUSE EDDENHOLD

KING HEXAR, Lord of Loran, four times married and widowed

The king's children, by their corresponding mothers:

- GARRETT EDDENHOLD, the crown prince, son of HARRIET
- LORANA EDDENHOLD, or ANA, steward, daughter of ALYSE
- ERICK EDDENHOLD, the deceased prince, son of ALYSE
- JASON WARCHILD, the bastard prince, son of SARAH
- HEATHER EDDENHOLD, the princess, daughter of ROMARA

The king's estranged brother, LORD SHADDON EDDENHOLD, exiled for his role in kidnapping a young ERICK EDDENHOLD

The king's advisors:

- JON APPLEWOOD, an apothecary
- CHARLES BURKE, the Grand Inquisitor and Lord of the Red Tower
- HANOR GRAXHOLD, a Tessian, Chancellor of the Exchequer
- DREXAN LORRAIN, known as the KING'S CROW, Chancellor of the Chancery

The king's knights, including:

- SIR CONNOR TOMAS, master-of-arms
- SIR DAVID BRIDGE
- SIR ASTIBAN HOARD
- SIR JEREMY HUNT
- SIR HAROLD MARC
- SIR ERICK SEAM
- SIR HORTUS GALLIVAR
- SIR SAM HORNBY
- SIR ROGIR LEVAN
- SIR BLAKE OXLEY

- SIR ANDREW WINDKIN

The king's Casaanite hostages, including:
- NAMONI of Tribe Chandiwe, who oversees the Casaanites
- ANYASHA of Tribe Nuur, or YASHA
- JHAZAR of Tribe Groth, also known as the INQUISITOR'S SHADOW
- MUSA and SAAN, brothers, both of Tribe Chandiwe
- ZURAN of Tribe Nuur, or ZUR

LORANA'S lady-in-waiting, LORNA DURROS

LOYAL COMPANYMEN

LORD EVAN SINCLAIR, Speaker of the LOYAL COMPANY, an underground political movement divided into two factions

SINCLAIR'S faction, the PETITIONERS, include:
- GEOFF DONOVAN, also known as the Whore Lord, a brothel owner and Assemblyman
- LORN GRANGER, a merchant and Assemblyman
- DREXYN LAUPHREY, a merchant and Assemblyman
- TRISTAN LOX, a fur trader and Assemblyman
- RATHOS ROBSWELL, also known as SILVERTONGUE, his deputy speaker
- TOM WEBB, a merchant and Assemblyman

REZLAN AMBROSE, a coal hand mockingly called the LORD OF SHOALTOWN, founded the LOYAL COMPANY with SINCLAIR

AMBROSE leads a faction called the REUBENITES, who include:
- LORD JACOB FARRYLL, a nobleman and Assemblyman
- LORD SAMUEL IRONKEEP, a nobleman and Assemblyman
- LORD JEFF MOHR, a nobleman and Assemblyman
- KARL REDMORE, a freeholder

- JON WATLEY, also known as FIREMOUTH, a rabble-rousing reader of the Free Beliefs

The PIGEONS, armed spies and messengers in service to the LOYAL COMPANY, help Companymen stay ahead of the men who want to apprehend or kill them. Their regiments include:
- The SOOTHSAYERS, composed of TOM GOODFIELD, JACOB, REED, VARN, and YULE
- The WATERFOWL

MASON GREXON, a co-conspirator, owns the Last Elflord Inn

NOBLE HOUSES, THEIR FAMILIES, AND SWORN MEN

HOUSE DURROS

LORD ALAN DURROS, Lord of Linwick Castle and Lord Warden of South Farcombe

DURROS'S child, LORNA DURROS, a lady-in-waiting

HOUSE FAWKES

LORD TOMAS FAWKES, Lord of Westerliche

FAWKES'S sworn vassal lords include:
- SHANNEN FOWL, Lord of Wesswood
- VENN LAMPOREAN, Lord of Ethelwood
- ORRENN SILVERSPEAR, Lord of Copper Grove

HOUSE GELDER

LORD TOM GELDER, Lord of Major Sunder, an Elvarenist

HOUSE MORLEY

LORD UTHRON MORLEY, Lord of Thorn's Keep and Lord Warden of Rosbury Village, husband to LADY CATHREEN MORLEY, a Magnesian noblewoman

Their children:
- SAM MORLEY
- BARBARA MORLEY
- HARRIETT MORLEY
- MAEDA MORLEY

The lord's cousin, UTHER BRUNE, an Elvarenist priest

The lord's knights:
- SIR BARDO LYM
- SIR LUC TOLOS

The lord's officers:
- SIR WILLARD RITTMAN, justice of the peace
- GEFFREY CHAFFER, a justice's deputy
- TOMAS LEER, also known as SWEET TOM, a justice's deputy

The lord's servant, MANNI

HOUSE SINCLAIR

LORD EVAN SINCLAIR, Lord of Caerdon Castle and Speaker of the Loyal Company, a band of traitors, once widowed

The lord's children by the late LADY FAYE HALIFAX:
- MINA SINCLAIR, lady and steward in her father's absence
- LEAH SINCLAIR, the so-called MAD LADY OF THE HERETICS

The lord's late sister, LADY SARAH SINCLAIR, the illegitimate third wife of KING HEXAR and mother of JASON WARCHILD

The lord's wards, sired by the late SIR MATTHUS ROBSWELL and his wife, ANNA, a castle laundress:

- RATHOS ROBSWELL, also known as SILVERTONGUE, a member of the Loyal Company
- DANA ROBSWELL

HOUSE SOTHOS

LORD GRAM SOTHOS, also called THE HAMMER OF THE COMMONS, LORDSBANE, and PINKHANDS, Lord of Saxhold Castle, Speaker of the Worthy Assembly's Wing of Lords. SOTHOS is husband to LADY TESS SOTHOS. Their children include LORD JUSTEN SOTHOS, their firstborn son.

SOTHOS'S sworn vassal lords include:

- PETOR ELLSBY, Lord of Odoro
- DOMIN GREATHALL, Lord of Ivanton
- JACOB HEXBROOK, Lord of Redforge
- JON REDOAK, Lord of Fordham
- DUMAS SUNOX, Lord of Ramsport
- ARON TULLER, Lord of Savon

SOTHOS'S sworn knights include SIR GORDON WHITECASTLE, a trapper

HOUSE THORNGALE

LORD GREG THORNGALE, also known as the OLD OAK, Lord of Thessela, a moderate Elvarenist famed for negotiating the end of the Long Summer Rebellion

THORNGALE'S children:

- DARREN THORNGALE, also known as the STORMSWORD, a hero famous for killing thirty-nine Uzmen single-handedly
- GAVIN THORNGALE, the eldest

    ◆ LUC THORNGALE, lastborn

HOUSE WEXLEY

LORD TREVOR WEXLEY, also known as the BULL, Lord of Eddenloxley Castle and unrecognized ruler of the Cloudlands, husband to LADY UTHRA WEXLEY. They have nine daughters.

WEXLEY is warder to the children and wife of his late brother SIR HANORR WEXLEY, a traitor:
- YOSAR WEXLEY, SIR HANORR'S widow, an Orranese woman
- HANORR THE YOUNGER
- TREVOR WEXLEY, named after his warder
- YASMEEN WEXLEY

WEXLEY'S sworn vassal lords include:
- DEREK CLABBARD, Lord of Whitecape
- ZAROLD ULBRIDGE, Lord of Hapry Springs
- RUSSELL WEXRENN, Lord of Sheep Hills

WEXLEY'S other sworn men include:
- SIR HALFORD IRONKEEP, a knight
- EORL, an apothecary

HOUSE WUTHERS

LORD SAM WUTHERS, Lord of Minor Sunder

OUTLAWS AND OTHERS

The HERETICS, a band of outlaws led by LEAH SINCLAIR, the so-called MAD LADY, and which includes:
- CREATURE, a madman
- GOOSE
- LETHABO, a Casaanite

- MURG, an Uzman
- STONEHANDS
- DUSTIN, her paramour
- JEFF THE GIANT, a dwarf
- LISHA, a Sylvanian
- PRETTY PHILLIP
- VENN

MERMAN JARROD, captain of *The Drunken Adventure*

FREDERICK MIDLICHE, known as the FOX, a merchant and Speaker of the Worthy Assembly's Wing of Knights

The LADY ORELLA, known as the ORACLE or LADY AT THE TREE, a mysterious griffon-tamer at the Great Tree of Loran, and those with her, including:

- SIR FEMI
- ABEBA

THE PEASANTS

Loran's peasants, also known collectively as THE COMMONS, or COMMONERS, the lowest social class

ROSBURY VILLAGE

SIR DAMIEN SOTHRON, a knight of House Morley

- ROSE SOTHRON, his wife
- SARA SOTHRON, his daughter
- DEVAN, his squire

Other villagers:

- LUC ALMSMAN
- CONNOR BAGMAN
- CALEB BARD
- ELFRED, a priest
- SETH BRIARFIELD

- FARMER GREY and his wife
- DESSA GORD
- ALFORD HEMLOCK
- GARY HENLEY, a reader
- CLYDE HOBBS
- HEXAAR OLMSTEAD
- FORD ROUNSEY
- CAM SUFFREY
- ASHLEY VAULD
- JACLYN WEBSTER
- PRAISE WHORESON

The villagers' children:
- ALFRID
- FROGFACE JENNY
- BRAM HOBBS
- PESH, or PESH THE PRINCE

Rumored Sylvanians:
- BILL
- TOM
- ORTHOS and OWEN, brothers
- JACOB WEESLAW, or SPITTLELIP

PEASANTS AT THE COLOSSUS

- RORYN COOK
- JAINA NADLEY
- JONATHAN SMITH
- SHANNON IRONKEEP
- TYLER ROLFE of South Farcombe
- SHREVE

SOUTHPOINT

LORD DAVID RENWORTH, also known as the LITTLE KING, mayor of Southpoint

Kitchen help at the Silver Walls:
- DORIAN FIELDER, friend to TYLER ROLFE
- ERIN, the baker's wife
- SEAN, a butcher, and his sons DONLEY and GAMLEN

RELIGIOUS LEADERS

MASTER READER JACOB SULLEY, the leader of Loran's Free Beliefs, member of the Worthy Assembly's Wing of Clergy

PRIESTKING PARLISIS, leader of the Elvarenist faith, rules from the LONELY ISLE, a kingdom in Eastern Ansara

The priestking's only child:
- EDENIA HIGHDAUGHTER, prieslenne and high priestess of their faith

The priestking's emissary in Loran:
- PESHAR GRATHOS, High Bishop, Speaker of the Worthy Assembly's Wing of Clergy

Acknowledgements

Writing a fantasy novel of this size is a lot like illustrating in pen and ink. You may outline a great plot, as you may create a terrific drawing . . . but it all comes down to execution.

I had help from a lot of amazing people to execute this dream. I'm grateful to my editor, Leigh Grossman, for tearing up my first two drafts. Sean Mallen, Mark Eckert, and Cassandra Shuptar critiqued early versions. Ryan Engen and Victor McDonald read the third draft, giving me invaluable feedback and helping me remember why I wrote it. Jason Niehaus went above and beyond, reviewing the third draft twice and returning annotated copies. A special friend encouraged me to finish this work and celebrated it by organizing a fabulous reading in Johannesburg, South Africa, and I'm grateful to her.

Western political theories informed this novel about inclusion, representation, and the dangers of denying others a seat at the decision-making table. I'm grateful to my professor, Richard Ruderman, for exposing me to the philosophers who inspired this work. Brendan Millan introduced me to new dead guys and read several chapters, evaluating the philosophically grounded ones with care.

Ted Nasmith's illustrations attracted me to the fantasy genre early on, and it was another dream realized to work with him on two glorious covers.

Finally, I want to thank my mother, Pat Schuette, for believing in me, supporting me, and making the earliest drafts possible.

My love and gratitude to you all.

About the Author

Ryan Schuette is the author of *A Seat for the Rabble* and *The Art of the Big Lie: Political Cartoons About the Fight for America's Soul*. He's also authored a romance novel under his pseudonym.

Before returning to fantasy fiction and art, Ryan wore a few hats. He's both illustrated and reported for National Public Radio and various trade publications, including *DS News* and *MReport*. He's also freelanced for Al Jazeera America. He lived and worked in Uganda as a 2008-2009 Rotary Ambassadorial Scholar and holds a master's degree from American University in Washington, D.C.

Somewhere along the way, he also started a nonprofit and fair-trade lingerie company that operated in West and Central Africa, respectively. Many of his friends still wear safari-print boxers.

Ryan lives in Texas, where he looks after his cat, Rusty.

To learn more about Ryan or his epic fantasy series, *A King Without a Crown*, visit RyanSchuette.com.

The following is an excerpt from
the next volume in Ryan Schuette's
exciting epic fantasy series

An End to Kings

the stirring conclusion to
A Seat for the Rabble

To Each a Chair

hen the portcullis began to shiver open, the swords and axes came out.

Shannon Ironkeep rushed in first, burying her axe into the first guard's chest. The second guard, a boy no older than Tyler, slid forward on Blackstaff's sword, mouth agape as he bled out, spilling intestines.

Blackstaff's impostor planted a foot on the boy's chest and kicked him off his sword. He seemed to lose himself in his rod's mystical aura, transfixed.

The woman boxed his helm as if it were the big man's ear. "Donna stand there like an oaf, Shreve. Work needs doin'." She swiveled on the peasants and thrust her bloody axe into the air. "*To each a chair!*" she cried lustily.

"*TO ALL A PIECE!*" the peasants thundered together.

With the pretender beside her, the warrior-grandmother led the way into the tunnel of the gatehouse, running with the light from Blackstaff's staff fidgeting all around them. Peasants disguised in silks ran after the bobbing light, swords in the air, their war cries echoing.

Lost in a loud, sweaty, silverstone-lit stampede through the gatehouse, Tyler tried to stay alive by staying on his feet. Running behind the pack, he nicked his chin on someone's shoulder and tasted blood; he stepped wrong on something and winced at the pain in his ankle. Ahead, past the charging people, at the end of the gatehouse, he glimpsed a sand arena.

He felt hope. Mad hope that mingled with his grief. Roryn Cook's van had managed to slip through the Golden Meadows almost entirely unnoticed and unsuspected. Walking alone, one cassocked priest, an Assemblyman, had made eye contact with their Blackstaff, but he didn't make inquiries or raise alarm.

Undraping his staff, the man called Shreve had knocked its stone against the portcullis a little lightly at first, harder the second time, after Shannon prodded him. Everyone held their breath when the impersonator misremembered Blackstaff's traditional exchange with the guards, stammering out, upon them querying his allegiance, "AYE, uh—*I'm for the king.*"

But no one took issue. No one questioned his identity or spied Commoners lurking beneath the archways of arcades, waiting for the portcullis to slide open. The man who donned Blackstaff's armor, who wielded his rod, was someone whose significance lay in ritual. Who feared treason from a symbol?

Roryn's plan was working. If they could take his kingly namesake's amphitheater—*if they could hold it*—they could hold the steward hostage and force the lords to return to the peasants what was theirs. Everything felt possible.

As Tyler ran through the gatehouse, he remembered what his tanner papa had once told him. It was a memory that stayed with him, one he'd shared with Jaina just yesterday.

Satin, he remembered.

"Satin," the elder Rolfe had told his son in their house one night, patting his rock-hard stool seat. "*Satin!*" he'd repeated with childlike wonder. "Can you believe it? When the Wing of the Commons still had seats, Commoners sat *on satin cushions* beside their lords, clergymen, and merchants. To this day, the Worthy men sit on cushions when they meet to make law." He remembered his father waxing serious. "As peasants will again . . . one day."

That day is here, Papa, Tyler thought as he ran toward sand and moonlight, toward salvation. *The long night of our Common folk is over.*

Arrows whistled at the entrance, studding sand and flesh. The peasants at the front of the van, who would've been the first Commoners to set foot in the Colossus in centuries, were the first to fall. A corpse heap formed at the entrance, slowing their advance. Tyler huddled with Shannon, Shreve, and other men under an archway as arrows peppered the sand feet away.

As he kept his eyes on the blitz of arrows, calamity arose in the Golden Meadows behind them, orders bellowed into the night, horses whinnying—and there, distantly, the peal of steel clashing against steel. *Be worthy of mercy and justice, Roryn.*

Tyler urged Shannon and Blackstaff's impostor to move forward, *for god's sake, move forward,* but his cries fell on deaf ears. "RORYN, RORYN," he shouted as he grabbed the woman by her arm. He jabbed his finger at the camps behind them and told her the Colossus had to be taken.

Battle was raging, peasants like Tyler were dying, but he took confidence in Shannon's unwavering gaze. She cocked her thumb at the sand arena. "*WE CANNA GET IN,*" he heard her say over the tumult.

Still the arrows rained down, catching dead men, *pfft, pfft.* With a crazed look, Shreve said something. Only afterward did Tyler read his lips and understand he spoke for the ages.

Into the storm strode Blackstaff, convulsing from impact as arrows lanced his greaves, arms, cuirass. Arrows appeared everywhere but on his helm, and by some miracle, the hero *still stood* nearly a minute in, bushed by so many that he looked like a shrub made of shafts. Shannon, Tyler, and the other peasants bounded over bodies. Tyler caught a glimpse of Shreve's eyes misting as he slumped sideways. Doing his duty by Roryn, by all peasants, he picked up the luminous rod.

Peasants fanned out across the arena to make themselves harder targets. That ploy might've served the remaining two-dozen peasants well, but a muck of wet sand slowed their pace dangerously. *The Second Trial,* he remembered.

Worse for the boy, the luster of Blackstaff's rod made him a well-lit firefly. He plodded through sand, ducking arrows. One plonked by his ankle; another singed his cheek. Commoners fought a skeleton crew of archers in mail and boiled leather—perhaps eight in all—but their nests in the middle and upper benches made them seem a hundred. The Colossus's sackers scattered like roaches, seeking cover or dying in the attempt.

Tyler sighted a crossbowman in the benches, not twenty feet off. Loading a bolt took precious time. Tyler charged with weights on his feet, his blade up.

His ankle exploded with pain. He collapsed in the soggy sand, got up, and fought to hop away on one foot, crying out every time he put pressure on his skewered ankle. His blood slicked the protruding arrow, dribbling a trail in the sand.

A bolt from the crossbowman whistled past his shoulder as he half-stumbled, half-crawled for cover. *But where?* Tyler forced himself to think through a wall of pain. He considered sheltering beneath a bench until he saw a peasant below one, hand dangling out, an arrow through his head. *WHERE, GOD?*

The One True God didn't disappoint. The answer was in front of him, a dozen yards off. Evading arrows, he hadn't yet noticed the giant cagehouse at the center of the arena; there was no missing it now. A silver tarp blanketed the enclosure, leaving visible only its sand-caked wheels.

The griffon, Tyler thought. Ruts in the sand led from the wheels to the gatehouse. The Assembly had carted the king's bird here for the Third Trial.

He staggered in the cagehouse's direction as people fought for their lives around him. An over-the-shoulder glance showed him that the crossbowman hadn't given up on his prey; their eyes locked as the enemy cranked his bolt.

Tyler reached the cagehouse. Seconds turned to hours as he struggled to ease himself flat on his belly, clenching his jaw to weather the fire lancing up his leg. Clutching his sword and staff, he crawled to safety beneath the cagehouse on his elbows. A crossbow bolt *thwopped* by his feet.

Perhaps the best I can do right now is keep the staff safe, Tyler thought. *We'll need it for Roryn to know we've taken the Colossus.* Despite their losses, despite the arrow lodged in his ankle, tides were turning. Fewer arrows pelted the sand as Commoners stormed the benches, cornering archers.

Tyler worked fast. He unbuttoned the gambeson, jerked out a wad of his cloth shirt, pulled it out and over his head. It was a good shirt and had served him for years; he ripped it in two pieces. Gingerly, he folded one piece around his inflamed ankle, the arrow too, trying to stanch blood loss.

As he finished tying the knot, thunder rumbled overhead. *A storm?* He gazed at the gatehouse, hoping that it was Roryn Cook arriving with his peasant army, Princess Lorana bound by rope. *Were the lords and their men-at-arms so easy to dispatch?*

Then he remembered what the enclosure contained. The sound of the creature's growl was enough to rattle iron floor, carry through sand, *vibrate* in his bones. It wasn't over. The cagehouse shook side to side violently, creaking, as if tussled by gale wind. Talons raked the iron floor from the other side; he kept waiting for them to shear through it.

In spite of his leg, he was still and silent. Until he saw the snake gliding over the sand. Not a snake—a tail. A griffon's tail. Thicker than his arm, the appendage plumed so thickly with fur at the end that it resembled a head. The tail moved almost with a will of its own, searching for the source of disturbance. His breathing quickened. *Please, god, donna let it take me.*

Tyler squinted at the aura pulsating from Blackstaff's rod. Roryn's warning returned to him: "You clothe that rod quick, an' keep it far, *an' I mean far,* from the beast's sight. He sees it, he'll raise hell."

As the tail wended by his cheek, he took the other half of his torn shirt and draped the rod. This accomplished precisely nothing; the pearl aura bled through the fabric radiantly. With the cagehouse over him shaking, he plunged the silverstone into sand. That mostly snuffed its light.

The shaking quelled. He realized he could hear himself breathe. Peasants were scouring the benches for archers, communicating in low voices. "Did Rolfe fall?" A man called out. "I donna see him," another answered. "But we need him, least that silverstone. He took it off Shreve."

Seconds passed before Tyler remembered he was alive. He crawled halfway out from under the cagehouse; he left Blackstaff's rod sheathed in the sand. "I'm here!" he cried.

Shannon Ironkeep descended from the benches. The old bewhiskered woman lumbered in his direction, dragging her axe listlessly through the sand. She, too, had taken an arrow; a broken shaft poked out of her arm, and she breathed heavily. She halted a distance away. Besieging the Assembly's seat of power and getting shot with arrows hadn't fazed the doughty peasant, but the sight of the cage blazed her eyes.

"Get up an' outta there, Rolfe," she urged him in a strained voice. "I dare nah get closer."

"I canna walk!" he whispered loudly, fearful of angering the beast. "I took an arrow in my leg."

"Then throw the rod. Roryn needs the signal. We've taken the Colossus."

Hope unlooked-for washed over Tyler. He was about to tell her he couldn't, that the griffon nearly smashed its prison to bits over silverstone light, when cheers and cries of joy filled the night air. Of the some forty people who'd breached Rorin's amphitheater, only ten still drew breath. Some of them tended to the wounded and dying. Others celebrated.

A young Midland farmhand ran around the arena for no other purpose than to rejoice. "*WE DID IT,*" he shouted as he leapt exultantly through sand. "*WE SACKED IT! WE DID IT! WE FUCKIN' TOOK THE COLOSSUS!*"

Shannon watched him wearily as he darted by. "It's not done, ya fool. Roryn'll be comin' with Her Highness. It's one thing to take a building; another to keep it, make demands."

Most ignored the grandmother. A man broke down and wept into his hands. Another lifted his hands skyward, giving thanks to the One True God of readers and peasants for their hallowed victory over vicious priests. The farmhand running laps started cartwheeling; he couldn't sustain it in the moist sand and fell splayed out. He laughed madly, triumphantly.

A middle-aged man savored the moment with dignity. He sat on a lower bench, face forward, back straight, hands round on his knees, as if he were a child in school. Blood oozed down his face from a gleaming head wound, but he didn't attend to it. It was as if he'd decided that nothing and no one would move him. Even if he bled.

That was when Tyler realized it. The benches were bare! *I'm here, Papa, I'm here for you and Jaina and everyone . . . but I donna see your satin cushions.*

The blaze in his ankle outweighed disappointment. Tyler motioned for Shannon. "Help me upstairs so we can give the signal," he said. "Roryn wanted me to do it."

A fletched bolt blossomed in Shannon's heart like a red rose, and she fell clutching her axe. Another bolt flattened the farmhand where he lay in the sand.

"*THEY'RE COMIN' FROM BELOW!*" someone shouted.

No, Tyler thought. Fresh archers swept across the arena, stringing their bows. With them were knights in heavy armor. They streamed out from the northern portcullis—from *below* the Colossus. There were more men than he could count.

It took the Assembly's forces under a minute to kill the remaining peasants. Tears falling off his face, Tyler shuffled back under the cage. Fear made him desperate. Trying not to scrape the arrow in his ankle, lest he cry out, he inadvertently nudged the staff. It was as if he'd dug up a moon. The blast of silvery radiance drew a *hissss* that Tyler felt through his back.

Near where Shannon lay, a company of men halted in their tracks. "There's one under the cagehouse," a dark-haired archer told the others.

"Is that . . . is that *silverstone* he has with him?" asked another, incredulous.

"Blackstaff's rod," said a crossbowman, an Eastlander by his accent. "It's how the little Common fleas got in. Good thing word reached

Redoak about Lordsbane's visit here. Elsewise, he might not've had us posted here tonight."

The same fear that had paralyzed Shannon Ironkeep lay in the archer's eyes. "A *griffon's* in there. I'll go no closer."

"You don't have to." The crossbowman approached with his weapon pointed. His footsteps came softly, as if he thought to reassure the griffon. "Is that a star ya got with you, lad?" he called out. "Bright light, that. I can see you clear as day. From here, I could stick you between your eyes. Kill ya quick."

He remembered their faces, their voices. Dorian. Sara of Rosbury. Roryn. Shannon. Shreve. His papa. Jaina most of all. They kindled his courage, but her face and hair and voice, her laughter, helped numb the fiery throb of his leg. He heard a low rumbling—not from above him, but *out there,* like the rush of a wave gaining momentum before it crashes ashore. The battle continued, and it was because of her sacrifice, the first of many.

Tyler took heart. "We're nah alone," he piped. "Nah t'all. An army's comin'. Big brutes with swords and armor. Let me live, an' I'll reason with their leader to let you men live. You've done nothin' wrong, just your duty and your lords' orders."

Guardsmen laughed heartily.

A maddening grin worked its way into the crossbowman's face. "*Nah,*" he mocked Tyler. "I'll let you live so we can ask ya questions. If you've got friends comin', well, this bolt will fly through your stomach instead of your head. Not so quick, that sorta death. And if ya stay under there, well . . ." He paused so that all anyone heard was the cagehouse-rattling growl. "I reckon that vicious beast might just save me the trouble."

Tears coursed down Tyler's face. *Forgive me, Roryn. I see no other way.* On elbows and knees, he crawled through muck, the rod with him, spilling light, throwing shadows wildly. The cagehouse squeaked as the creature paced about anxiously. The drag of his injured leg dragged out the surrender.

The crossbowman sighed impatiently. "Gods, what is this one, a snail or a peasant? I repeat myself, I s'ppose." Laughter rang around the Colossus. "Sitting, resting, taking your sweet time—that's for lords and priests. Not for dumb serfs like you."

Tyler held aloft the rod of light; the cagehouse quaked about in response, jingling iron bars. The plumed tail curled out, silver tarp rising with it. He trembled under the glare of a massive eagle's eye, a golden disc forked with amber. He saw his reflection in its black pupil.

The crossbowman was still snickering when Tyler Rolfe tossed the spear of Blackstaff's rod into the cagehouse.

The scream was monstrous and frightening. Inside, the rod spun round like a bottle, scrambling darkness with light, offering fleeting glimpses of vast arched wings, the mustard beak and sickle talons working furiously to uproot iron bars. A few bars gave way, but a few was all it'd take. The cagehouse tilted over him precariously.

Give me mercy and justice, beast. I've never had none.

The enclosure capsized the other way, the staff twirling out and away, its static light fogging a swath of sand. Iron sheets and iron bars whirled through the air. A great shadow vaulted free of the cagehouse, wings beating air, whipping up a gritty sandstorm that flung Tyler and the archers away like leaves in the wind.

There was no mercy in how the fall broke the boy's legs, or justice, as many of the guardsmen fled to safety. But before debris tumbled down on top of him, darkening his world, Tyler saw a shadow angel spreading its wings, blotting out stars, and he remembered why peasants worshipped griffons.

9 7 9 8 9 8 8 5 9 8 6 0 2